DARKENING SKY

DARKENING SKY

Alison Joseph

This edition first published in Great Britain in 2006 by
Allison & Busby Limited
13 Charlotte Mews
London W1T 4EJ
www.allisonandbusby.com

Copyright © 2004 ALISON JOSEPH

The moral right of the author has been asserted.

A catalogue record for this book is available from
the British Library.

10 9 8 7 6 5 4 3 2 1

ISBN 0 7490 8107 4
978-0-7490-8107-2

Printed and bound in Great Britain by
Bookmarque Ltd, Croydon, Surrey

Acknowledgements

I would like to thank Professor John Took of the Department of Italian, University College London. I would also like to thank Sister Anne-Marie, Ian Willis, Michael Jecks, Dr Amyas Bray and Leigh Skelton, Clinical Director of Combat Stress. I especially wish to thank Mark Hiscott, Brian Lloyd and Easton Thomas, who served in the Falklands.

Also by Alison Joseph in the Sister Agnes series

Sacred Hearts
The Hour of our Death
The Quick and the Dead
A Dark and Sinful Death
The Dying Light
The Night Watch

Chapter One

Sometimes I think he's still alive. Sometimes I think, the way he's staring at me, those big dead eyes, I'm waiting for them to blink, waiting to see the life come back into them. And then he'd laugh and sit up and say, 'What you standing there for you big pillock?'

And when I'm thinking all this, I'm smiling aren't I? Thinking that the old bastard might just get up and tell me it's my round. And then I remember. I remember that when I looked down at him he had no legs. Shot to bits, weren't they. After his arse he just stopped.

I sat there next to him, him staring at me with them dead eyes, shells flying all around us. I told him, 'Lucky, mate, I ain't going to leave you. Not in that state, mate.' It felt like hours, I was sitting there.

They had to drag me away from him.

Agnes read the crumpled pages, then re-read them. Walker had thrust them into her hands the night before, saying 'Read these – then you'll understand,' before downing the rest of his can of brown ale and stumbling out into the London streets.

So much for helping, she thought. Trying to explain to a drunken ex-soldier that he had forfeited his place in the hostel by drinking, trying to tell him that he knew the rules, he knew that Rule Number One for being able to stay in the hostel was that you stay dry and clean, and appearing drunk on the premises meant you were in breach of trust and therefore had to go – it had fallen on deaf ears, and after shouting incoherent abuse at her, he'd fished in his pockets for these scraps of paper and then gone.

He'd have blagged enough to drink all night, the start of a long bender that would last days, if not weeks, at the end of which he might stumble back to the hostel, promising he would change, managing to stay sober for long enough to begin to talk about what had brought him here in the first place.

Or he might not. I might never see him again.

She looked out at the darkness, the rainy London night. Walker Mc Fadden, sometimes known as Andy, was a man of wiry strength and thinning grey hair. He was taciturn and reserved, although at times you'd find him tucked into a corner of a lounge with a resident, listening quietly. When he laughed, a wide, expansive laugh, it was like a burden briefly lifting.

Recently, he'd decided that the garden of the hostel, a scrubby bit of back yard, needed attention. He had set to, declaring that it wasn't gardening, it was archaeology, appearing in the kitchen with various finds, old flower pots, a tea-cup, a half-rotten teddy bear. 'Where do you want these, sister,' he'd say. The day before yesterday he'd come into the kitchen half-hidden behind a huge self-seeded sycamore that he'd dug up. 'Where do you want this, sister?' he'd said. She'd shooed him out of the kitchen, scolding him about the trail of earth that he'd brought in, and he'd cowered, laughing, calling for help, shouting about mad nuns.

She wondered what had changed. Something had started him drinking again, just a day or two ago. Some memory, perhaps, some horror revisited. She hoped he'd come back.

When the order had first suggested that Agnes be seconded to St Christopher's House, Sister Madeleine had warned her that the work could be dispiriting. 'Sometimes I think we're just contributing to a cycle of failure,' she'd said. But Agnes knew that taking the job meant she could stay in her little Bermondsey flat in solitude, instead of having to return to the community house in Hackney.

'Drunks?' her best friend, Athena said, when she'd told her. They were sitting in a restaurant, just off Fulham Broadway, picking at ciabatta bread. 'Have another glass of Sancerre.'

'Not just drunks,' Agnes said. 'Drugs too, heroin addicts, anyone referred to us, really.

'Oh dear, are you sure you'll manage?'

Agnes looked at Athena. 'Of course I will.' Athena was concentrating on dunking some bread in olive oil, and a curl of long black hair fell across her face. 'That's a nice sweater,' Agnes said.

Athena looked up. 'It was a bargain. Cashmere, a third off the marked price. They had it in lilac too.'

'That grey's very nice.'

'You could get one. You've been wearing those old things for years.'

Agnes laughed. 'I'm not supposed to think about my appearance. These old things – ' she glanced down at her jeans, her cream Aran sweater – 'will just have to do.' She looked at Athena, her heavy earrings, the slash of red lipstick, her dark eyes fringed with thick black eyelashes.

'And you could grow your hair,' Athena said.

'No,' Agnes said. 'Short brown hair. Or grey, increasingly. We all have it, it's like school uniform.'

'Well, I think those old nuns are very mean. You have a good figure, and very good bone structure, your parents might have been hopeless but at least they were good stock- '

Agnes started to laugh.

'I'm serious,' Athena went on. 'With a decent haircut and some properly tailored clothes, you'd look great. And it would be good for the order too, people would look at you and think, well, if that's being a nun, I might reconsider. I would have thought those nuns would be glad of new recruitment strategies in these times of falling vocations.'

'I'm surprised you take the rise of secularism so seriously,' Agnes said.

Athena poured them both some more wine. 'By the way, any

handy tips for cutting down on the booze, do pass them on.'

'You can't mean that.'

Athena pouted, shrugged. 'There's those limit things, aren't there, sweetie. Brussels or someone has passed a law. Men are allowed 95 units a week, and women allowed about two. Something like that.'

Agnes laughed. 'We don't drink too much.'

'You're French, you don't understand.'

'And you're Greek.'

'I was. A long time ago. I've been with Nic so long now, I must be as English as he is.'

'I thought he was Welsh.'

'Not very. Just fashionably Celtic.'

'We're both Londoners,' Agnes said. 'And anyway, I'm only half French.'

'Talking of which, have you sold your place in Provence yet?'

Agnes topped up both their glasses. 'I'm stuck, you see,' she said at last. 'What I'm supposed to do is take my final vows and hand everything over to the order, including that house.'

'Sweetie, you can't. It's out of the question.'

'A nun can't own a house in Provence – '

'With how many bedrooms? And how many acres of orchards?'

Agnes sighed. 'Precisely.'

'But it was only left to you last year. You haven't been orphaned long, they can't expect you to make snap decisions so soon after your mother's death. And what if you decide to leave the order? You'll need a bolt-hole.'

'The point of taking final vows is that there's no going back. It's just that. Final.'

'No one can make a decision like that.'

'Julius thinks it'll be helpful to me.'

'Oh, well, obviously for Father Julius it's been easy.'

'I don't think it has – ' Agnes tried to say.

'He's a lovely sweet old priest – do you know, whenever I see him, I always want to ruffle his fluffy white hair, one day I'm just going to do it. And that soft Irish accent of his, it's so cute – but you see, sweetie, I know you've known him for ever and all that, but I don't think he's the best person to give advice to someone like you. He's so perfect, he's barely human, so he can't understand what it would be like for a mere mortal like you. Or me. You see, sweetie, it's just not in human nature. It's like Nic trying to get me to live in Barcelona.'

'What?' Agnes stared at her friend.

'Didn't I tell you? He's been offered some work opportunity there, setting up a therapy and counselling centre with some friend of his, he's been banging on about fresh starts and a new life, and me going with him – '

'Barcelona?'

Athena shrugged. 'I know, sweetie. I'm not keen, really. Mainly because if I do that then Nic is all I have. I mean, once I get there, you know, before I make new friends, find work, that kind of thing – and what kind of work am I going to find anyway? Working in the art gallery here suits me, and anyway, I don't speak Spanish or whatever it is they speak there...' She sipped her wine. 'So then it's just me and Nic. And to be honest...' She glanced up at Agnes, looked down again, fiddled with her knife. 'We don't even live together, sweetie. All these years, we've kept our own separate flats. And the idea of being thrown together with him – to be honest, I've no idea if we're strong enough for that.'

'But at least you'd find out.'

Athena met her eyes. 'Yes. But do I want to?'

Agnes picked up the empty wine bottle and peered at it. 'You don't get much of this to the pint, do you?'

It changes you, you see. Being a soldier. I thought I knew what that meant, when we all signed up. It was a laugh, weren't it, and me the big man, walking in there, saying, yeah, sure, I'll join. And I was the hardest new boy they'd ever seen. Throw cold water over me? I laughed. Tie me to a post all night? When they found me, I was standing there with a smile on my face. That's where my name comes from, Walker. Walker McFadden. Got stranded twenty miles from our base due to that bastard sergeant driving off without me. I walked, all night. Reported for duty the next day like nothing had happened. So when they said it was war, I had my bag packed ready to go.

I was another person then. Pitch said that to me, one night, we was sat by the fire, and he looked at me, and he said, remember the Kings Arms? In Southwark? Down by the river? And I said, yeah, sure. And he said, remember that night, we was on the ale, weren't we? And we put the same song on the jukebox, over and over again? And I said, yeah. It was that one by Queen. And he said, yeah. And then we sat there, staring at the fire, listening to the shells. And he said, we ain't never going to do that again. And I said, Pitch, don't be a git, 'course we are. And he looked at me again, and he said, "No, what I mean is this: Even if we were to live through all this, go back to that pub, sup the same ale, put on that same music – it won't be us, Walker." And he held his two first fingers up, pointing at his face, and he said, "Look, look at my eyes." And I looked, and he says, "See? The light's gone out of them. Like it has for you."

We was all like that, though, running around blank-eyed, you could see it in every man, all of us high as kites, all of us with bloodshot eyes with the light gone out of them. Except for one. One what I'm not going to even write his name, but you ask anyone from our barracks about the one who was the devil himself, and they'll tell you. In my dreams when I'm in the mud after the helicopter crash, trampling them bodies smashed up like offal, I look up and I see him. And in my dream I'm thinking, one day he'll kill me. If I don't kill him first. And then I wake up, and there's my old friend the demon rage, the anger burning in my brain, sometimes so bad that I have to hold on to the sides of the bed to keep me there, to keep me from running out into the street...'

Agnes turned the page. The writing had come to a halt. She folded the battered pages together and put them down on her desk in the hostel. Outside it was dark, the roar of evening traffic on the wet roads. There was a knock at the door, and she jumped.

'Yes?'

A young man put his head round the door. 'Sorry, Sister...'

'Oh, Dan. I was about to go home.'

'I just thought I'd brief you about our new resident.'

'Sure.' Agnes gestured to the chair opposite. 'By the way, Andy McFadden's gone.'

Dan sighed. 'Walker?' he said. 'Again.' He sat down, took out a packet of cigarettes and lit one, drawing on it deeply.

'So?' Agnes prompted.

'She's called Jeanie. She says her surname is Clark. She's from Hull, originally. She was in care from age five, absconded a few times, disappeared altogether for a couple of years. Bit of a record, various charges, shoplifting mostly, something rather nasty involving an assault on another girl. She did time for that. It's not very clear but it seems that heroin was involved, and some kind of boyfriend who was also a dealer. She refers to him as Ash, and she's terrified of him. He's local, which doesn't help, some of the other residents know him.'

'Is she clean now?'

Dan shrugged. 'She says so. When she was inside, she asked to be transferred to a drug-free wing.'

'When you say she says her surname is Clark – ?'

'There are other names in the paperwork. McKinnon is one, but she says that's her stepfather's name from way back.'

'And Clark?'

'That's her mother's maiden name. I think she adopted it quite recently.' His blond hair flopped across his face and he pushed it back. 'I'll leave you the file, shall I?' He placed a thin folder on the desk in front of her. Outside a lorry rumbled past. Rain pattered on the darkened windows, and Dan looked up at her. 'Are you OK?'

'Has Andy ever shown you his writings?'

Dan glanced at the pages heaped on her desk. 'They're a difficult read, aren't they?'

'He told me they'd explain everything.'

Dan nodded. 'And he takes you into his confidence, and presses his papers into your hand, and makes you feel special, like he's picked you out as someone he can trust...'

Agnes picked up a pen, put it down again.

'And then it turns out,' Dan went on, 'that it's not all true.'

'Isn't it?' She felt suddenly tired.

'He had a few sessions with a counsellor before you joined us. It's quite clear he's got Post Traumatic Stress Disorder, he's had it for years. We've been trying to get him proper counselling from people who work with ex-soldiers, they're the ones who know how to deal with people like Walker. He's on a waiting list. They're terribly overstretched. Loads of unmet need among ex-soldiers.'

'So, he was in the Army? He often mentioned it.'

'Oh, yes, that bit's true. He trained with the Scots Guards. The bit about walking all night is true, getting that nickname. And he served in the Falklands. That's where all his nightmares started. He saw terrible horrors, apparently. But you see, he needs real help. Half the stuff in the writings is true, but he's still trying to make sense of most of it. He's been living with the flashbacks for twenty odd years, with no one to help him.'

'Is that why these writings are unreliable? Does war change your reality?'

'The real nightmare stuff gets burnt into your brain. You don't make that stuff up.' He sighed. 'Poor Walker.'

There was a sudden burst of loud music from upstairs. 'Jayce,' Dan said. 'Again.' He left the room, and Agnes heard his footsteps on the stairs. A few minutes later the music stopped.

Agnes fingered Walker's writings, then got up and went over to the window. The rain had softened to a drizzle, and she could see the moon, almost a full circle, rising above the glass towers of the City in the chill, February night. She yawned, turned back to her desk and stuffed the pages into a drawer. Then she left, locking the office door.

She walked through the rain, hearing the distant rattle of the trains at London Bridge. She passed the strips of new buildings, the flats with riverside views, sleek balconies and high steel gates.

Then she turned away from the river, past the old post-war estates which were hunched and shabby, sheltering fractured and desperate lives.

Her flat was cold and dark. She switched on lights and lit the gas fire, then went and ran a bath. She paused in front of her reflection in the bathroom mirror. Her face stared back at her. She pulled at her short brown hair, dismayed at the amount of grey she could see. She frowned, watching the lines deepen round her eyes.

If I was Athena, I'd rush out and dye my hair and have my eyebrows shaped and have a facial and spend a fortune on anti-ageing face cream. And some new clothes.

But I'm not, she thought.

She turned away from her reflection, turned off the bath.

Mind you, she thought, watching her jeans and sweater land in a heap as she got undressed, that cashmere jumper of Athena's was very nice. I wonder if they've got one in camel.

Final vows. The end of all that. No longer to attach any importance to worldly things. To see adornment and vanity for the illusions that they are.

She pulled on a white towelling dressing gown and went into the kitchen and poured a large gin and tonic with lots of ice. Then she went back into the bathroom, and hesitated before opening a bottle of Issey Miyake bath essence, given to her some time ago by Athena, and tipping a generous amount into the steaming water.

She lay in the scented bubbles, sipping her gin.

I might as well be part of the world while I can, she thought. And anyway, even if I do see all this as illusory, as mere vanity, that doesn't mean I can't enjoy it. And it will be Lent soon, I should make the most of it.

She splashed her face with water, and remembered that there was a very nice crab paté in the fridge for supper.

The darkness of the pre-dawn shrilled with her alarm. Agnes switched it off, aware of fading dreams, images of bubble baths and mud baths and trenches and camel coats. She fell out of bed and went in search of a clean pair of jeans. Ten minutes later, she left her flat, running down the stairs to the ground floor in the chill grey light. The spire of Father Julius's church was visible between the tower blocks, and she wrapped her scarf round her neck and quickened her pace as she heard the bell ring for the first mass of the day.

'Though I walk through the valley of the shadow of death...' The straggling congregation intoned the psalm, four thin voices reedy in the empty space. 'I shall fear no evil, for you are with me...'

Agnes thought of Andy Walker McFadden, keeping company with his dead friend while the shells flew around them. She heard Father Julius reciting the liturgy, and the church seemed to echo with his voice, with his deep faith.

She came out blinking into the bright morning. There was the rumble of traffic heading for the City, and beyond the church gates she could see the silver strip of the Thames.

'Agnes?' Julius appeared from the door.

'How are you?' She wondered how he always looked so young, his eyes such a clear blue despite his age. She smiled, remembering Athena wanting to ruffle his hair.

'It's nice that your order could spare you from Lauds.'

'Julius, as you very well know, for me to join my community for Lauds I'd have to find a bus to Hackney in the middle of the night. Anyway, they see enough of me.'

Julius laughed. 'Have you had breakfast? I could make us some toast.'

'How well you know me.'

Agnes sat on a worn red velvet chair and watched Julius making a pot of tea. The sun broke through the leaded window behind her, throwing criss-crossed shadows on to the old polished floorboards.

'How's the new job?' Julius was saying.

'Fine, thanks.'

'I thought it was your kind of thing.'

'You mean, it takes one compulsive excessive addictive personality to know one.'

'Now have I ever called you excessive or addictive?'

'Only politeness has prevented you, Julius.'

'That's possibly true,' he said, bringing two mugs of tea over to his desk.

'Anyway, you'd be right. I'm drinking more than ever and spending my days counselling people who are trying to give up.'

'And why's that, then?' Julius leaned back in his chair, his hands clasped round his mug. 'The drinking, I mean.'

'Oh, look at you,' Agnes said.

'It'll be about final vows, will it?'

'It certainly will, Julius.'

'And no doubt Athena's taking you out for bottles of Chardonnay.'

'It's not her fault.'

'I never said it was. Every nun needs an Athena.'

'And anyway, we seem to be on Sauvignon Touraine these days.'

The toaster made a whirring noise, and Julius got up to deal with it. 'That's where we met,' he said.

'Sorry?'

'You and me. Touraine. The Loire Valley.'

'So we did.' Agnes cast an affectionate glance at the back of his head.

'I was just starting out as a curate. Ah well.' Julius began to open and close cupboards.

'Don't say Happy Days,' Agnes said. 'We were both utterly miserable. And the butter's over there, on that shelf.'

'Yes, we were,' Julius said, reaching for the butter dish. 'You were still married to your violent French husband-'

'And you had run away from the love of your life on the misunderstanding that it was what God wanted.'

Julius buttered toast. 'It was a long time ago. We're both old and wise now.'

'I'm just old, Julius.'

Julius handed her a plate of toast. 'The thing is, taking final vows, it won't make any difference.'

'But it will. It means giving up – '

'But it doesn't. You're focusing on all the wrong things. Nothing will change. It's just that instead of pretending to yourself that you have all these options, you won't have to worry about them any more. It'll give you a structure, a framework, within which you'll be free to live your life. It'll be very peaceful, you know.'

Agnes looked at him. 'But I'm not pretending. About the options, I mean. Right now I really do have choices. I could leave. I could go and live in my house in Provence – '

'That's just what I mean. That house is a huge distraction. If you take final vows you can get rid of it. It'll simplify your life.'

'But what if I don't want to get rid of it?'

Julius cut a piece of toast in half. 'Tell me, Agnes, do you want to leave the order?'

'No.'

'Well then.'

'Well then what?'

Julius smiled at her. 'If you don't want to leave, then there are no what-ifs, are there?'

Agnes went over to the teapot and topped up their mugs.

'But there's bubblebath, and cashmere sweaters, and gin and tonic – '

Julius laughed. 'That never goes away. Final vows or no.'

'So you mean, it'll make no difference either way.'

'Not at first, no.'

'It's the long game, then, Julius?'

Julius nodded.

Agnes said, 'I'm not sure I'm very good at the long game.'

She walked to the hostel in the sharp cold and slanting sunlight, and let herself in to the office.

'Hi, Agnes – ' Petra, one of the co-workers, appeared in the doorway, struggling with a large pile of files, which she dumped down on the other desk. She pushed spiky brown hair away from her face, straightened her baggy jeans. 'Sometimes I think this job is just paperwork. These are all referrals. There are loads more files to do, but I'm on my own this morning, since Mary didn't turn up.'

'Again?'

Petra nodded.

Agnes glanced across at her. 'Has she said why?'

Petra shook her head. 'She looked in briefly yesterday, but went off again.' Petra looked at the floor.

'I'll sort it out,' Agnes said.

Petra seemed relieved to change the subject. 'Dan told me Andy McFadden has left us,' she said.

'Seems so – '

'They can choose Now. Or they can choose Then. He's running back to something.'

'Only temporarily,' Agnes began, but her attention was caught by a thin straggle-haired figure standing in the doorway. She seemed translucent in the sunlight.

'Oh, Jeanie,' Petra said. 'Come in.'

The young woman ventured in, glancing from one to the other.

'Have you met Agnes?'

Jeanie shook her head. Agnes put out her hand, and Jeanie leaned forward and brushed Agnes's fingertips with her own, then withdrew.

'Sit down,' Petra said. Jeanie obeyed as if it was an order. 'How are you getting on?'

Jeanie opened her mouth to speak, closed it again. The phone rang, and she winced.

Agnes picked it up. 'Sister Agnes.'

'Oh. Detective Sergeant Russell here, Vine Street CID. Do you know an Andrew McFadden?'

'Yes,' Agnes said.

'Resident of yours?'

'Yes.'

'Bad news I'm afraid.'

'He's dead?' Agnes wondered afterwards how she'd been so sure, just then, just at that moment.

'Died last night. Some kind of brawl down at Charing Cross, seemed to be about someone nicking someone else's patch, everyone out of their heads, couldn't get any sense out of anyone, we're still trying. Two of them stabbed, one just a scratch, but your bloke was DOA at the hospital. They need someone to do the identification, can I give you the number there?'

Agnes wrote down the number, then rang off.

She looked up at Petra. 'Walker's dead,' she said. Her voice sounded loud in the room. 'Stabbed in a drunken fight in the West End.'

They both glanced at Jeanie. She was sitting motionless, her pale eyes fixed on the floor, her bare arms wrapped around her tiny body.

Chapter Two

Agnes stamped her feet with cold. The cemetery chapel was deserted. Julius had gone to find someone who might know where Andy was being buried. Gravestones stretched away in neat rows, their edges softened by the mist, tinted with pink in the afternoon sun. She heard footsteps on the gravel, and turned to see a figure appear beside her.

'I'm – I was looking for – ' his voice was low, muffled in the still air.

Agnes met his eyes, which were shadowed under a strangely formal black trilby. 'Andy?' she said.

'Yes.' He put out a hand to shake hers. 'I'm Alasdair. Alasdair Brogan.'

Early forties, Agnes thought. With a lived-in face. Or maybe just young for fifty. 'Are you a relative?' she said.

He hesitated. 'Yes. Sort of. Brother. Well, not really. Kind of.'

In the distance, Agnes saw Julius reappear from the chapel and turn towards one of the aisles. 'It's this way,' she said. They followed Julius, crunching gravel underfoot, and reached a newly-dug grave. There was no one to be seen. Agnes hugged her coat around her and stared into the damp earth.

A priest appeared, followed by two men carrying a coffin. Julius glanced at Alasdair, then at Agnes. Alasdair took off his hat. The priest looked up, then began to intone the burial service. Agnes caught the name Andy McFadden. The coffin was being lowered into the grave, when they were aware of a noise, a shrieking emerging from the fog.

'Where is he? Where's my Walker?' A blonde woman dressed in a short black fur coat was running towards them, her high heels kicking up the gravel. 'Is this it?' She reached Agnes, breathless, and grabbed her arm. 'Is this his grave? Is that my Walker there?'

The priest had stopped, transfixed and hostile. Alasdair didn't move. Agnes linked her arm with the woman, and murmured, 'Yes, this is Walker's funeral.' She lowered her eyes, and after a moment the woman did likewise, and the priest continued.

'... our brother, Andrew,' he muttered, 'May his soul rest in peace.'

'Amen,' the woman echoed.

'Rest eternal grant to him, O Lord, and let light perpetual shine upon him...'

'Amen,' she said again, and a sob caught at her voice.

Agnes gazed at the coffin. She noticed the heavy wood, the ornate brass handles. She glanced at the woman at her side, who was casting steely looks at Alasdair.

Afterwards the priest melted away into the mist. Alasdair Brogan ignored the blonde woman and offered his hand to Agnes. 'It was nice to meet you,' he said, and she wondered at his composure. She noticed that his eyes were a clear blue, and his hair was dark, almost black, greying at the temples. He hesitated a moment.

'We're from the hostel,' Agnes said. 'Where Walker was living. I'm Sister Agnes.' She looked over at Julius, who had wandered off and was reading the inscriptions on headstones.

'Well...' Alasdair shook her hand again, nodded at her and turned to leave. 'Goodbye, Trina,' he said. They heard his footsteps retreat into the silence.

The blonde woman smoothed at her coat with gloved hands. She glanced up at Agnes. 'Thanks,' she said.

'That's all right.'

They looked at each other.

'A holy sister?' The woman crossed herself. 'Why aren't you

wearing them things, then?'

'We don't have to.'

'Makes things confusing,' the woman said. 'Don't know where we are any more if people don't dress the part.' She glanced nervously behind her.

'And you are – '

'Trina.' She giggled.

'How did you know Andy?'

Trina dug her stiletto toe into the gravel. 'From way back.'

'When he was a soldier?'

Trina flicked Agnes a glance. She frowned, then nodded. 'Yeah. And before that.'

Julius reappeared. 'Would you like a lift?' he asked her.

She shook her head. 'No, thanks. Someone's meeting me here.'

'Trina – ' Agnes began.

'Yeah?'

There were footsteps approaching at a distance, and Trina looked nervously in their direction.

'Did Alasdair pay for that coffin?'

'No,' she said. 'Mean bastard.'

The muffled crunching on the gravel got nearer. Agnes could see a stocky figure in a leather jacket coming towards them.

'Gotta go,' Trina said.

'But – '

'Trina? I ain't got all day.' The man's voice was rough.

'Really. I've got to go.' Trina fled towards the man, who took hold of her arm and led her away.

Julius came and joined her. They looked at the fresh earth of the grave, the half-buried mossy stones of its neighbours.

'There ought to be a last post,' Julius said. 'A lone bugle to play out a soldier from this life to the next.'

The lines of graves stretched away from them, vanishing into the twilight. 'He wasn't a soldier any more,' Agnes said.

Julius glanced at her, then took her arm, and they walked together back to the car park. 'I could drop you home,' Julius said. 'Unless you fancy sharing a bowl of soup with me.'

'I'd love to. But Athena wants to try some middle-eastern place in Bayswater or somewhere, she says that Simon, you know, her boss at the art gallery, he's been raving about it.'

'I thought red wine, sweetie.' Athena handed her a menu. 'There's a very nice red Burgundy on the list, look. How was your funeral?'

'Oh, OK. Just me and Julius, and this man, who said he was his brother, and then an odd woman turned up. But what was so strange was – '

'Oh, I nearly forgot – ' Athena reached down into her bag and brought out a parcel. 'It's for you,' she said.

Agnes took the parcel, which was soft, and wrapped in gold tissue paper.

'Happy birthday,' Athena said.

'But it's not my birthday.'

'It was.'

'Ages ago. And you've already given me a present.'

Athena shrugged. 'I give you Chanel perfume every year. I thought I'd make a change. Happy Un-birthday, then. You might as well open it.'

Agnes unwrapped the tissue paper, and pulled out a camel-coloured cashmere jumper.

'I couldn't resist it,' Athena said. 'I went back for the lilac one, and I thought of you in your rags, and they're such good value, and now you've gone all unworldly I knew you wouldn't buy one yourself, and anyway I got a nice surprise commission from a painting I sold in the gallery last month, and – and you can see it as a loan, offset against your estate in Provence when you get round to selling it.'

Agnes laughed. 'Thank you,' she said. 'It's lovely. Julius said that every nun needs an Athena.'

'Perhaps he was being sarcastic.'

'Julius doesn't do sarcasm. Anyway, he gave up worrying about my soul some time ago. I rather thought I'd have the couscous with lamb shank, what do you think?'

'Mmm.' Athena looked at the menu.

'They're hardly rags,' Agnes said suddenly. 'My clothes.'

'I just hate seeing you wear the same old things. I might have couscous too. Unless I have the sea bass.' She waved at a waitress.

'The thing about this funeral...' Agnes said, 'I mean, what was so odd about it, was that – '

'Ah, yes,' Athena said, as the waitress came and took their order. 'Couscous, and – oh, dear, I can't decide. Um, sea bass, yes. With rice. Lovely. You were saying – ' Athena turned back to Agnes.

'The coffin was really fancy.'

'What coffin?'

'The coffin, at the funeral. It was a pauper's grave, but the coffin was one of those ones with brass handles and everything.'

'So?'

'Well, who'd have paid for it? There was no one there apart from this woman and his brother. And his brother was – '

'His brother was what?' Athena glanced up at her.

'Oh, I don't know.'

'What don't you know?' Athena's expression was searching. Agnes shrugged. 'I hardly spoke to him. He was wearing a really nice coat, expensive-looking.'

'You can tell a lot about a man from his coat,' Athena said, eyeing her.

'Don't you start.'

'Was he good-looking?'

'Yes, but – '

'Well, then.'

'Not "well then" at all. I'm a nun.'

'A nun. Of course.' Athena studied the menu absently. 'Maybe the woman paid for the coffin,' she said.

'Maybe.' The wine arrived, and Athena poured a generous glass each.

'I still think it's odd,' Agnes said.

'You always do.'

'What's that supposed to mean?'

'You always see mystery in things that are quite

straightforward. Which is weird, when you think about it. You'd think it would be people like me, who don't have your God, who'd find things mysterious, not people like you who have an explanation for everything.'

'But it is mysterious. Our Walker vanishes from the hostel, is then murdered, and we don't know how. We arrange a basic funeral, and there's a "sort of" brother who appears from nowhere and now this posh coffin. I think it's very strange.'

'Didn't you ask the woman at the funeral?'

'I did, but she was dragged away by a chap in a leather jacket before she could answer.'

'So all that's a mystery too, I suppose.' Athena swirled the wine in her glass, which glinted ruby-red in the low light.

'It certainly is.'

'I don't suppose – ' Athena hesitated, then went on, 'I don't suppose that all this is about your final vows.'

'You're beginning to sound like Julius.'

'I just meant, that deciding that all this funeral business is very mysterious would be a good distraction from having to make a huge decision. It's like me; every time Nic asks what I think about Barcelona, I just go shopping.'

'For cashmere sweaters.'

'I do think camel is very you.'

'So do I.'

'More wine?'

'Just a little. I'm on an early shift tomorrow.'

Agnes sat at her desk in the hostel, yawning. It was not yet eight o'clock, and the grey dawn struggled to break through the heavy sky. Rain slashed against the windows. She went into the kitchen, made herself a huge mug of tea and went back to her desk.

'Jeanie Clark,' she read from the file in front of her. 'Referred by Southwark Social Services Department – '

There was a loud hammering on the front door. Agnes jumped up and went out to the hall. One of the residents, a quiet, middle-aged man, appeared sleepily at the top of the stairs. 'If that's for me, I'm not in,' he said. 'If they ask for Aberdeen Bob, say I've gone back home.'

The hammering continued. Agnes hesitated, then opened the door.

A thickset, dishevelled man was standing there. His jacket was soaked, his dark hair fell in strands, dripping with rain.

He stared at her. 'Who are you?' he said.

'Can I help?'

'Is Sister Helen here?'

'I'm Sister Agnes. Helen doesn't work here any more.'

He seemed to crumple slightly. 'Am I too late?' he said. His voice was rough, with an accent Agnes couldn't place.

'Too late for what?'

'He's dead, isn't he?' His breath made clouds in the cold air. 'Walker? He's dead.'

Agnes could smell whisky. She nodded. 'Yes,' she said. 'He's dead.'

The man put one hand against the doorpost to steady himself. He shook his head. 'I knew I was too late,' he murmured. He turned to go.

'Wait – ' Agnes heard herself say.

He turned back, his feet on the stone steps. 'I can't come in there. I stayed there once, dried out, clean I was for months. Not now.'

'I'll come with you, then,' Agnes said. She ran and got her coat, and told Aberdeen Bob, who had wandered into the kitchen, that she'd be at the cafe on the corner if anyone needed her.

The man was still standing on the front steps.

'Breakfast?' Agnes said to him.

He looked at her, and for the first time he smiled. 'Sure,' he said. 'Breakfast.'

It was still raining. The drab tower blocks of the estates cowered under heavy grey skies. In the distance the smart new developments looked insubstantial, as if their sleekness was a mere surface, a veneer liable to dissolve in the rain.

Agnes pushed open the door of the cafe, and was met by the familiar warmth. They found a table tucked away in a corner.

'The usual, love?' The woman behind the counter wiped her hands on her thick white apron.

'Times two,' Agnes said. 'Please.'

'So you're called Sister Agnes,' the man said, studying her.

'And you are – ?'

'Michael,' he said. 'Michael Cordaro.'

'Do you know Trina?' Agnes watched his expression shift at the name. The waitress put two mugs of tea down in front of them. Michael nodded, slowly. 'Trina,' he repeated. 'You're not going to tell me she was there. At the funeral?'

'Yes. And so was Alasdair.'

'Who?'

'Alasdair Brogan. He said he was a sort-of brother.'

Michael shrugged. 'Don't mean nothing to me. Never heard of no brother. Though that family, they were all over the place, they were.' He took a mouthful of tea. 'Trina, eh? And was she dressed up to the nines?'

'Yes,' Agnes said. 'She was.'

Michael shook his head. 'And was it my Walker this and my Walker that?'

Agnes sipped her tea. 'Yes, it was. The coffin,' she went on. 'The coffin looked as if it had cost a lot.'

Michael looked up from his mug. 'Did it?'

'Yes. Oak, I thought. Brass handles.' She watched him.

'You mean, who'd pay for all that?'

'I did wonder.'

'Maybe this brother.'

'I don't know. He didn't seem involved.' Their breakfast arrived, and Michael attacked his hungrily. Agnes speared a fried egg and watched the yolk spread over her toast. 'How did you know Walker, then?' she asked.

Michael finished chewing a large mouthful. 'The army,' he said. 'We were soldiers together.'

'In the Falklands?'

Michael shook his head. 'No. Not me. I never got there. Glad really, although it cost me my mates in a way. Them that went, they came back different. I was in Belfast, you see.'

'How did you know he was dead?'

'I'd heard from someone, that's all. Hoped I wasn't too late, I'd have liked to pay my respects. They said he was stabbed.'

'Yes. There was a fight last week, in Charing Cross.'

Michael nodded. 'It was his patch, but I suppose he'd been away for a while. I know some of them boys there.'

'Who's Trina?' Agnes asked.

'She and Walker, they nearly got married. Way back. She knew him from when we was all kids on the estate in Stepney.'

'But who told you Walker was dead?'

Michael concentrated on smearing margarine on a piece of toast. 'Word gets out,' he said finally.

'Did you know Lucky?'

Michael nodded. 'Poor bugger.'

'He died in the Falklands?'

Michael raised his eyes from his plate in surprise. 'Lucky was only a soldier for a few months. Never went to the Falklands. No, he died here. Smashed up his bike, didn't he? Always was a reckless bastard.'

'In Walker's writings, he says that he and Lucky were together in the Falklands.'

'What writings?' His tone was suddenly sharp.

'Walker wrote a diary thing, over the months he was in the hostel.'

'He did?'

'It was a sort of therapy.'

'I bet it was.' Michael was eyeing her. 'Where are they now, these writings?'

Agnes hesitated. 'I've got them,' she said.

'On you?' he said, urgently.

She shook her head. 'They're locked away.'

He put his knife and fork carefully together. 'Don't suppose I'm in it, am I? This so-called diary?'

'No,' Agnes replied, thinking about the stack of pages that she hadn't yet read. 'It was mostly about fighting the war. There was someone he mentioned, though – '

'Yes?'

'He doesn't name him. But there's some sort of threat, implying that if he ever saw him again – '

'That's Walker all over, that is. There's about ten blokes that Walker had it in for. It's probably all rubbish, like Lucky being in the war.' The tone had softened again, and he smiled at her. 'Shall we go?'

'Sure.'

He helped her on with her coat, and they headed for the door. 'That Trina,' he said, as he held the door open for her.

'Yes?'

'Don't believe a word she says.'

They stood out in the street, their breath making mist. 'I don't suppose I'll see her again,' Agnes said.

'You see,' Michael said, as they started walking back to the main road. 'Walker, he was on borrowed time. Death wish, that boy. Stuff he'd got up to, he was lucky to live as long as he did. We always said that, we did, we always said that when Lucky had his smash, the Bloke up there was having a laugh, weren't he? Lucky died, Walker survived. And now Walker's dead too. Funny, isn't it? I'm going this way. Thanks for the breakfast.' He ambled off to the traffic lights and crossed the road. Agnes watched him go into the pub at the corner, then turned and headed back to the hostel.

That evening, she sat at her desk in the quiet that descended at the end of the day. She opened a drawer to replace a file, and saw Walker's crumpled pages. She pulled them out, and began to read at random.

'... So he tells Tin that back in Peckham, his brother Nigel's been shagging his bird, and we laugh, because we all know he hasn't got a brother and even if he had he wouldn't be called Nigel, would he? And Tin looks like he's going to start crying, and it isna funny, so we laugh more. That's how hunky-bloody-dory it is out here, and now Pitch has gone it's like the life's gone out of me too, drained away with his blood in that fucking mud-bath last week...'

There was a ring at the doorbell. Agnes closed the diary, then went to the door.

'We weren't expecting anyone – ' she began. 'Oh.'

'Hello.' Alasdair Brogan was standing there. She hadn't remembered he was so tall. The black wool coat, she'd remembered perfectly. 'I don't suppose you're free for a drink?' he said.

'I was just finishing my shift,' she said.

'Surely you're too grand to keep to shifts,' he said.

'No,' she said. 'I'm just a nun.'

He smiled at her. 'Just a nun,' he repeated, as she went to get her coat.

Chapter Three

'Will this do?' Alasdair pushed open the door of the wine bar. 'I thought it would be nice to be by the river.'

Agnes nodded, breathless from trying to keep up with him as he strode through the night beside her.

He found a corner table, and picked up the wine list. He handed it to her. 'You choose. I'm not drinking.'

'Oh.' She scanned the list. 'I'm rather keen on Sauvignon Blanc at the moment,' she said.

She watched him at the bar, watched him return some moments later with a bottle and one glass.

'It's New Zealand, but I believe they're rather good at this stuff,' he said. He studied her as she tasted it. 'Is it OK?'

She smiled at his concern. 'It's very good,' she said.

'I wasn't sure whether...' Surprisingly, he blushed. 'Nuns, I mean. You know, all this...' he gestured around him. 'I only know about medieval monastic life, and it's probably changed a bit since the fourteenth century.'

Agnes laughed. 'It has, a bit.' She sipped her wine. 'Do you ever drink?'

'No. Not now.' It was the end of the conversation.

'I can't manage all this,' she said.

'We can always ask for a cork.'

'Why fourteenth century?' she said.

'It's my work.' He brought out cigarette papers and tobacco

and began to roll a cigarette. 'I'm a translator. Italian, mostly. These days I seem to get rare Tuscan writings from book collectors to work on. Although at the moment, I'm translating Dante, which will tie me up for a while. Do you mind?' He indicated the cigarette.

'No, not at all. Why Italian?'

He lit the cigarette and puffed on it. 'Don't know. It just kind of happened. I did Languages at university. And...' His voice tailed off.

'And what?'

'My mother was Italian,' he said. In the silence she sensed his hesitation, his pausing at the brink of speech. Then,

'Andy and I – we weren't really brothers,' he said. His voice cut through the surrounding hubbub and Agnes looked up at him. 'I mean, not in any blood relative sense. His mum came and lived with my dad, we were thrown together. I hardly knew him really.'

'So why... I mean, the funeral?'

'When the police contacted me – and then you people – '

'He had you down as next of kin.'

'Yes. I know.' Alasdair turned his cigarette in his fingers. 'I suppose there was no one else left, after Eileen died, his mother.'

'But – '

Alasdair looked up.

'Andy was from the East End,' Agnes said.

'Not to start with. We grew up in Glasgow. His mum met my father, she was widowed, they got together. Then my father died, and she and Andy moved back to London, where she was from. I hardly saw him after that, I went to college, he joined the army...'

Agnes sensed that he was waiting, wanting to say more.

'We were very different,' he went on. 'He hung about on the estate, I went away to school. I was taught by monks for a while,' he added, smiling. 'They thought I'd make a good priest.'

'A priest?' She looked up at him.

'It would have been a mistake.' His eyes darkened as she met his gaze. There was another silence, until she looked away.

'Why did you come and find me?' she asked, staring at the table.

'Because – ' he stopped.

She looked up at him. He was tracing the grain of the wooden table with his finger.

'He was killed, you see.' Alasdair was speaking very quietly. 'Andy... Walker. He was murdered.'

'But – ' Agnes wondered what he was talking about. 'But everyone knows that. The police came to tell us. They're looking for a down-and-out called Mitch, someone said he was holding a broken bottle. He's vanished for the moment.'

Alasdair was shaking his head. 'No, I mean, it wasn't a street brawl. It was deliberate. They came for him. It was a carefully planned killing.'

'You mean, not this Mitch?'

'No. Not some down-and-out in a random killing.'

'Who, then?'

'That's what I don't yet know.'

'So what makes you think it was deliberate?' she asked.

'There were clues. There are things he's said, over the years, not that I've had much to do with him, but... All I know is, there were old scores to be settled, and this is the result.'

'Did you pay for the coffin?' Agnes heard the words blurt themselves out.

He glanced at her, then nodded. Agnes wondered why she didn't believe him.

'So,' she said, 'these old scores – ?'

'There's all this rubbish, you see, all this stuff about the Falklands and his friend Lucky, he's gone on about it for years – it's covering something up.'

'But he was a soldier.'

'A soldier, yes.'

'And he did see active service?'

'Well, yes. But the battles he fought out on the field, they were nothing compared to the ones he was fighting in his head.'

Agnes drained her glass. 'What are you going to do?'

Alasdair stared at his hands. He fiddled with a signet ring on the index finger of his right hand. He looked up. 'Will you help me?'

'Why?' she said. 'Why do you have to find out more? What is it to you?'

This time she met his searching gaze without looking away.

'Because...' Alasdair took a deep breath. 'My father was not a good man. Andy's mother, Eileen, wasted several years of her life on my father, and it did Andy no good. Andy deserved better, that's all. I think of him dying in the gutter, and I know that it falls to me to... to do what's right. And I need your help. Will you help me?'

I cannot say yes, Agnes was thinking. I mean, just because Walker had some dark past, as all such men do, and just because this distant not-even-brother suddenly wants to make amends, for reasons which are not at all clear... Of course I can't say yes. If I say yes...

'Yes,' Agnes said.

Alasdair reached across the table and grasped her hand. 'Thank you,' he said, his voice thick with feeling. Agnes stared at the bright white strip of shirt cuff, at the wrist that held her own. The noise around them was suddenly much too loud.

'Well, just tell him you can't, sweetie. Just say you've changed your mind.' It was evening, and Agnes lay on her bed, listening to Athena's voice on the phone. 'Or even better,' Athena was saying, 'tell him that one of those bossy nuns has forbidden it. Or God even.'

'Athena, really, I can't – '

'I mean, sweetie, it must be so darn useful being able to have God as an excuse, you might as well make the most of it. Maybe I should try it, next time Nic's going on about Barcelona, I can just say, God tells me that I mustn't. Nic was brought up a Methodist or something, it might work.'

'But I don't want to.'

There was a brief pause down the line. 'Don't want to what?' Athena said.

'I don't want to say no to Alasdair. It's just that saying Yes is a very bad idea.'

'You don't half complicate things, sweetie. I mean either you say No, and concentrate on taking these vow things, and doing as you're told – and getting rid of your lovely house in Provence, God, if I had the money I'd buy it – OR – you say Yes, and find yourself embroiled in some plot with a mysterious and gorgeous man who goes on about murder and lies about coffins. Well, it's obvious which path you're going to choose, isn't it?'

'Is it?' Agnes felt suddenly tired.

'Oh, listen to you, darling. You've already chosen it.'

Agnes lay on her bed. There was the swish of cars in the rain, flashes of passing headlights. She looked at a strip of white light on her ceiling, and remembered Alasdair's grip on her wrist. As they left the restaurant he had taken her hand again, only relinquishing his hold as they had come out into the street. He had faced her, hunched into his collar in the night air. 'I'll phone you,' he'd said. 'Tomorrow.'

'Tomorrow,' she'd agreed, then turned away and crossed the road to the bus stop. When she glanced back, he'd gone.

It doesn't feel like a choice, she thought. It feels inevitable.

She stirred from her bed, crossed the room and lit her candle. She reached for her prayer-book, and stood, turning the pages to find the readings.

'...Jesus turned round in the crowd and said, "Who touched my clothes?" And his disciples said to him, "You see the crowd pressing in on you – how can you say, 'Who touched me?'" He looked all around to see who had done it. But the woman, knowing what had happened to her, came in fear and trembling, and fell down before him. He said to her "Daughter, your faith has made you well. Go in peace, and be healed of your disease."'

Agnes knelt in prayer. 'Daughter, your faith has made you well...' The words sounded in her head.

If only, she thought. If only one could find oneself in the presence of One who would make it all better. To touch the hem of their robe, and be healed... To be healed by one's own faith.

My faith is too weak, she thought. What would it be like, she wondered, to be so loved? To be able to believe in that kind of love, to abandon oneself to the belief that one is loved.

She thought about Athena, and Julius. She thought about her mother, and tears pricked her eyes. There is no one left who knows me as a child, she thought, and wondered why she was crying. Why this wave of loss? Even when my mother was alive, she didn't even like me. I am no more lonely now than I was then.

'Go in peace, and be healed...' It is enough, she thought, to love. To love Athena, and Julius; to love life itself.

She wiped the tears from her eyes, and settled in prayer, and dismissed the image of Alasdair that briefly passed across her mind.

The morning was bright and sunny. Agnes made breakfast at the hostel, washed up, made coffee, and every time the phone rang she jumped. Jayce's probation officer arrived and Jayce refused to see her. Dan found some money missing from the petty cash box, and Aberdeen Bob said he'd seen Archie Crane in there last night, and what with his gambling problem the finger pointed at him.

During a lull, Agnes went through all the hostel paperwork on Andy McFadden, but found nothing of interest.

By lunchtime there was no word from Alasdair, and Agnes wandered across to the Rising Sun on the corner, in the hope of seeing Michael Cordaro. There was no sign of him. She was greeted by a one-time resident, a grizzled-haired ex-sailor who'd worked in the London docks but whose life had fallen apart some time during the seventies when the love of his life, a jeweller, had emigrated to Australia. He raised his glass to her, and she smiled back, and wondered whether if he'd stayed at the hostel it could have made his life better, or whether for him this was the best it could get, sitting with a pint and a cigarette and dreaming of Karen setting diamonds in Melbourne.

Back at the hostel everything was calm. She unlocked her desk drawer and took out the crumpled sheaves of paper that made up Walker's writings.

'... They talk about circles of Hell here. I don't know about circles, it just seems like it has no end and no beginning. Every time I close my eyes I see Pitch staring at me from the pilot's seat of the helicopter, and I think, thank Christ he's alive, and then I see he's got no legs, and I remember that I'm laughing then, when I think about it, I'm laughing and I think, how's the poor bugger going to walk?...'

Agnes turned over a few pages.

'... I remember walking up the hill after Goose Green, in the silence, the smell that was like death. I remember the wind blowing, but I'm not sure if I've added that bit in. What I do remember, though, is thinking, if it wasn't for her, I'd be dead. It was like she'd kept me alive, thinking of her. And I remember walking up the hill thinking all I need to do is go back home and tell her how I feel. And now, all these years later, I see him, the man I was then, walking up the hill in that silent dawn, and I think, you poor sod. 'Cos she said she'd love you for ever. And you believed her.'

The door opened, and Agnes looked up. Jeanie had crept in, like a shadow, and was now standing there, uncertain. She wore huge, pink fluffy slippers.

Agnes smiled at her. 'Hello.' She folded Andy's papers and put them back in the drawer.

Jeanie continued to stand there. Her eyes flickered, glancing at the floor, at the filing cabinet, then out of the window, where something had caught her eye.

'How are you?' Agnes tried.

Jeanie's gaze came to rest on Agnes. 'Someone came,' she said. 'When Walker went, that day, someone came and asked for him. I answered the door and there was this woman there, and she said, was he there, and I said no. I didn't know if he was in or not, but I was scared, opening the door like that, Mary was supposed to be here but she didn't answer the door so I did. And this woman just said, can you say I called. And I said yes, and shut the door, because I know it's against the rules to answer the door, I don't know why I did it. And then I didn't see him, and then he'd gone and I didn't know.'

She seemed to sway, drained by the effort of saying so many

words at once, and Agnes drew up a chair for her.

'Did she give a name, this woman?'

'No.' Jeanie flopped into the chair. 'I thought it was strange, but I was panicking, I thought what if Ash comes past.'

'What did she look like?'

Jeanie frowned. 'A bit like you. Younger. Red hair. She had a coat. There was a man there too, standing behind her. He was kind of big and hairy.'

'Thank you for telling me,' Agnes said.

Jeanie sat, hunched, staring at her knees. 'It's my fault,' she said, in a small voice.

'What's your fault?'

'He died, didn't he?' She raised fierce eyes to Agnes. 'If I'd found him and told him about this woman, things would have been different.'

Agnes leaned across to touch Jeanie's hand, and Jeanie snatched it away.

'It is not your fault,' Agnes said, withdrawing her hand. 'Andy died in a brawl. It was an accident. And anyway, if this woman had something to say to him and knew where he lived, she could have come back. She could have come another time. There's no connection. It's just one of those things.'

Jeanie stood up. 'The only person who ever cared about me drove his car into a tree. Is that just one of those things?' She turned and left the room.

Agnes stared at Andy's file sitting on her desk. The phone rang and she snatched it up.

'Sweetie, it's me.'

'Oh.'

'What's the matter?' Athena asked.

'Nothing.'

'Listen, can we meet for a drink this evening. I really need your advice. How's the lovely man?'

'What, since last night? I've no idea. And he's not lovely. Well, he is, but that's not the point.'

'No. Of course not, sweetie.'

'He said he'd phone today.' In the background, Agnes could hear the hostel doorbell ringing.'Must go,' she said, 'someone at the door – '

'The Crazy Bear, Shoreditch. Eight o clock?'

'I know it – ' the doorbell was now sounding continuously. 'See you then.'

Agnes heard Dan answer the door, heard him raise his voice in argument with someone there – a woman's voice, she thought. She locked the desk drawer and went to see what was going on.

'That's the one – ' the voice was shrill, the finger pointing at her was tipped with a long, bright red nail.

'Hello, Trina,' Agnes began.

'He wouldn't let me in,' Trina said. She was standing in the doorway, her short fur coat golden in the sunlight. Dan was standing in the doorway, apologetic.

'I didn't know you meant Agnes,' he said.

'It's not my fault I couldn't remember her name,' Trina said. She brushed past Dan and came into the hall. 'That man phoned me,' she said to Agnes. 'Alasdair. It upset me. I don't like people upsetting me.'

'Um, no...' Agnes said. 'Would you like – '

'Yes. I would. Coffee, please,' she said, turning to Dan. 'Black, two sugars.' She walked past Agnes into the office.

'No, really, don't worry, it's fine,' Dan said, heading for the kitchen, 'I like being staff.'

Trina arranged her fur coat over the back of an armchair, and sat down. 'Scott was upset too,' she said.

Agnes sat down opposite her. 'So Alasdair phoned you?'

'Scott wanted to know who he was, what he was to do with me. I said, no one, 'cos he isn't, is he? But that made it worse. Scott don't like no one saying no one.'

'And Scott is – ?'

Trina opened wide eyes. 'My old man. You know.'

Agnes remembered his appearance at the funeral, the rough

voice and leather jacket emerging briefly from the mist to carry Trina away.

'I'd say my husband,' Trina was saying, 'only he isn't. But we've been together that long, we might as well be. Common Law, isn't it?'

'And what did Alasdair want?'

'He was asking me all these questions about Walker's last days, like I should know? The way those two were, you wouldn't even know he had a brother. Then Scott grabbed the phone, and said a few words. And then Scott hung up, and said, that Alasdair, he won't be bothering us no more.' She laughed, a bare twitch of the lips.

The door opened, and Dan appeared with a tray, on which were two mugs. He put the tray down, bowed deeply, and left.

'And what did Alasdair want?'

Trina picked up a mug of black coffee. 'He said, Walker had been killed on purpose, and did I know anything about it.' She blew on her mug, glossy red lips in a puff of steam.

'And what did you say?'

'What do you think I said? I said, don't be stupid, if Walker wants to get himself glassed in Charing Cross, what am I going to do about it? And that's when Scott grabbed the phone.'

Agnes tasted her coffee, and wished it wasn't instant. 'And why did you decide to come and see me?' she said.

Trina smoothed her short black skirt over her knees. 'Because I want that man off my back,' she said.

'Alasdair?'

'Yes. Because Scott will kill him if he tries to talk to me again.'

'Oh.'

'And I thought as you seemed to know him, you could tell him.' Trina put down her mug. 'OK?'

'OK.'

Trina stood up. She picked her coat up, and threw it over her shoulders. Agnes sat still, watching her.

'Trina – '

'What?'

'Why did you really come and see me?'

'I just told you, didn't I.'

'You knew Andy McFadden well, didn't you? For years, you said.'

'Mmm.' Trina pulled her coat around her.

'You knew him well enough to find me here. You knew this hostel?'

'Maybe.' Trina stared at the floor.

'You'd known him a long time.'

Trina met her gaze. Her eyes welled with tears.

'He had few friends in life,' Agnes said, searching for the right words. 'Maybe in death...'

Trina crumpled back into her chair. 'I loved that man for years, and if he hadn't changed I'd have loved him still – ' she stopped for breath, between sobs – 'He was always saying that there were some who had it in for him, someone was going to get him in the end, but what I reckon is, they was in his head. It was life that messed with him, and the army, it messed with his head, but underneath it all, he was straight as a die, and loyal. But no one could see...' Another sob, a sniff. Agnes passed her a tissue and she dabbed at her nose.

'Trina – the night he died...'

Trina looked up. She sniffed again. 'Sister, if I start to tell you the list of people who had an account to settle with Walker, we'd be here all bloody day.'

'How about the first ten?'

She managed a smile. 'When he came back from the Falklands, he was an angry man. He made a lot of enemies in those days after the war. But none of them would've killed him. I mean, I can tell you the blokes what would like to have a go at Walker, but to stab him like that, one clean blow, Scott said, you'd have to really mean it, really plan it, wouldn't you.' She picked up her handbag, took out a compact and peered at her reflection. She patted her face with powder, snapped the compact away in her handbag and stood up. 'I'd better go. Scott don't know I've come here.'

Agnes stood up to show her out. 'Alasdair said he paid for the coffin,' she said, opening the wide front door.

Trina stood at the top of the steps. 'Well he's a lying bastard,' she said.

'He might have done, surely – '

'No, he didn't.' She hesitated, then said, 'It was me. I paid for it.' She put out her hand. 'It was nice to talk to you,' she said.

Agnes took her hand. 'You paid for the coffin?'

Trina smiled. 'I told Scott the money was for this coat, and then I got my mate to nick the coat for me, she goes shopping, professional, like. I planned it all. Nothing but the best for my Walker.' She giggled, like a child. The sudden sunlight softened her blonde curls. 'If you find out any more about what happened to him, will you let me know?' she said.

'How do I contact you?'

Trina pulled out a scrap of paper and scribbled a number on it. 'That's my mobile,' she said. 'If Scott answers, just say who you are, put in the Sister bit, then he won't mind.' She turned to go.

'Trina – '

She turned back. 'What?'

'How did your Scott know it was one clean blow?'

'I don't know what you mean.'

'You said, just then. About Walker being stabbed. One clean blow.'

Trina tried a light laugh. 'Did I?'

'You said that's what Scott said.'

She pouted, shrugged, laughed her little laugh. 'That's Scott for you, isn't. Makes it his business to know everything. Better go.' She turned her back. 'Bye, then,' she said.

Agnes watched her teeter down the stone stairs in her high heels. At the end of the street, she glanced back and waved, then was gone.

'And I bet he hasn't phoned you.' Athena chose an almond from the bowl of roasted nuts in front of her.

'Who hasn't?' Agnes raised her voice. It was a Wednesday night and the bar in Shoreditch was very crowded.

Athena raised an eyebrow. 'Who indeed. The man, of course. The one who's lovely but we're not supposed to notice.'

'No, actually. He hasn't.'

'You see? He's a man.'

'And you were right about – ' Agnes blinked as the icy vodka hit her lips.

'Told you their martinis were good here.'

'They remind me of my old life in France, for some reason. My ghastly ex-husband.'

'Typical of Hugo to pretend to be James Bond.'

'I think the Bond martinis were gin, weren't they?'

'You know best, you're a nun, after all.' Athena took another nut. 'What was I right about?'

'It was Trina who paid for the coffin.'

'Trina?' Athena looked blank.

'The woman at the funeral.'

'Oh, her, of course.' Athena smiled, pleased. 'Trust me, sweetie, I'm a great judge of character.'

'So, if you're so clever, you can tell me – why did Alasdair lie? And why did he say he'd phone and then not?'

Athena took a sip of martini and sighed. 'Oh, sweetie, you really are a nun, aren't you? Because he's a man, of course.'

'But surely they're not all – what's that noise?' Agnes could hear a beeping coming from under their table.

'It sounds like someone's mobile.'

'Honestly, it's such a nuisance, the way people – oh. I think it might be mine.' Agnes rummaged in her coat and took out a phone. 'Hello?'

'Hi.' She could hear Alasdair's voice, faint against the noisy crowd.

'Hello,' she said.

You're blushing, Athena mouthed at her across the table.

'How are you?' Alasdair was saying.

'I'm in a bar,' Agnes said.

'It sounds like it.'

'Did you get anywhere?' Agnes said.

'Yes. Lots to tell you.'

'I can hardly hear you.'

'I'll phone you later.'

'I'll be home by ten,' Agnes said.

'Fine.' He'd gone.

'Do I press the red button?' Agnes said to Athena.

'Honestly,' Athena said, 'if your order is going to issue you with mobiles, you'd think they'd show you how they work.'

'It's for the hostel, we're not supposed to use them for idle chat.'

'Does God need to communicate by phone these days?'

Agnes sighed. 'Heathen times, you see. He has to make the most of whatever technology's available.'

Athena nodded. 'Mmm. I can see that.'

'And I wasn't blushing.'

'Either that or an early menopausal hot flush.'

'Obviously not that.'

'Obviously,' Athena agreed.

Agnes sipped her drink. 'What did you want to ask me about?'

'Nic's going to Barcelona next week, to have a look round. He wants me to come too.'

'And?'

'I don't have time, sweetie. We've got a new exhibition opening on Monday, she's a temperamental German woman, a sculptor, it's all bronze cubic things that look like naked men. Simon's relying on me. I bought a new suit specially for the opening, it's beautifully cut, but it's lime green, I'm really not sure about it.'

'Have you told Nic you can't go?'

Athena sighed. 'Yes, but – he said he needed me to show that I was willing to support him in this.'

'In other words, he's cross.'

'He's a therapist, sweetie. Sometimes it's hard to tell.' She took a mouthful of her drink. 'I love Nic. And I love my London life. And I don't want to have to choose between them.'

'I wish I could help.'

'We're in the same boat, really, you and I.'

Agnes frowned. 'We are?'

'Having to make irrevocable life choices.'

'Oh. Yes. I suppose we are.'

Athena raised her glass. 'To gorgeous men. To Nic and – and what's-his-name.'

'Alasdair,' Agnes said, raising her glass. 'But he's not gorgeous. Well, he is, but – '

'Oh, just shut up.'

At ten minutes to ten, Agnes let herself into her flat. She put the kettle on, hung up her coat, picked up her book of the Daily Office, turned to the Psalms, glanced through the pages as she stood in the middle of the room. At five to ten she put a peppermint tea bag into a mug and poured boiling water on to it. At ten o'clock her mobile phone rang.

'Hi,' she said.

'Can you hear me now?' Alasdair seemed to be shouting.

'I'm at home.'

'Oh. Good.' There was a brief pause. 'What is home?' he asked, his voice quieter now.

'A tiny flat in an interwar social housing block in Bermondsey. Almost a bedsit really. I love it.'

'Oh. Don't you miss having a garden?'

Agnes started to laugh. 'A garden?'

'Have I said something funny?'

'My order has a huge house in Hackney, with a large garden. If I lived there, which is what they want, I could garden to my heart's content. Roses. Herbs. Potatoes, probably. Whenever I wanted.'

'But -?'

'I love roses. But given the choice between roses and solitude, there's no contest.'

'Mmm.'

'What about you?'

'What about me?' he said.

'Where do you live?'

'I have a house. In Hampstead. Well, Hampstead borders really.

We just tend to say Hampstead.'

'We?'

There was another hesitation. 'I live alone.'

Agnes heard his breathing. 'So,' she said.

'I spoke to Trina,' Alasdair said.

'So did I.'

'You did?' He seemed surprised.

'Yes, she came to see me. You'd upset her.'

'I'd upset her? – ' Alasdair's voice was suddenly harsh. 'When – ?'

'This afternoon. At the hostel. She said you'd phoned, and she wants you "off her back", I think that was the expression she used. And she said Scott will kill you if you try to contact her again. And Scott seems to know rather more than anyone's saying too.'

Alasdair was silent for a moment. 'We have a bit of a history, Trina and me,' he said at last. 'She's never liked me.'

'And – ' Agnes took a deep breath. 'And she said she paid for Walker's coffin.'

'Do you believe her?'

Agnes hesitated. 'Yes,' she said. 'Yes, I do.'

'She's a stupid woman.'

Agnes listened to the change in his voice. 'You said you had lots to tell me,' she tried.

'Oh. Yes.' He sounded distracted. 'Are you around tomorrow?'

'I'm on the afternoon shift at the hostel. Before that I'll be at the community house,' Agnes said.

'Tending your potatoes.'

It sounded sarcastic, and she regretted having trusted him.

'I love my order,' she said.

'Just as well, in the circumstances,' he said. There was a silence. 'I'll phone you,' he said, and rang off.

Agnes took the bag out of her mint tea, which was still hot. She picked up her prayer book where she'd left it, and found she was reading Psalm 77.

'In the day of my trouble I sought the Lord, my hands were

stretched out by night and did not tire; I refused to be comforted...'

Something had happened, just then, on the phone.

'The waters saw you, O God; the waters saw you and trembled; the very depths were shaken.

'The clouds poured out water, the skies thundered; your arrows flashed to and fro;

'The sound of your thunder was in the whirlwind; your lightnings lit up the world; the earth trembled and shook...'

Outside Agnes could hear the siren of a passing ambulance. She closed the prayer book, and picked up her mug of tea. She wrapped her hands around it, wondering why she felt so cold.

Chapter Four

The chapel echoed with women's singing. Agnes scanned the pews. She could see Sister Madeleine, Sister Felicity, Sister Karina. She joined in the hymn, as the early sun touched the east window, lighting up the flowers by the pulpit, the irises and yellow roses, flecking the oak benches with blue and gold.

This will be my home, she thought. I will have to belong here.

The kitchen was warm and brightly lit.

'Tea, Agnes?' It was Madeleine.

'Thanks.'

'How are you since we swapped jobs.'

'Oh,' Agnes said. 'You know.'

Madeleine smiled at her. 'Is life complicated?'

'Yes,' Agnes said. 'How's the homeless children project?'

'Fine.' Madeleine leaned against the table. 'We miss you. Julius misses you most of all, I think.'

'Silly old Julius,' Agnes said.

Madeleine laughed and went over to the cupboards in search of mugs.

'Madeleine,' Agnes began. 'Did you have much to do with Mary? Mary Holbeck.'

'Oh. Mary.'

'She seems not to like me. I mean, I know I'm a tricky person, and I'm used to people finding me difficult, because I am, but – '

Madeleine was holding up her hand. 'It's not personal.'

'Whenever I'm on a shift, she vanishes. She's been doing nights because I'm mostly on days. How can you say it's not personal? Poor old Petra, and Dan, neither of them want to say, but they know, they can see – '

'It's not you.' Madeleine interrupted. 'It's because you're a sister.'

Agnes was silenced. 'But – how – ?'

'I had exactly the same problem. I thought I'd offended her in some way. It was only when I mentioned it to Sister Karina, who knew the background, that I found out what was going on. She used to be a nun, Mary did. She was in a closed order, up north somewhere, Carmelite, I think. Karina found out by chance, from one of the residents. She won't talk to any of us.'

'So, what happened?'

'There was a man that she loved. She met him before she joined the order. I think she thought it would all wear off if she became a nun.'

'It never does.'

Madeleine handed her a mug of tea. 'No. From what Karina could gather, it went on for years. This terrible conflict, between staying in the order and running off with the man she loved. And in the end, after about fifteen years of waiting for her, he came to see her. And they had a long heart-to-heart, a conversation that went on for days. And then he left. And then, a few days later, he died. The man she loved. Natural causes, a huge heart attack.'

Agnes put her hand to her mouth.

'Exactly,' Madeleine went on. 'And so Mary had a crisis, which resulted in her leaving the order, giving up the church, giving up everything.'

'She told Dan she was an atheist.'

'There you are. She trained in social work, apparently, and ended up specialising in addiction. So you can imagine her horror when she gets a job attached to a hostel and finds it overrun with us lot.'

'How awful.'

'I mean, really, someone should talk to her, help her find a different job.'

'It just burdens the others,' Agnes said, 'Dan and everyone, if she keeps slipping away.'

'Are you busy there at the moment?'

'Well – ' Agnes took a deep breath. 'One of our residents was killed. Stabbed in a street brawl.'

Madeleine rubbed the side of her head. 'That's all you need.'

'Andy McFadden. Known as Walker. Did you meet him?'

'He was in the Falklands.'

'That's right,' Agnes said.

'Went back on the drink?'

Agnes nodded. 'Got involved in some argument down by Embankment.'

Madeleine went over to the sink. 'It's all so tenuous, isn't it,' she said. She picked up a mug from the draining rack and dried it with a tea-towel. 'Our grip on life. It all seems so Here, doesn't it, so solid and definite and certain, and then one flick of a knife and it drains away to nothing.' She put the mug away in a cupboard.

Agnes sipped her tea. The two women stood in the kitchen, as the morning sun crept in through the window.

She took the bus from Kingsland Road to Whitechapel. She thought about Walker's writings, locked away in a drawer at the hostel. She changed buses, got off the bus at Tower Bridge Road, and walked to the hostel in the midday sun.

As she arrived at the front steps she could hear loud drum and bass music blasting out of Jayce's open window.

The office door was open. Mary was sitting at one of the desks.

'Hello – ' Agnes began.

Mary looked up and saw Agnes. She got up from the desk, and stood, straight backed, her grey hair pulled into a tight bun at the back of her head. She walked out of the office.

Agnes opened her drawer and took out Walker's writings. She searched through the pages, but they were un-numbered and tatty from having been folded and unfolded. She chose a page at random.

'... the counsellor said I needed Anger Management. I laughed. I told her, if you'd been through what I'd been through you'd be angry too. She went on about the war but I said, Listen, Hen, I was angry before the war, I was angry during the war and I'm angry now. When I was a kid I broke down doors in our house, until my mum moved in with another man and I was too scared of him to be angry...'

She heard a ring at the door. She jumped up and went to answer it. Alasdair was standing on the front steps. .

'I'm sorry about last night,' he said.

His black coat was open, and he was wearing a crisp white shirt underneath.

'Have you had lunch? I know it's rather late, and I'm sure you've already eaten, there's a place by the river I know, it's very good – '

'No,' Agnes said, rather louder than she meant. 'No, I haven't already eaten.'

They sat in the glass-walled roof terrace restaurant, and she turned her wine in her hand, watching flecks of light fall on white linen.

'I'm sorry I lied,' Alasdair said.

'About the coffin?' Agnes said.

He nodded. 'I didn't pay for it.'

'Do you often lie?' Agnes asked him.

'It was the way you put me on the spot. I felt terrible, you see, I still do. He's sort of my brother and yet I've had so little to do with him.' He paused while the waiter arranged plates of scallops on the table.

'I've brought you a present,' Alasdair said. He fished in his pocket and brought out a crisp rectangle, a bookshop bag.

Agnes drew out the book. 'The Divine Comedy,' she said. 'Dante.'

'It's the second volume,' he said.

'The *Purgatorio*,' she said.

'It's an odd American edition, but it's my favourite translation,' he said.

'Apart from your own, of course.'

Alasdair smiled at her. 'If only.'

Agnes turned the book over in her hands. It was a handsome, compact hardback with an eggshell blue cover. 'It's lovely,' she said. 'Thank you.' She placed it carefully on the table. 'Shouldn't I start with the *Inferno*?'

Alasdair considered the book as it lay on the tablecloth. 'Probably. But I like the *Purgatorio*. In the *Inferno*, the poet, Dante, is led through the layers of Hell, encountering sinners being horribly punished. In the *Purgatorio*, he's climbing a mountain towards Earthly Paradise, or the Garden of Eden. You see, the sinners in Hell are there because they can't acknowledge that they have sinned. They are blind to the truth of their actions. The sinners in the *Purgatorio* have the chance of salvation, because they can see clearly the nature of their failings.'

'Oh.' Agnes sipped her wine. 'In that case, I fear for my soul.'

He laughed. 'You'll be all right.'

'You don't know me well enough to say.' She looked at him. 'And what about your chances?'

'Perhaps that's why I'm drawn to it,' he replied. 'Out of a kind of terror.'

In the silence that followed, she wondered why the death of a step-brother with whom Alasdair had so little connection should affect him so much.

'It's guilt, you see.' Alasdair echoed her thoughts.

'Guilt?'

He smiled. 'I'm a naturally guilty person. It's in my character, always to blame myself.'

'Does that make you a Catholic?' she said.

He shook his head. 'Only by birth. Now I'm just an atheist and a scholar of medieval Italian.'

'But how can you understand *The Divine Comedy* without knowing Dante's God?'

'There's a long answer to that,' he replied.

'Which is?'

He took a deep breath. 'I mean, obviously, for Dante, who was writing in the early fourteenth century, then the presence of God is unarguable.'

'And for you?'

'No. Not for me. I'm a translator. And a poet. But I wouldn't call myself religious.'

'Why *The Divine Comedy* then?'

He leaned back in his chair. 'Because a wealthy American publisher is paying me an unusually large amount of money and giving me an unusually lengthy amount of time to work on it. And so I said yes. And also, because I think I can do it well. My thesis was about the emerging Italian language in the thirteenth and fourteenth centuries, about the choice to use the vernacular for a work of literature, rather than Latin. Dante was very conscious of the language he was using, *The Divine Comedy* is a deliberate exploration of poetic style, it is a reflection on its own poetry.' He sipped his mineral water.

'Wasn't Dante in love with Beatrice?' Agnes said.

'Beatrice is his second guide, in the *Purgatorio*.'

'But wasn't she a real person?'

'She was, yes.'

'So, isn't it a love poem too?'

Alasdair frowned. 'It's true that, Dante himself, when he describes the first time he set eyes on Beatrice, the real woman, he said that if at that moment anyone had asked him a question, about anything, the only answer he would have given would have been "love".'

'She must have been very beautiful,' Agnes said.

'But it's not that simple,' Alasdair went on. 'She's also an allegory. In the poem, the characters all have meaning.'

'And what does she mean, then?'

'She's spiritually pure. She's able to intercede on behalf of the poet. And then he follows her to Earthly Paradise, or the Garden of Eden.'

'Well, that's a tough one,' Agnes said. 'I wouldn't like a man to expect that of me.'

Alasdair laughed. 'It was different in the fourteenth century.'

'So,' Agnes said, 'without a Beatrice, we don't get a chance of salvation?'

He shook his head. 'Not at all. It's a very optimistic work. *The Divine Comedy* is about love, and it's about the path of the soul, but it's also about being human. As far as Dante is concerned,' he went on, 'we are in Hell, and Purgatory, and Paradise, all the time, now, in this life. We are constantly making that journey.' He stopped, flushed with argument.

'I can see what he means,' Agnes said. 'But paradise is a bit difficult, isn't it? I mean, to live in now.'

'I thought your God promised you Heaven?'

She looked at him. 'Yes,' she said. 'For those brave enough to believe in it.'

'Not you, then?' he said.

Agnes watched the light catch the bubbles in his water glass. 'Personally,' she said, 'I'm happier with Purgatory.'

He laughed. 'Me too.'

In the frosty pink sunset, she walked across the little graveyard that led to Julius's church. She looked at the burial stones and thought about sin and the chance of redemption. She thought about the restaurant table flooded with sunlight, his eyes meeting hers above the bright circle of his glass.

She tried the side door of Julius's church, which opened, heard his muffled greeting from the office, which was down a small flight of stone steps.

She put her head round the door. Julius was sitting at his desk. In front of him was an ancient, heavy, black typewriter. He looked up and smiled.

'Is it that time already?'

'And what time would that be, Julius?'

'Tea time, I'd say. Your arrival usually signals either coffee-time or tea-time, unless it's lunchtime. But I'd say in this instance, it's tea-time.'

'I'll put the kettle on, then.' Agnes crossed over to the sink.

'No cake?' Julius bashed a key of the typewriter.

'I've had rather a large lunch,' Agnes said, searching for the teapot.

'That Athena,' Julius tutted.

'No, actually. Not Athena.'

Julius looked a question at her, got no answer, returned to his typing. He bashed another key. 'Half of these letters don't work,' he said.

'Why are you using it, then?'

'Mrs Featherstone donated it to the parish on Sunday, as they've upgraded to a plasma screen, she told me. It seemed churlish to refuse.'

Agnes poured tea, carried two cups across to his desk and sat down beside him.

'Julius – '

'What?'

'What if – what if this is all a mistake.'

'You mean, wasting time drinking tea with me when you could be doing whatever it is you're supposed to be doing.'

'Seriously,' Agnes laughed. 'What if it's wrong to turn away from love and life and... and everything?'

'You're not turning away from life,' he said.

'The vows I'm supposed to take in a month are all about relinquishment. If I practise self-denial, then I'm turning away from life.'

'No,' Julius said, 'That's not true. Relinquishment is liberation. If you look at a rose, you can see that it's beautiful. You can love it for its beauty, precisely because of its transience. If you were to say, there's no point appreciating that rose because it will be dead tomorrow, then you'd be denying life.'

'And love?'

Julius considered her for a moment. 'Who did you have lunch with, then?' he asked.

'A man called Alasdair, but that's not relevant,' Agnes said.

Julius paused for a moment. Then he said, 'I can pour a glass of wine, and drink it with great pleasure. Or, I can drink the whole bloody bottle, and maybe another after that. The wine we offer in the eucharist is a celebration of life, but sometimes, it's a human failing to love life too much.'

'Like the people in my hostel.'

He smiled at her. 'Yes,' he said. 'Like the people in your hostel.'

Agnes considered this. 'But their drinking is as much about running away from life as embracing it.'

'No,' Julius said. 'Not running away from life. Running away from yourself. The self can be a dead weight. That's why taking final vows is liberating.'

'There's a woman who works at the hostel, Mary, she's called. Sister Madeleine might have mentioned her to you.'

'Perhaps,' Julius said, pushing his glasses up his nose again.

'She was a Carmelite. She loved a man, she tried to give him up. After fifteen years of struggling she decided never to see him again. And then he died.' Julius rubbed his forehead. Agnes went on, 'Mary calls herself an atheist. She left the order. Left everything.'

'Yes,' Julius said. 'I can see one might.'

'If I walk into a room, she walks out. She hasn't said a word to me since I started work there.'

Above them the church bell chimed the half hour, echoed across the river by distant peals from the City.

'I mean,' Agnes went on, 'I know you had your doubts too... I know it wasn't easy for you either...'

Julius inclined his head. 'I made my peace with it all,' he said after a while. 'But this poor woman is still at war.'

'But what if she's right?' Agnes said. 'Everyone would say, she should have left the order and married the man. Wouldn't they?'

'That seems to be what she thinks.'

'That's what I mean. And what if, at the end of my life, it's quite clear to everyone that I shouldn't have signed up, shouldn't have thrown it all away...'

'But Agnes, your case is completely different. There isn't anyone in your life whose sudden death would throw you into turmoil. Athena, maybe – '

'And you, Julius. But you'll go on for years.'

He went to pick up his tea, and the cup rattled on the saucer.

'Julius – ' Agnes said. 'What is it?'

'What's what?'

She looked at him, at the serenity of his smile, at the light behind him, the window brushed pink with the last of the day.

'Julius,' she said, 'tell me.'

He put his cup down and sighed. 'Must you be telepathic?' he said. 'It's not even part of our theology.'

'Go on.'

'I didn't want to tell you yet.'

'Tell me.'

He sighed. 'It's probably nothing. I really shouldn't be worrying you – '

'Julius, for Heaven's sake – '

'Just a few tests,' he said, staring at the floor. 'The doctor sent me off for them. Waiting for results.'

'Tests? What – medical tests? But you don't believe in doctors.'

'I don't believe in telepathy either.'

She smiled, but she could feel her hands shaking in her lap.

'Father Sean suggested I go,' he was saying. 'Few funny symptoms, digestive, mainly. Engine coughing, I'm sure that's all it is, not that young after all...'

'Julius, do stop mumbling. This is important.'

'They had to have a bit of a look. Rather nasty, actually, pumping air into me. Biopsy too.'

'Julius – will you stop being so bloody calm?'

He met her eyes. 'I don't know how else to be.'

'All right – I'll be the one to make a fuss then. Which bit of you are they investigating?'

'Colon,' Julius mumbled.

'Julius, if this turns out to be serious, I'll rant and scream and shout and cry on your behalf. OK?'

He smiled, shook his head.

'And I won't mind who's looking,' she went on, 'I'll be there in the hospital corridor, weeping and wailing, you'll have to pretend you don't know me.'

'It's a deal,' he said. 'Shake on it.' As their fingers touched, her eyes filled with tears.

'Julius,' she whispered, 'I can't live without you.'

'Agnes,' he replied, 'You'll never have to.'

'I thought you didn't believe in ghosts,' she said, trying to smile.

'I didn't believe in doctors either,' he said.

She left in the twilight, the night clouds gathering as she walked along the rush-hour streets. She had promised to come to mass on Monday, and she had made Julius promise to tell her everything from now on, though he continued to protest that he felt fine, really, and it was only because we inhabit a diagnostic paradigm that anyone would describe him as ill, which he wasn't, never felt better really, apart from when he was a young man in Ireland, in those days, of course, he could run up the hill at the back of his seminary and would hardly be out of breath...

She walked fast, her head down, shivering. She thought about the sunny restaurant with Alasdair, and it seemed to have happened in another time, to another person. She'd joked about Purgatory, but now here she was, weighed down by the thought of going through the rest of this life without Julius as her guide.

He will be all right, she thought. There is no alternative.

Instead of turning down Borough High Street, she crossed over to St Thomas's Street and turned left.

It was now quite dark, and a misty chill had descended. She turned towards the lights of the Rising Sun and pushed open the door. She was aware of men glancing towards her and away again, and then she saw Michael. He was sitting with another man, deep in conversation. He looked up as she approached.

'Sister Agnes,' she reminded him, reaching out a hand.

'Of course,' he said, shaking hands, bear-like in a heavy jumper. 'This is Tom Connolly,' he said, indicating his companion, who nodded at Agnes. He was wearing lived-in denim and a rough growth of greying beard.

'I'm sorry to interrupt,' Agnes began.

'Not at all,' Michael said, getting up. 'What will you have?'

Agnes glanced at their whisky glasses. 'Same as you, please,' she said. 'With ice,' she added.

'You a nurse, then?' Tom Connolly turned to speak to her, as Michael queued at the bar.

'No, a nun.'

'Ah.' Tom nodded. After a moment he said, 'You're allowed the whisky, then?'

'Yes,' Agnes said.

He turned his empty glass round in his hand. 'No harm in the whisky,' he said.

'So,' Michael said, returning to them, 'what brings you here?'

'It's about Walker,' Agnes began. She tasted her drink, and wondered whether it would have been rude to ask for a single malt. 'The day he died,' she went on, 'someone came to the hostel to warn him not to go out. A woman. I thought it might be someone you know?'

Michael frowned at her. 'Who told you that?'

'Someone at the hostel.'

'Was it Trina who came to warn him?'

'No. She doesn't match the description.'

'Trina wouldn't have known if Andy was in danger in any case,' Michael said. 'She'd lost touch with him.'

'Scott seemed to know quite a lot about him.'

Michael's expression hardened. 'He would. I'd keep away from him if I were you.'

'The police are looking for one of the men who were with him at Charing Cross. A chap called Mitch.'

'I know Mitch. Mitch O'Grady. It couldn't have been Mitch. Typical of the man to admit to it, too drunk to know what he's doing.'

Tom swivelled in his chair towards Michael. 'Is this your friend that got killed?'

Michael nodded.

'Terrible business,' Tom said, turning back to his whisky. 'It's the army,' he went on, addressing the table. 'You put a man in uniform, it does terrible things to him. Terrible.'

'They wouldn't take Tom,' Michael said, leaning towards Agnes. 'Failed the medical.'

'Didn't want to join up anyway.' Tom raised his voice. 'Irish, me. No place for me in Her Majesty's Forces.'

Michael laughed. 'Tom's as Irish as I am. And I'm from Cyprus, well, my dad was. Although originally Italian.' He took a large mouthful of whisky. 'Tell you what, talking of Cyprus – is Haz around at the moment?

Tom nodded. 'He stood me a pint only last night. Night before, maybe. Now him,' he said, waving a finger at Agnes, 'he had no more place in Her Majesty's Forces than I had. A Turk. Centuries of war between those two empires, eh? No love lost between the English and the Ottoman. And then he goes and signs up as a soldier.'

Michael was laughing. 'But he wasn't fighting Turkey, was he?'

'No. He was fighting the Irish. Belfast. Make of that what you will.' Tom returned to his whisky.

'Listen,' Michael was saying to Agnes, 'Haz – Hassan – he was a mate of Walker's. He runs nightclubs now. I'll ask him what he knew. If he's about I'm bound to bump into him in the next day or two. Are you at the hostel?'

'Most days, yes.'

'She works at the hostel. St Chris's,' Michael said to Tom, tipping his head in the direction of the street.

'But she said she was a nun,' Tom said.

'They have them there,' Michael said.

Tom picked up his glass. 'Ah. Good. Holy Sisters. God knows we need them,' he said, nodding at his drink.

Agnes drained her glass and said her goodbyes. It's from wearing jeans, she thought, as she left the pub. No one knows where they are with you. She imagined herself wearing full habit, swishing out into the street in heavy folds of black. At least in habit, everyone knows you're a nun, she thought, crossing Jamaica Road, straightening her back as she felt the weight of fabric around her.

Mind you, if signing up to the order meant signing up to that, I'd never do it.

And yet, she thought, turning down Tooley Street, metaphorically, it's still all the same. It's just not so obvious to anyone else.

She was aware of shouting behind her, a loud gang of jostling men, a sudden fierce argument between them. She crossed the street, hearing their shouts die away in the traffic noise. She imagined the swirl of the habit as she walked on through the evening traffic, and wondered whether she'd feel more or less visible, safer or less safe, dressed head to toe in black robes and veil. She was aware that her mobile was ringing, and she pulled it out of her pocket, but it had stopped. 'Missed Call' it said, and when she pressed a button it told her it was Athena.

I'll phone her when I get home, she thought. After all, I'd look ridiculous walking along the street talking on the phone in full habit.

Chapter Five

'You in a habit, sweetie? Don't be silly.' Athena linked her arm with Agnes's, as they went into the bar. It was smoky and crowded. 'Although, they're very good quality, aren't they, those nun clothes, they always hang very well. Perhaps with a bit of tailoring, the odd pleat, shorter of course, and a decent pair of high heels... What shall we drink, sweetie?' Athena waved at a harried young man behind the bar.

'I think I'd better stick to whisky,' Agnes said. 'That's what I've been drinking so far this evening.'

'You nuns,' Athena said. 'I'm having wine.'

'Single malt,' Agnes prompted. 'With ice. Please.'

They found a small table tucked away by a wall. 'So,' Athena said. 'Does the gorgeous man drink whisky?'

Agnes shook her head. 'The gorgeous man doesn't drink.'

'Doesn't drink? How very restrained. He must be a Capricorn or something. Or a Scorpio, maybe, but they're trouble – '

'It wasn't the gorgeous man. And anyway, he isn't gorgeous. I was just trying to find out a bit more about Walker, you know, the guy who was killed – '

'Because the gorgeous man asked you to.'

'Because I want to.'

'Hmm. So what happened?'

'When?'

Athena sighed. 'When you spoke to him – last night?'

'Oh, it was very odd. He got kind of shirty, just because I questioned his version of events, about pretending that he'd paid for the coffin, when that woman Trina had.'

'I told you he was trouble.'

'But then, today, he came and said sorry, and he bought me lunch.' Agnes tasted her whisky.

'Oh. And how was that?'

'Do you know that restaurant just by Blackfriars Bridge? It has a terrace overlooking the river, it's lovely. And I had plaice with capers – '

'And?'

Agnes looked up and smiled. 'And what?'

Athena sighed. 'You know what I mean.'

'He gave me a book.'

'A very bad sign,' Athena said.

'This.' Agnes handed her the copy of Dante's *Purgatorio*.

'Isn't there Hell before Purgatory?' Athena turned the book over in her hands.

'It's the book he's working on. He's translating it.'

'Into what?'

'English.'

'But this is in English.'

'Athena – '

Athena handed the book back. 'So, what happened after your romantic lunch?'

'Anyone would think you were jealous.'

'How can I be jealous, sweetie, you're a nun.'

'Quite.'

'I mean, if I were to have a lovely lunch with a gorgeous man, it might lead to, ooh, all sorts of things. Whereas if you have lunch with a gorgeous man, it can't lead to anything at all. Even if he does give you a book.'

'Thank goodness,' Agnes said.

Athena was looking at her. 'Yes,' she said. 'Thank goodness.'

Agnes put her glass down on the table. She met Athena's gaze.

'I mean it,' she said.

Athena leaned back in her chair. 'And anyway, sweetie, it's probably true that I'm jealous. You're being wined and dined by a sexy man in an expensive coat, and Nic is just grumpy and self-obsessed, and still expecting me to go to Spain with him. He's found a place in some fashionable suburb of Barcelona, he's investigating prices. It's a kind of studio, and he says there's a flat upstairs, and we could live there.' She drained her glass of wine. 'One day soon I'm going to say, but what about me? What the hell do you think I'm going to do there, all day, while you ponce about doing multi-lingual holistic dance-based therapy or whatever it is this new business partner is going on about – and don't say teach English because I refuse, I haven't the patience, and it's not even my first language, and who out there will want to learn Greek?' She stopped, breathless.

'I didn't say sexy,' Agnes said, after a moment.

'What?'

'Just then, about Alasdair, you said, sexy. I've never described him as sexy.'

'You've never had to. It's obvious by the way you talk about him.'

'Oh.' Agnes turned the melting ice around in her glass. 'Is it?'

'I'm afraid so.'

'Oh dear.' There was a pause. 'Nice nail varnish,' Agnes said.

'I wasn't sure at first, it's a bit orange.'

'It'll be nice for spring,' Agnes said.

Much later, Agnes sat by her window. The bells of the city struck twelve, pealing across the night in waves. She looked out at a square of sky, clear midnight blue pricked with stars, and wondered why she hadn't told Athena about Julius.

But I know why, she thought. Because, if I say it out loud: 'Julius is ill. He might be seriously ill...' If I say that out loud, then it becomes true. And it can't be. It simply can't be true.

She found her prayer book and lit her candle.

'O Lord my God, I cried out to you, and you restored me to health;

You brought me up, O Lord, from the dead; you restored my life as I was going down to the grave...'

O God, keep him safe, she prayed, as her eyes filled with tears.

She woke on Friday morning to leaden skies and driving rain. There were two envelopes on her mat; one was thick, yellow parchment postmarked Paris, the other was from London, hand-written in neat, black ink. She ignored them both and left for the hostel.

She crossed Jamaica Road, pulling her scarf over her head, as muddy water splashed against her legs. She walked up the hostel steps, blinking rain out of her eyes.

Mary Holbeck was sitting at the main desk in the office. Agnes stood in the doorway. Rain puddled at her feet. Mary got up from the desk, and took a step towards the door. 'Hello.' Agnes didn't move. She pushed back her scarf, feeling it damp against the back of her neck.

'I was just leaving...' Mary began.

'No you weren't.' Agnes held the door shut behind her.

Mary stood, blinking. 'I was going to get some tea,' she tried.

'This can't go on,' Agnes said. 'It's not fair on Dan and Petra.'

'I have no idea what you're talking about,' Mary said. 'Someone's trying to come in,' she said, pointing at the door.

Agnes had to stand aside. Jeanie came in, and Mary darted into the hall and disappeared into the kitchen.

'Morning.' Agnes took off her coat and hung it up.

'Is she all right?' Jeanie gestured with her head towards the door.

'I don't think so, no.' Agnes smiled at Jeanie, and Jeanie almost smiled back. She perched on the edge of a chair.

'What can I do for you?' Agnes asked.

Jeanie pushed a letter across to her.

Agnes took the letter. It was from a Social Services Department in Hull, addressed directly to Jeanie, and it said that Jeanie's aunt was offering to take her in.

'Do you want to go there?' Agnes went over to the filing cabinet and took out Jeanie's file.

Jeanie shook her head. 'I'm not going back to Hull, that's my mum's sister, I'm not having nothing to do with them.'

'But you can't stay here for ever.' Agnes sat down and opened the file.

Jeanie was silent. The window shivered with raindrops.

'What do you want to happen?' Agnes asked her.

Jeanie shrugged.

'Where did you live before?' Agnes tried. 'In London, before you came here?'

Jeanie stared at her hands in her lap. 'I'm not going back there neither.'

'Why not?'

'I owe him.' She was almost whispering.

'You owe who?'

Jeanie shook her head. 'He don't know I'm here, if he did he'd come after me.'

'Who, Jeanie?'

Jeanie closed her eyes, then opened them again. 'I was using Heroin. He was my boyfriend. When I got sent down, I got away from him. Then I came here.'

'Where does he live?'

'Around. Not far, but he don't know where I've gone.'

Agnes heard the doorbell ring. 'Wouldn't you be safer out of London? You must have some family?'

Again, the doorbell, followed by someone answering it.

Jeanie shook her head. 'I don't need no family.'

Aberdeen Bob put his head round the door. 'Someone asking for you, Sister. A foreigner. And someone with him.'

Agnes sighed, stood up, put the letter in Jeanie's file and put it away. She leaned her hand briefly on Jeanie's shoulder, then went out to the hall.

'I shouldn't be opening the bloody door,' Bob grumbled, going back upstairs. 'No one else to do it.'

Michael Cordaro was standing in the doorway, with another

man. 'Here she is,' Michael said to his companion. 'Hassan,' he said to Agnes. 'Told you I'd bring him.'

Hassan raised his eyes to hers. She took in his angular, olive-skinned face, framed with smartly clipped black curls. 'Let's go to the cafe,' Agnes said.

They sat tucked into a steamed-up corner.

'Someone tried to warn him, you see,' Michael was saying to Hassan. 'Someone went to the hostel on the day he died. A girl.'

Hassan was hunched over his mug of black coffee, stirring the spoon round and round. 'Any description?'

'Red-haired,' Agnes said.

Hassan shrugged. 'No one I know,' he said. 'But girls change their hair all the time, innit.'

'How did you all know each other, then?' Agnes asked.

'Andy came to our school, didn't he,' Haz said. 'He came to live in the flats.'

Michael smiled. 'We all arsed around for a year, and then we left school. And then Andy made us all join up.'

'Scots Guards as well, innit.' They both laughed.

'Not an Englishman between us,' Michael said. 'And all serving Her Majesty, too.'

'Did you all go to the Falklands?' Agnes held her mug to warm her hands.

'Nah,' Haz said. 'We all started at the same barracks, and we all did a tour of Germany, didn't we. And then Lucky dropped out, he couldn't hack it. And me and Michael, and some of the other lads from the barracks, we did our tour of Belfast. And it was just chance, Andy was delayed in Germany and he was in England when the call came for the Falklands. He was supposed to go on leave and instead he was off on one of them ships, heading for the other side of the world.'

'And we were right jealous,' Michael added.

'Yeah. A real war, we thought. Jammy sod.'

They fell silent.

Agnes picked up a slice of soggy toast, and put it down again.

'And how do you know Mitch?'

They glanced at each other. 'Michael got into bad ways, after Northern Ireland,' Haz said. 'Your hostel saved him.' Michael nodded. Haz went on, 'He spent some time on the streets. So did Andy. And Mitch was one of them good ol' boys, weren't he?'

'He's all right, Mitch,' Michael said. 'But no one can help him.'

'And now he's gone and told the old bill that he's a murderer.' Haz shook his head. 'That's all he bloody needs.'

'Might he have done it?' Agnes asked.

Again, they exchanged a glance. 'You can ask him yourself, if you like,' Haz said.

'How?' Agnes wondered what he meant.

'I know where he is. He's living rough, he's hiding out. But we trust you,' Haz added. He laid his spoon on the formica table, where it made a small brown puddle.

'Could I bring Alasdair too?'

'Who's Alasdair?' Haz frowned at her.

'He's a kind of step-brother. From Scotland. Trina knows him.'

'You remember him,' Michael said. 'Posh bastard.'

'Yeah,' Haz said. 'OK.' He glanced up, a sudden piercing gaze. 'These writings of Andy's, what do they say?'

Agnes shrugged. 'They're about being in the army. They're about the Falklands, and Lucky – '

'Lucky?' Haz's interest was intense.

'Some of it may not be true.'

Haz smiled. 'He always was a liar.'

'Why do you think someone might want him dead?' Agnes asked.

'It was all them bad years,' Haz said. 'He made enemies.'

'He was a right difficult bastard when he came back from the Falklands,' Michael said. 'People gave up on him.'

'There was that girl he loved,' Haz said.

'Yeah,' Michael nodded. 'She gave up on him too. Married someone else.'

'Which girl?' Agnes said.

'She was from back home in Scotland. We never knew her. Teenage romance, Andy never forgot her.'

'Silly sod,' Michael said, and they both laughed.

It was still raining. They stood huddled outside the cafe. 'I'll let you know.' Haz raised his voice above the traffic. 'Tomorrow, maybe?'

'Tomorrow,' Agnes agreed, turning back towards the hostel.

'Thanks for the breakfast,' Michael called as they crossed the street.

'Anytime,' Agnes called back.

The hostel was reverberating, again, with Jayce's music. Agnes sat at her desk in the office, in the damp, dull afternoon. She switched on the desk lamp, and began to sort through Andy's writings. She heard Aberdeen Bob shouting upstairs; the music's volume lowered, slightly.

'... They talk about circles of Hell here. I don't know about circles, it just seems like it has no end and no beginning...' Agnes turned the page.

'And I remember walking up the hill thinking all I need to do is go back home and tell her how I feel. And now, all these years later, I see him, the man I was then, walking up the hill in that silent dawn, and I think you poor sod. 'Cos she said she'd love you for ever. And you believed her...'

She thought about the girl in Scotland, who Andy had always loved. She thought about him coming back from the war, damaged, drinking, on the run from himself.

Circles of Hell, she thought, turning the page.

'... When I was a kid I broke down doors in our house, until my mum moved in with another man and I was too scared of him to be angry...'

She dialled Alasdair's number.

'It's me, Agnes.'

'How nice to hear from you.'

'I've spoken to two people who knew Andy. Michael and Haz, they joined the army with him, but they went to Belfast. They know Mitch, they know where he is, they said we could speak to him. Tomorrow, maybe.'

'Why don't they turn him in?'

'What, to the police? Because they think, like you, that maybe he didn't do it. And that even if he did, he didn't mean to. They said Andy made enemies, after the Falklands.'

'Yes. He did.'

'There's a bit in the writings,' Agnes said, holding the page nearer the light. 'About Andy's mum moving in with a man who he was frightened of.'

Alasdair was silent.

'Was that your father?' Agnes said.

After a moment, Alasdair said, 'Yes. That was my father. He wasn't a nice man.' He was silent, then said, 'I'd like to see those writings.'

'You can,' she said.

'What are you doing now?' he said.

'Just finishing here at the hostel. Then I'm going back home to open two very difficult letters.'

'From admirers?' The cheerful tone was slightly forced.

'Admirers would be easy, not difficult,' Agnes said. 'One letter is from the order, making arrangements for me to take final vows. The other is from my French lawyers, asking me what I want to do with a very beautiful house in Provence that I happen to have inherited on the death of my mother last year.'

He didn't say anything.

'You see?,' she said. 'I told you that you didn't know me well enough to offer me guarantees of salvation.'

He laughed. 'Tomorrow, then?'

'Tomorrow,' she said.

The wind got up as night fell, dashing rain against the windows. At home, she lit guttering candles and knelt in prayer.

'... For behold, you look for truth deep within me,
And will make me understand wisdom in secret.
Cast me not away from your presence,
And take not your holy spirit from me...'

Cast me not away from your presence.

But Julius seems so well, she wanted to shout. He's perfectly all right. How can he be dying?

In the midst of life, we are in death.

She thought about Julius's words, about loving the rose, not in spite of its transience but because of it.

She thought about the promise of eternal life in the eucharist; the cup of salvation.

The death of the self isn't the end, she thought.

She remembered that in the letter from the order, Sister Christiane had asked to have a meeting, early next week perhaps, to discuss the arrangements for her final vows.

The death of the self.

She picked up her prayer book again.

'... For you will not abandon me to the grave, nor let your holy one see the Pit. You will show me the path of life... As it was in the beginning, is now and ever shall be, Amen.'

I don't care about the eternal bit, she thought, closing her prayer book. I want Julius here, now. For ever.

That night the wind invaded her dreams. She seemed to be descending through layers of darkness, in some kind of machine, a helicopter, it seemed to be, but it wasn't her in the helicopter, it was a soldier, and it had crashed into some kind of hellish pit, there was screaming, and sirens. And there was someone who had to be rescued from the wreckage, and there were more sirens, and she had to save him, whoever it was, but the sirens were shrill and loud...

Her phone was ringing. It was still dark outside. She was awake, she realised. No helicopter. No inferno.

She picked up her phone.

'It's Petra.'

'Oh.'

'I know, I'm sorry. It's just, there's been a break-in, here, at the hostel, some time during the night. In the office. Glass everywhere. The police are here, we're trying to find out if anything's missing.'

'I'll come right over.'

Agnes sifted through the heap of clothes on her floor to find something to wear. Her clock said 5:30 a.m. Next to the clock, on her table, were the disordered, tatty sheets of Andy McFadden's writings.

Chapter Six

All the lights were on in the hostel. In the kitchen, Petra was pouring mugs of tea from a huge teapot, yawning. Two uniformed police officers, a man and a woman, sat at one end of the table. Archie sat at the other end, clutching a mug of tea, staring at the table. Next to him, Aberdeen Bob was voicing various theories about burglary and the value of particular types of computers.

Agnes went into the office. Dan was there, with a plain-clothes policeman. Glass littered the carpet, covered the desk.

'Hardly a professional job,' the policeman was saying.

'The computer printer's gone,' Dan said to Agnes.

'What else?' She stared at the jagged window, broken despite the bars across it, which were wrenched apart.

'Nothing else. The filing cabinet's been raided, though.'

Papers were scattered across the floor, letters and forms and the cardboard envelopes of files, torn open.

Dan looked at it, scratching his head. 'It'll take us ages to sort through that lot.'

'How's Jeanie?' Agnes said.

'Don't know. Haven't seen her,' Dan said.

Agnes went upstairs and knocked on Jeanie's door. It was opened a crack, and Jeanie stood there, pale and thin in a huge t-shirt. She let Agnes in, and went back to her bed, hugging her duvet around her.

'I told you,' she said. 'I never thought I could get away from him, and I was right, weren't I?'

'Your dealer-boyfriend?'

Jeanie nodded. 'He never forgets a debt. That's why he drives around in a BMW.'

'What do you owe him?'

Jeanie stared at her bedcovers.

'It may not be him.' Agnes thought about the files thrown around the office.

'Who else?'

'It may be about Andy McFadden.'

'He's dead, though, isn't he? It's me who's still here.' Agnes looked at her. She was pinched and white and shivering, gathering her bedclothes around her.

The morning passed in statements to the police, in more cups of tea; then breakfast, and clearing up. Agnes picked shards of glass off the carpet, wearing a pair of gardening gloves which she'd found in a kitchen drawer. Dan and Petra began to gather up papers, matching them with files. After an hour, the room looked just the same.

They sat in the kitchen, drinking coffee. Agnes was surprised to hear her phone ring.

'Hello? It's Haz. We can go and see Mitch this afternoon. Do you want to meet me in the Rising Sun?'

'Sure. We'll be there, Alasdair and me.'

'Two-thirty OK?'

'Fine.'

She dialled Alasdair. She got an answering machine, and left a message, asking him to come to the hostel at two. Mary Holbeck appeared and Petra explained what had happened. Mary went straight to the office, and somehow, after half an hour the room was useable again.

At two, Alasdair appeared on the doorstep of the hostel.

'Are you all right?' he said. 'You seem flustered.'

'We had a break-in, last night,' she said.

'Oh. Anything missing?'

'Computer stuff.'

'It must happen all the time,' he said. 'Shall we go?'

'Nice coat,' Alasdair said, as they set off towards the Rising Sun.

'No it isn't. It's very cheap. Athena's always trying to get me to dress properly, but I'm – '

'A nun,' he finished for her.

'Exactly.'

'It's a good thing,' Alasdair said, as they crossed the main road. 'It's a good thing to turn away from consumerism. The whole world's going mad. Everyone goes shopping. All the time. It's good if people like you show that you don't have to be part of all that.'

'Mmm. I suppose so,' Agnes said. Two women passed them, heels clicking on the pavement. Agnes was aware of a well-cut suit, a slick of red lipstick, the swing of a tailored, belted coat. 'I like that look,' she said, her gaze drawn towards the women as they receded. 'Fifties tweed, elegant shoes.'

Alasdair looked at her and smiled. 'Perhaps the anti-consumer movement could find a better spokesperson after all.'

'Did I say I wanted the job?' Agnes stopped outside the pub. 'Hassan said he'd meet us here.'

'I'll wait outside,' Alasdair said.

'You can come in if you like,' Agnes began, but he shook his head.

'I don't like pubs,' he said.

A few minutes later, Haz was leading them towards Tower Bridge Road. 'Be kind to him,' he was saying. 'He's not a bad man. I've known him that long, I know what he's like. And now he thinks he's killed someone, and he's feeling really bad, and he'll just drink more. And it could have been any of us, we could have gone down that road, it's only because I found my faith that I don't drink, not a drop, not any more.'

'Your faith?' Agnes turned to him, as they waited for the lights to change.

'Islam,' he said. 'We don't drink.'

'You Catholics could do with some of that,' Alasdair said, so quietly that only Agnes heard. He was close enough to elbow in the ribs, but she thought better of it.

'And the Rising Sun?' she asked Hassan.

He smiled at her. 'My mate Mehmet there, he's the new barman. Does a fantastic Turkish coffee. Now that,' he said. 'That's my addiction. Too many of those each day, I never get to sleep at night.' He laughed.

The wind had died down overnight, and the day had dawned damp and chill. They turned off Jamaica Road towards an estate of flats. Behind them, a new riverside development glittered in the thin sun.

Haz suddenly darted into a scruffy cafe, and emerged with a breaded chicken drumstick and two cans of beer.

'Hungry?' Alasdair asked him.

Hassan looked at him, blankly. Then he said, 'Oh. No, these aren't for me.'

Agnes and Alasdair exchanged glances, and set off again behind him. They went under a railway bridge, and came out by a series of tower blocks.

'He'll be down at the bottom,' Hassan said. He glanced at Alasdair, an up-and-down look that took in his coat, his Italian shoes. 'You ain't got no phone on you, have you? They'll have it off you if you don't watch out.'

'It's just in my pocket,' Alasdair said.

Hassan shrugged. 'The kids here, they might be OK if they see you with me – ' He was interrupted by a vicious growling, which seemed to have come from nowhere. She froze, aware of Alasdair a step behind her. The dog leapt up, and she thought perhaps she'd screamed as it came snarling towards them, teeth bared, and then it had passed them in a flash of black and tan, and was devouring the chicken leg that Hassan had thrown for it, growling and pawing at the bone as if it might be still alive.

'Come on.' Hassan broke into a run, and they hurried across the central courtyard of the estate. A couple of stones landed behind them, thrown from some unseen balcony, as they reached a staircase. 'He'll be down here,' Hassan said.

They picked their way through broken glass, syringes.

'He lives in the garages,' Hassan explained, as they started down a second flight, the daylight fading out above them. In the stench and darkness they could hear shouts, the thump of music. A woman's voice scolded in a foreign language.

They came out onto a concrete floor. Blinking in the dim light, between the looming pillars, Agnes could see one car, then another, burnt-out shells, no wheels, smashed windscreens. Slits of light from beyond made gaps in the darkness. In the distance there were children's voices.

'Mitch?' Hassan's voice echoed. 'It's Haz. Are you there?'

'I'm here,' came an answer. 'Follow the smoke.'

They picked their way across the car park. Round a corner they came upon a few meagre flames, and screwing up her eyes against the smoke Agnes saw a ragged figure hunched behind them. He had sparse white hair; a bruised, reddened face.

'I've brought visitors,' Hassan said. 'They're OK.'

Mitch nodded, and gestured to a heap of wooden boxes. Hassan set them out for Alasdair and Agnes. Mitch stretched out shaking hands, wrapped in woollen scraps that were once gloves. Hassan opened a can of beer for him and handed it to him. Mitch downed most of the can, then set it down carefully beside him. He looked up, peering through the smoke.

'This is Sister Agnes,' Hassan said. 'And this is Alasdair.' Mitch nodded again. Haz went on, 'It's a bit of a tricky one, this. Andy McFadden, you know, Walker – '

Mitch interrupted him with a wave of his arm, a groaning noise. He buried his face in his hands.

Haz glanced at Alasdair, tried again. 'It's OK, Mitch. It's OK.'

Mitch was shaking his head. Haz laid his hand on Mitch's arm. 'No one blames you,' he said.

Mitch lifted his head from his arms. 'I do,' he said. 'I blame me. I killed a man, Haz. Not just a man. A friend. No reason, nothing. A broken bottle, a fuckin' mist of rage, and vroom. I can't even remember it all. I remember the red mist, everything happening like it's in a fog. There was a bloke there, that's who I was angry with. Walker was with me, and this bloke was having a go at him, shouting at him, and I wasn't having that, so I joined in. And then he's waving a bottle, and – ' He broke off. He shook his head, reached down for the can at his feet and took a large mouthful.

'I remember afterwards,' he said, talking to the can. 'I remember I looked down, and I was soaked with blood. That stink, you know?' He put the can down and looked across the fire at them. 'I remember that.' He shook his head. 'The blood of my friend, and I'm awash with it. That's my Hell, see.' He looked up at Haz. 'They'll send me down, won't they? But, see, I've killed my friend. No prison is going to be worse than the one I'm in now.'

Haz patted his arm. 'We're on your side, Mitch.'

Mitch shook his head. 'Where I am, I'm on my own now.'

Agnes cleared her throat. 'Mitch,' she said. He frowned at her, as if trying to recall who she was. 'This man who was there, who was being abusive to Walker – who was he?'

Mitch blinked at her through the smoke. 'I don't know. Don't remember him. I didn't know him.'

'What was he saying to Walker?'

Mitch scratched his head. 'He called him a coward. Yellow. I remember that. Only, in different words, you know.'

'Did Walker know him?'

'I think so, yes. They was yelling at each other.' He downed another mouthful of beer. 'Connor might know,' he said. 'He knew some of Walker's mates, didn't he?'

'Connor?' Agnes asked.

'My brother,' Mitch said.

'Carpenter,' Haz said. 'He works for me sometimes.'

'He done good, our Connor,' Mitch said. 'He lives over on the Peabody now, with his family. You know what I've been thinking all this time? Walker had a brother, didn't he? And one day, in this life or the next, I'm going to be talking to a bloke and I'll find out, he's Walker's brother. And I'm going to have to say to him, I killed him. I killed your brother. And that will be what hell is. Saying to a bloke, I killed your brother.'

Agnes was aware of Alasdair beside her. She reached out a hand, feeling for his.

'They can lock me up,' Mitch was saying, 'but I'm in prison now.'

Haz placed both his hands on Mitch's shoulders. 'It'll be OK,' he said. 'You'll get sent down, you'll get help. You can put all this behind you. They dry you out in prison. They teach you stuff. A new start, you know?' He got up, shaking one leg, then the other. Agnes and Alasdair stood up too.

Mitch looked up at them. The smoke blurred all expression from his face. 'I do remember something. It's like a dream. Perhaps it is a dream...' He screwed up his eyes. 'There was a woman there. When Walker was... ' He swallowed, then carried on. 'There was blood everywhere. And she was holding him, crying. And I didn't know who she was. And she was saying, Don't leave me. She was saying, I love you, don't leave me. Holding him like a baby. And him making this weird gurgling noise. I remember the blood. That's not a dream, not blood like that.'

'Who was it?' Haz crouched down again next to him.

'I don't know. Really.'

'Trina?'

Mitch spat at the fire. 'Nah. Not Trina. Can you imagine her? Nah, not her. This girl was for real, crying and that.'

'Wouldn't the police have seen her?' Agnes asked.

His eyes focused on the fire. 'Don't know. I remember sirens, I remember standing there, holding a broken bottle. Don't know where it came from.'

Haz stood up again. 'We'll talk to Connor,' he said. He reached into his coat and took out the second can and stood it down on the heap of blankets. He patted Mitch's shoulder. 'You'll be all right, mate,' he said.

They turned to go, picking their way back across the car park, up the stairs, so many stairs, emerging, breathless, in the courtyard.

They blinked in the daylight. There was no sign of the dog.

Hassan shook his shoulders, brushed down his sleeves, as if getting rid of something. He looked at Agnes, then at Alasdair. 'Well – ' he shrugged. 'That's Mitch, that is.' They came out into the street. He combed his fingers through his hair. 'To be honest,' he said, 'it's amazing he's still with us at all. Medical bloody miracle, the amount he's put away over the years.' He slowed his pace, glancing at Alasdair as if about to speak, but said nothing.

'I almost told him,' Alasdair said, after a while. 'For a second, back there, I thought, if I tell him, it might help him. And then I thought, no, it'll make it worse. He doesn't need me to point out what he's done.' He turned to Haz, his tone conversational. 'Do you have a Hell in Islam?'

'Sort of. It's not quite like yours.'

'I've read quite a lot of the Q'ran,' Alasdair said.

'Then you'll know,' Hassan said.

'I used to read the Arabic version, but I'm rather enjoying it in Urdu at the moment.'

Hassan looked at him.

'Show-off,' Agnes said. They laughed, walking along the embankment, breathing in the daylight, the gentle splashing of the Thames.

At Tower Bridge, Haz shook their hands. 'Got to see a man in Soho,' he said. 'There's a bar I've got my eye on, but the money's wrong at the moment.'

'Do you think the police will look for Mitch?' Agnes said.

'It's only a matter of time before they find him, I'd have thought. He's got nowhere left to run.' Haz scanned the street for a taxi. 'Still, he's right about talking to Connor, I'll see what I can do.' He hailed a cab, and then was gone.

Alasdair and Agnes stood on the street corner. Alasdair shifted his weight from one foot to the other. 'Well...' he said.

Agnes looked beyond him to the river, which sparkled in the sun.

'Maybe – ' Alasdair began. 'Maybe that's all it is. A street brawl. A drunken rage. A broken bottle. Maybe that's all you need to take out a life.'

'Mmm.' Agnes scuffed the pavement with her toe.

'Maybe I was wrong.'

'And yet...' Agnes looked up at him. 'This stranger shouting abuse, that Mitch remembered. This woman cradling him in her arms... and they're both people that Mitch had never seen before.'

'Do you really think Mitch's memories are reliable?'

'Alasdair – when we first met, you were sure there was more to it. You said he'd made dark hints about old scores to be settled. You said there were battles being fought in his head.'

'Yes, but – '

'You managed to convince me.'

Alasdair glanced at her, looked away again. 'I didn't really know him very well. I just felt I ought to make amends. For the sake of the two kids that we used to be.' He pushed his hair away from his face. 'Perhaps I was wrong.'

'But what if you're not?'

He met her gaze. After a moment, he said, 'This woman that Mitch remembered, she might be the same one.'

'The same one that came to the hostel to warn him? I thought that. I'll talk to Jeanie about it.'

'And we might as well see what Connor's got to say. If he knew some of Andy's friends, at least we'll hear about that.' He brushed Agnes's arm with his hand. 'I'll phone you.' He turned to go, then turned back. 'Thanks,' he said.

She watched him cross the street, through the glint of passing windscreens.

Twenty minutes later she was at the hostel, knocking on the door of Jeanie's room. There was silence, then it opened a crack.

'What is it?' Jeanie came out on to the landing.

'Can I have a word?'

'If it's about sending me away from here – '

'It isn't.'

They sat in the deserted lounge, trying to ignore the thumping beat coming through the ceiling. Agnes brought two mugs of instant coffee, and watched Jeanie ladle four spoonfuls of sugar into hers.

'Just because that bastard – ' Jeanie began. 'Just because he thinks he can come here and put the wind up me, I don't want to leave here, not yet, OK? I'm not going to let him frighten me, if I leave here I'll go back on the gear and I don't want to, not now.'

'You don't have to leave.'

'I'm not safe, though.'

'Jeanie,' Agnes said. 'If it was this bloke you're frightened of, he'd have stolen more, wouldn't he?'

Jeanie shrugged. 'Maybe.'

The music stopped, and then started again with a new track, even louder. 'He drives me mad,' Jeanie said, jerking her head towards the ceiling.

'You know the woman who came to warn Walker,' Agnes said. 'What was she like?'

'I already told you.'

'You said she had an accent,' Agnes tried.

'I told you. Maybe Scottish. She only said a few words.'

'How old?'

'Older than me.'

'Younger than me?'

Jeanie studied Agnes. 'Difficult to tell. If you dyed out the grey in your hair you'd look younger, see.'

'That's what my friend Athena says too.'

Jeanie nodded.

'And how did she seem?' Agnes asked.

Jeanie frowned, dredging her memory. 'Don't know. Worried. There was a man too, they kept looking behind them, like they might be being followed. I told you, it was a few seconds on the doorstep, and then she ran off. And I sat here, thinking I should knock on Walker's door, but I didn't know what to say, and then he went without me seeing him.'

'And would you have changed his mind?'

Jeanie shrugged, nursing her mug between pale fingers.

Agnes sighed. 'Sometimes people just do what they're going to do.'

Jeanie turned to face her. 'When my Chris died, in his car, I could have stopped him. I could have changed his mind.'

'Jeanie, it was an accident – '

Jeanie shook her head. 'He drove into a tree. On purpose. He killed himself, see? We'd fallen out–' she hesitated. 'And then one night he got into his car and went down the A228 when there was no one about and smashed it into a tree.'

Agnes reached out a hand and touched Jeanie's arm. She felt Jeanie shrink from her, and took her hand away again.

'It was still his decision,' Agnes said, quietly.

'Well, it was a bloody crap one,' Jeanie said. The pulse from upstairs changed beat. Jeanie suddenly stood up, rushed to the door, flung it open, strode into the hall and up the stairs. Agnes heard hammering on a door, followed by a stream of abuse from Jeanie. Then a door slammed shut. The music stopped. There was silence, then footsteps. Jeanie appeared in the lounge.

'He's not a bad kid really,' she said.

'I didn't know you could shout so loud,' Agnes said.

'Only when I need to. Do you mind if I go now?'

'No, not at all.' Agnes stood up, pulling at her hair. Out in the hall, she put her face close to the mirror. 'There's not that much grey,' she said. But Jeanie had gone, back upstairs to her room.

Dan was in the office, dealing with paperwork for Aberdeen Bob's return to Scotland. 'I'll miss him,' he said. 'No one to organise us.'

'Is it really only the printer that's missing?' Agnes glanced at the square of dust marking the place on the desk where it had been.

'Yes. All the files are back in order, nothing seems to be missing.'

'Andy McFadden's file?'

Dan nodded. 'It had been seriously raided, but nothing's missing,' he said, as Agnes's phone rang.

'Hi, it's Haz. I've spoken to Connor, Mitch's brother. He can see us tomorrow.'

'Sunday?'

'Is that a problem?' Haz said.

'No,' Agnes said. 'No, not a problem at all.'

Athena opened a packet of ready-washed salad and put it in a bowl.

'You know,' she said, putting the bowl on her kitchen table, 'I'm going to starve in Spain.' She took a quiche out of the oven and put it on a plate. 'I bet they don't have supermarket quiche in Spain.'

'I'm sure they do.' Agnes re-filled both their glasses.

'No, sweetie, it's full of housewives rustling up their traditional home-made paella, I've seen it on the telly.' She sat down opposite Agnes and took a mouthful of wine. 'I'm not going, sweetie, I'm not. I don't know how to tell him, but I can't possibly live there.'

She carved the quiche into slices, and served out one each. 'Do you think,' she said, 'Do you think, when a man tells a woman he loves her, it means the same as when a woman tells a man she loves him?'

Agnes shook vinaigrette from a bottle on to her salad. 'I don't know,' she said. 'How could one measure it?'

'I just have this feeling,' Athena went on, 'I mean, I know Nic says he loves me, but I wonder whether it's like they have a kind of limit, men, you know?'

'Would it matter, though?' Agnes said. 'It's all an approximation, isn't it? I mean, we're all trying to use the same words to mean roughly the same thing, aren't we?'

'No, but you see, what worries me, is this. OK, so a man says to a woman, I love you. And he's expressing some kind of need, or desire. So the woman says to him, I love you too. And she's saying something different. And he senses the difference. He senses the power of what she's said, and he kind of knows that maybe he can't match it, even if he likes the idea of loving her and her loving him. It's as if something contractual has happened. And so the man panics.'

'What happened, to bring this on?'

'Nic and I went out for dinner last night, we tried that new Thai place on the corner, and it was all lovely, and I was trying to be positive about everything, and so I said, whatever happens, we'll survive. Even if Barcelona doesn't work out, we'll survive, him and me. And I said, because I love you. And then he went all quiet.'

She moved a lettuce leaf around her plate. 'It was as if it was top-heavy, as if I'd overbalanced the conversation. As if there was too much of it. And after a while he said, I love you too, but it was thin. That's what made me think about it.'

Agnes put her wine glass down. 'Maybe I'm not the person to ask.'

'You know loads about love, sweetie. Even when you were married to Hugo – '

'That wasn't love. Well, he claimed it was, but he couldn't tell the difference between love and hate, really. Alasdair says- '

Athena smiled. 'What does Alasdair say?'

'Alasdair says that in the fourteenth century, there was a concept of love that was all about spiritual purity. And that's why Beatrice can offer the poet the chance of salvation.'

'Heavens, sweetie, no wonder he's single.'

Agnes laughed.

'Although,' Athena went on, 'it's a bit like you and Julius. That kind of love.'

'I'm not sure Julius and I can offer the other the chance of salvation,' Agnes began, but then her eyes welled with tears.

'What is it?' Athena leaned forward with concern.

Agnes shook her head. 'It's probably nothing, he's had some tests, they had a look at his colon, they've done a biopsy- '

'Oh my God.' Athena put her hands up to her face. 'That word. That's a serious word. Even I know that.'

'I know,' Agnes said, her voice thin as she tried not to cry.

'When will he know?'

'Early this week.'

'How is he with it?'

'You know Julius,' Agnes said. 'He's being calm. Mostly.'

Athena sighed. 'It's so annoying, he makes the rest of us look so bloody flaky by comparison. Listen, sweetie, when they tell me I've got cancer, don't expect anything courageous from me. I'm warning you now. I'm going to be such a bloody drama queen about it all that when I do finally die you'll all be glad of the peace and quiet.'

Agnes smiled through tears.

'Dearie me, what with your mother dying, and now this – '

'My mother's death set me free,' Agnes said. 'But I can't live without Julius.'

Athena picked up her glass and took a sip. 'It's like what I was saying to Nic last night. I said, we've only got one chance, let's not blow it. God knows we've screwed up enough in the past, him and me, but we're still here, still together.' She sighed. 'I care about him very much. I don't want it to go wrong. It concentrates the mind, doesn't it, sweetie, the thought that we're not here for ever... that he might not be here for ever...' She stared at her glass, turning it round in her hands. Then she looked up. 'He'll be fine, Julius will. Of course he'll be fine. He's young for his age. Everything will be fine. We'll all live forever.' She raised her glass. 'To eternal life,' she said, and they both laughed.

Chapter Seven

'It's broken our mam's heart, you know?' Connor O'Grady hugged his knees, curled up on his navy blue sofa. The white walls of his flat dazzled in the sunlight. Next to him a vase of golden roses exploded with colour.

Agnes leaned back in her blue armchair and glanced across at Alasdair, who was balancing a bright yellow cup and saucer on his lap. 'You're twins?' she said.

'Our mam's always saying, two boys, same Mum and Dad, same birth, couldn't be more different.' He laughed, a flash of white teeth under his sandy fringe. 'She says she'd swear one of us was swapped at birth, if it wasn't that she never let us out of her sight, not once. Mind you, I'm not saying I was good as gold neither, both of us tearaways in our time. But there was always something about Mitch, some devilment. Like with the drinking, I mean, don't get me wrong, I like a pint same as the next man, but with Mitch it was never just a pint. Never.' He shook his head. 'And now this.' The thought of his brother passed across his face like a cloud.

'When did you meet Andy?' Agnes took a sip of coffee from her large blue cup.

'Through Mitch, it was. It was after the Falklands, when he was invalided out of the army. I was trying to help Mitch, he was living at a men's hostel down by the docks, and Andy pitched up there for a bit, and they got to be mates. Looked out for each other, didn't they?' He turned to Haz. 'And then there was Haz, here, and Michael, trying to get help for Andy, and we all sort of got to know each other.

'Were you a soldier too?' Alasdair asked.

Connor shook his head. 'Not me, mate. We come from Donegal,' he added. 'Moved here when I was a wee lad, grew up on the Isle of Dogs, we did. Mitch and I, left school with about two and a half 'O' Levels between us. But I was never one for up here – ' He tapped the side of his head. 'Our dad was a carpenter, before he died, and I took after him. You give me a bit of wood with a nice grain to it, and I'm happy. I did a City and Guilds, and I met Roy, he's my boss, well, business partner really, and he said I had talent, and took me on in his business, and I never looked back.'

'He's good,' Haz added. 'When I do a refit of a space, I often get them in, him and Roy.'

'Mitch said there was someone there, on the night Andy died...' Agnes leaned over and put her cup down. 'He can't remember it properly, but he said there was a man shouting, and a woman, who held Andy when he was dying. He didn't recognise them.'

'Street people?' Connor addressed Haz.

'He thought so, yes.'

'Thing is, anything could happen around Andy.' Connor frowned, flicked at a speck of dust on his knee. 'It was the Falklands that changed him. He came back different, didn't he?'

Haz was nodding. 'An angry man, he was, after that. He'd laugh about it, wouldn't he, about them Argie boys, about nicking packets of fags off them dead bodies, and we'd laugh too, but then he'd shout and swear and say it wasn't funny, what was we laughing for?'

Connor sighed. 'After a while we kind of gave up on him. I wish we hadn't. People get help these days, don't they, those Gulf War lads, they get counselling and stuff. We didn't know enough about it.'

'Maybe it wouldn't have helped.' Haz stood up and went over to the window, peering down through the blinds onto the street below.

'And then Lucky died,' Connor said. 'And it's like something of Andy died with him.'

'Have you seen Betty recently?' Haz said, still watching the street.

'Last week, Saturday, it was. Did a bit of shopping for her.'

'Betty is Lucky's mum.' Haz turned away from the window. 'Perhaps prison will do it for Mitch. They're bound to catch up with him, he'll get sent down, it'll give him some breathing space.'

'Prison? Give me a break. How's that going to help him?'

'No booze for a start.'

'No, just everything else.' Connor picked up his cup, put it down again. 'Nothing's going to change that boy. It's like there's a switch in his head, like it's set to self-destruct or something, and nothing you can do will turn it off. My mam's tried, I've tried, Rachel, my girlfriend, she's tried. She's off out with Lily at the moment, our little girl.'

'Tell you what,' Haz said. 'Betty might know something about Andy's past. Being a Scot and that.'

'A Scot?' Alasdair looked up.

'Yeah. Gorbals, Betty was, wasn't she?'

'So were we,' Alasdair said, 'originally.'

'You might know her,' Connor said. 'Betty O'Donovan.'

'That would be her married name,' Haz said.

'True.'

Alasdair scratched his head. 'Doesn't ring a bell. But it's a long time since I lived in Glasgow.'

'You could talk to her, if you like,' Connor said. 'She'd like the company. She gets lonely these days. She lives over in Hackney, near the Queensbridge Road.'

'My convent house is near there,' Agnes said. 'I could pop in at the same time, they see little enough of me as it is.'

Out in the street, Haz wrapped his scarf round his neck. He shrugged. 'It's tough on Connor, dealing with Mitch,' he said. 'And it's about to get a lot more difficult when they catch up with him. Poor Connor.' he said. He looked away, down the street, where a woman, hunched with age, struggled against the wind, her feet dragging in slippers along the pavement, threadbare coat flapping. 'Poor everyone,' he said. He held out a hand to Agnes, then Alasdair. 'See you around,' he said. 'I've got to be in town in an hour.'

Agnes and Alasdair watched him go. Grey clouds scudded across the sun, and the street was suddenly bathed in sunlight. Alasdair looked at Agnes. 'Lunch, I suppose,' he said.

'Lunch,' she agreed.

They sat on high chrome stools, raising their voices above the cappuccino machine.

'I'm not sure how much longer I can afford this,' Alasdair said.

Agnes glanced up at him from her cup of coffee.

'Bankrolling impoverished nuns whose idea of a cheap lunch is organic smoked salmon,' Alasdair said.

'I'll buy the next one,' Agnes said, squeezing lemon between two slices of brown bread. 'Anyway, you're lucky they didn't have lobster,' she added.

This made him laugh. Agnes sipped her coffee and watched him. The collar of his shirt was crisp and white against his neck.

'Nice shirt,' she heard herself say. 'The American publisher must be paying you well.'

'It was in a sale,' he said. He looked across at her. 'You always need an explanation, don't you. It's something about you.'

'I don't know what you mean.' Agnes raised her cup, to hide behind it.

'It's funny for someone who's supposed to live with faith,' he went on. 'You see an expensive shirt on someone, and you immediately seek out some kind of reason that explains that particular shirt on that particular person.'

'I see no conflict.' Agnes put her cup back on its saucer. 'My faith doesn't need to concern itself with how much people's shirts cost. My faith is about life, love. Continuance.'

'Not whether there was a sale at Yves St Laurent last summer?'

She looked up at him. 'Do you know, I don't think Yves St

Laurent is even mentioned in the Bible.'

Alasdair picked up his sandwich, then put it down again. 'When you say love...' He stared at his plate.

'Go on.'

He looked at her. 'What kind of love?'

'All kinds. God's love.'

He shook his head. 'That isn't all kinds.'

'Oh, but it is. It's what my friend Julius says, about loving the rose. Even though it's going to die...' She heard her voice tremble.

'It's easy to love a rose. A rose is beautiful.'

'But it won't last. The point is, you love it anyway, knowing that it won't last. You take that risk. That's what Julius said.' Agnes concentrated on her sandwich.

'Anyway, loving a rose, that's not the same as the love between two people.'

'I wouldn't know about that.'

He looked at her. 'Wouldn't you?'

'My friend Athena – you should meet her, you'd like her – she reckons that men and women mean something different when they use the word love.'

'She does?'

'Yes. She says, when a man says to a woman, "I love you," he's expressing something masculine. You know...'

'Desire?'

Agnes stared at the table. 'Yes. But more than that too. A sort of yearning, maybe. But women understand it differently. And then the man senses that the woman thinks that something contractual has happened, and it worries him. And he feels out of his depth, so he's reluctant to use the word Love any more. And that's the beginning of that sense of inequality that women have in relationships...'

She glanced at him. He was looking at her, amused. 'So,' he said. 'It takes a nun to tell me this.'

'I'm only quoting Athena.'

He shook his head. 'She's wrong. The only time in my life I

have used the phrase "I love you," I said it with my whole heart and soul.'

Agnes was aware of the loud roaring of the expresso machine behind the bar.

'But – ' she began.

'What?' His eyes shone with a kind of challenge.

'Isn't that because it was unrequited?'

He stared at her. 'It takes a nun to tell me that as well.'

They finished their sandwiches in silence. Alasdair paid the bill. Agnes got down from her stool and put on her coat. He took her arm as they went out into the street.

'Who was she?' Agnes said, muffling herself against the wind.

Alasdair turned away to light a cigarette, shielding the match from the wind.

'Your Beatrice,' Agnes said.

'Perhaps.' He took a breath of cigarette smoke.

'Can you get away with it these days?' Agnes said.

Alasdair took her arm again as they set off towards the tube station. 'Get away with what?' he said.

'That sort of love,' she said. 'Being guided by the beloved away from Hell, towards Paradise. The redemptive power of the ideal woman.'

He stopped and faced her as they waited at the traffic lights. 'Well, if you're still allowed to lock yourself up in a cloister after all this time, then I don't see why I can't have medieval love.'

She laughed.

'You see,' he said, 'That world never went away. You just scratch the surface of this time that we inhabit, and the fourteenth century lies beneath. Anyway,' he went on, taking her arm again as the lights changed and they crossed the road, 'I wasn't pursuing an ideal. She was real. She just didn't happen to feel the same way that I did.' He shrugged. 'Not courtly love at all. Just the normal mess of human relationships. I'm taking the tube from here.' He paused at the steps of Southwark station.

'Alasdair – '

'What?'

'Here.' Agnes pulled out a sheaf of Andy's writings and handed them to him. 'Look after them.'

'I will.'

'There's another thing – ' she scuffed her toe on the ground, then looked up at him. 'How is it that Scott knows how Andy died?'

Alasdair looked at her blankly.

'Trina said,' Agnes went on. 'One clean blow to the head.'

'Yes. You told me. I really wouldn't trust her account of anything.'

The sky had cleared, and the clouds were edged with pink. 'How do you know Trina?' Agnes persisted.

'Through Andy. I already told you.'

'You seem to know her well.'

Alasdair wrapped his scarf more tightly round his neck. 'When Andy came back from the Falklands, I saw quite a lot of her then. We both tried to help him. But in the end, I could see it was over between them. I helped her leave. But she blames me, for some reason. No one could help Andy in those days. Least of all her.' Alasdair leaned towards her, his fingers brushing her arm. 'I'll phone you.'

'Sure.' She watched as the station engulfed him, as he merged with the crowds, descending into darkness.

She let herself in to the hostel, and stood in the hall. It was very quiet. Not even the beat of Jayce's music. Above her on the landing, she heard a door open and shut, and then the sound of someone crying.

She went up the stairs and knocked on Jeanie's door. 'It's me, Agnes,' she said.

The sound of crying continued from inside the room.

'Can I come in?'

Agnes tried the door and it opened. Jeanie was lying on her bed, face down under her duvet, sobbing.

'Shall I go away?' Agnes said.

Jeanie's tear-stained face appeared over the top of the duvet.

'What do you want?'

Agnes looked at the tree outside the window, its bare branches fingering the sky.

'Shall we go for a walk?' she said.

'Is this what you do?' Jeanie strode along beside her as they crossed the park.

'What do you mean?'

'Going for a walk. It's just a funny thing to do, that's all, for someone like you.'

'It's such a lovely afternoon.'

'Me and Chris used to walk in the park. It was one of the things we did. After he died, I didn't think I'd ever walk in a park again.' She dashed the back of her hand against her eyes. 'But here I am, eh?'

A Yorkshire terrier yapped across their path in pursuit of a ball. Jeanie stopped to watch, smiling like a small child. 'That's the sort of dog we were going to have, me and Chris. Something like that. We were going to get a rescue dog, we'd worked it all out.' Her eyes filled with tears again.

'Jeanie – what's wrong?'

'I'm all right.' Jeanie kicked at a twig underfoot.

'If this is how you are when you're all right – ' Agnes began, but Jeanie stopped still. In the silence the birds announced the ending of the day.

Jeanie set off again, Agnes at her side.

'Look at all these trees,' Jeanie said, waving a vague arm in their direction.

Agnes nodded. The bare branches were brushed with pink with the last of the sun.

'Must have been the last thing he saw, my Chris. The tree he went into. And then smashed-up metal and glass. And blood.' Jeanie's voice was chill in the crisp air. 'Sometimes – ' she quickened her pace, breathless. 'Sometimes, I think maybe people who die that way, maybe they become like the trees. Maybe if you smash yourself into a tree then you kind of take root, and live and grow, and maybe you're not really dead at all.' She was almost shouting, and now she turned, pink-cheeked, to face Agnes. 'What do you think?' she said. 'Because it's true isn't it, no one should decide when to die, even if you do it to yourself and not to anyone else, it's still violence, isn't it? And so maybe your soul is trapped, like in a tree, because it was never up to you in the first place, it was never something that was for you to decide...' She stopped, her breath making clouds in the space between them.

They stood under a tree in the gathering twilight. 'In my tradition,' Agnes began, 'we pray for souls that are stuck.'

'Pray?' Jeanie scuffed her toe against a stone. Agnes could hear home-time sounds, the shouts of children. Above them, birds settled on branches, silhouetted in the dusk. 'Pray for him?' Jeanie said.

They turned to go. 'If you want to – ' Agnes said.

Jeanie shook her head. 'Don't know how to pray.'

They walked in silence towards the park gates, emerging into the yellow lamplight of the street.

'It was nice, that,' Jeanie said. 'Walking in the park. I did it with Chris and I think I must have done it when I was a little girl. Going to the swings. I remember the swings.' They turned away from the park towards the hostel. 'That's another thing I must have done when I was a little girl,' Jeanie said. 'Praying. I remember saying my prayers. At school, in Hull. We all said our prayers then. So I must have known how to do it once.'

'You could try again.'

Jeanie glanced up at her. 'What, for him? For Chris stuck in his bloody tree? It'll take more than the Our bloody Father to rescue him.' The laughter had left her face. 'What he did – what he did to himself, and what he did to me – Oh my God.' Jeanie broke off and was staring across the street.

'What?' Agnes tried to follow her gaze.

'It's her.' Jeanie was whispering. 'See that woman there?'

Agnes saw a woman pass under the streetlight; a flash of red hair, a pale raincoat.

'It's the one who came to see Walker, on the night he died.'

'The woman?'

'Yes, I'm sure of it.' They walked on, their heads down. Agnes glanced back, took Jeanie's arm and crossed the road, keeping the woman at a distance in front of them. They followed her for some yards. She reached a shabby terrace of houses, turned into the rusted gate of one, went up the steps and rang the bell. After a moment a man opened the door and greeted her, pulling on his coat. They left together.

'Shall we follow them?' Jeanie tugged at Agnes's sleeve.

'Are you sure it was her?'

'Positive.'

Agnes hesitated. 'We've seen the house. Let's go back when we have something to ask her.'

Agnes walked Jeanie back to the hostel. 'Are you coming in?' Jeanie said, standing on the steps, shifting from foot to foot.

Agnes shook her head. 'Not my shift. I'll be back in the morning.'

'It'll be that horrible Mary on duty then. She's always there when you're not.'

'Talking of souls stuck in trees – ' Agnes stopped herself.

'What?'

'Nothing. It's just that you and Mary have more in common than you think.'

'Oh, great. Well, I'm not going to end up like her.'

'Good.' Agnes smiled. 'You've got time on your side.'

Jeanie nodded. 'Thanks for the park,' she said, turning to go up the stairs. 'Next time it's the swings, OK?'

Agnes laughed. 'OK.'

The flat was in darkness. Agnes dialled Trina's number. A man's voice answered.

'It's Sister Agnes,' she said. 'Is Trina there?'

'Who?'

'Sister Agnes,' she said.

'Are you that nun?' The voice was gruff.

Agnes heard him carry the phone through to Trina. There were raised voices, 'Why did you answer my bleeding phone in the first place then. Hello?'

'Trina?'

'Hi.'

'Is this a bad time?'

'It's always a bad time with him around. Yes, you,' Trina seemed to be shouting to someone in the background. 'Fine. Fuck off then.'

'Shall I call back?' Agnes could hear doors slamming.

'It's OK. He's gone.'

'I wondered whether we could meet,' Agnes said.

'Why?'

'I met Michael Cordaro,' Agnes said. 'And Haz.'

'Haz, eh? How is he?'

'Fine.'

'Is he still doing clubs?'

'I think so.'

'He promised to book me as a singer once. He never did. Could've changed my life.'

'I thought maybe we could have a drink together,' Agnes said.

'With Alasdair?'

'Not unless you want to see him.'

'No. I don't want to see him.' There was a pause. 'OK. When?'

'Tomorrow?'

'Yeah, OK. The Rising Sun?'

Agnes was surprised. 'I thought you'd want somewhere nearer to you.'

'If I come into town, he won't know where to find me.'

'Scott?'

'Stupid bastard. Seven o'clock?'

'OK.'

Agnes rang off. She was sitting on the edge of her bed, chilled in the darkness. A passing siren pulsed blue light across the room. She thought about Jeanie. She thought about Jeanie's boyfriend, smashing into a tree.

She thought about Walker, snuffed out on a London street.

There was a pealing of church bells, calling the faithful to Sunday evening prayers. She thought about Julius, waiting for his test results.

I should have gone to mass, she thought. She lit her candles, and turned to the pages of her prayer book.

'... For since by man came death, by man came also the resurrection of the dead. For as in Adam all die, even so in Christ shall all be made alive; for the wages of sin is death; but the gift of God is eternal life through Jesus Christ our Lord...'

She shivered, got up on her bed and pulled the bedclothes around her.

Chapter Eight

Rain, again. Agnes found herself following Connor up the shabby concrete staircase of a 1960s tower block.

'Isn't there a lift?' she said, stopping for breath on the third floor landing.

'You don't want to go near the lift. Even if it's working.'

'How does she manage, then, Lucky's mum?'

'Like everyone. She just does. They've been promising to find her sheltered accommodation for about six months, but fat chance. No Alasdair?'

'He says he's got to work.'

They reached the fifth floor, and pressed the buzzer on one of the doors, which opened immediately.

'I knew it was you,' came a voice. 'When I saw you on the intercom downstairs. And who's this?'

'This is Sister Agnes. I told you, remember? When I phoned. I said I'd be bringing a nun with me.'

Mrs O'Donovan peered up at Agnes, her eyes diminished behind thick lenses. 'A nun, eh?' She patted at her tight white curls of hair.

'You remember, don't you.'

'She wanted to talk about my boy, didn't she?'

'That's right.'

'If I'd known there was company I'd have made a cake.' Mrs O'Donovan turned sharply and shuffled along the corridor. They followed her into a small, overheated living room. She went to a large armchair by an electric heater and sat down into it. Agnes took the sofa, which was squashed low and rust-coloured.

Mrs O'Donovan picked up some knitting and went at it, surprisingly fast.

Connor was still standing. 'I'll make us some tea, shall I, Betty?'

Mrs O'Donovan looked up from her knitting and smiled. 'That would be kind of you, dear.'

She seemed to be waiting for Agnes to say something. She held her knitting close in the glow from the lamp and the fire at her feet, the amber light from the tiled fireplace behind her with its false electric coals. On the mantelpiece there were two china ladies in crinolines, supporting an array of family photographs.

'Are those your children?' Agnes broke the silence, gesturing to the portraits.

Mrs O'Donovan nodded, still knitting.

'Is that one Lucky?

She shook her head. 'No, that's his brother, Tom. My younger boy. Oh, dear me, now look...' there was a flurried rearrangement of stitches, then she said, 'I've only got the one proper picture of him. In his uniform. I couldn't put it up there, it's not true, you see.'

'Not true?' Agnes leaned forward towards her.

'He only signed up because all his friends were. He was never a soldier, my Alf always said that, never a soldier, that boy. And there you are, you see, he left, didn't he? I hope you got out the proper cups dear,' she added, as Connor appeared with a tray of tea things. 'He should never have signed up, should he dear,' she said to Connor, as he stirred two sugars into her cup of tea.

'No,' Connor agreed.

'Andy, Eileen's boy, it suited him, the army. He did well, there, didn't he, awards for bravery and all sorts. But not my boy, oh no.'

'What did he do after the army?'

The clicking of the knitting needles stopped.

'It was the motorbikes, you see. Connor here will tell you. He loved them bikes. My Alf wanted him to go into a proper business, fix him up with a shop and that, but our Lucky had to do the bikes, didn't he?'

She started knitting again.

Agnes stood up and went to the mantelpiece. 'Are these your other children?'

Betty glanced up. 'That's my Carol, with her two boys. She lives in Nottingham. That was last year that photograph, on holiday, they're bigger than that now. And that one, with the mountains in the background, that's Doug. He lives back home in Scotland, went to the oil rigs, ended up settling up there. He's done very well for himself. Nice girl he lives with. Nice girl, she is... pass slipped stitch over, there we are.' She looked up from her needles. 'We called him Lucky. Always called him Lucky. It's like he was born smiling. I used to sit by his cradle and sing to him, and he'd smile and smile. Christened him Francis, after my Alf's father, but he was always called Lucky. And he was, wasn't he Connor? Sailed through life. Always had money, somehow. Always had the girl he wanted. And then...' She put her cup down on the tray. 'I didn't think luck could run out like that. Never thought it would happen. You hear the news, you hear there's been an accident, and you think – no. Not him. Not my Lucky...' Her eyes misted over as she peered at her work. 'Knit three from cable needle...' she murmured.

'Agnes wanted to know about Andy,' Connor said.

'And that's another one,' Mrs O'Donovan said. 'That's one that should still be with us. Although at least his mum wasn't there to see him go, God help us. It would have broken her heart, that would. And there's your brother...' She glanced up at Connor, lost for words. 'I used to sing with Eileen, you see,' she said, addressing Agnes. 'Eileen and I, we'd work the pubs, just from time to time, nothing professional, but they liked us, didn't they Connor? We'd do folk nights down the Red Lion, do you remember? A lot of people didn't have much time for Eileen, but I liked her. It was the Scots connection, I always thought, it made us like family. Glasgow. Gorbals people, we were, way back, then our Dad got work in Govan and we moved there. And then I married, and came here, and then my sister Kathleen and her husband took a house on one of the Schemes, the new estates, you know. Castlemilk. Didn't work out for everyone, but she settled. Lovely it was, your own bathroom, all electric. She still lives there, you know.'

Connor smiled at her as he picked up the tea things. He took them into the kitchen, and in the silence, Betty O'Donovan began to hum a thin, reedy tune, but as she added the words, Agnes could hear the sweet, strong voice she must have had, years ago. '"Hush, my baby, hush, my pretty one,

Soon it will be dawn..." Oh, I had a good voice,' Betty said, as if in answer. 'I could have made a career of it, my Alf said, but...' She shrugged. 'Sometimes life takes over.'

'We should go,' Connor said, coming back into the room.

Agnes hesitated. 'The thing is,' she said, 'Andy wrote a sort of diary, about the war. And he keeps talking about Lucky in it, as if he was there, even though he wasn't.'

'They were good friends.' Mrs O'Donovan picked out a new colour of wool from the basket at her feet.

'And we thought that Lucky might have known – ' Agnes glanced at Connor.

'Andy had enemies,' Connor said. 'We think Mitch might have been set up.'

Mrs O'Donovan put her work down on her lap. 'When my Lucky died...' She started again. 'You can always think that way, you see? When I heard about my boy, I thought, that isn't how it was. It can't have been an accident. They've got it wrong. Someone must have caused it. Because – ' she picked up her knitting again – 'it's too cruel for it to be an accident. The good Lord wouldn't have willed that my Lucky should be taken from us like that. That's how you think. You think, if this is the world, I don't want to live in it. And then after a while, a few months, maybe, or years, you get used to it. You change your ideas about the world you live in, and then you find that you can still live in it. After a while.'

Agnes stood up and took her coat from the arm of the sofa.

'They were good friends,' Betty O'Donovan said again. 'They

stood by each other. When Andy was picked up for fighting, it was years ago now, there was a fight down Wapping way. It was over a girl, Lucky said.'

Connor smiled. 'Doesn't surprise me.'

'And our Lucky turned up in court, in a suit, he borrowed one of my Alf's old ones, and he's all charm, and he goes on about how Andy's a fine upstanding member of the community, and then suddenly all the charges were dropped...' She laughed. 'He was like that, our Lucky. Charm itself.'

'Well...' Connor hesitated in the doorway.

'Let yourselves out, won't you,' she said. 'My legs aren't what they were.'

'Thank you for seeing us,' Agnes said.

As they made their way down the dark hallway to the front door, Agnes could hear the sweet, clear notes of the folk tune again, as Mrs Donovan sang to her knitting.

Out in the street, Connor pulled up the collar of his leather jacket against the drizzle.

'I thought she might have known more,' he said.

'I suppose Lucky wasn't the sort to confide in his mum,' Agnes said.

'I always got the feeling that Lucky knew Andy better than anyone else. That they shared secrets, you know? When Lucky died, Andy was in a right old state. Mind you, he was often in a right old state, it was difficult to tell.' They were interrupted by his ringtone, and he pulled out his phone. 'Yeah? Yeah. OK. Later.' He rang off. 'I've got to go,' he said. 'Do you need a lift?'

'No, it's OK,' Agnes said. 'My convent is just round the corner there, I said I'd visit. And this evening, I'm having a drink with Trina. Do you know her?'

'She was keen on Andy once, years ago, wasn't she. Yes, I've met her. I'm surprised her old man has allowed it, from what I've heard of him. I suppose, you being a nun, you count as safe.' He laughed. 'Phone me if you need to.'

'Thanks,' Agnes said. She watched him splash across the gutter back to his car, then turned towards Mare Street, to walk to the convent.

Sister Christiane paced the three steps to the window, then turned. She stood, framed in the arch of red Victorian brick. Outside the trees shook drops from their branches as the rain eased.

'Sister Agnes,' she said. 'It seems to me that there is no difficulty.'

Agnes was silent. She sat, her hands folded in her lap. Her eye was caught by a glass paperweight which lay on Christiane's antique mahogany desk.

'You've served your novitiate,' Christiane was saying. 'You are a valued member of the community. More to the point, I am not aware that you have expressed any doubts about your vocation.'

Agnes raised her eyes to Christiane's. 'No,' she said.

'So,' Christiane said, then smiled. 'It's a simple matter of disposing of this house of yours, and then you'll be free.'

'Free?' Agnes heard herself say.

Christiane sat down opposite her, in a flurry of skirts. 'Property is such a hindrance in discerning the will of God,' she said. 'I find it inspiring, don't you, that in monastic life we have the opportunity to shed all encumbrances and just possess only what is necessary, and no more. Goodness knows, such a state of affairs is fortunate in these acquisitive times.'

Agnes nodded. The paperweight crushed the pale sunlight into a bright, narrow beam.

'So,' Christiane said, in conclusion. 'We're agreed that all you have to do is dispose of this house in France, and then we can proceed. Obviously, our trustees will need to know how much money is due to them from the sale, but you can let me know about all that in due course.' She smiled again in termination of the interview.

Agnes found she had risen to her feet. 'Of course, Sister,' she said. She gathered up her coat. 'Thank you.'

She walked out of Christiane's office, along the thickly carpeted corridor and out into the hallway. She opened the heavy front door, went down the stone staircase. The afternoon was fresh and bright after the rain. 'What am I going to tell Athena?' Agnes thought.

'You've agreed what?' Athena's voice on the phone was shrill.

'I couldn't think of any argument against it.'

'Next time you go to see one of these women, I'm coming with you. I'll hide under your coat and whisper the right answer, OK?'

'She said it would make me free.' Agnes sat on her bed, her phone in one hand, a mug of tea in the other.

'Free?'

'Yes. Unencumbered by possessions.'

'Well, that's a great philosophy, but, sweetie, it really doesn't bear close examination.'

'It doesn't?'

'Freedom is having enough money to go to the Yves St Laurent sale without having to worry.'

'Oh.' Agnes sipped her tea. 'That's funny.'

'What is?'

'Alasdair gets his shirts from the Yves St Laurent sale.'

'I must meet this man.'

Agnes rang off. Almost immediately, her phone rang.

'Hi,' Alasdair said.

'We were just talking about you,' Agnes said.

'We?'

'Me and my friend Athena.'

'What were you saying?'

'Oh, nothing. Just about clothes, really.'

'Clothes?'

'Yes. The philosophical connection between spiritual freedom and the Yves St Laurent sale.'

'Again.'

'Funny, isn't it?'

'How was Lucky's mother?' Alasdair said.

'Sweet. But not very informative. How are the writings?'

'Interesting,' Alasdair said. 'Have you read the bit which

mentions his commanding officer? Major Braybrook, he's called, he looked after Andy after the Falklands. I thought I might track him down. There's all this talk about revenge, something that happened during the war, I thought if there was someone who was out to get Andy, this man might know about it.'

'Good idea.'

There was a small pause. Outside it had begun to rain again.

'What are you doing now?' Alasdair said.

'Drinking tea.'

'I meant, this evening?'

'I'm about to meet Trina for a drink at the Rising Sun.'

'Shall I – ' he began, but Agnes interrupted.

'No. It's a big concession on her part. Don't ruin it.'

'OK. Well,' he said, after another pause. 'Tomorrow, maybe? We could meet up?'

'I'm at the hostel, I'm on the early shift.'

'I'll phone you.'

Agnes sat in the Rising Sun. It was 7:15. Agnes sat by a steamed-up window, looking at the old ship's clock on the wall, the minutes ticking by, the flickering of the fire reflected in the glass. She drained her whisky, went to the bar, ordered another. It was 7:35.

The door swung open, and in a swish of shiny white mackintosh, Trina arrived.

'Oh God, am I late, I tried to get out, I thought he was going over to Mikey's to watch football, but he cancelled, so I sat there like a lemon until he went down the snooker club...' Trina flopped down in a chair next to Agnes.

'What can I get you to drink?' Agnes smiled at her.

'Do you know, I really fancy a vodka and tonic, if that's all right.'

While Agnes queued at the bar, Trina fished a mirror out of her bag and patted at her hair. Agnes wondered about a third whisky, but settled for mineral water, fizzy, with ice.

'So Scott doesn't know you're here?' Agnes said, returning to the table.

'No. And he won't be pleased if he finds out, neither.'

'Why not?'

Trina sipped her drink. 'He's just like that,' she said. 'Stupid bastard.'

'Why do you stay with him?'

She put down her glass, circled it on the sticky table. 'Sometimes I think I love him,' she said at last. 'And sometimes I think I don't.'

'But you loved Andy?'

'When I was a kid, when he came to London... He was lovely, he was.' She smiled across at Agnes. 'Everyone said we'd get married, all them lads, Michael and that. You ask them.'

'So what went wrong?'

'He signed up, didn't he. Him and Lucky and the others. Went off to Germany. Then Andy came back, and then straight off to the Falklands. And then after that...' She stared into her glass. 'I always felt I'd let him down. I knew it was the war that made him like that, I knew the old Andy was still there, somewhere underneath it all. I tried to get him help, but none of the doctors he saw seemed to understand what he'd been through. And one day I was sitting at home, and Alasdair called on us. And Andy was out, somewhere, as usual. So I made Alasdair a cup of tea, and he sees the bruises on my arms. And he tells me I should leave.'

'Alasdair told you to leave?'

'He arranged it all. He found me a room in a flat, one of his mates. He said Andy was never going to change.'

'And was he right?'

'No. Not really. I was vulnerable. I was in no position to choose.' Trina picked up her empty glass, put it down again.

'I'll get us another,' Agnes said. 'Same again?'

This time she had a whisky.

'Is that why you're so cross with Alasdair, then?' she said, coming back to the table.

'I'm not.

'You are. And Alasdair's shifty about you.'

Trina smiled a tight smile. 'He's always shifty, that one.'

'All this claiming to have paid for the coffin,' Agnes said.

'I'll tell you what it is. It's guilt. Both of us. Alasdair thinks he could have done more for him. They weren't even real brothers, were they? It was Alasdair's dad who died in Scotland, not Andy's. And then because of that, Eileen brought Andy back to London, where she was from in the first place. And Alasdair went off to university. So it's like, after Eileen died, Andy had no one. Just Alasdair. And the army. And they both let him down.' She crunched an ice cube, then went on, 'That's why he was so angry. For years, after the war, he was angry. Because everyone had let him down. Alasdair said, that boy will go to his grave being angry. And it turned out he was right. It's like when Alasdair's dad had that accident...'

Agnes glanced across at her. 'Go on.'

Trina met her eyes. 'He fell out of a window, Jim Brogan did. Roaring drunk he was.'

'And?'

Trina shook her head. 'That's all, really. He lived in one of the high rises up there in Glasgow, and he came home drunk. Eileen was nice though,' Trina said, in a deliberate change of tone. 'I liked it when she came to the estate. She'd had a hard life, Andy's dad died in an accident in the docks, when Andy was only a kid, and then she met Jim. She was a bit like a mum to me, I didn't get on with my mum and Eileen kind of looked after me.'

Agnes put her glass down on the table. 'Trina – who are all these people who wanted Andy dead, all these people in the writings?'

'It's like I said before, Sister. Maybe they were all in his head.' She finished her drink. 'I'd better be getting back before he notices I'm gone – ' Her eyes flashed towards the door. 'Uh-oh, here we are.'

Agnes turned, expecting to see Scott, seeing Alasdair instead. He came over to their table.

'Hello.' Agnes felt his hand rest briefly on her shoulder.

Trina was looking up at him. 'Did you tell him I'd be here?' she said to Agnes.

'I – ' Agnes began.

'I was just going anyway.' Trina stood up.

'Trina – ' Alasdair took a step towards her.

'What?' She glared back at him.

'What did he tell you? About my father's death?'

'I'm not trading secrets with you. Not after what you did to drive us apart – '

'I rescued you – '

Trina pulled her coat around her, and picked up her bag. 'Maybe. But you were wrong.' She was standing close to Alasdair, almost close enough to touch him. 'It was me he needed. And you drove us apart.'

'In the writings, he says he's talked to you about that night that my father died – '

Trina put a hand up to stop him. 'I don't care. If you hadn't split us up, he'd still be here today.'

'If I hadn't got you away from him, you'd be dead by now.' Alasdair's voice was tight. 'It's not my fault you went from one violent man to another – '

'Oh, and I suppose you're a bleedin' knight in shining armour, are you? Well, I'm not buying it.' Trina was shouting now, and people were staring. 'Don't blame me for your guilt, Alasdair Brogan.' She turned to Agnes. 'Thanks for the drinks,' she said, before turning on her stiletto heels and click-clicking out of the door.

Agnes turned to Alasdair. His face was drained of colour. 'Do you want a drink?' she said.

'That's not the right question,' he replied. 'If I start now I won't stop. Let's go.'

He took her arm and they left by the other door, away from the direction that Trina had taken. They stumbled outside into the splashing of the passing cars. He walked fast, still holding on to her arm, his face set against the rain.

'Can we slow down?' Agnes asked, after a while.

He stopped and let go of her arm. 'I'm sorry,' he said. He stood looking down at her. The rain was sheeted yellow in the street light. 'Shall I walk you home?'

She smiled at him. 'Sure.'

This time he didn't take her arm. They walked in silence, crossing the end of Jamaica Road, passing the estates on the corner.

'Do we pass the hostel this way?' Alasdair was saying, and Agnes was about to say no, when she noticed the woman that Jeanie had recognised turn into the street ahead of them.

'Yes,' she said, and she took his arm and began to hurry, almost to run, dragging him with her.

'What's the matter?'

'Look,' Agnes whispered to him, 'that woman there, she's wearing a pale raincoat, and boots, can you see her – ' she broke into a run, Alasdair alongside her.

They gained on her. The woman had reached the house they'd seen before, and now stood under a street lamp, rummaging in her bag.

'Who is she?' Alasdair said. 'Why are we – oh.' He stopped, his eyes fixed on the woman, just as she raised her eyes, her keys in her hand, and saw him.

'Janet?' Alasdair took a few steps towards her.

'Alasdair,' she said. 'What are you doing here?'

'I could ask the same of you.'

They stood in the rain, uncertain. Agnes held out her hand.

'I'm Agnes,' she said.

Janet looked at her, then back at Alasdair. 'Well,' she said, 'you'd better come in, I suppose.'

Chapter Nine

The hallway was dark and smelt of damp. Janet pressed a light-switch. Nothing happened. She continued up the stairs, Agnes and Alasdair following. On the first floor she took out her keys and opened a door.

'Hi,' she called.

There were lights on, and a steady beat of music.

'Hi,' a man's voice replied.

'We've got company,' Janet called. She opened the living room door. A bare light bulb hung from the centre of the ceiling. There was a thin, grey carpet, and one sofa, covered by a yellowing bedspread. On the sofa a man was sitting, nodding his head to the music. He looked at Janet and their two visitors, then flicked a remote control towards the CD player, and the music stopped.

'So who's this?' he said. Agnes noticed his accent was the same as Janet's.

'This is Agnes,' Janet said, with a wave towards her. 'And you know who this is.'

The man on the sofa stared at Alasdair. There was a silence, then he said, 'It isn't.'

'It is,' Janet said.

Alasdair's gaze was fixed on him. 'Sean,' he said.

'Alasdair,' Sean said, getting up from the sofa, his arm outstretched. He was clean-shaven, blue-eyed, with a broad smile.

They shook hands, standing in the middle of the room, grinning at each other. 'How on earth did you – ' Sean said.

'What are you doing here – ' Alasdair said, at the same time, then they both laughed.

Sean patted Alasdair on the back, then returned to the sofa. Janet found a chair for Agnes, a floor cushion for Alasdair. 'I'm sorry,' she said, 'we've not got much here.'

Alasdair turned to Agnes, smiling. 'I've known Sean here since we were kids. In Glasgow.' He shook his head. 'I can't believe you're sitting there, in front of me, like nothing's changed.'

'Me too,' Sean said, and laughed. 'Find them a drink,' he said to Janet. 'There's some beers in the fridge.'

Janet went out to the kitchen. Sean sat, still smiling. 'Who'd have thought?' he said.

'In all of London...' Alasdair said.

'How did you – ?'

'We bumped into Janet,' Alasdair said. 'Out there, out in the street.'

'By chance?'

Agnes was aware of Alasdair not looking at her. 'Yes,' he said, after a moment.

'I work in a hostel,' Agnes said. 'Across the way there, in the next street.'

'Andy stayed there,' Alasdair added. 'That's how I ...' his voice tailed off.

Sean's smile died. 'That was terrible news,' he said. 'I was so sorry when I heard...'

'Yes,' Alasdair said.

'He must have been all the family you had,' Sean said.

'All I had left,' Alasdair agreed.

'I heard from Gordon,' Sean said. 'This is his flat, him and Janet here. Gordon came down here looking for work, couple of months ago. And Janet joined him. And then I thought, what the hell, nothing doing up in Glasgow, might as well try my luck in London too.'

'How did Gordon hear,' Alasdair said. 'About Andy, I mean?'

The door swung open, as Janet appeared with some cans of beer and some glasses.

'Janet,' Sean said to her. 'How did Gordon know about Andy?'

Janet flicked a glance at him. 'It was in the papers, wasn't it?'

'You could have come to the funeral,' Alasdair said.

'We found out too late,' Janet said. 'Gordon said that, didn't he, Sean? He said, it was a shame we didn't know in time for the funeral. And Sean here, he wasn't even here at the time, were you?' She put the tray down on the floor, and settled next to it.

'But – ' Agnes began.

Alasdair turned to Agnes. 'I grew up with these boys. My father was from Castlemilk, we lived on the estate there. And then my mum got ill... No thanks,' he said to Janet, as she offered him a beer. 'And then Andy's mum took up with my dad, and they joined us.'

'He was the clever one, Alasdair here,' Sean said, laughing. 'He went to the school in town. And Andy came to our school, didn't he?' Sean clicked open a can, and took a mouthful. Agnes poured some beer from her can into a glass.

In the silence, Janet said, 'Gordon'll be back soon.'

'He went to see someone about a job, in a club. Bouncer,' Sean explained.

'I don't want him to take it,' Janet said. 'It's too dangerous.'

'He's worked the clubs back home,' Sean said.

'It's different there. He knows what's going on. If someone starts something ugly, he knows what to do.'

'England, see – ' Sean laughed. 'Foreign country.'

'It is,' Janet said.

There was a small silence, broken by Alasdair. 'When did you leave the army?' he said.

'I did my time,' Sean said. 'Germany. Then Belfast. Then Bosnia.'

'Bosnia?' Alasdair turned to him. 'I didn't know that.'

'Peacekeeping,' Sean said. He held his can, turning it round in his hands. 'I left after that.'

Janet glanced across at him. 'Gordon said – '

'Oh, aye,' Sean said. 'Gordon reckons it changed me. It's true enough, it is, I've seen things no one should have to see. Peacekeeping, they call it. I've had to stand by and watch man's brutality to man, and not do a thing to prevent it. Andy used to say, when we'd talk about these things, he'd say, if that's peace I'd rather have war.' Sean laughed, looked up at the others as if to share the joke.

'But you got out.' Janet spoke quietly.

'Och, aye, I was lucky.'

Janet stretched her legs out in front of her. 'Unlike Andy,' she said.

Sean nodded. 'He was wrong. He did see war. The Falklands, you see. Like I said, I've seen some ugly things in my time, don't get me wrong, but the boys in the Scots Guards...' He shook his head. 'They were out there, in '82. You see them now, in the pubs, back home.' He stared at his shoes. 'Broken men, some of them.'

'It changed Andy, didn't it?'

Sean nodded. 'Never the same.'

'And you were the only person he'd talk to about it,' Janet said.

'Maybe I was the only person who could understand.' Sean took a large mouthful of beer, as the room fell silent.

Agnes turned to Janet. 'So, when you came to the hostel, the day Andy died – '

Janet looked blank. 'When?'

'You came to find him, that afternoon. Before he went out.'

'No I didn't. We didn't know he was there.'

'But you did, you came to the hostel.'

'No I didn't. If I'd known he was there, of course we'd have come to see him. That's why it was all so sad, when we heard.' Janet tucked her knees under her, staring at the floor.

Agnes glanced at Alasdair, then fell silent.

'How's Gemma?' Alasdair said.

Sean looked up, met his gaze. 'Fine,' he said.

'Good,' Alasdair said. 'And Iain?'

'Fine,' Sean repeated. 'They're both fine.'

'Their kids must be quite old now,' Alasdair said.

'Aye,' Janet said. 'Robbie's near fifteen now, and Ellie's twelve. And Gemma is thinking of going back to teaching.'

'Good,' Alasdair said. 'That would be good.'

Another silence, then the sound of a key in the door. Janet jumped up. 'That'll be Gordon,' she said, going out into the hallway. Agnes heard a voice, answered by Janet's, then Janet came back into the room, followed by a man. Agnes saw thick, greying hair, a red checked shirt.

'Alasdair,' Gordon said, holding out a broad hand and smiling warmly.

Alasdair stood up and greeted him, shaking his hand.

'We found him in the street,' Janet said, and laughed. Alasdair laughed too, as he sat back down again.

'Eh, it's a bad business with Andy,' Gordon said, opening a can of beer and settling into a corner of the sofa next to Sean. 'We felt for you all, didn't we, pet?' He looked across to Janet, back in her corner on the floor.

'How was the meeting?' Sean said to him.

'Not bad,' Gordon said. 'Not bad at all. They need someone to run the bar, I said I'd rather do that than the door, and they took one look at me and agreed.' He laughed, a loud, booming laugh. 'And our Janet here can do shifts too,' he said.

'That would be great,' Janet said. 'Then we can move from this dump and get somewhere nice.

'I thought you couldn't wait to get back home,' Sean said. 'I thought you said you couldn't breathe here.'

'Well, maybe I've changed my mind,' Janet said, then turned to Alasdair. 'You've settled here, haven't you?'

'Well, yes,' Alasdair began.

'His heart was never in Scotland,' Sean said. 'He's not like us.'

'Is that so?' Alasdair flashed a smile across at Sean.

'Oh, aye,' Sean said, smiling. 'His heart is in Italy.'

'You think so? Even now?' Alasdair returned, but Agnes could see that the smile in his eyes had died.

'Och, I wouldn't know about now,' Sean said, then turned to

Gordon. 'So, Gordon, you're taking this job?'

Gordon nodded. 'It's not great pay, but the shifts are good, there's loads of overtime.'

Janet stood up, and began to gather up the empty cans.

'How's about some dinner?' Gordon said to her. Janet stood in the middle of the room in the thin electric light. She glanced at Alasdair, then at Agnes, and smiled, tightly. 'We'd love to stay,' Agnes said, 'but I've got to get back to the hostel.' She stood up to go.

Janet breathed again. 'It's been great you being here,' she said to Alasdair, as he gathered up his coat.

'I'll see you out,' Gordon said, pulling himself up out of the sofa. He followed Agnes and Alasdair out to the hall. Behind him, Sean called out that it was great to see them, any time they wanted, they must call by. Janet went into the kitchen, and Agnes heard her finding saucepans, opening tins.

'Well,' Alasdair said to Gordon, in the doorway, but Gordon suddenly grabbed his arm and led him out onto the darkened landing.

'I need to talk to you,' Gordon said. 'Don't you think it's strange, that here we are, right across the road from Andy's hostel?' His voice was low, compressed.

'We did think it a bit odd,' Alasdair began, but Gordon was glancing anxiously at the door of the flat.

'I can't talk now,' Gordon said.

'Come to the hostel. Tomorrow,' Agnes said. 'I'm on the afternoon shift, come any time after about three.'

'Right you are,' Gordon said. 'Tomorrow. It'll be four, maybe four-thirty, before I can get away.'

'Alasdair can be there too, if you like.' Agnes said.

Gordon nodded. 'See you then. Goodbye,' he added, stepping back inside the flat, his voice loud again.

The door slammed, and Agnes and Alasdair felt their way down the stairs in the dark. Out in the street they stood in the yellow shadows and looked at each other.

'A drink?' Alasdair said. Agnes looked at her watch. 'I

promised Julius – ' she began, then glanced up at Alasdair. 'A drink,' she said.'

She breathed in the smoky warmth of the pub, folding up her coat into the corner of the seat while Alasdair went to the bar.

'There you are.' He reappeared with a glass of sauvignon, taking the seat opposite her. 'It's not Touraine, it's from the South, but it's quite reliable.'

'For someone who doesn't drink, you know a lot about it,' Agnes said.

'I know too much. That's why I don't drink,' Alasdair said. 'With a father like mine, it would be fatal. I almost went down that path. Drink became a good friend of mine. I thought it was about loving life, embracing life, but you can love life too much.' He took out tobacco and papers and rolled a thin cigarette. 'So,' he said, 'what was all that about?'

Agnes watched the steam rising from his cup of coffee. 'I was hoping you'd tell me,' she said.

Alasdair stirred sugar into his cup. 'They must have known,' he said. 'They stayed away from his funeral, but they must have known. That's what Gordon was trying to say.'

'But were they close to Andy?'

Alasdair gathered up some spilt sugar with his finger. 'Not once he left. No.'

Agnes put her glass down. 'Perhaps Jeanie was wrong,' she said. 'Perhaps the woman who came to the hostel to warn Andy, the day he died, perhaps it wasn't Janet. Perhaps everything Janet said today was true.'

'But then, what was all that just now, with Gordon? Mind you,' he added, 'it's not like Janet to lie. She was always a nice girl,' Alasdair said. 'I liked her, when we were kids. She was honest, not like some of the other girls on the estate who'd say one thing to your face and another to your back – why are you laughing?'

'I was just imagining what you were like when you were young enough to care about all that,' Agnes said.

'Oh, I cared,' Alasdair said.

Agnes sipped her wine. 'In which case, there's some other woman out there who tried to warn Andy. Or,' she continued, 'Jeanie was right. In which case, Janet is lying. And, either they knew about Andy's death and stayed away on purpose. Or they knew about Andy's death and stayed away because they didn't care.'

Alasdair re-lit his cigarette. 'Well, we'll just have to wait for Gordon tomorrow.'

'Mmm.' Agnes watched him breathe the smoke away from her. 'And Gemma?' she said.

'Ah,' he said. 'Gemma.' He tapped his cigarette on the edge of the ashtray. 'Gemma is Sean's sister. She's married to a bastard called Iain. She should have married Andy. Sean knows that, Janet knows that.'

'So what happened?'

'Andy went to war, that's what happened. Gemma waited for him, but when he came back, nothing was the same. As you know. Gemma decided to get on with her life. I don't blame her for that. It's just a shame she chose to share her life with Iain.'

'What's she like, Gemma?'

Alasdair turned his cup round in its saucer and smiled. 'Lovely. Like Sean, he's a straight kind of guy too. They've got a brother, Gray. Nice lot.'

'Short for Graham?'

Alasdair smiled at her. 'Yes.'

'She's not in the writings,' Agnes said.

'No. But then, the writings are about rage, and anger and madness. Being trapped in Hell, as he puts it. There's no place for love there.'

Agnes considered this. Then Alasdair said, 'it's like *The Divine Comedy*, you see. Beatrice doesn't appear until the *Purgatorio*. There's no place for her in the *Inferno*. She's the glimpse of salvation, of redemption.'

Agnes looked across at him. 'How clever of your brother to know that.'

Alasdair took a long drag of his cigarette. 'There's no need to tease me. If you see everything refracted through God's vision, then why shouldn't I see everything through Dante's?' He drained his cup of coffee. 'Anyway,' he went on, 'maybe some more of the writings will turn up. We might not know the whole story.'

'That's true,' Agnes said. 'Although, I don't know where we'd find them, his room's been stripped bare.'

'Another drink?' Alasdair said.

'It's my turn,' Agnes said.

'Coffee, then,' Alasdair said. 'Please.'

'You were looking at your watch,' Alasdair said, when she returned to the table with another glass of wine and a cup of coffee.

'Mmm,' she agreed, sitting down.

'So,' Alasdair said. 'Who's Julius? And what did you promise him?'

Agnes laughed. 'Julius is my best friend.'

'This is the Julius you mentioned, who loves roses even though they'll die?'

'Yes,' she said. 'That one.'

'I thought that woman was your best friend. The one with views about love. And men.'

'Athena. Yes, she is too.'

'How many best friends does a nun need?'

'Just the two, thank you,' Agnes said.

'So, this Julius – '

'He's a priest. Catholic, Jesuit. His church is just across the way there. In fact, you can probably see the spire from this very window.'

Alasdair peered through the glass. 'It's dark out there.'

'And I promised I'd go to mass this evening.'

'Ah.'

'And now it's too late.'

'And you've had two glasses of wine.'

'Oh, he's used to that,' Agnes said.

'So – ' Alasdair added more sugar to his coffee. 'So, when you say best friend...?'

Agnes leaned her chin on her hands. 'Yes,' she said. 'Just that, really.'

'What does it mean, best friend?'

'Oh, you know.' She picked up her glass of wine and took a sip from it. 'Rescuing me from almost certain death at the hands of my violent ex-husband in France. Finding me a safe place in England, in an enclosed convent, even though he had to tell the Holy Father in person that I was good enough, which was blatantly untrue. Covering for me when I ran away from that order several years ago and joined the one I'm in now. Usual best friend kind of things.'

'Really in person?'

Agnes looked up at him. 'What?'

'Did he really have to see the Pope in person?'

Agnes laughed. 'I don't suppose so. Not really, no. But various scary nuns had to be appeased, which was probably even more of a challenge.'

Alasdair nodded. 'Yes, I can see that.'

'And now he's ill.' Agnes wondered how those words had appeared, like that, spilling into the smoky air.

'Ill?'

Agnes nodded. She could feel tears, taking her by surprise, a wave of grief and fear that had come from nowhere. She tried to speak. 'Tests, you know. Something not right at all. Losing weight, that kind of thing...' And now the tears came, and there was no point pretending to be brave.

A silence enfolded them, in the midst of the pub's noise. Alasdair handed her a large, neatly-folded cotton handkerchief. 'When will you know?' he said.

'Very soon, Julius said. But he won't tell me the truth, he's trying to protect me, I think, but of course that doesn't work.'

'No,' Alasdair agreed. He stubbed out his cigarette.

'If the worse thing in the whole world is going to happen to you, then nothing can protect you, can it?' Agnes dabbed at her face with the handkerchief.

'I'm sorry,' he said.

She looked up, surprised. 'Whatever for?'

'For talking about redemption. As if it's something we can all hope for. It must have sounded hollow to you.'

'Do you believe it?'

Alasdair rolled another cigarette and lit it. 'What I think is,' he said, drawing a breath of smoke, 'I can see how Dante believed it. I can see how his contemporaries believed it. But to believe it now, in this century, here...'

Agnes watched the smoke rise from his cigarette. 'But you envy them,' she said.

He glanced at her, then smiled. 'Yes,' he said. 'Yes, I suppose I do. I envy them their certainties.'

'Oh, I don't suppose they had any certainties,' Agnes said. 'Faith isn't about certainty. It can only be about doubt. You have to be brave, to have faith.'

'So your friend Julius – ' Alasdair stopped himself.

'Even Julius has no promises from God,' Agnes said.

Alasdair's coffee was cold, but he drank some anyway.

'It must help to understand Dante if your heart belongs in Italy,' Agnes said.

Alasdair's cup clattered in the saucer. 'What makes you say that?'

'Sean said it, didn't he. That your heart is in Italy. I just wondered who it was, that's all.'

'You don't miss a thing, do you?'

'Not when it matters,' Agnes said.

Alasdair shot her a glance, but she was concentrating on her glass of wine.

'She's called Laura,' Alasdair said. 'In fact, Sean's wrong, she lives in Paris. She is Italian, though.'

'And you and her...' Agnes wondered if it was Alasdair's smoking that was making her crave a cigarette.

'She lives with her husband,' Alasdair said. 'In a large apartment, in the seventh arrondissement.'

'Lucky them,' Agnes said.

'Yes, it's nice.'

'So, is she your Beatrice?'

Alasdair shook his head. 'No. I suppose I might have thought she was. Once. But that's just it, isn't it? Beatrice was a real person, she has a real historical truth like lots of the characters in *The Divine Comedy* – but in the end, she's also an ideal. She's allegorical. Her role in the story is more than just being a woman who Dante may or may not have loved in real life. She meets the poet in Purgatory and becomes his second guide, after Virgil. She is the path to redemption. She has a meaning.'

'So love in real life can't be about ideals, then?'

'No. If you make someone your ideal woman, then the whole relationship is destined to failure, isn't it?'

'Right.'

Alasdair balanced his cigarette on the edge of the ashtray. 'What's funny?' he said.

'Nothing. I was just wondering when you stopped loving Laura.'

'I learned not to believe in love,' he said.

'When?'

'A long time ago.'

'I don't agree. Love is...' Agnes sighed. 'Isn't it?'

'In my experience, no. I think two people who claim to love each other, all they're seeing is their own reflection. You can never love totally, there's always a holding back, a sense of offering one's best self. I think, in the end, that love is an exercise in relinquishment. It's about loss. We might aim for the ideal, but it always falls short.

'Oh.'

'Don't you think so?'

'Me?' Agnes put her empty glass down on the table. 'I'm really not the person to ask. But I'd say, that where love is concerned, it's like faith. You have to be brave.'

Outside, the damp clung to the night. Alasdair tucked his scarf around his neck. 'I'll walk you to your friend's church,' he said, taking her arm.

'So,' Agnes said, as they set off across the road, 'if Beatrice has a meaning in Dante's work, what does Laura mean in your life?'

Alasdair paused, breathing in the cold air. 'If my life was a story,' he began, 'then I suppose she'd be some kind of learning curve.' A bus passed close to them, its windows a pulse of warm light. 'But you see, in life, people can't have meanings, can they? You can't pin people down, you can't limit them in that way. We have no boundaries, no beginnings, middles or ends. Is this the church?'

They stood at the gate. Beyond them, the dim light of the gravel path, the church door at the end. He looked down at her, then bent and kissed her cheek, very lightly. 'I'll see you tomorrow,' he said. 'When Gordon comes. If that's OK.'

'Of course,' she said.

'And I ought to find this Major Braybrook. I'll phone the regimental office in the morning.'

She watched him stride off into the night, then turned and crunched down the path to the little side gate.

Chapter Ten

'You see, Alasdair says we all have meanings. Or rather, he doesn't say that at all. He says we would have meanings if you could pin us down. Why are you smiling?' Agnes flung her damp coat over a chair, then sat down next to Julius's desk.

Julius handed her a cup of tea. 'Sometimes I have no idea what you're on about,' he said.

'You look well,' Agnes said, as he sat down in his chair.

'Do I?'

Agnes put her cup down on the edge of his desk. 'Alasdair says we don't have beginnings, middles and ends, but of course we do. That's just the trouble, isn't it. Oh, I do wish I could stop this weeping, it seems to come quite unbidden, I cried with Alasdair earlier and I hardly know him.'

'I expect he had a large white masculine handkerchief to lend you.'

Agnes pulled Alasdair's handkerchief out of her pocket and looked at it in surprise. 'And I never gave it back.'

'So you missed mass because you were crying with a man you hardly know who believes in meanings.'

'It's not a good excuse, I know.'

'I've heard worse.' He sipped his tea. 'And you were talking about endings.'

'Yes.' Agnes dried her eyes. 'And he said in real life people don't begin and they don't end, but of course he obviously hasn't thought about death, has he? And if he had a friend like you who might be about to...' She sniffed, wiped away more tears. 'If he thought about death,' she said again, 'he'd know that ending is exactly what we all do.'

Julius was frowning. 'If he knows about Dante, he'll know about Paradise.'

'He thinks it's just a metaphor.'

'Oh. Right. Whereas, you and I know that Heaven is real.'

Agnes glanced up. Julius laughed. 'You thought I was serious, didn't you?' he said.

'For a moment,' she said.

'No wonder you looked worried. No sooner will you get rid of me from this life, than you'll find yourself reunited with me in the next – and that one's for ever, just think of it, Agnes. We'll have eternity to annoy each other.'

Agnes was clutching Alasdair's handkerchief. 'You know, then,' she said. Her voice was small.

'I know what?'

'That you're going to die before me. Everything you've just said...'

Julius fell silent.

'Tell me,' Agnes said. 'The tests...?'

'It's not good news, no.'

Agnes waited. After a moment, Julius said, 'There's a tumour. That's what they saw, when they had a look at the bowel, it's amazing, isn't it, they know more about my body than I do – '

'Julius, tell me. What's going to happen?'

'An operation. To remove it.'

'When?'

'As soon as they can. '

'It might be benign – '

Julius shook his head. 'That was my hope too, but they had the histology results too – "adenocarcenoma", it said. You can't argue with a long word like that, can you?'

'But – ' Agnes felt her eyes well with tears.

'There's hope. It might be small, it might not have spread, it looks like early stages but they can't tell. It's the liver, you see,' Julius said. 'If it's gone to the liver...' He didn't look at her.

'Why?' Agnes seemed to be shouting.

'Why what?'

'Why have you got cancer?'

Julius shrugged. 'Lot of it about,' he said.

'But you're healthy, you don't smoke, you drink far less than I do, you're a good person, you don't deserve to – to –'

'To die?'

Agnes couldn't think of an answer.

'I did think of being cross,' Julius said. 'With myself, firstly, as if somehow I could have prevented it. And then I thought about being cross with God. I thought I could go out into the streets and rail against my fate, like one of the prophets. I could curse the heavens, and shake my fist, and shout.'

Agnes managed to smile. 'It might do wonders for your congregation numbers.'

'All I know is,' Julius said, 'is that I may not have as long as I thought I had. But then, that's the human condition, isn't it. We all know that. Come on, I'll walk you to the gate.'

Agnes put on her coat. Julius switched off the bar fire.

The sky had cleared to bright stars and sharp cold. They walked arm in arm up the church drive.

'How are you really?' Agnes said.

Julius stopped still. His breath made clouds in the chill air. He looked down at her. 'I am absolutely terrified,' he said.

They reached the gate. Suddenly he held her, caught her into his arms. They stood there together, as traffic swished past. Agnes heard him say something, close to her ear.

'What did you say?'

This time, it was Julius who had tears in his eyes. 'I said, pray for me.'

'I do,' she said. 'All the time. But really, it's praying for myself.'

"For a thousand years in your sight, are like yesterday when it is past, and like a watch in the night. You sweep us away like a dream; we fade away suddenly like the grass..."

Agnes closed the book, and the echo of the Psalm died away. She stood up, the lamp still unlit, and paced her room. At the window she paused, and stared out for a while, the stars blurred through the glass. Eventually, aware of a chill draught, she drew the curtains and switched on the light.

Alasdair's gift to her, the copy of Dante's Purgatory, was sitting on her desk, and she picked it up.

"... And now I will sing of that second realm, where human souls are purged, ready to rise up to heavenly joy..."

She closed the book.

All these words, she thought. All this fluency, this poetry, this hope of a hereafter.

And when it comes to it, there's nothing. Only grief, and pain, and tears. And rage.

She lit a candle, and arranged her prayer cushions. Pray for me, Julius had said to her. Yes, she'd said. Of course.

And now there were no words. Only tears. And rage. And silence.

A persistent chirping broke her sleep. Blackbird, she thought. Birds and clouds and spring... no, phone. Phone, she thought, sitting up, grabbing it, pressing buttons.

'Sweetie, it's me.'

'Oh. Hello.'

'Are you all right?'

'I'm not sure yet.'

'Breakfast, I thought,' Athena said. 'Somewhere nice. It's raining, or sleeting or something horrible, I can't wear my new heels which is so annoying, but it's either that or fall over which I really can't risk at my age. And Nic's left me.'

'Oh,' Agnes said, searching for appropriate noises. 'What?' she said, as the words registered.

'Well, he's gone to Barcelona. Without me. I mean, he doesn't think he's leaving me, but then, he doesn't think. Full Stop. How about that nice new delicatessen with the almond croissants just near Borough Market? I'll go on to work afterwards. Simon won't mind me being late, we had our exhibition opening last night.'

'Fifteen minutes?'

'Twenty. I can do it in a cab.'

Athena spooned chocolatey milk froth into her mouth. Outside a sleety snow settled on the grey streets.

'Barcelona, eh?' Agnes said.

'It's twenty degrees there,' Athena said. 'I looked, in the paper this morning.'

Agnes sipped her cappucino with extra whipped cream.

'How was the exhibition opening?'

'It went very well. Lots of serious bearded German gentlemen, for some reason.'

'And the lime green suit?'

Athena frowned. 'I didn't wear it, sweetie. Went for black. Again.'

'Did Nic go?'

'He popped in for a drink. Didn't stay long. Silly old Nic,' Athena said.

'What are you going to do?'

Athena stared into her mug. 'Do you know what really annoys me?' she said, after a moment. 'He never really thought I wouldn't go with him. Whenever he's mentioned it in the last few days, I've told him what I thought, about not being happy about it, about having this big exhibition on and not being able to go this week; when we went out for dinner, I told you, we talked about how he and I might continue as a couple with me here and him there... and it's quite obvious he wasn't listening. And there's him, making a fortune running workshops on listening skills...'

'Cobbler's children...' Agnes murmured.

'You what?'

'The cobbler's children go unshod. Isn't that an English expression?'

Athena shrugged. 'All I know is, listening skills or not, he hasn't heard a word I've been saying.'

'Did you have a row?'

Athena shook her head. 'And that's the other weird thing. During supper on Sunday, he took out the two airline tickets for this morning, and I said, but I'm not going. We've got the big do at the gallery on Monday, as you know, and I'm not going to rush off the next day. And he just shrugged and said, please yourself.'

'That's not like you two.'

'Exactly. Normally we scream and shout and throw stuff, or at least I do, and that's how we know we love each other...' Athena's eyes welled with tears. 'And it's not as if I don't want to go at all, I'm quite happy to see the place and think about how it might work – just not this week.'

Agnes sighed. 'Men, eh?'

'They're not like other people,' Athena agreed. She pulled off a chocolatey piece of croissant. 'And how's your lovely-man-who-isn't-lovely-at-all?'

'Alasdair. He's OK. It turns out he was in love with an Italian woman who's married and lives in Paris.'

'Oh. How very glamorous. Is it really over, do you think?'

'Difficult to tell.'

'And how's the quest for the truth?' Athena said, through a mouthful.

'Which one?'

'I meant the dead brother business.'

'Oh. That one.'

Athena put down her cup. 'You're not yourself, you know.'

'No.' Agnes took a deep breath. 'Julius is going to have an exploratory operation, they think it's cancer, it just depends how far it's got...' Her voice faltered on the edge of tears.

Athena reached across and took her hand. They sat that way for a while, until Athena said, 'I think we need more coffee. And more things with chocolate in.'

'So, when will Julius know?' Athena said, putting down two large mugs topped with whipped cream.

'Soon. They're hoping to take him in next week.'

'And is he still being cool and calm?'

'Not really, no. Would you?'

'I've told you. Absolutely not.' Athena bit into an almond croissant.

'I was reading Dante last night,' Agnes said.

'The one your chap gave you?'

'Yes, actually. It's all about people making their way towards Paradise, painfully aware of their own failings. They have to climb a mountain.'

'How very metaphorical.'

Agnes managed a smile. 'It is. But you see, Alasdair claims not to be spiritual, except in a fourteenth century sense. And then I was reading the Psalms too, and I thought, in the end, it makes no difference, does it? We're born, we die. We can have inklings that there's more to it, but it makes no difference in the end. We fade away, we wither away like the grass.'

'Sweetie, now's really not the time to be questioning your faith.'

Agnes managed a smile. 'Seriously, though. What difference does it make? Alasdair's right, really. And also, there's things he's not telling me, about this Laura woman who lives in France, there's something between them, or maybe there was and it really is over, but there's something he's hiding. And with Trina, I met her in the pub the other night, she escaped from the ghastly Scott, and she was telling me about Alasdair's dad, who took up with Andy's mum. And then Alasdair appeared in the pub and they had this huge row, it was all about how Alasdair's dad died.' She looked up. 'He has a way of shutting down, Alasdair has. He can be open and generous and interesting, and then I'll ask him about something to do with Trina or his family or this woman in Paris, and it's like some huge iron shutter has come down and I can't get through to him.'

'He must be a Capricorn.' Athena said.

'You're no help.'

'Although I was thinking Gemini with all this languages and communication and stuff. Don't look at me like that. And what's happening about the brother who died? Are they going to charge someone?'

'There's poor Mitch, yes, who was found holding the broken bottle. But, you see, we went to see this woman, Jeanie recognised her. There's a group of men from Scotland who Andy and Alasdair grew up with, and one of them rented a flat near here, and now his wife's joined him, and another bloke called Sean who Alasdair knew. But Alasdair was wondering what the Scottish lot, as he calls them, are doing in London, and so near where Andy was living, apart from looking for work which they might be quite legitimately doing, except as Gordon said, why are they so near the hostel, and Janet came to find Andy on the night he died, except she lied when I asked her, and she spoke to Jeanie, who's frightened of her dealer and that's another problem I should be addressing really. And Gordon's going to come and see Alasdair and me this afternoon – '

'Isn't that your phone?'

Agnes was aware of a ringing from her bag. She pulled out her phone and answered.

'Ask him if he's a Capricorn,' Athena mouthed to her.

'Hello Alasdair,' Agnes was saying.

'Agnes,' Alasdair said. 'I've spoken to Major Braybrook. He said, can we come and see him this evening at his club? It's in St James'. I thought we could go after seeing Gordon, if you're free.'

'OK.'

'I'll let him know – who's that in the background?'

'It's my friend Athena. It's very embarrassing. She wants to know if you're a Capricorn.'

'No, I'm not,' Alasdair said.

'What are you then?' Athena was now leaning across the table and shouting.

'Guess,' Alasdair said, and hung up.

'He's gone,' Agnes said.

'Well, that's typical Capricorn behaviour. Perhaps he just doesn't know, lots of men don't. Anyway, here's me having been left altogether, and there's you with a gorgeous Capricorn-like man asking you out for the evening.'

'It's not a date, Athena.'

'Hmm.'

'He's my guide through Purgatory, that's all.'

'Well it sounds dodgy to me,' Athena said. 'You've decided it makes no difference whether you believe in God or not, and now you're allowing a lovely man to lead you up a metaphorical mountain. Call yourself a nun?'

Agnes laughed, and reached for her coat. 'I've got to get to the hostel,' she said.

'And it's still trying to snow,' Athena said, as they gathered up their things. 'It's February, for God's sake. It ought to be spring.'

They stood on the street corner in the traffic's roar, blinking against the icy rain.

'I'm going this way.' Athena gestured towards the embankment. 'There's bound to be a cab up there.'

'You could get the Jubilee Line all the way to Green Park.'

'Oh, no, sweetie, not trains. Do you know, the tube map looks the same whichever way up you hold it? No, I can't afford it, but taxi it is.' She took both Agnes's hands in hers, brown woollen gloves held by soft leather. 'It'll be all right,' she said. 'Julius will be OK. And the Barcelonans will turn their Spanish noses up at male-centred drumming therapy and we can all come home.'

Agnes nodded. 'You're right. It will be all right. Somehow.'

'Do you think Barcelonans is the right word?'

'Probably not.'

Athena kissed her cheek. 'Speak soon, sweetie.'

Agnes stood in the hostel hallway and listened. Drum and bass from upstairs. A pall of murmured conversation and cigarette smoke from the lounge. She went into the office, where Dan sat, on the phone.

'... You can't just swap to earlies without telling us. No. I'm finishing at eight today...'

Agnes hung her coat near the radiator.

'... Yes, she's on the same shift as me. No, it's not fair on Petra.'

He glanced at Agnes. 'What? Yeah, OK. Nights, then. Sure. I'll see you this evening then.' He rang off.

Agnes watched her coat begin to steam quietly. 'Mary,' she said. Dan nodded. 'Perhaps one of us has to go,' Agnes said.

'It's not a good solution,' Dan began. There was a ring at the door.

'That'll be our new resident.' Dan jumped up. 'They rang this morning. He's been referred from the probation service -' He got up and went out, then reappeared. 'It's not him at all. It's for you.'

Agnes found Connor standing in the hall. 'I'm sorry to bother you here,' he began, but she ushered him into the kitchen.

'It's fine,' she said. 'Tea? Coffee?' She put on the kettle.

'Mitch has been charged with manslaughter and remanded in custody.' He sat heavily at the table. 'It's no surprise,' he added.

'No.' Agnes sat next to him. The kettle began to murmur in the silence. 'Still, it might be better than the garages,' she said.

'Mixed blessing,' Connor agreed. 'A roof over his head. And he'll have to come off the drink. Just heroin instead – '

There was a sudden loud shouting above their heads.

'...so, what you lying for, girl? Everyone knows you're a whore – '

'... I ain't no fuckin' whore, Jayce, and you can fuck off – '

A door slammed, feet hammered down the stairs, Jeanie flew into the kitchen, red-faced and tearful. 'Keep him away from me before I slap him,' she said, then saw Connor and stopped.

'Jayce?' Agnes said, making space for her at the table.

She flung herself on to a chair. 'He says he saw Ash, down on the main road.'

'When?' Agnes asked.

'Don't know. Yesterday. I don't know.' She glanced at Connor, then back at Agnes.

'Ash – ' Agnes began. 'Your boyfriend? Dealer?'

Jeanie stared at the table. 'He's trouble, Ash, and it's true I was using when I was with him, but I'm clean now, and now he's going around saying wrong things about me. And he knows I'm here, and that's why he broke in the other night.'

'It might not have been him.'

'It's just the sort of thing he'd do.'

A loud burst of music broke out upstairs.

'I'm going to have to move from here,' Jeanie said, standing up. 'Just don't send me back home, that's all.'

She left the room. Connor glanced at Agnes, just as the doorbell rang.

Agnes went to open it. Alasdair was standing there.

'Connor's here,' Agnes said, leading him through to the kitchen. 'They've caught up with Mitch, he's been remanded in custody.'

'I'm sorry to hear that,' Alasdair said, joining Connor at the table.

Connor shrugged. 'It was bound to happen. Maybe it's justice. Maybe he did do it, even if he didn't mean to.'

They sat at the table. The kitchen was dim, the windows dark with the wintry day.

'Andy always talked about someone who was a threat,' Alasdair said. 'From his time as a soldier. And in the writings, he talks about someone who wants him dead. He keeps referring to it.'

Connor looked up. 'Do we trust the writings?'

'And anyway,' Agnes said. 'Mitch remembers those other people there, when Andy died. The woman, and the man.'

'Do we trust Mitch's memories?' Connor said.

They sat, not speaking, the rhythms of the music reverberating from above.

'Isn't this Ronnie Size?' Alasdair said. 'I like his stuff.'

'Gordon's late,' Agnes said, looking at her watch.

'I might as well go,' Connor said. He stood up. 'Keep in touch. Have you got my mobile number?' He wrote it down and handed it to Agnes.

Agnes showed him out, then went back to the kitchen.

'How's your work?' She sat down again at the table.

'It's OK. I'm doing the Wrathful,' he said, and she laughed. 'It's not funny,' he went on. 'They're all submerged in the black mud of the Styx, it's very unpleasant.'

'Why are they in the mud?'

'Oh, it's a fantastically wise symbolism. They reject pity, you see. Like all the horrors of Dante's Hell, the physical discomfort is only a symbol of the mental agony. They're bogged down in a refusal to accept their guilt, and if anyone offers them compassion, they see it as a further personal slight and throw it back. I'm trying to keep to a kind of blank verse, to keep the rhythm of the poetry but not to sacrifice the meaning by creating rhymes. It's very hard, and everyone who's gone before me has made a better job of it. What time is it now?'

'It's after six.'

'We should go. I promised Braybrook we'd be there in half an hour.'

The club was in St James', a terrace of creamy stone staircases and solid elegance. They went up the steps, muffled in scarves in the freezing evening. The hallway was warm, and they waited, taking off wet gloves, folding up umbrellas.

'Denham Braybrook,' came a deep voice; an outstretched hand, a clean-shaven, shiny pink face, a loud check jacket. 'Yes, yes. Come and have a drink.'

The lounge was high-ceilinged, heavily draped, warm with a roaring fire.

Braybrook gestured to a table in the corner. 'Sherry? Brandy?'

'Dry sherry, please,' Agnes said. 'With ice.'

As they sat down, Braybrook peered at Agnes. 'Ice,' he said. 'Good heavens.'

A waiter took their order. Major Braybrook turned to Alasdair. 'Were you ever a soldier?'

Alasdair shook his head.

'Not blood brothers, of course.'

'No,' Alasdair agreed.

'Brave man, McFadden.' He dropped his gaze, his eyes clouded with memories of a distant winter.

The waiter returned with two glasses of whisky, and a tumbler of iced sherry. Braybrook watched the glass being set down on the table, watched its way to Agnes's lips. She thought she saw him wince.

'So young, you see,' he said. 'Lads like McFadden. Battalions been training in the Brecon Beacons, suddenly find themselves on Mount Longdon. Mind you, mud just the same. Frostbite just the same.' He smiled at Alasdair. 'They had to learn fast. But by God, they did learn. Brave, brave men.' He sipped his whisky. 'When you told me what had become of him, I was sorry to hear it. Very sorry. He deserved better than that.'

'We wondered,' Alasdair began. 'We think that there's more to it.'

'He kept a diary,' Agnes said.

'We wondered whether you'd mind – ' Alasdair glanced at Agnes. Agnes brought the battered sheaf of paper, now in a new file, out of her bag and handed it to the Major. 'He wrote down his memories, about the war.'

'Would you mind looking at it?' Alasdair said.

Major Braybrook held up the file. 'I can't imagine I can help. Not after all this time. But – certainly, I'll cast my eye over it. McFadden was a good lad, yes, yes, least I can do.'

Half an hour later they left the marbled hall of the club and walked out into snow. Alasdair took Agnes's arm as they skirted the edge of St James' Park. A white hush had settled on the city.

'Why are you smiling?' Agnes said, after a while.

'We should be wearing big fur coats and hats,' he said. 'Look – you've even got a snowflake on your nose.'

They walked on, the snow creaking underfoot. 'Westminster Bridge?' Alasdair said. 'And then probably a bus.'

'Don't you have to go to Hampstead?' Agnes said.

'Oh, eventually,' Alasdair said.

'I thought I'd call in to the hostel,' Agnes said. 'Before I go home. Perhaps Gordon left a message.'

They reached Westminster Bridge. Traffic swished past them. The face of Big Ben was freckled with still-falling flakes.

'Funny to think of those chaps in there, sending our boys into war,' Alasdair said, looking back towards Westminster. They walked on, as crisp white turned to grey slush at their feet. 'What would it be like,' Alasdair went on, 'to serve one's country?'

'Your country would be Scotland. Or Italy. And mine would be France.'

'Really?' He stopped and turned to her.

'No. Not really. I'm a Londoner,' she said. 'Which is why I suppose I've got to get rid of the house in Provence. Cut my ties. Become stateless.'

'At least you've got the Kingdom of Heaven to fall back on,' Alasdair said.

'If only it was that certain,' Agnes said.

They walked on, the snow brushing their faces. As they crossed into Westminster Bridge Road, a bus loomed out of the night.

'I hope Gordon's all right,' Agnes said, as they settled into seats by the steamed-up windows.

At Borough High Street they got off the bus. They turned off the main road towards the hostel. The sky had cleared, the pavement was icy underfoot. Through the crisp air Agnes heard sirens, realising as they approached the hostel that the blue flashing lights were there ahead of them.

'It's us,' Agnes said, breaking into a run, Alasdair close behind her.

Then she was there, at the steps, the door wide open, policemen standing there, a policewoman too, Dan and Petra both in the hallway. People seemed to be talking, arms signalling distress. Agnes was confused, struggling to hear what they were saying, unable to understand in the surrounding sense of panic.

'We don't know him,' Dan was saying.

'He wasn't a resident,' Petra said.

The policemen stood there, pens and notebooks and the crackle of radios.

'Agnes,' Dan said, looking up.

'He was dead,' Petra said. 'In the street.'

'Just there.' The policeman pointed.

'When?' Agnes said. 'Who?'

'I heard shouting,' Dan said. 'I called them. We found him. Just now. No one knows who he is.' Dan suddenly slumped towards the ground and sat on the floor, blinking.

'Hadn't we all better go inside?' Agnes said.

As they turned to close the door, Agnes glanced out into the darkness. A woman was standing at the foot of the steps. A figure, pale coat against the night, chalk-white face. 'Janet,' Alasdair whispered. Agnes took a step outside, about to call her, but she had gone.

Chapter Eleven

The kettle was boiling. Petra was handing out mugs of sweet tea. The colour had returned to Dan's face. He sat at a corner of the table, giving a statement to the policewoman. Radios crackled.

'No,' one of the policeman was saying to the other. 'No ID. Nothing on him at all. Pockets emptied.'

'He was bashed over the head,' Petra said. 'With some kind of weapon. We heard the shouting, me and Dan, we ran outside. I think he was still breathing when we got to him, but by the time the ambulance came...' Her fingers were clutching the mug of tea. She looked up at Agnes and gave a little shrug.

'Was he Scottish?' Agnes said. She was aware of Alasdair, slumped on the old fake leather armchair in the corner. He glanced across at her.

'No idea,' Petra said. 'He didn't speak. The police think it was a robbery.'

The door opened and Mary Holbeck came in. She cast a look around the room, went straight to the teapot, poured a mug of tea and left again.

Dan looked round to Agnes. 'Jeanie's in the office.'

Agnes stood up. Alasdair was leafing through an old newspaper. Agnes left him there and went to find Jeanie.

She was wrapped in a cream blanket, huddled on a chair in the office, her pink slippers on the floor. She was clutching the tea that Mary had brought her. Mary sat down next to her. Jeanie looked up at Agnes, wide dark eyes sunk in a pale face. 'It's my fault,' she said. 'It's always my fault.'

Agnes sat on a black plastic swivel chair, on the other side of Jeanie. 'Was it Gordon?' she said.

'It was the one who came the other day, with that Scottish woman. She asked me to warn Andy not to go out. The man standing behind her, it was him. I heard the shouting, I heard Dan and Petra, I ran out and I saw who it was, he was just out there, by the steps, lying down. His head was all twisted round...'

'It's not your fault.' Agnes spoke gently.

'It was Ash.' Jeanie's voice faltered at the name. 'It was Ash who killed him. And it was my fault. That man who died just now, he must have been coming here, and Ash was out there, I know he was, I'd seen him earlier, I've been hiding from him all day, and Ash saw that man coming up the steps and had him.'

'You don't know any of this for sure,' Agnes began, but Mary cut in.

'Why can't you leave her alone?' Her face was pinched and hard. Wisps of grey hair trailed from the loose bun at the back of her head.

Agnes turned back to Jeanie. 'What would you like to do now?'

Jeanie held the blanket close to her. 'I'd like her to go.' She jerked her head towards Mary.

Mary stood up. She strode to the door, glanced back at Jeanie for a brief moment, then left the room.

Agnes sat with Jeanie in the silence.

'She means well,' she said, after a moment.

'No she doesn't. She's a nosy cow,' Jeanie said.

'Jeanie – ' Agnes began. 'Why would – why would Ash have attacked Gordon?'

Jeanie shrugged. 'Because he thinks he owns me? Because any man approaching that door looks to him like a threat? I don't know why.'

'It might not have been him.'

'It's his weapon of choice. Baseball bat. It has all the signs of being him. The last time I saw a body in that state, it was because of Ash.'

'When was that, then?' Agnes asked.

'It was up by Kings Cross, when I was...' her voice tailed away. 'Don't matter,' she said. She slid her feet into her slippers and stood up, still draped in her blanket. 'There's nothing anyone can do,' she said. 'I'm the angel of death, I am.' She turned and went out of the room. Agnes heard her footsteps softly on the stairs. She got up, and opened the door, thinking she'd go and find Alasdair. Mary was standing in the hall, and now she brushed past Agnes and stood, facing her, in the office.

Agnes shut the door again, and waited.

'You should be ashamed of yourselves, you people.' She spoke with flattened, Yorkshire vowels. 'The poor girl needs practical help, not an empty promise of heaven.'

'Mary, with all due respect, I don't think I've ever – '

'And now you've involved her in something that should never have concerned her,' Mary went on.

'Perhaps you'd like to explain how a violent street robbery is anything to do with me?' Agnes tried to restrain the anger in her voice.

'I know what you people are like.' Mary stood, facing her, tight-lipped and pale. 'You should be ashamed of yourselves.'

'Hasn't it occurred to you that I might know more about her life than you do?'

'Well, that's where you're wrong. Sister.' Mary placed heavy emphasis on the word. 'The reason she doesn't want me around is that I've rumbled her. Hasn't it occurred to you that she's still using?'

'Using?'

'Heroin.' Mary smiled with empty triumph. 'Don't you know anything? She's thin. She's pale. She's often sick. Do you think that young man has been hanging around because he loves her? He's her dealer. I'm surprised she hasn't told you,' Mary said.

'Do Dan and Petra know?'

Mary shook her head. 'I didn't want her to lose her place here.'

She went over to the door.

'Is that why she's so hostile to you?'

Mary nodded. 'I've been telling her a few home truths. It's not what she wants to hear. She'd rather listen to you talking about angels and everlasting love. Even though it's nothing but bloody rubbish.' The door clunked shut behind her.

Agnes waited for her footsteps on the stairs, then left the office, locking the door behind her. Alasdair stood up as she came into the bright warmth of the kitchen. Dan and Petra were sitting at the table.

'Have they gone?' Agnes asked.

'The police?' Dan said. 'Yes. Just now.'

'I wish we could have helped them more.' Petra was dabbing furiously at her sleeve, at a dirty brown stain across her elbow. 'I held him,' she said. 'I held him, whoever he was. I knew he was dying. And I've no idea who he was.'

'We know who he was,' Agnes said. Petra stopped rubbing her arm and looked up. 'Jeanie recognised him. He lived in a house on the next street.'

'Is that why you asked if he was Scottish?'

Agnes nodded.

'So why did he die?' Petra's eyes welled with tears.

Alasdair was standing next to Agnes. 'Wrong place, wrong time,' he said.

'Who's on the night shift?' Agnes asked.

Daniel looked up from his empty mug. 'Mary,' he said.

'We could all go home,' Agnes said.

'Look – ' Petra was pulling at her sleeve. 'Look at this shirt. Those stains. Those are...' She began to cry.

Agnes went over to Petra. She took off her jumper and handed it to her. 'Give me your shirt,' she said. She stood there in a t-shirt while Petra stripped off the shirt and put on the jumper, and Alasdair and Dan found a sudden interest in the newspaper.

Agnes put the stained shirt in a carrier bag. 'The hostel can buy you a new one,' she said.

Petra shivered, wrapping her cable-knit arms around her.

'If Jeanie knew him, we'll have to tell the police...' she began.

'I'll do it,' Agnes said. 'We've all had enough for one night.'

Dan stood up. 'Come on,' he said to Petra. 'Let's share a cab.'

'I'll walk you home,' Alasdair said to Agnes.

The streets felt late and empty. 'Will she give it back?' Alasdair said to Agnes. 'Your sweater?'

Agnes found herself wanting to laugh. 'It was old and horrible. It was probably from Oxfam, about a hundred years ago.'

'So, not an act of charity at all?' Alasdair said.

'It was just... the blood...'

'I understand.'

They walked on a little way. 'Anyway,' Agnes said, 'I was rather fancying a cashmere sweater in lilac.'

'Lilac cashmere, eh?' Alasdair turned to her as they reached the entrance to her block. 'I don't suppose your friend Athena has anything to do with that.'

'It looked very nice on her.' Agnes fished in her bag for keys.

Alasdair suddenly took her arm. 'What are we going to do?'

Agnes met his gaze. 'I don't know,' she said.

'Why should someone have killed Gordon?'

'Because he was about to tell us something,' Agnes said.

'I didn't dare say it,' Alasdair said. 'It makes us responsible.'

'Jeanie's blaming herself too,' Agnes said.

'Does that mean Janet's in danger?'

'Oh God.'

Alasdair let go of her arm. 'Tomorrow we'll have to go to the police. Tell them what we know.'

Agnes nodded. 'We should visit Mitch too, you know. He was there when Andy died, he might be able to tell us more.'

'What if – ' Alasdair began. 'What if Jeanie's right. What if it was just wrong place, wrong time.'

'He's her dealer,' Agnes said. 'Mary just told me.'

'Even worse.'

'Do you really think it might have been Ash?' Agnes said.

'When I was seventeen, my dad fell out of a window and died.

An accident. In my view, anything can happen.'

'But then, why did they all move in so near the hostel?'

Alasdair looked down at her. 'Coincidence?'

Agnes shrugged.

'No,' Alasdair said. 'You're right. Another journey towards the centre,' he said. 'That's what we've got to do. Another level of Hell. We've got to find Mitch. Have you got Connor's number?'

'Do people like Mitch stay in the inferno for ever?' Agnes handed over the scrap of paper and Alasdair typed the number into his phone.

'No,' he said, handing her back the paper. 'His sorrow is his salvation. He'll be in Purgatory, not Hell.' His hand brushed her arm. 'I should go home.'

'Are we going to talk to Braybrook again?'

'If you haven't been blackballed from his club for having ice in your sherry. Sleep well.'

She watched him go, watched him fade into the yellow lamplight. She unlocked the front gate and climbed the stairs to her flat.

'My soul waits for the Lord...'

Agnes stood, yawning, in Julius's darkened church. Behind the altar, the window was grey with the dawn. She added her voice to those of the few early-morning worshippers.

'My soul waits for the Lord; more than the Night-watch for the morning..."

She watched Julius light the incense, prepare the communion wafers, the chalice for the wine.

The body and blood, she thought. The promise of eternal life.

In her mind, Agnes saw a blood-drenched field. She saw a legless man. She saw Walker McFadden sitting by the body of his friend Pitch.

'The Lord redeemeth the soul of his servants; and none of them that trust in him shall be desolate...'

Walker's life, Agnes thought. Walker's death. And how are we redeemed by blood? How does the blood of one innocent crucified man redeem the battlefields of human history?

Julius poured the wine into the chalice.

An image flashed through Agnes's mind, of an altar in the ancient world, the sacrificial blood dashed against the stones.

An empty promise, Agnes thought. The lamb that dies so that we can live. And yet we all must die.

'... If you would save your life, then you will lose it, but if you lose your life for my sake, then you will save it.'

As they knelt at the altar rail for communion, the first rays of the sun broke through the incense smoke.

'They're going to have to know, of course.' Julius spooned tea into a pot and poured on boiling water. 'I mean, the bishop knows, all his people know. But the congregation – how am I going to tell them?'

'Poor Julius,' Agnes said, sitting in her usual chair. 'All those women who'll want to minister to you. You won't get a moment's peace.'

Julius sighed. 'Exactly.'

'That's why I'm so good for you,' Agnes said, taking the mug of tea that he handed to her.

He smiled at her.

'Does it hurt?' Agnes said. 'Cancer, I mean?'

He sat down at his desk. 'That's why it's all been such a shock,' he said. 'A few minor problems, which I put down to being an old man – '

'If you're old then I am,' Agnes said. 'Which is obviously impossible.'

He laughed. 'All right, not old. But yes, who'd have thought the body to be so resilient in the force of such an invasion?'

'Have you got a date yet?'

'It'll be very soon. I have to have a scan first, in the next day or two, to look at the liver. And then the operation after that.'

'And, afterwards, will you have to... I mean, if they've removed bits...?'

He shrugged. 'It may involve all sorts of direct involvement with certain bodily functions that I've hitherto managed to ignore. On the other hand, apparently these days they can cut out very little and stitch it all up again and you're as good as new. Or, in my case, old.'

'Julius, I've warned you.'

'Sorry. Not old. Not old at all.' He stood up and gathered up their mugs. 'The funny thing is, I feel absolutely bloody ancient. Since I got my results, I seem to have aged about twenty years. I have symptoms I'd never have thought of before. I limp slightly, have you noticed? I never used to do that.' He poured more tea and handed her mug back to her. 'I've gone from being a sprightly middle-aged man to a hobbling invalid on his last legs – and all in a matter of days.' He sat suddenly, heavily, into his chair.

'Julius – it will be all right.' Agnes heard the empty certainty of her words, and her eyes welled with tears.

'Yes. To be sure.' Julius stared into his mug of tea. She saw his pallor, the shadows round his eyes. 'All will be well, as Julian of Norwich tells us.' He looked up and met Agnes's gaze. 'But the way it seems to me now, none of this feels like any kind of Divine Plan. This feels like chaos, and mess, and terror. I find myself saying, this can't be happening to me. As if I deserve something different, something better. As if I've gone into someone else's life by mistake, and that poor bugger is having a hell of a time.' He looked at his watch. 'And now I'm supposed to be going to the Archdeaconry for a meeting about church repairs, so I am.'

'I should be at the hostel,' Agnes said, staring at her hands in her lap.

'Life goes on,' Julius said, getting up from his desk, gathering up papers. 'Or in some cases, not.'

'Julius – ' She looked at him. 'Julius, you're not alone.'

'Oh, but I am. That's what seems to be the hardest thing of all.'

They climbed the staircase to the side door of the church, blinking in the sunlight as they came outside.

'No,' Agnes said. 'I will be with you. Whatever this journey of yours, I will be by your side. For as far as I can.'

Julius bent and kissed the top of her head. 'I might have known I couldn't get rid of you that easily.'

The wind was gusty, and Agnes let herself into the hostel in a flurry of raincoat, to be met by Dan.

'Thank God,' he said, ushering her into the office.

'What is it now?' Agnes went over to the coat-stand. She felt tired, felt the energy drain from her as she sat down.

'It's Jeanie,' Dan said.

'Is she still with us?'

Dan frowned. 'Yes, she's upstairs. What made you say that?'

'A sudden sense of dread, that's all.'

'She's in her room. But she's in a state. About half an hour ago there was a man outside, and she went out to talk to him, and then she came back in and fled to her room, and no one's seen her. No breakfast, nothing.'

'You think I can help?'

'I think she'll talk to you.'

Agnes clasped her hands in her lap. 'If anyone knows Jeanie, it's Mary.'

'Mary? Jeanie can't bear her.'

'That's because Mary's worked out that Jeanie is still doing heroin.'

A gust of wind rattled the window, a sudden burst of sunlight. Dan glanced outside, then back to Agnes. 'She promised me she wasn't,' he said.

'Perhaps Mary's wrong,' Agnes said, but Daniel shook his head. 'Never trust a junkie,' he said, getting up, opening the door. 'Your job might not be so easy,' he said.

Agnes stood up. 'You mean, talking to Jeanie?'

He nodded. 'Good luck.'

Agnes hesitated outside Jeanie's room, then knocked. Silence. She knocked again. 'Jeanie?' she called. 'It's Agnes.'

Shuffling of feet. The door opened a crack. 'Has he been back?'

Jeanie's voice was a whisper.

'No,' Agnes said.' No one's been here. Can I come in?'

The door opened just enough to admit her, then closed again. Jeanie locked them both in. She sat on her bed, her eyes huge in her thin face, her skin taut. She waited.

'Dan said you were frightened,' Agnes began. 'Is it about Gordon?'

Jeanie shrugged. 'Is that his name?' she said.

Agnes nodded.

A door slammed, somewhere far away.

Jeanie's hands worked in her lap, her fingers pulling at each other. 'You'll talk to them, won't you,' she said. 'They were here last night, and you said stuff to them, and they'll come back, and you'll talk to them.'

'The police?' Agnes asked.

Jeanie nodded. 'You'll talk to them, and Ash'll think it was me, and then I'll be dead. He said so, he said if I talk to the cops them I'm dead.' Her eyes flickered to Agnes, then back to her hands. 'I might as well kill myself, do it for him.' Her voice was quiet. 'He always means what he says.'

'But you haven't talked to the police,' Agnes said.

'He won't know that. I asked him, this morning, he was out there, I went out to him, I said, did you kill him? And he said, I don't know what you're talking about, girl.'

'Perhaps he doesn't know. Why should he know about Gordon's death?'

Jeanie curled her fingers together. 'He was coming here, wasn't he? The bloke who died. And Ash's always been on at me, since I moved in here, about blokes coming to see me here.'

'Jeanie – ' Agnes's voice was loud, and Jeanie raised her head at last and looked at her. 'Jeanie – what is Ash to you?'

'He thinks he's my boyfriend. But I loved Chris, you see, but Chris died – '

Agnes shook her head. 'No,' she said. 'I don't want this rubbish. I'd rather have the truth.' She faced Jeanie and waited.

Jeanie turned to look outside, at the wintry tree, its bare

branches fingering the windowpane.

'He's not your boyfriend,' Agnes said. 'Ash – he's not your boyfriend.'

'No?' An empty smile, as she turned back to Agnes.

'He used to be your dealer.'

'Yes,' Jeanie said.

'And he still is.'

The same smile, a thin gash in the pallor of her face. She said nothing.

'Am I right?' Agnes said.

Jeanie dragged her eyes to meet Agnes's gaze. She shrugged. 'So what if he is?'

'Oh, it doesn't matter to me,' Agnes said. She stood up. 'It doesn't matter at all. It's your life, after all. The question is,' she said, 'who killed Gordon? Was it your dealer, suspicious of any man coming to the hostel? Which would explain the lack of subtlety, I suppose. Someone with more sense might not have used a baseball bat. Or was it to do with the house across the road?'

Jeanie wrapped her arms around her thin body and stared at the floor.

'The problem is,' Agnes said, 'that whatever we do now, Ash will think it's come from you.'

Jeanie didn't move.

'I wish,' Agnes said, her hand on the door handle. 'I wish you'd told us you were still using. Before it got dangerous.' She opened the door.

Jeanie looked up. The hollow smile, again. 'Never trust a junkie,' she said.

Agnes stood in the doorway. She looked at Jeanie, huddled on her bed, then quietly closed the door behind her and went back downstairs.

Dan was in the office. 'Well?' he said.

'Mary's right,' Agnes said, as the phone rang. Dan answered it, and handed it to Agnes.

'Hi.' Agnes heard Alasdair's voice.

'Hello,' she said.

'I've spoken to Mitch's solicitor. We can visit him today, about half past one. He's only down the road, they've remanded him to Belmarsh, although they'll move him eventually, Connor said.'

'Half past one. OK. Shall we have lunch first?'

'Maybe afterwards,' Alasdair said. 'I've got to work.'

'It was a joke,' Agnes said.

'Oh.'

Agnes heard his silence. 'Are you all right?' she said.

'Why shouldn't I be?'

'Will you tell Mitch your connection to Andy?'

'No,' Alasdair said. 'It's not fair on him.'

'No,' Agnes agreed. 'See you later.'

'Sure.' He hung up.

Agnes frowned at the phone.

'Everything all right?' Dan said.

She looked at him. 'At the moment, it feels as if everything's all wrong.'

'I know the feeling.' Dan stood up. 'Aberdeen Bob is leaving us today. He was the voice of reason.' He smiled at her. 'The lunatics will take over the asylum,' he said, closing the door behind him.

The prison officer selected a key from the large bunch at his waist, and unlocked the door. They went through; Alasdair, Agnes and James, the solicitor. The officer locked the door behind them. They followed him along a high-walled corridor, in flashes of sunlight from the strips of windows above them, until they reached the next door. Again, the jangle of keys, the unlocking and locking, the striding through the stripes of light.

'Here we are,' the prison officer said at last, and showed them into a visiting room. A few moments later, Mitch appeared from another door. He shuffled towards them, nodded briefly at his lawyer, then sat down behind the glass screen. He was grey-faced and thin, and his hands were shaking.

'Connor sends his love,' Agnes said, and Mitch nodded again. 'How is it?'

He shrugged. 'No worse than before. I can dry out here as well as anywhere. I've asked to be on drug-free, no point ending one problem and starting another.' He managed a thin smile.

James leaned towards the glass. 'Can you remember anything more? The more you remember about that night, the better we can work for you.'

Mitch shook his head. 'I thought maybe giving up the juice... thought it might make my head work better. But no...' He seemed to have aged, the greying fuzz of beard, the gaps where he'd once had teeth. 'The noise, you see,' he went on. 'It's so noisy here. Where I was before, down in the garages, it was quiet at night apart from the kids. Here there's noise, there's the locking and the gates and the slamming and the shouting and the wireless they turn up so loud, so very loud...' He broke into a fit of coughing, exhausted by so many words.

'We'll get you out of here,' James said. Agnes heard his well-spoken confidence and wanted to believe him.

'And people wanting to know, people asking me what happened. My brief – ' he turned to James – 'no disrespect, mate – and Connor, he means well, but all these questions. Even had Scott down here yesterday, you know, Trina's bloke. Wanting to know, did I remember any more about Andy's death?'

'Scott?' Agnes glanced at Alasdair.

Mitch shook his head. 'Couldn't help him. Never liked the bloke in any case.' Another fit of coughing. He wiped his mouth with the back of his hand. 'I'm always dreaming,' he said. 'I dream about that night. I remember the lights from the cars. The moon, way up in the sky. And the blood, the life blood draining out of the man. And the woman, the one I told you about, the one holding him. And she's singing. In my dream she's rocking him on her knee, singing him a lullaby, and the tears pour down her face and the blood drenches the very stones.' His voice cracked to a whisper.

Agnes looked at Alasdair. 'What does she look like, this woman?' she asked.

Mitch shook his head. 'No one I know. Long hair. Long dark

hair. But it was night, it was dark. And anyway, it's only a dream. When they came, the police, there was no woman. It was me, drenched with the blood of the man. It haunts me, I can tell you, the smell of the blood.'

Alasdair glanced at Agnes, then said, 'The song she sings. In your dream. Do you know it?'

Mitch took a breath, then tried to sing. A few notes formed in his rasping voice. He nodded. 'Yes,' he said. 'It always seems familiar, when I think about it.' He tried again, a longer phrase. The melancholy tune hung in the air.

'Maybe it wasn't a dream,' Agnes said. She saw the prison officer standing by the door, saw him tapping his watch.

'I've thought about it,' Mitch said. 'But if it was true, where did she go? In my dream, she's soaked with blood. The police came, I remember the sirens, the blue lights. She couldn't have just vanished, could she?' He stood up, as the officer approached them. 'Thanks for coming,' he said. 'Say hello to Connor for me. At least he knows where I am these days, it must be a weight off his mind.' He managed a smile. They heard him take up the tune again as he followed the officer back to the landings. The mournful notes faded into the slamming of gates, the lockings and unlockings, the loud shouts and radio noise.

Chapter Twelve

Outside the prison, in the crisp bright air, they breathed again. James shook their hands, promised to be in touch, hailed a cab back to the city.

Agnes and Alasdair looked at each other. 'I really need a coffee,' he said. 'But don't expect me to bankroll a lobster sandwich.'

'Smoked salmon bagel?' Agnes said, as they set off in search of a cafe. 'Or even chips, if they're nice ones.'

'Don't you people carry money?' Alasdair said.

'Me and the Queen both,' Agnes said.

'I suppose it spoils the line of your clothes, to have pockets full of small change. How about that one on the corner there?'

They pushed open the door, and found themselves in steamy warmth and faded chrome. They headed to a table at the back, and sat by a wall which was papered with yellowing photographs of film stars, some signed, some curling at the corners. 'Actually,' Agnes said, 'this is my treat. What will you have?'

'Lobster sandwich, then,' Alasdair said.

Agnes threw him a look, and went to queue at the counter.

'They only had crab,' she said, returning some minutes later with a tray of coffee and sandwiches.

'I hope it was expensive,' Alasdair said, stirring sugar into his cup.

'Very,' Agnes said.

He smiled at her. Behind him, a gleam of sunlight caught the edge of the young Judy Garland. Agnes felt suddenly glad to be here, glad to be with him.

'How did your work go this morning?' she said.

'Oh, you know...'

'Badly, then.' Agnes said.

'I'm a bit distracted.'

'What is it?'

'What's what?'

'You're not yourself,' Agnes said.

'You know me that well, do you?' he said. There was a flicker of his eyes, like a shutter coming down.

'Right,' Agnes said, suddenly business-like. 'What do we do next? And what do we think about this dream-woman of Mitch's.'

'I don't know. Do we think she's real?'

'Did you recognise the song?'

Alasdair shook his head. 'I don't think we should attach much importance to it all. As Mitch said himself, the woman couldn't have just vanished, not in the middle of the West End of London. I think we should talk to the police,' he said. 'Tell them about Gordon.'

'The problem with that is – '

'What?'

Agnes looked at him. 'If Gordon's death is to do with Jeanie's horrible pimp, and if we put the police on to him, then Jeanie's in danger.'

'But what if it's not that? What if Gordon was coming to tell us whatever he knew about Andy?'

Agnes cut the crusts off her sandwich. 'If we tell that to the police, they'll go and question Janet and Sean, won't they?'

'Good. Perhaps they'll find out what Gordon wanted to tell us. Don't you eat crusts?'

'Me and the Queen both,' Agnes said.

They walked out of the cafe into the late afternoon.

'I ought to work,' Alasdair said. Again, the closed-off expression on his face.

'So,' Agnes said, 'do I just phone that nice policewoman and tell her what we think?'

He fell into step next to her. 'We could just go to the local police station,' he said.

Agnes began to laugh. 'They'd think we were mad. Or dangerous. They'd have us locked up.'

Alasdair feigned crossness. 'I look perfectly respectable, thank you very much.'

'No you don't.'

'Look at this coat,' he said. 'Those coppers, they'd recognise quality if they saw this.'

'They'd know it's a criminal's coat,' Agnes said.

'At least I don't dress from charity shops.'

Agnes stopped dead. 'If I can look this good from Oxfam, think what I'd be like in Chanel.'

He faced her, standing in the street, the wind whipping his hair. 'I think, for the sake of both our souls, it would be better if I didn't.'

She waited for him to laugh, but his face was serious. He took her arm and they walked in silence to the main road. He placed a finger under her chin and raised her face to his. 'Talk to the police,' he said.

'But – ' she began.

'What else can we do?'

She met his eyes. 'OK,' she said.

'Dante calls,' he said, glancing at his watch.

'Is it still the wrathful?'

'The poet has passed the river, and he's about to enter Nether Hell. But his soul has begun to stir with the need to fling himself on God's mercy.'

Agnes glanced at him. 'And does that mean he will be saved?'

'Yes. It means that he can move freely through Hell, unlike the souls who are stuck there.' Alasdair began to turn away from her. 'I'll speak to you tomorrow,' he said.

'Have a nice evening,' Agnes said.

'I'll try,' he said.

She watched him lope away from her, his dark coat blending with the deepening dusk. She shivered, although the evening was mild.

'Long lunch, then?' Dan looked up from his desk in the office.

'We need to talk to the police.' Agnes flung her coat over the back of her chair. 'There's stuff they should know.'

'They've been phoning. That nice woman police constable, from last night, Sheila Kelly, wants to talk to Jeanie, I suggested she wait until you were here. I said I'd let her know when you were back.'

'Oh. Good.'

Dan leaned back in his chair, his hands locked behind his head. 'Do you think, that man last night – do you really think it's connected to Walker having been killed?'

'I don't know.'

'You knew the dead man?'

Agnes nodded. 'He was from Scotland. Glasgow. Alasdair knew him. We'd been to see them. There's a little group of them, they live in a house, in one of those old terraces, you know, round the corner.'

'Jeanie thinks it's all her fault.'

'I know.'

Dan sighed. 'We've hardly seen her today. Mary took some lunch up to her earlier.'

'And did that help?'

Dan glanced at Agnes, but said nothing.

Agnes stood up. 'I'll go and talk to her.'

When she knocked at Jeanie's door, there was no answer. She tried again. A small voice said, 'Fuck off.'

'It's Agnes,' she tried.

'So?' The voice was louder.

'The police want to talk to you.'

'They can fuck off too.'

'Jeanie, please.'

There was silence.

'Jeanie,' Agnes said. 'You need to get away from here. We need to find you somewhere else to live. That's what we need to talk about.'

More silence. Then, the sound of shuffling feet, and the door opened. Agnes went inside.

Jeanie climbed back on to her bed and clutched her duvet around her. 'Where can I go?' she said.

'That's what we need to discuss. We've had Walker's death, and now Gordon's. None of it is to do with you. Even if Ash's involved, he's not your problem. We need to get you away from him.'

'He is my problem.'

'No,' Agnes insisted. 'If we get you onto a methadone programme, then you can sever your connections with him – '

'Methadone?' Jeanie seemed to be laughing.

'To get you off the heroin,' Agnes said.

Jeanie shook her head, still giggling.

'What's so funny?' Agnes asked.

'Did you really believe her?'

'Who?'

'Did you really believe Mary when she said I was using?'

'I believed you, when you told me you were.'

'I never said I was.' Jeanie looked like a sullen pixie, perched on her bed.

'You didn't deny it.'

Jeanie sighed. 'You don't know nowt, you don't. That's why I'm stuck. That's why I can't get away from him. If it was just gear, I'd go.'

'So what is it, then?'

Jeanie shook her head. 'No one knows,' she murmured.

'Tell me.'

'If anyone finds out, it'll be me next, dead in the street, like those other two.'

'If anyone finds out what?' Agnes felt weary of the game. Never trust a junkie, she thought.

'I'm not doing drink, and I'm not doing drugs, and if anyone had any sense they'd have asked themselves why. Why would someone like me stop? I ain't never stopped before.' A patch of colour appeared on her cheeks. 'Before, there was just me to think about. But now there's more than just me. Why do you think I've been throwing up?'

Agnes stared at her.

'Or maybe,' Jeanie went on, 'maybe you nuns really don't know nothing about it. Maybe you think all babies are like the baby Jesus.'

Agnes found her voice. 'How many months?'

'About twelve weeks. I counted.'

'Do you know – ?'

'Do I know who the father is? Is that what you were going to say?' Jeanie was dry-eyed, her voice sharp.

Agnes nodded.

''Course I know. Chris. He was the only man I loved.'

'Did you tell him?'

'I was going to. And then he – and then he did what he did.'

They sat in silence. Outside, they heard a bird call, a distant chorus in reply.

'If I'd told him... maybe he wouldn't have done it.' Jeanie said.

'Why didn't you tell him?'

Jeanie's fingers picked at the duvet cover. 'I was scared,' she said. 'No one had ever been with me the way Chris was. He was kind to me.' She lifted her face. 'You know, like when we were crossing a road, he'd hold my hand. And if there was only one seat on a bus, he'd let me sit down. And he'd say that he loved me. He said he'd never felt like this about anyone else. He said I'd changed his life.'

'How did you meet him?'

Jeanie smiled. 'There was a cafe I used to go to. Near Kings Cross. It's knocked down now, for the railway. One minute it was there, the next it had gone. He used to work there. We'd just talk, when I'd be in there of a night. And then when we got to know each other, I'd go to his place. He had a room in a house, up the

Caledonian Road. We'd sit on his sofa and watch telly, and we'd laugh at those programmes when those designers come in and make everything leopard skin and things and the people are supposed to be pleased. We laughed... And he knew I was working, you know, doing business, and it didn't make no difference to him. And then when we... when we were like, going out, like... he said I should stop working. He said he'd look after me.' Her face glowed in the thin light from her bedside lamp.

'And what happened?' Agnes asked.

Jeanie sat silent, chewing her lip. She shook her head.

'He got upset?' Agnes prompted.

Jeanie's eyes filled with tears. 'It was my fault. He used to say I was the first person he'd ever trusted,' she said. ' And I told him I'd stopped working for Ash, I told him I'd stopped using...' The words poured from her. 'And I tried but Ash wasn't having it, and one day he found out about Chris, he made me tell him, and he...' She swallowed, stopped. 'I went to Chris. I told him we couldn't carry on. I was scared. He asked me why, I said because I had to be with Ash. He said, he's made you say that, hasn't he. I didn't know what to say. I was so scared. I didn't know I was pregnant then.' She breathed, then went on, 'But he guessed that Ash had beaten me up, and Chris said I should stay with him, so I did for a few days, and then Ash came, with some other people, I think. We were asleep. They put lighted rags through the letter box downstairs. One of the tenants there was awake, they put the fire out, it was luck, really. Next day, I sat on Chris's bed, in the dawn. I looked at him, sleeping, and I thought about how he'd be better off without me. And I picked up my coat, and I looked around his room, and I thought, this is the place where I was happy. The only place in my whole life where I was happy. There was a photo of us on the telly, we'd got someone to take it for a laugh, when we were in the park once. And I put it in my bag, and I thought, if I don't have proof I won't believe this ever happened.'

Outside the night settled on the city streets. Agnes broke the silence. 'Do you still have the photo?'

Jeanie reached into the drawer of her bedside table and drew out a plastic frame. Agnes saw two happy faces, a lake in sunshine, ducks gathering. Even the ducks seemed to be smiling. She handed the photograph back.

'He was lovely, Chris,' Jeanie said, looking at it. 'His mum's Jamaican, he had this lovely skin... my baby will look like him, won't it?'

'What happened then?'

Jeanie put the photo back in the drawer. 'Chris looked for me for days. But I'm good at hiding if I want to. And then...' she hesitated. 'Ash scared him,' she said. 'And he went back to Essex, where his mum lives, and he got in a car and...' Her face tightened.

'How did you find out?'

'Someone at the cafe remembered me. She told me. And I wouldn't believe her, and I phoned his mum, I'd kept her number, and she told me it was true. She wanted to see me but I couldn't face her, 'cos it was me, wasn't it? If it wasn't for me her son would still be alive...' She was pale, dry-eyed, her fingers clawing at the duvet cover.

A motor-bike roared past, leaving a tail of noise.

'So why can't you get away from Ash? – ' Agnes began, sensing a doubt at the corner of her mind.

Jeanie's fingers pulled at a loose thread.

'He knows you're pregnant.'

Jeanie said nothing.

'He thinks it's his?' Agnes tried.

The thread tightened round her finger. 'He says he'll kill us both. Me and the baby.'

'Well, then you have to get away.'

Jeanie lifted her head and looked at Agnes. 'Where?'

'We'll find you somewhere.'

'Don't send me back home. My mum'll kick me out again, and then I'll be back where I started.'

'There must be a unit you can stay in. Out of London somewhere.' Agnes stood up. 'I'll go and make some calls. I'll tell the police you've got nothing more to say.' She went over to the bed and sat down next to Jeanie. She took her hand, felt Jeanie's fingers stiffen.

'Jeanie,' Agnes said. 'What are you really frightened of?'

Jeanie stared out of the window.

'Why should I believe a word you're telling me?' Agnes said. 'So, you're pregnant. So, it's definitely Chris's, even though he died before you could tell him.' Agnes addressed the back of Jeanie's head.

'I am pregnant.' Jeanie didn't turn round.

'And it may not be Chris's,' Agnes said.

Jeanie snatched her hand away.

'As you said, we nuns don't know much about these things,' Agnes said. 'But I know what it's like to have sex against your will. And I wish I didn't.' Jeanie's head turned a fraction.

'You chose sex with Chris. You didn't choose sex with Ash. And now there's a baby. And that's what made Chris so upset, because Ash must have told him, and no doubt he made out it was his baby, not Chris's – '

Jeanie suddenly turned to her. 'It's got to be Chris's.' The words seemed to burst from her, a sudden wail of grief. 'How can you make a baby out of hate? I loved Chris, I want this baby, I want it to be his.' Tears poured down Jeanie's face. 'When Chris died... I wanted to kill Ash. And I thought, everything's going to be different now. And I went to the clinic, and I told them I wanted to stop using, and then there were loads of forms to fill in, and then I came here. And I thought maybe I'd got away from him. No more working for him, no more allowing him to – and, then I saw him out in the street. And I realised, I'd never get away from him. And if it's his baby, then I'll never ever ever get away from him... Her voice was drowned in sobbing.

'And that man, he's ruined everything. When I came to live here, I told him no. No more. No more working for him, no more allowing him to – and, then he found out about me and Chris. And he got angry, more angry than I've ever seen him. And that's when...' Her voice was drowned in sobbing.

Agnes put her arms around her, felt Jeanie curl into her like a child. 'It will be all right,' she heard herself say. 'It will be all right.'

She left Jeanie tucked up in bed with promises of a new life. She went back to the office, which was empty. She picked up the phone, and dialled the main convent house in Hackney, asked for Sister Madeleine, and almost cried with relief when Madeleine came to the phone. A brief conversation later, and Madeleine had promised to find a room in a mother and baby unit run by the sisters in Hertfordshire. 'I feel like Mother Teresa,' she said. 'Except, St Albans is probably not much like Calcutta. Although, I've heard the curry's better,' she added, as she rang off.

Almost immediately, the phone rang again. It was Alasdair.

'I went back to see Braybrook,' he said. 'He phoned me. He wanted to give me the file back.'

'Had he read it?'

'Yes.' There was a pause. 'He said there's someone he wants to talk to, a training officer, he knew Andy and Lucky and the others in the barracks. He might be able to shed more light on Andy's writings. He's going to get back to me. He sounded quite moved by Andy's memories, actually – '

There was a ring on the doorbell.

'Alasdair, I must go – ' Agnes remembered that Dan had finished his shift and Petra wasn't due on until the morning. The doorbell rang again.

'We'll speak later,' Alasdair said.

Agnes heard voices in the hall. Then Mary put her head round the door. 'Bye,' Agnes said to Alasdair, and hung up.

'There's a policewoman here,' Mary said. 'I thought she wanted to speak to Jeanie. I told her she couldn't.'

'Can you send her in here, please?' Agnes stood up and began to clear files from one of the few comfortable chairs.

Mary sighed, loudly. She left the office and a moment later WPC Sheila Kelly appeared.

They shook hands. 'How are you?' Sheila said.

'All right, I suppose,' Agnes said.

'You must have to be tough for this job,' Sheila said. She sat down in the cleared chair. 'I gather you wanted to speak to us.'

'Yes.' Agnes wondered whether to offer her some tea.

'He wasn't known to us, the dead man. Gordon Tait. We've been to talk to his widow.'

'Janet? How is she.'

Sheila shrugged. 'Devastated. They'd been planning to buy somewhere, start a new life here. I expect she'll go back to Scotland now. The thing is, Sister – '

'Agnes.'

'Agnes. The only lead we have to go on is that it looks like a drug-related crime. The violence of the attack, the fact that Mr Tait was robbed. There's a couple of people round here we've had our eye on, and I know that one of them is connected to one of your residents.' She raised her hand. 'Yes, I know there are issues of confidentiality too.'

Agnes leaned back in her chair and ran her hand through her hair.

'It's not just Jeanie,' Agnes said. 'I wanted to talk to you about Walker's death. Andy McFadden, a resident of ours. He was stabbed in a brawl, about three weeks ago.'

'I know the one,' Sheila said.

'Andy knew Gordon Tait. He spent his teenage years with a group of lads on an estate in Glasgow. And then, twenty-five years later, some of them turn up in a house across the road. Gordon was on his way to see us, you see?'

Sheila took out a notebook and started writing in it.

'When Andy was fifteen,' Agnes continued, 'he moved to London, with his mother, Eileen, who was an East Ender by birth. So he finished his education, if you can call it that, here. After that he signed up to the army, with a couple of mates from the East End. One of them died in a motorbike accident. The others ended up training with the Scots Guards, which brought him back into contact with his Glasgow friends. Some of them stuck it, most left. Andy went to the Falklands. He was the only one – '

Sheila held up her hand to interrupt. 'But – if I was to link every alcohol-related death amongst the homeless of London,' she began, then stopped, suddenly weary. 'Post Traumatic Stress Disorder,' she said. 'Ex-servicemen, substance abuse, homelessness, street violence...' she sighed. 'If you ask my personal opinion, I'd say that yes, war damages people, more than anyone is prepared to admit. I see that damage, time and time again. But that said, Agnes, is there any reason why I should see a connection between these two deaths?'

'Gordon Tait was coming to see us.'

'Gordon Tait was hit over the head with a baseball bat and robbed. And I'm almost certain who did it, and I'd like to see this individual off our streets. Your other resident, Mr McFadden, I'll happily re-open the file on him if there's other evidence. But for now...'

Agnes sighed. 'You want to talk to Jeanie about Ash.'

'Presumably she's reluctant to talk to us.'

Agnes nodded. 'She's absolutely terrified of him. I promised her she wouldn't have to.'

Sheila frowned. 'It would help her too, surely, if we got this man off the streets. He's got form, has Ash – Simon Ashleigh, to give him his proper name.' Sheila opened a file and took out a photograph, which she passed to Agnes. Agnes saw a pale, narrow face, pale eyes, shorn blonde hair.

'But – you know, as well as I do – ' she handed back the photograph. 'He'll be out again in months, and Jeanie will be in greater danger.'

'And is she safe as things are?'

Agnes shook her head.

'What do you want for her?' Sheila asked.

'Me? What I want is for her to be safe. Far from here, in a supportive home, and that man off the streets.'

'Well then,' Sheila said.

Agnes stood up. 'I'll go and get her,' she said.

When Agnes reappeared a few moments later, she was white. 'She's gone,' she said. 'I knocked, there was no answer. Mary and I had to get the master-key. I thought perhaps she was asleep. But – '

Agnes sank into a chair. 'She's not there.'

'Perhaps she's popped out – ' Sheila reached for her radio.

'No. She's packed a bag. She's taken most of her belongings.' Agnes buried her head in her hands.

Sheila stood up. 'We'll send out a search.'

'I was only talking to her a while ago – ' Agnes looked up at Sheila.

'Then she can't have got far.' Sheila smiled. 'We'll find her. Don't worry.'

'I'm sorry – ' Agnes began.

'It's not your fault.'

'It is. I let her down.'

Sheila shook her head. 'No. She's let herself down. I see it over and over again. We reach out a helping hand, to drag these people out of a hole they've got themselves into, and they refuse to take it. If I go and look for her, it will only be because we've already had one of your residents bleeding to death in a London street, two if you count your Scots bloke outside. I don't want to clean up another one.'

Agnes stood up and opened the door for her. 'You must have to be tough for your job,' she said to her.

Sheila smiled. 'Let me know if you hear anything.'

Agnes sat in the silence and stared at the phone. There was nothing to do, except wait. She got up, paced the room, sat down again.

Mary came into the office and sat down opposite her. They looked at each other.

'What are we going to do?' Agnes said.

Mary didn't answer.

'Sheila says it's not our fault,' Agnes tried.

Mary turned towards the window and looked out at the twilight.

'She's pregnant,' Agnes said. 'Jeanie is.'

Mary turned to look at her. Her mouth opened, closed again.

'She's not using drugs, she's not drinking. She's expecting a baby.'

'I don't believe you.' The words seemed to come out with difficulty.

Agnes shrugged. 'It makes no difference. She's still in danger. We've let her down.'

'No.' Mary stood up. 'You have. You've let her down.' Mary's eyes seemed to have filled with tears. She turned and fled from the room.

Some time later, Athena phoned. 'Where are you, sweetie?'

'At the hostel.'

'Still? It's late.'

'I know – '

'I wondered if you fancied a drink. I'm really feeling low, to be honest. With Nic gone, it feels like an ending.'

'Athena, I can't, I'm sorry. Jeanie's absconded, I'm waiting for news.'

'Oh, well, I can always drink alone, I seem to be getting rather good at that.'

'Don't overdo it.'

'Me? Overdo it? I'll be fine, sweetie. Good luck.'

Agnes sat at her desk. Distant bells chimed the hour, across the river, muted by the mist. She thought about Jeanie, back on the streets. Agnes put her head in her hands.

I couldn't save her, she thought. Lord, forgive me. I couldn't save her.

A sound at the front of the house; a tentative knock at the door. Agnes lifted her head and listened. Again, a knock at the door.

Agnes jumped up. Of course, she thought. Jeanie. She's come back, she's seen sense, she's realised she was better here with us than out on the streets... Agnes flung open the front door.

Janet stood there. She looked drawn, her eyes shadowed in the sallow lamplight.

Agnes let her in, and locked the door behind them. They went through to the office without speaking. Janet sat down with her hands clasped in her lap.

'Can I get you anything?' Agnes said.

Janet shook her head. Agnes sat down and waited.

'He was on his way here,' Janet said at last. He was coming to speak to you. About Andy.'

Another silence. Janet looked away, towards the window, the urban night beyond.

'Why did you deny it?' Agnes said.

'Deny what?' Janet's sharp blue gaze met her own.

'When we came to your house, Alasdair and I – you said you hadn't been here.'

Janet stared at her lap, her pale fingers twisted together.

'You came to see Andy,' Agnes said. 'And then he died.'

'We felt terrible,' Janet said. She bit her lip, hiding tears. 'We wished we'd come before. But we knew it would do no good. It was the army,' she went on. 'It ruined him. Andy had no one, and when we moved to London, Gordon wanted to find him, and we got this address for him, but you see...' She stopped, took a breath. 'I think you should know, in recent times there wasn't much love lost between us lot and Andy. I'd have thought Alasdair might have told you, although maybe...' She seemed to check herself, then went on, 'It was the war, you see, the Falklands, it changed him. People who cared about him gave up on him after that. We tried, Sean tried, our Iain tried, my Gordon tried. But he was destroyed, Andy was. Too much drink, too much fighting...' She reached into her bag and took out some papers. Agnes recognised at once the narrow feint, the biro scrawl. Janet held them out to her. 'We found these writings. They're Andy's. They're about the war, I found them in Gordon's things, they're all about the Falklands. Angry stuff, terrible stuff. He was always angry, see, after the war.'

'Why did he give them to Gordon?'

Janet hesitated. 'I don't know. Gordon kept giving him another chance, maybe that's why.' She raised tearful eyes to Agnes. 'He was a good man, my Gordon. The best...' She slumped forward, covering her face, and her words were drowned in sobbing.

Agnes waited for the tears to subside. 'When Andy died – what did you all think?' She handed Janet the box of tissues from her desk.

Janet took a tissue, wiped her eyes. 'We thought the same as everyone else. Andy was always first to pick a fight. He just came off worse this time. When he went for our Iain – '

Agnes heard the hesitation in her voice. 'When was that?'

'Oh, some years ago now. He did time for it. I'm surprised Alasdair hasn't told you. Mind you...' Her voice tailed off.

'Mind you what?'

Janet shot her a glance. 'It's not for me to say. All I meant was, that was the last time we gave him a chance. When I saw my brother there, his face cut, that was it as far as I was concerned. And to think they'd been so close, him and Sean and our Iain. It was Gordon, see, who kept on, trying to help him. He was right, of course.' She shifted on her chair. 'It caused a bit of trouble between us sometimes...' Again, her eyes filled with tears.

'When Gordon arranged to visit us – he implied it was secret.'

Janet sighed. 'He didn't want Sean to know. You see, Gordon was the first to come down South, and he wanted to see Andy again. He chose the area because he'd heard Andy was in your hostel. He wanted to help him. But Sean didn't approve, and neither did Iain. They felt they'd given Andy too many chances, and there was nothing we could do. And then we found out he'd died, and Gordon felt bad that we'd missed the funeral. I think he was coming to see you to find out as much as he could about Andy's death, to put his mind at rest. Sean didn't want to get involved. In the old days, in Castlemilk, Sean and Iain, they loved that man like a brother. They got the worst of it when he changed. It was difficult to forgive.' She dried her eyes, threw the tissues into the rubbish bin by the desk. 'You know, I never wanted to come down South. And I was right. It's brought nothing but grief.'

'Do you think – I mean, when Gordon was attacked... ?'

'You mean, do I wonder why Gordon was killed? All the time.'

Agnes wondered how to phrase her question. 'He was on his way to see us, about Andy. Andy had already been killed. I've had to ask myself – '

Janet's voice was loud. 'No. The police reckon it was some

crackhead. If I thought that Gordon's death was to do with Andy...' Her voice faltered. 'I can't think that way. It will drive me mad.'

'Janet – ' Agnes hesitated, then went on, 'the hostel was broken into. On Friday night.'

Janet looked surprised.

'I wondered,' Agnes said, 'whether you or Sean knew anything about it.'

She frowned, shook her head. 'No,' she said. 'Why would any of us do that?'

Agnes looked at her open face, her genuine puzzlement. She shrugged. 'Never mind,' she said. 'It was probably just some bungled robbery.'

Janet gathered up her bag on to her lap. 'I should go.'

'What will you do now?'

'I'll wait for the police investigation. And then I'll go back up North, I suppose. I can stay with Mam and Dad, sort my life out.'

'And Sean?'

Janet shrugged. 'I don't know. He's got to work out what he wants to do. Me, I don't care.'

It was as if there were no more words to say. The tears on her cheek glistened in the light from the anglepoise lamp.

Agnes picked up the sheets of Andy's writings. 'Do you want these back?'

Janet looked at them. She shrugged. 'Who is there left to care about him?'

'Surely you know someone who – '

Janet was shaking her head. 'Not now.' She stood up, belted her coat around her waist. 'The Andy that we knew... we loved him. But the way he changed...' She looked at Agnes with her clear blue gaze. 'It's all very well Alasdair claiming him as his brother, but he never knew him. I know I'm speaking out of turn, but if Alasdair's decided to fight Andy's corner, it's for reasons of his own. He never knew him. It's not as if they were ever really brothers. Alasdair's dad...' She stared at the floor, traced a thread in the carpet with her foot. 'It's not for me to say,' she finished.

Agnes stood up too. 'What do you mean?'

Janet flicked her a glance, then looked back at the floor. 'He never really settled in Castlemilk, Jim. And Alasdair was off at that posh school. If he thinks it's up to him to pursue the truth of Andy's death, he's wrong. He'll not find out any more than that Andy got angry and was killed in a brawl. It was always going to be that way. In a way, who can blame him? He was thrown together with Andy, because of their parents. He feels bad, that's all. The cards were dealt out and he got the best hand.' She turned to leave.

Agnes showed her to the front door. 'It's late,' she said.

Janet shrugged. 'I'll be OK.'

Agnes opened the door for her. On the steps, Janet put out her hand to her, as if it was an unaccustomed gesture. Agnes shook her hand.

'Thank you,' Janet said.

'I've done nothing,' Agnes said.

'Are you a Catholic?' Janet asked, then added, 'Silly question. I don't think us Protestants have nuns.'

'I think you do,' Agnes said. 'Although I don't know about Scotland.'

For the first time, Janet smiled. 'I don't know either.'

Agnes looked out into the hush of the London night. 'Will you be all right?'

Janet looked out too. 'It's not far.'

'I didn't mean – '

'You mean, now that Gordon's dead?'

Agnes nodded.

Janet was biting her lip. 'I loved him,' she said. 'It was love at first sight, like in all the stories. I was fifteen, I went to a disco, he asked me to dance. That was it.' She took a step outside. 'We got married. We waited for children. They didn't happen.' She turned back to Agnes. 'It was enough for me, to be with him.'

It was a clear night, with twinkling stars. They both looked upwards. Janet broke the silence. 'I don't know what I'm going to do.' She gestured towards the sky. 'What use is all that, without him?'

Janet stared towards the heavens, silenced by grief. It was Agnes who spoke first. 'I'll keep in touch,' Agnes said. Janet nodded, vaguely. 'Sure. See you.'

Agnes watched her as she went down the stairs, pale in her raincoat, vanishing, ghostly, into the night.

Chapter Thirteen

Agnes held the phone in one hand, a mug of tea in another. She listened to the ringing, imagining the hallway of Alasdair's Hampstead home, black and white tiled floor, the phone, black bakelite of course, trilling into emptiness.

'Hello?'

'It's Agnes.'

'I know.' His voice was muffled with sleep.

'Did I wake you up?'

'Do you care?' he said.

'Are you standing in the hall in your pyjamas?'

'Is this some kind of kinky nun thing?'

Agnes laughed.

'No,' he said, 'I'm in bed. Of course. The phone woke me.'

'Sorry.'

'It's still dark outside. I suppose you've been praying since the small hours.'

'Are you in bed in your pyjamas?'

'This is some kind of kinky nun thing.'

'You like it really,' she said.

'Now, that really is enough.' They smiled in the silence. 'Did you phone me for a reason?' he asked.

'Yes. Janet came round to the hostel. Very late last night. She gave me some of Andy's writings, Gordon had them, apparently.'

'Have you read them?'

'Yes. They're more of the same. But there are still all these references to being frightened of someone, someone in his regiment.'

'Is that what Gordon wanted to talk to us about?'

'I think so. Janet said he was the only one of that lot to still care about Andy.'

'That's true.'

'She also told me that Andy did time for injuring Iain in a brawl.'

'Yes. Some time ago. Before he was diagnosed with Post Traumatic Stress Disorder. In those days he'd pick fights with anyone. Iain's her brother, that's why she gave up on Andy, I think. The poor girl had to take sides. Does she have any views on Gordon's death?'

'Only that it was bad luck. She agrees with the police, that it looks like a mugging gone wrong.'

'Mmm.'

'Do you have a black bakelite phone in your hallway?'

'How on earth do you know that?'

'You mean, you do?' Agnes rather shakily put down her mug of tea. 'Black and white floor tiles?'

'You are one spooky nun you are. Either the Saints spy on your behalf, or you're a crazy mad stalker person with secret cameras hooked up everywhere. Or you've broken in here without my knowing.'

'Which is most likely?' Agnes asked.

Alasdair sighed. 'With you, anything's possible.'

'What shall we do next?'

'I'd like to see these writings. And as soon as Major Braybrook gets back to me, we should find out about this training officer who was in the barracks with Andy.'

'OK. Although I can't go far, in case there's news of Jeanie.'

'Won't the Saints keep an eye on her too?' Alasdair said.

'Why else do you think I've been praying since the small hours?'

As she rang off, she was aware of a snatch of music flitting through her mind, an echo from a dream. A woman's clear voice; a lullaby. Then her phone rang.

'Hi.'

'Athena – '

'Did I wake you?'

'No. I've been up for a while,' Agnes said. 'You sound terrible.'

'Why else would I be up at this hour? I've been awake since about six, that's how bad I am.'

'Breakfast, then?' Agnes said.

'I think so. Borough Market?'

'I've got to get dressed yet.'

'See you in half an hour.' Athena rang off.

At ten to eight, Agnes was sitting in the window of the coffee bar. A heavy dawn had crept over London; the streets were washed pale grey. People hurried past, their faces set with intent, their well-cut coats and sharp-edged briefcases signalling a destination of open-plan glamour, of creative thinking, of hot-desking and cool water and real coffee. Agnes flicked through a newspaper and thought about the people left behind, like the old people of Julius's congregation, who'd worked in the leather industry, or in the docks, or on the railways; who would tell you how it was before 'They' knocked it all down; before they put up all this; before the docks closed; before the war.

The door swung open, and Athena was there, scarlet coat and patent leather boots.

'You look great,' Agnes said.

'No I don't.' Athena plonked herself down on the sofa.

'OK then. You look terrible.'

'That's better.'

'I'll get the coffee,' Agnes said. 'Tall? Grande? Cream? Froth? De-caff? Skimmed milk? Caramel? Cinnamon?'

Athena shaded her eyes with her hand. 'Coffee. Strong. Proper milk. Don't care about the rest.'

Agnes put two mugs of cappuccino down on the table, with two croissants. Athena grabbed a croissant and took a large bite of it.

'So,' Agnes said, sitting down next to her on the sofa, 'what is it?'

'Nic phoned last night. From Barcelona.'

'How is he?'

'Very happy. It's 22 degrees there. Sunny. He's found a house he could buy, needs a bit of work but it's lovely. He's had a meeting with some backers, a holistic therapy centre is just what the area needs, apparently. It's all wonderful.'

'How sickening.'

'Exactly.' Athena took another large bite of croissant. 'The house has white walls and a courtyard, it's perfect, of course. Oh, and he's met a massage therapist, she's been very helpful about local contacts. She has an interesting theory about how people internalise their family history in muscular stress, and how with massage you can actually solve not just physical problems but long-term emotional ones too.'

'Even worse.'

'Sweetie, it's a disaster. I'm going to have to go over there and fight her off.'

'I can see that.' Agnes spooned froth into her mouth.

Athena looked out of the window. The early morning light fought through a creeping drizzle. She shook her head. 'I can't bear it, sweetie – '

Agnes's phone trilled. She snatched it from her bag. 'Hello?'

'Agnes? It's Sheila Kelly.'

'Sheila. How are you?'

'OK. Any sign of Jeanie?'

'I was hoping you'd have one,' Agnes said.

'I was hoping she'd have had second thoughts and gone back to the hostel.'

'No such luck.' Agnes took the spoon out of her mug and licked it.

'We've got a possible sighting, in Brixton last night. I just wanted to check she wasn't with you. I'll pursue it, OK? Keep in touch.'

'OK,' Agnes said. 'Thanks.' Sheila rang off. Agnes locked her phone and put it back in her bag.

'You're getting quite good at that thing,' Athena said.

'Thanks,' Agnes said. 'Another croissant?'

'The thing is,' Athena said, when Agnes returned to their place, 'I'm cornered. I've got to go. I'm going to have to go and sort out this white-walled sun-washed paradise, and I bet you anything that when I get there it'll turn out to be some tumble-down old shed with a bit of yard attached, that's the problem with foreigners, they see someone like Nic and they just take advantage – what's so funny?'

'You're a foreigner,' Agnes said.

'So? At least I know how to behave.'

Agnes sipped her coffee. 'When will you go?'

Athena pulled a face. 'I don't know. Soon, I suppose.' She glanced out of the window. 'Whoever would have thought that I'd be reluctant to swap London in the rain for Barcelona.'

'It must be true love,' Agnes said.

'True love?' Athena raised an eyebrow. 'Do we still believe in all that?'

'I don't know. I thought you did. You and Nic have been through a lot together.'

'Mmm.'

'Alasdair says – ' Agnes began.

'What does Alasdair say?'

'There's no need to give me That Look,' Agnes said. 'Alasdair says falling in love in real life can't work. He says that Beatrice is an ideal, an allegory. Love in real life is an exercise in relinquishment, it's about the loss of the ideal.'

'That can't be right, can it sweetie? It's a love poem, for goodness sake. Beatrice leads the Poet to Earthly Paradise and beyond.'

'Since when were you an expert on medieval Italian poetry?'

'All I know is, it's not an exercise in relinquishment to fall in love. Taking a chance on Earthly Paradise – we can all have a shot at that, can't we?'

'But in real life – '

'Of course in real life. Doesn't he know anything about human relationships?'

Agnes sighed. 'I don't think Alasdair's very good at those.'

'You're telling me.'

'Don't judge him harshly, you haven't met him yet.'

Athena pushed croissant crumbs across her plate with a shiny red nail. 'No, but sweetie, it's obvious. There she is, this glamorous Italian bird stashed away in Paris, and here he is, moping around London in his posh coat, going on about Beatrice as an idealisation of love.'

'And hanging out with nuns.'

'That's different. You're not just any old nun.' Athena smiled at her friend. 'That jumper really suits you.'

'Thank you.' Agnes smiled back. 'But, you're right. He is stuck. Something about his life is weighing him down. I think he's been weighed down for years.'

'And anyway – ' Athena drained her mug of coffee. 'Look at me, letting Nic go off to Spain and then mouldering away here in London. You're right, it's time I took action.'

'What will you do?'

Athena sighed. 'All I know is, if I don't go over there, it'll be the beginning of the end for me and Nic.'

'Mmm.'

'But then, perhaps it already is.'

They gathered up their bags and coats and emerged into the street. 'Are you going to your hostel now?' Athena asked.

Agnes shook her head. 'There's a service at my community house this morning.' She wrapped her scarf around her neck against the cold. 'To be honest, I can't face the hostel. Andy is dead, Gordon is dead, and Jeanie's run away. That's how good I am at my job.'

'Sweetie, don't be silly. People make their own choices. You can't be responsible for everyone.'

A train rumbled overhead. The red brick railway arches faded away into the distance, muted in the soft rain. 'Jeanie could be anywhere,' Agnes said.

Athena squeezed her arm. 'It'll be OK,' she said. 'Everything will be OK. Julius. Everything.'

'You and Nic?'

Athena nodded. 'Yup. Everything.'

'The lord takes up the weak out of the dust; and lifts up the poor from the ashes...'

The reedy voices recited the Psalm.

'Lord, I shall sing to you a new song...'

Again, that whisper, that echo, of the lullaby from Agnes's dream. A clear, female voice, rising in her mind above the murmur of the nuns.

'Glory be to the Father, and to the Son, and to the Holy Spirit...' Agnes joined in the ending of the service, and the Gaelic rhythms ebbed away.

'There's a letter for you,' Madeleine said to Agnes. They stood in the kitchen, waiting for the kettle to boil.

'Is nothing private here?' Agnes opened a jar of teabags and sniffed it.

'It's from the Provincial,' Madeleine added.

'Perhaps you'll tell me what it says, too?' Agnes closed the jar. 'That's the problem with communal living,' she said. 'Horrible cheap tea, and people steaming open your mail.'

'The decent Assam is in the other cupboard.' Madeleine pointed above Agnes's head. 'And I don't think anyone goes so far as to actually steam open the mail. We just hold it up to the light and peer at it a lot.'

Agnes laughed. She took a teapot from the cupboard, and a packet of tea. 'Anyway,' she said, pouring boiling water into the pot, 'it's obvious what's in my letter. The dates for taking final vows, and some kind of form to fill in about disposing of my property.'

'I remember all that,' Madeleine said. 'It's such a relief, to get rid of everything.'

'That's what Julius says.' Agnes immediately regretted saying his name.

Madeleine smiled. 'I'm sure he does. How is he, the old sweetie?'

'Oh. Fine. You know.' She turned away, opened the fridge.

'The milk's on the table,' Madeleine said, watching her.

Agnes poured the milk. 'By the way,' she said, 'did you find a place for Jeanie?'

'Bad news on that front.' Madeleine took the mug of tea that Agnes handed her and went and sat down. 'The mother and baby unit is full. Sister Constanza said she'd try to contact another unit, in Essex. She'll let me know – '

'Jeanie's absconded.' Agnes sat heavily at the table opposite her.

'What?'

'Our nice copper came round to talk to her about her horrible pimp, and she'd gone.'

'Where?'

Agnes shrugged, and then suddenly her eyes welled with tears. She shook her head. Madeleine reached across and took her hand.

'It's not your fault,' Madeleine said, after a while.

'She didn't believe we could help. She didn't believe anyone could help.' Agnes pushed her mug around the table. 'Mary said I'd let her down.'

'Did you tell Mary about the baby?'

Agnes nodded.

'You mustn't take to heart what Mary says,' Madeleine said. 'It will be the last straw, won't it? No wonder Mary's cross with everyone. Are the police looking for Jeanie?'

Agnes nodded. 'Needles in haystacks, but yes, they are.'

'We must have faith.' Madeleine stood up and went over to the teapot.

'And I must sign a form which means I belong, irrevocably, to the order.'

'You do anyway.' Madeleine smiled across at her. 'Were you considering an alternative?'

Agnes shook her head. She got up from the table. 'I'll go and rescue my letter from all those nosy nuns,' she said. 'And then I must go back to the hostel.'

She found Dan and Petra in the office.

'Sheila's phoned,' Dan said. 'The sighting was false. She wanted to know if Jeanie had a patch in London she might have gone back to. We couldn't really help.'

'Technically, she was referred from the probation service in Hull,' Petra said, as Mary came in and sat down in the one remaining chair.

'But that dealer of hers, Ash, he's from somewhere near,' Dan said. 'She must have been working in London before we found her – '

'Kings Cross.' Mary's voice broke in. 'She used to work in Kings Cross. Which you'd know if you'd ever bothered to ask her,' she added, looking at Agnes. 'Instead of believing all this bloody rubbish about babies.' She got up again and left the room.

'Babies?' Dan asked, in the silence.

Agnes nodded. 'According to Jeanie, she's pregnant.'

'That's all we need.' Dan sighed heavily.

'Is it true?' Petra said.

'I think so. I know she's not that reliable, but – '

'We have to find her.' Dan picked up the phone and dialled. 'Sheila Kelly please,' he said, when it was answered. 'Oh. OK. Can you tell her, Jeanie might have gone to Kings Cross? She'll understand. Thanks. Bye.' He rang off and looked at Agnes. 'Unless Mary's lying too, of course,' he said.

Agnes spent the evening making supper for the residents. She grilled sausages and mashed potatoes, all the time aware of a thought just beyond her reach. She stirred a large saucepan of baked beans, thinking about bakelite telephones and black and white floor tiles. Once she'd called everyone to come and eat, she left the kitchen and took refuge in the office. She checked her phone but there were no messages. She switched on the desklamp and sat there, holding the phone in her hand, gazing at the shadows beyond the light. The wind gusted outside.

She punched up Alasdair's number on the phone. Then she cancelled it.

If it hadn't been for him, she thought, she would never have followed this path into Andy's past. Without Alasdair, she would have had no reason to question Andy's death and Mitch's culpability.

She recalled Janet's hesitancy when speaking of Alasdair, her implication that Alasdair was acting for reasons of his own.

She walked home through the rainy dusk and let herself into her flat. She went to her desk, and rummaged through bits of paper. She pulled out a number, picked up her phone and dialled it.

'Connor O'Grady,' said a voice.

'Hello, it's Sister Agnes.'

'Oh, hi, how are you? How was my brother when you saw him?'

'He said, at least you know where to find him these days.'

Connor laughed. 'It's the truth, it is. I'd never have thought that prison would be the making of him.'

'He seems to be remembering more about the night that Andy died. He said he remembered a woman singing a song, a kind of lullaby – '

'I know, I know,' Connor interrupted. 'The lullaby. The ghostly woman. You see, whatever happened that night, and whether it's the truth or some figment of his imagination – it's like he's re-playing it in his head, over and over. He's haunted by it.'

'Do you know anything about this woman, or the song?'

'Nothing at all.' Connor hesitated, then went on, 'The thing is, Sister, if you've lived with Mitch and his ghosts all your life as I have, you know not to get too caught up in it all. I know it sounds harsh, but, a lad like Mitch...'

'I understand,' Agnes said. 'But it was the same song that Betty O'Donovan sang when we went to see her. It's been on my mind since Mitch sang it to us.'

'If it's one of them tunes from the old country, it wouldn't be surprising if they both knew it. Those old songs are in the air, you know, for the Irish.'

'I suppose so.'

'I'm going to see Betty tomorrow,' he said. 'I keep an eye on her, there's no one else to do it. You can come along if you like. It'll keep her amused, she loves company, and you can ask her about it if you want. She loves talking about those old songs, she does. Bring Alasdair too, if you want.'

'Oh. OK. I'll check with him.'

'Tea-time, she told me. That'll be around three o'clock. I'll warn her there'll be three of us and she'll make us a cake. If we're lucky.'

'Fine. See you there. Thanks,' she added.

She rang off, and almost at once her phone rang again. 'Agnes, it's Sheila. We think we've got a sighting of her, at Kings Cross. It's a bloody building site there with the new railway construction, but there's a group of girls who hang out behind the station. The thing is, they're not going to betray anyone's secrets to the likes of us, so I might need you to come down with us. I'll keep you posted.'

'Thanks.'

'Bloody awful night to be looking for someone,' Sheila said.

'I know.'

'We'll find her,' Sheila said.

'Thanks.' Agnes rang off. She thought about Jeanie walking the streets in the stormy night; she thought about Jeanie's despair.

She took off her wet shoes, and sat down at her desk. From her bag she took out the envelope from the convent and stared at it. Then she ripped it open, and extracted a letter, several sheets long. She read through it, slowly. Outside the sky deepened into night. Eventually she finished. She turned to the last page. She picked up a pen, ready to sign her name where it was indicated. Her phone rang. She put the pen down.

'Hello?'

'Agnes, it's Julius.'

'Oh.' She felt like bursting into tears at his voice.

'Are you all right?'

'No, not really. I've got the letter from my provincial to sign, about the house in Provence.'

'And you're not ready to sign it.'

'Julius, I have to be ready. As you keep saying, as Madeleine keeps saying, it's not as if I want to do anything else.'

'Hadn't you better have a chat with your French lawyers first?'

'What?'

'What I mean is,' Julius said, 'it's always best to check these things thoroughly. It would be awful if it turned out that by some loophole it hadn't been properly signed over to the Order, or something.'

Agnes began to laugh.

'What's so funny?' Julius sounded aggrieved.

'We seem to have swapped places. I'm about to sign my life away to God, and you're suggesting delaying tactics.'

'I don't suppose a couple of weeks' delay will make much difference to God.'

'No. You're right.' There was a comfortable silence, broken by Agnes. 'How are you?'

'I had my scan today.'

Agnes heard her heart thump in her ears. 'And?' she managed to say.

'Oh, it was all right. Very noisy, you go into a kind of tube thing.'

'No, I meant, what was the result?'

'They all seemed rather jolly, the doctors. They were looking for how far it might have spread, lumps in the liver or something. Anyway, it seemed to be good news on that front, so it's full steam ahead for surgery now.'

'Metastases in the liver. And lymph nodes.'

'How do you know?'

'I – I went on the internet. At work.'

'Oh. Is it helpful?'

'It's great for hypochondriacs, I imagine. Anyway,' Agnes went on, 'it sounds encouraging.'

'Yes. Perhaps.' There was another silence. 'It's still cancer,'

Julius said, quietly. 'It's still surgery.'

'I know.'

'I keep reading the Psalms.'

'Does it help?' she asked.

'"I am all poured out like water, and my bones are out of joint... my tongue cleaveth to my mouth; and thou hast brought me into the dust of death..." No, it doesn't help. Nothing helps.'

'Julius...'

'I had no idea. The Psalms, they're full of lament for the passing of life, the body torn apart by death. Strange, you can know a text so well, and yet some event can endow it with a whole new meaning. One's enemies at the gates, gnawing away at one's life...'

'But – '

'You're right, I shouldn't go on like this. It's probably blasphemy.'

'Julius, it's going to be all right. Your scan was good news.'

'Ah. Yes. Good news.'

'I'll come and see you on Saturday,' Agnes said.

'Yes. That would be nice...' his words were muffled, as if by tears.

'Saturday,' Agnes said.

They rang off.

Look after him, Agnes found herself saying. 'Look after him,' she repeated, muttering, as she wandered through her flat. 'Don't let him die,' she murmured. She gathered up some candles, three altogether, and arranged them on the floor, on the rug, and lit them. She knelt in front of them with her prayerbook.

She turned to the Psalm:

"My heart is sore pained within me; and the terrors of death are fallen upon me..."

Don't let him die. She wanted to shout it out loud, the words silent within her. Don't let him die. The candle flames guttered in the draught from the window. Behind their feeble light the dark rain battered the glass.

Chapter Fourteen

The alarm clock woke her. She blinked in a band of brilliant sunshine that broke through a gap in the curtains. She switched off the alarm. Friday, she thought, staring at the ceiling. She reached for her phone and dialled Alasdair's number.

'Hello,' he said.

'It's me.'

'Is this another question about what I wear in bed?'

'No. Not this time,' she said. 'Do you want to come and meet Lucky's mum this afternoon, with Connor?'

'Yes,' he said. 'Yes, I do.'

'It might involve cake,' she said.

'That's fine by me. Cake I can do.'

'I'll give you these new writings from Janet when I see you.'

'Great,' he said. 'Thanks.' There was a pause. 'Where are you?' he asked.

'What, now?'

'Yes, now.'

Agnes hesitated. 'I'm about to get up,' she said.

'And what are you wearing?' he asked.

'I refuse to be teased by you,' she said.

'I'm not teasing. I'm genuinely interested.'

'I'm sure you are,' she said. 'But I'm going now. Find me at the hostel about two.'

'Bye, then.'

'Bye.' She clicked off her phone.

She watched the sunlit shadows flicker on her ceiling from the tree outside her window. Then she got up and had a shower.

The first thing she did when she arrived at her desk at the hostel was to phone the police station and ask to be put through to Sheila Kelly.

'Agnes, how are you?' Sheila came on the line. 'I was about to phone you. I went to Kings Cross last night. No sign of Jeanie, but I spoke to one of her friends. Sweet kid, actually. She said Jeanie was terrified of this pimp of hers. He wants to kill her, something about the baby she's expecting.'

'Yes. That's why she ran away from us.'

'I'm having a think about it at the moment. What I'm thinking is, if we could haul him in for something, some kind of minor drug offence, it might make her feel safer. I'd like to ask him a few questions about the death of Mr Tait too.'

'Can you do that?'

'Leave it with me. I've got to check a few things here.'

She settled at her desk, and took out the sheaf of notes from Andy that Janet had given her.

'...this time I hit the deck again, and waited for the explosion, but there was none, just the noise of a helicopter's blades spinning. It was the down draught that had knocked me flat... we got back onto our feet, and we could see it, a Sea Hawk, bobbing up and down, with blokes being knocked over by the draught and slipping in the mud...

'...Me and Lucky, we used to talk about it when he was still alive, about our time in the barracks in 3 Company. If it wasn't for Lucky, I'd have been dead then, even if he hadn't tried to kill me, I'd have killed myself, done it for him...' The page ran out, and Agnes turned to the next page.

'...The Paras called it a Tactical Advance to Battle. We called it a forced march, with Stanley seventy miles away and our kits weighing about a hundred pounds each, and the blizzards and the muddy ground. Some of the boys got frostbite...'

Agnes sifted through the pages, searching for the name Lucky.

'...They say shouldn't have ever called him Lucky,' she read. 'With a name like that, someone's going to have it in for you, aren't they. Lucky was all right until he met Billy Lee. Then Billy died. That's when his luck ran out...'

Agnes turned the page. The other side was blank. She wondered how old these writings were, how long Andy had had them, when he'd given them to Gordon, whether he'd shown them to anyone else.

She heard the doorbell ring, heard Dan answer it. She folded up the papers and locked them into her desk, as Dan put his head round the door.

'Do you have the paperwork for Bernie Meek, new resident? He was referred by Southwark Social Services, homeless, ex-drinker, ex-gambler..?

Agnes handed him a file. 'What's he like?'

'Quiet. He's sitting in the kitchen listening to Jayce's life-story.'

'All nineteen years of it,' Agnes said.

'They might be there some time. We're on the second step-dad so far, and Jayce was only six at the time.'

The sun had gone in when Agnes and Alasdair arrived at the estate in Hackney. Connor was standing in the entrance of block B. 'She gave me the code,' he said. 'Saves me buzzing her.' He punched some numbers onto a keypad, and the door clicked open. 'We'll take the stairs again,' he said. 'Too many breakdowns, that lift.' He laughed and headed up the stairs, and Agnes and Alasdair followed him.

'Betty, it's me,' Connor called through the door. He pressed the buzzer. 'I've brought Agnes with me, like I said,' he added, as Mrs O'Donovan opened the door. 'And Alasdair.'

She nodded at them, then turned and shuffled back along the narrow corridor into her living room. 'I made a cake,' she said. 'I hope there's enough.' She lowered herself into her armchair and picked up her knitting, breathing fast.

'How's your little girl?' she said to Connor.

'She's doing fine, thank you.'

'You must bring her to see me again,' Betty said. 'She liked my fireplace, didn't she?' She turned to Agnes. 'She liked the pretend fire there, couldn't keep her away from it, could we?' She laughed, and turned back to Connor. 'The tea things are all ready, dear.'

Connor got up and went into the kitchen.

'This is Alasdair,' Agnes began. 'Andy's sort-of brother.'

Betty stopped knitting and peered at Alasdair. 'So you're the boy,' she said. 'It was your dad what Eileen took up with, all them years ago.'

'That's right,' Alasdair said.

Betty considered him for a moment. 'Well, I feel sorry for you. If it's not a liberty to say so.'

'It's not a liberty at all,' Alasdair said. Agnes felt the warmth of his charm, like the glow from the plastic logs in the hearth.

Connor reappeared with the tray of tea things, the cake perched on its doily.

'If you wouldn't mind doing the honours, dear? It's my fruit-cake recipe, came from my mother,' Betty said. As the cake was cut and distributed, she looked at Alasdair, her head on one side. 'You knew Trina, didn't you?' she said.

'Yes.' Alasdair balanced his plate on his knee.

'Hmm.' Betty nodded to herself.

Connor stirred two sugars into her cup, then handed it to her.

'Eileen always liked her, that Trina,' Betty said. 'She even left her a few bits and pieces in her will. Daughter she never had, you could say.' She glanced across at Alasdair, then back at her knitting.

'Very good cake,' Connor said, dusting crumbs from his knee.

'Thank you dear,' Betty said. 'Never fails, as my mother used to say.'

'Do you know Scott?' Agnes's question, once uttered, seemed to her to be intrusive.

Betty looked up from her work. 'Oh, yes, we all know Scott.'

She nodded at Agnes. 'I'm glad Eileen's not here to see it,' she said. 'She had such hopes of Trina and her boy, not that everyone saw eye to eye with her on that, neither. But there's no doubt that Trina would've been happier with Andy than she is now. That Scott, he's just like his dad, you can trust me on that. And his dad, wouldn't do nothing unless there was something in it for him. That man, he went to his death believing the world had cheated him out of dues.'

'And you think Scott is the same?' Agnes pushed cake crumbs around on her plate.

'You can say what you like about Trina,' Betty said, 'But I feel sorry for her. If Scott didn't think there was something in it for him, he wouldn't still be with her.'

'You don't think it's just that he cares about her?' Connor smiled at Betty as he took her cup for a refill.

Betty looked up at him as he handed the cup back to her. She shrugged. 'Maybe. It's not my business, in any case.' She glanced across at Alasdair, then concentrated on stirring her tea.

'Mrs O' Donovan,' Agnes said. 'In Andy's writings, he says that Lucky protected him from someone. He implies that it was during their time in the barracks.'

'But that was such a short time, dear,' Betty said. 'They started their training together in the Scots Guards, but Lucky left after a few months.'

'He didn't mention anyone who was a threat to them?'

Betty shook her head. 'It was a long time ago, dear,' she said. She picked up her tea cup and drank from it.

Agnes broke the silence. 'When Andy died...' She took a deep breath. 'The thing is, Mitch thinks there was someone else there, the night that Andy died. A woman. And he remembers her singing a song to Andy.' She looked at Connor, then went on, 'The song he remembers was one that you were singing. Last time we were here.'

Betty smiled at her. 'Are you sure, dear?'

'Yes. It's a kind of lullaby, I think.'

'A lullaby?' Betty looked blank.

'Perhaps if I sing it,' Agnes tried, 'you might recognise it.'

Betty folded her hands in her lap. 'You can have a go, dear. My ear's not what it was.'

Agnes took a deep breath, trying not to look at Alasdair. Then she repeated the notes that Mitch had sung to her in prison, that had been with her on waking yesterday morning, that she'd been dreaming, she now realised, as the tune came back to her, since Mitch had first sung it to her.

And then there were two voices singing, as Betty took up the tune and sang it with her. Agnes stopped, and Betty carried on until the end.

'Hush, my baby, hush, my pretty one,

Soon it will be dawn,

The storm will quieten with the daybreak,

The waves' roar will be a whisper when you awake,

The ships will come back safely in the morn...'

' I used to sing that to my little ones,' she said. She turned to Connor. 'Do you recognise it?'

He shook his head.

'Funny that your brother should know it,' she went on.

'Mitch remembered it from this woman,' Agnes said.

'Long hair,' Alasdair said, and everyone turned to look at him. 'Mitch said the woman who sang it had long, dark hair.'

'Irish, it is. Lucky's dad, my Alf, he was from Derry, he always said it came from his people. My sister Kathleen always used to argue with him about it, our mam sang it to us and Kath wouldn't have it being Irish. Which was silly, because our mam was part-Irish anyway.'

'Do you know why this woman – ' Alasdair began.

'Oh, this woman,' Connor interrupted. 'She might not even exist. If you've known Mitch as long as I have, you know not to trust the stories from his dream world.'

'But the song is real.' Alasdair was emphatic, leaning forward on his knees. 'Betty here knows it. Even Betty's sister knows it.'

Betty shrugged. 'It's a common enough song,' she said.

'Mitch might have heard it himself, a long time ago.' Connor stood up and began to gather up the tea things. 'He's been on the booze that long, he doesn't know what's true and what's not. It was a lovely cake, Betty.'

Agnes and Alasdair helped to gather the tea cups. They began to go, murmuring their thanks, going to find their coats. Connor walked with them down the stairs, then said he'd go back and make sure that Betty had some supper ready.

Agnes and Alasdair stood in the gusting wind. Grey clouds scudded above the sandy yellow tower blocks.

'Scott,' Agnes said.

'What about him?'

'From what Betty said, he makes it his business to know anything that might be useful to him.'

'And?' Alasdair began to cross the courtyard towards the main gate. Agnes followed him.

'He must know a lot about all this,' she went on. 'He knows Trina, he knew Andy. He let slip that detail about how Andy died, you remember?'

'He's an idiot,' Alasdair said. 'What can we do? Go and cross-examine him? He'll pretend to know more than he does, it'll be a waste of our time.'

'Oh.' Agnes fell into step next to him. 'And the lullaby?' she said.

Alasdair shrugged.

'Perhaps it goes back to Lucky,' she went on. 'If Betty knew it from her mother, and sang it to her children, perhaps whoever sang it to Mitch was someone from Andy's past here, on the estate?'

'Perhaps,' Alasdair said.

'What shall we do then?' Agnes went on. 'Go and chase this shadow of a long-haired woman who might have sung an Irish lullaby to Andy in his dying moments? It's like Dante's Beatrice,' she said. 'The woman who will lead us to the truth.'

They had reached the main road. Alasdair glanced down at her as they waited for the lights to change. 'No it's not,' he said. 'Dante knew Beatrice. It was the purity of love that saved him, that led him through Hell. Whereas this...' The traffic lights beeped, and they crossed the road.

'Yes?' Agnes prompted him.

He turned to her. 'Connor's probably right. Mitch dreamed it.'

A light rain was beginning to fall. 'Why did you choose *The Divine Comedy*?' Agnes asked. 'Why did you choose to work on something that's all about love and faith if you don't believe in either?'

Alasdair looked down at her. Raindrops misted his hair. 'Don't you think we're all drawn to the thing we can't do? It must be the same for you, signing up to your convent. All I know is, I recognise the lack. We both have a gap we'll never cross, but we try just the same.' He brushed the rain from his forehead. 'We're getting wet standing here.'

He set off again, along the main road. Agnes followed. At the bus stop they paused. 'I'm going back to Hampstead,' he said. 'Work to do.' He looked at her. 'What will you do?'

'Me? I'm going to the hostel. And then probably I'm walking the streets of Kings Cross in search of Jeanie.'

He nodded. 'I'll phone you.'

'When you speak to the Major,' she said, 'can you ask him about Billy Lee? It seems from the writings that he was in the army with Lucky and with Andy. And he died.'

'Oh. OK. Look, here's my bus.' He squeezed her arm, as the bus swished to a halt at the stop. The doors slid open, and he got on. She turned and headed back down the main road, wondering about Beatrice and folk songs, and love and faith, and the gap she had to cross to take her vows, and what it was about Alasdair that made him suddenly hide from her, as if he could become invisible at will.

She stood at the bus stop in the rain. After ten minutes or so, she decided that Alasdair's other secret power was being able to summon cabs and buses whenever he needed them. She pulled out her phone and dialled Trina's number. There was no answer, so she left a message asking her to call. As she put her phone back in her bag, a bus loomed out of the downpour.

She arrived at the hostel soaking wet. Mary was sitting in the office.

'That policewoman has been trying to get hold of you,' she said.

'Thank you,' Agnes said, hanging her scarf over a radiator.

'She wants you to go and look for Jeanie,' Mary said.

'Yes, I know.' Agnes took off her wet shoes.

'I offered to go with her,' Mary said.

Agnes sat down at the desk.

'But she said you should go, the policewoman said.'

'Right,' Agnes said. 'I'll phone her.' Agnes shifted some papers on her desk, aware of Mary staring at her. She didn't look up until Mary had crossed the room and gone out into the hall, slamming the door behind her.

Chapter Fifteen

They walked along the side of the railway arches in the floodlights from the building site. The rain rattled above them. Beyond the pools of light the night was black.

Sheila raised her voice above the weather. 'The girls are usually up here,' she said. She was wearing jeans and a short hooded jacket.

They came out on to York Way into the darkness and the pouring rain.

'Are you sure?' Agnes said, peering into the deserted shadows.

'Wait for the cars,' Sheila said, slowing her pace. A few moments later a car dawdled past and came to a halt. From nowhere there appeared three young women in short skirts and high heels. There was a brief exchange between one of the girls and the driver, while the rain sparkled in the headlights' beam. Then she got into the car, which slid away into the darkness.

The two remaining women linked arms and teetered back into the shadows. Agnes and Sheila followed them. They had taken shelter under a bridge, and were sitting on the wall.

'Watch out,' Agnes heard one of them say, as they approached.

'We're looking for Jeanie,' Sheila said. 'Jeanie Clark. Or maybe Jeanie McKinnon.'

'Don't know her.' The young woman's tone was hostile. She stared out from under a fringe of bright red hair. 'Who are you?' The second girl had thin blonde hair and looked very young.

Agnes stepped forward. 'I'm Sister Agnes. I'm a nun. She was staying in our hostel. She left us, and I'm worried about her.'

The blonde girl nudged her friend, and whispered to her. Agnes heard footsteps approaching behind her. A woman in black high-heeled boots appeared; behind her, a short, dark-haired girl in a black PVC raincoat.

'Trouble?' The woman in the boots glanced at Agnes and Sheila, drawing heavily on a cigarette.

'Hi Babs,' the red-haired girl said. 'They're looking for someone called Janie – '

'Jeanie,' Agnes corrected.

'She's a nun.' The blonde girl tilted her head in Agnes's direction.

The woman in the boots threw her cigarette butt on to the pavement and ground it underfoot. 'She don't look like one.'

'I know Jeanie.' The girl in the shiny raincoat came forward. 'She's the one from Hull, she lived on the estate where my cousin lived.'

'That's her,' Agnes said.

'She was here the other night. We ain't seen her since.' The other women glanced at each other, tight-lipped, but the young woman still addressed Agnes. 'She's scared, she is.'

'What is she scared of?' Agnes spoke gently. The woman in the boots had lit another cigarette and was eyeing Sheila and Agnes in turn.

'Someone got killed. Jeanie was involved with this guy, she was trying to get away from him, and then someone got killed. Down South London way. She'd got away from him once, she'd met this bloke who really cared for her, they were going to have a family and everything...'

Babs made a snorting noise. 'That's likely, isn't it.' The other two women laughed. 'We've all heard that one in our time.'

'He died,' the young woman said. 'The boy she loved, he died. And now she's got no one, and that's why she's scared.'

In the silence, Babs drew on her cigarette; rain dripped from the bridge. The two women on the wall stared at the ground.

'Will you tell her we were looking for her?' Agnes said. 'If you see her.'

'Sure.' Babs nodded.

'Daisy's taking a while,' the blonde girl said, peering towards the road.

'Nah, here she is,' Babs said. A flash of headlights, a car pulling up, and a young woman emerged from the darkness. The car revved its engine and drove away.

'Anyone got a fag?' Daisy said.

'Here.' Babs held out a cigarette to her.

'We'll be going, then,' Sheila said. They nodded their goodbyes and set off back towards Kings Cross.

The rain had eased. Above the curved roof of the station, the sky was pricked with stars.

Sheila pulled out her radio and talked into it briefly, then put it away again.

'Have you seen Janet?' she asked.

'Not for days. I thought I might call on her,' Agnes said. 'Though I don't know what to say.'

'If Jeanie's told all that to her friends...' Sheila began.

'Yes?'

Sheila sighed. 'It does sound as if Ash was involved in Gordon's death.'

'If that was our Jeanie. If she knows anything at all.'

'We're no further on, really.'

A police car pulled up alongside them, and the passenger door opened.

'Come on,' Sheila said, holding the door for Agnes. 'We'll drive you home.'

Agnes let herself into her flat and switched on the electric bar fire. She sat in front of it. In her mind she saw old brick arches in the dripping dirty rain, Babs and Daisy and the others, their teetering heels silhouetted in the headlights. She moved nearer to the fire.

Her answering machine was flashing at her, so after a while she got up and pressed play.

'Hi, Agnes, it's Athena. Nothing urgent, I'll try your mobile.'

'Hello?' Julius's voice was hesitant. 'Oh. Just to say, I've got a date for the hospital. Um... well... Goodbye.'

The third message was a woman's voice. 'I hope that's you,' it said. 'It's Trina here. Your mobile was switched off. You can phone me this evening if you want.' She gave her number.

Agnes sat with her phone in front of the fire. Julius, she thought. He wanted to talk about the arrangements for his operation. She looked at her watch. It's too late to phone him now, she thought. She replayed Trina's message and dialled the number.

'Hello?' Trina was almost whispering.

'It's Agnes.'

'Oh, Sister. It's you. You wanted to talk to me.'

'Yes.'

'About Andy?'

'Yes.'

There was silence. Then Trina said, 'Don't know if there's anything else I can tell you.'

'What does Scott think he'll get out of it?' Agnes kept her voice light.

'Scott?' Trina's voice wavered.

'Yes. It must be difficult for you,' Agnes hazarded, 'when you were so fond of Andy.'

'Too right it's difficult for me.' Trina's voice was suddenly loud. 'Stupid bastard banging on about the money.'

'Shall we meet up?'

'OK. Tomorrow,' Trina said. 'I've got to come into town anyway, I said I'd go shopping. Oxford Street?'

'Sure. Where?'

'The Chanel counter of Dickins and Jones.'

'Oh. OK.'

'Midday,' Trina went on.' See you there.'

Agnes went into her kitchen. She opened cupboards in a vague way and then closed them again. She wondered why the idea of meeting Trina by the Chanel counter of Dickins and Jones should have taken her by surprise. She decided she wasn't hungry, went back to her phone and dialled Athena's number.

'Oh, sweetie, it's you, I'm so sorry I haven't been in touch...'

'That's OK – '

'How's Julius?'

'Not brilliant.' Agnes sighed. 'He's had a scan, he's got a date for being operated on.'

'I hate it,' Athena said.

'You hate what?'

'Everything. Ageing. Dying. Sometimes I wonder what the whole point of it is.'

'Mmm,' Agnes agreed.

'Going grey, for example. I mean, I'm naturally black haired, as you know.'

'Naturally.'

'But under the dye, there are more and more grey hairs, I'm sure of it. It's all very annoying. And I noticed the other day that the skin on my neck is different.'

'Athena – '

'I'm just waiting to go back to normal, that's all. It's not much to ask.'

Agnes smiled at the phone. 'Athena, why are you spending so long staring in the mirror these days?'

'Why do you think? Because I've got to go over to Spain and sort things out with Nic, and if this holistic massage therapist is a real threat then I've got to be on top form, haven't I? Did I mention she was a blonde? Originally from Sweden, Nic said. I nearly booked a flight to Barcelona on the internet yesterday, but something stopped me.'

'Yes. I nearly signed my house in Provence over to the order the other day, but something stopped me. And then Julius said I should consult my lawyers before doing anything–'

'Julius did?'

'Yes. I thought it was odd, too.'

'It's mortality. It's enough to make anyone reassess their deal with God, I would have thought.'

Agnes was silent.

'Oh, God, listen to me,' Athena said. 'Julius has got cancer and I'm going on about grey hair. I always do it. I'm so sorry – '

'It's all right, really – '

'And then to go on about Julius's deal with God, when the man is practically a saint... you know I'm very fond of him, you know that, it's only because I know he's going to be OK that I'm saying ridiculous things, honestly, I mean, if it was really bad, I'd be properly sympathetic, you know I would...'

'I know.'

'I'm sorry,' Athena said again.

'It's OK.'

'Are you free tomorrow?'

'Yes. I'm meeting Trina at the Chanel counter at Dickins and Jones at midday, but I'll be free for a late lunch.' Athena was silent. 'What's wrong?' Agnes asked.

'Nothing.'

'Athena – ?'

There was a pause, then Athena said, 'You won't buy anything, will you? Without consulting me, I mean?'

Agnes laughed. 'I'm asking her about Andy. I'm hardly going to be choosing lipstick with her, am I?'

'Oh. Good.'

'I think she's only there because she shoplifts to order.'

'Difficult place to steal from, I'd have thought,' Athena said.

'Yes, I thought so too.'

Athena started to laugh. 'What kind of nun are you? Hanging out at make-up counters with shoplifters...'

'A very bad kind of nun,' Agnes said. 'That's probably why Julius advised me to delay signing.'

'I'll see you tomorrow. 1:30? The basement cafe at Liberty's?'

'Fine. See you then.'

She sat by her desk. Outside, car headlights streaked the unforgiving night. She thought of Jeanie, out there somewhere in the city. She thought of Julius, making his own dark journey. She thought of the residents in her hostel, and then she thought of all the others, unknown to her, homeless or drunken or abused, surviving on London's streets.

Or not surviving, like Andy. And Gordon.

She went to brush her teeth, resolving to call on Janet the next day.

Everything glittered. Displays offering a flawless complexion, pots of cream promising eternal youth, lipsticks in every shade. Agnes picked up a tester and looked at the colour. She tried to remember the last time she'd worn lipstick. She associated wearing make-up with Hugo, her ex-husband; a never-ending and ultimately futile quest to please him, along with trying to cook him what he wanted, dress as he wanted, behave as he wanted...

'It would suit you, that colour.' Agnes turned to see Trina clicking towards her on high black court shoes, her hair newly platinum blonde, carrier bags swinging from her arms.

'Been shopping?' Agnes said, replacing the tester.

'You could say that, yes.' Trina took her arm and steered her towards the doors. The swing of the glass flashed sunlight, and they were out in the street. 'I'll buy you a coffee,' Trina said.

They settled down with two elegant white cups in the crowded hubbub of a coffee bar.

Agnes stirred her coffee, then looked across at Trina. 'I had tea with Betty O'Donovan,' she said.

'You did?' Trina was wide-eyed. 'When? How is she? Lovely lady, she is. I'd love to see her again.'

'Yesterday. She was talking about Eileen.'

'She was very fond of Eileen, she was. Thing about Eileen, when she moved onto the estate, she didn't know her way about, if you know what I mean. Made a few mistakes, got on the wrong side of people. But Betty, she could always judge a person right. They were great mates, they were. Used to go singing together, that was a right laugh too.' She giggled.

'She said Eileen was very fond of you.'

Trina looked suddenly serious. She twiddled her spoon around in her cup. 'Yeah. Like I told you, she was like a mum to me.' She was silent, blinking in the noise. She looked across at Agnes. 'You know the coffin, for Andy? That I paid for? That was for Eileen, really. She left me a bit of money when she died, some jewellery and that, and I thought, she did right by me. I'll do right by her boy.'

'And is that why Scott – ?'

Trina interrupted. 'He won't give up, you know? He used to go around with Lucky's dad, Alf, and Alf had some story about Jim Brogan being in the money and that was why Eileen never seemed to lack for nothing after he died, which was stupid anyway because Eileen worked bloody hard when she moved down here, waitressing and that. And then when Eileen died, you see, people thought maybe Andy was going to inherit. It was something about Jim's first wife, the Italian woman – '

'Alasdair's mother.'

Trina nodded. 'Alasdair's mother.' She stared into her cup for a while. 'And it's true, if you think about it, there was money there, 'cos Alasdair went to all them posh schools and look at him now, fancy clothes and that.'

'But there's surely nothing to connect Alasdair's mother with Eileen leaving money to Andy, is there?'

Trina smacked her hand down on the table. 'That's just what I say to my Scott. Why is he sniffing around what happened to Andy, talking to Haz and the others about it? He even went to see Mitch in prison. He won't drop it.'

'But what's in it for Scott?'

Trina sighed. 'When I got them bits and pieces, after Eileen died, the bloke we went to see, the solicitor, he said there was money for Andy, but it was tied up, you know, in a trust. Because by then Andy was drinking and that, and Eileen didn't think he could handle his own money. And she was right, weren't she? And so Scott got the idea that when Andy died, there'd be this trust money sitting there, and that I'd be put in charge of it, because I was the only other what-d'you-call-it, beneficiary. Which is stupid, isn't it, because that lawyer would have been in touch with me if there was anything to say. And anyway, I don't want to think about Eileen like that, I have good memories of her, she was a sweet lady and a real friend, and it's typical of bloody Scott just to see everyone in terms of what he can tap them for.' She stopped for breath, and began to drink her coffee.

'You and Scott – ' Agnes began, but Trina held up her hand.

'Don't say it. I know he don't do himself no favours, and I know people think I could do better for myself, but they don't know him like I do.'

'Last time we met, you said that sometimes you think you love him, but sometimes you don't.'

Trina picked up her cup and put it down again. 'You're a nun,' she said. 'Even if I was to tell you how I love him, you wouldn't understand.'

Agnes watched her as she dipped her finger into the foamy milk at the edge of her cup and then licked it.

'No,' Agnes said. 'Perhaps you're right.'

'Perhaps I don't know anything about love,' she said to Athena. It was twenty to two, and Agnes was sitting in the basement cafe of Liberty's.

'Don't be silly, sweetie. Shall we order some coffee?'

'Not more coffee,' Agnes said. She leaned her head on her hands.

'Wine, then?'

'Much better idea,' Agnes said. 'Lots.'

Athena called the waitress over and ordered a bottle of Pouilly Fumé.

'But that's very expensive,' Agnes said.

'Look, sweetie, you've obviously had a ghastly morning having to look at lipsticks with a horrible shoplifter who's made you doubt yourself as a woman, and this morning I booked myself a ticket to Barcelona, and when I phoned Nic he sounded like he didn't care either way whether I joined him there or not – the least we can do is have a decent bottle of wine.'

'I agree,' Agnes said.

'And I'm going to have the asparagus omelette.'

'I'll have the goat's cheese salad.'

The wine arrived and was tasted, and two glasses were poured.

'So – ' Athena sipped from her glass. 'What's all this nonsense about knowing nothing about men?'

'It's just that Trina seems to be with a really awful man. I worry about her, she's genuinely frightened of him, it seems to me – and she claims that she loves him and that as I'm a nun I wouldn't understand.'

'You know all about loving abusive men,' Athena said. 'You lived with Hugo all those years.'

'Yes.' Agnes drank a large swig of wine. 'I haven't got round to telling her that.'

'Did she nick anything nice for you?'

Agnes laughed. 'She had armfuls of shopping. For all I know, she paid for it all.'

'How very disappointing. I was hoping to pick up some tips. If Nic and I are going to break up, then subsidised shopping might be the only way I can keep up my own standards.'

Agnes smiled at her. 'So – what did he say?'

Athena shook her head. 'I said, darling, I've got a ticket, I'm coming over on Wednesday. And he said, Oh. And so I said, I thought you wanted me to join you, I thought this was our new life together, blah blah, you know the stuff – and he sort of agreed in a weedy kind of way, and then that was it really, he said he had to go.' She topped up both their glasses.

Agnes broke off a piece of bread roll. 'It'll be better when you see him,' she said.

Athena sighed. 'I suppose so. I just keep thinking, if this is what it's like after about a week apart, maybe we haven't really got a relationship. Maybe it was just familiarity keeping us together, and now he's doing something new and exciting he realises he doesn't need me.'

'Even if that were the case – which I doubt – ' Agnes said, 'how would you feel?'

Athena pursed her lips. 'Terrible,' she said, after a moment.

'The fact is, I'm a difficult person, I've never managed to have a stable relationship with anyone but Nic, and he puts up with me, and when I go mad he's calm, and when I decide that life is too awful, and threaten to leave my job, or tell Simon at the gallery exactly what I think of him, or throw away all my clothes and get an entire new wardrobe, he talks me out of it, and he makes me feel that it's possible to carry on after all with the job or the boss or the clothes that I've got.' She drank some more wine. 'And we have great sex.'

Agnes shrugged. 'Well, then.'

'Well then what?' Athena waited for an answer, as the food arrived.

Agnes speared an olive with her fork. 'I would have thought that if you have great sex, everything else is going to be OK too.'

Athena nodded. 'Though it takes a nun to tell me,' she said.

'It'll be OK,' Agnes said. 'You and Nic.'

Athena raised her glass. 'To everything being OK. Me and Nic will fall in love all over again, and Julius will be well, and my grey hair will go back to normal.'

Agnes laughed and raised her glass. 'To everything – ' she began, as her phone trilled in her pocket. She pulled it out and answered it.

'It's me,' Alasdair said.

Athena mouthed 'Alasdair?'

Agnes nodded. 'Hello,' she said, into her phone.

'Braybrook wants to talk to us.' He sounded fired up, engaged, unlike the taciturn, near-invisible Alasdair of the day before.

'What about?'

'He said he's been having a bit of a think, his words. He wondered if you could make tomorrow, it's Sunday I know, but it suits him – at his club, he thought we could find a quiet room somewhere.'

'Sunday's fine,' Agnes said, mentally rearranging her plans to attend chapel. 'By the way, I was going to call on Sean and Janet, do you want to come?'

'I'd love to, but Dante's gone sticky, and I've just got to get on with it. But I'd love to see them soon.'

'I'll tell them.'

'It sounds very noisy there,' Alasdair said.

'I'm in Liberty's.'

'With Athena,' he said.

'How did you guess,' Agnes said.

There was a silence. 'I'd better go,' Alasdair said. 'Phone me later.'

'I'm going to mass,' she said.

'After that.'

'OK,' she said.

'Pray for me,' he said, and then he'd gone.

Athena yawned, patting her mouth.

'Don't say my salad's getting cold,' Agnes said.

'Your salad's getting cold,' Athena said. 'And you're blushing.'

Agnes took a mouthful of goat's cheese.

'So, when are you seeing him?' Athena said.

'Tomorrow. And there's no need to tut like that.'

'You see,' Athena said, as if in explanation, 'I have to hang on to Nic, don't I. Any other available man gets snapped up by you.'

'I thought you didn't fancy Sagittarians,' Agnes said. 'Or something.'

'I never said that,' Athena said. 'All I said was that Scorpios are trouble.'

'Maybe I won't introduce you after all.'

'Anyway, he's not a Sagittarius.'

'How do you know?'

'I can tell.' Athena drained her glass. 'Finish your salad, and we can go and practise our shoplifting.'

It was twilight when she pushed open the side door of Julius's church and went down the stone steps to his office. She could hear a rhythmic clatter. She knocked, then put her head round the door. His desk was a pool of warm light, throwing the edges of the room into shadow.

'I thought it was you,' he said, not looking up. He bashed some keys of his typewriter, then stopped and peered at the paper.

'The "h" has stopped working,' he said. 'I'm going to have to write it in with biro. Either that or find a different word for "hermeneutic".'

'You shouldn't be writing words like hermeneutic,' Agnes said, settling into a chair.

'You mean, in my condition?'

For some reason, they both laughed.

'It's not funny really,' Agnes said, after a moment.

'No,' Julius agreed. 'Did I tell you they've given me a date?'

'You left me a message.'

'So I did. Tuesday next week.'

'That's very soon.'

'Yes,' he said. 'I've had to tell everyone now. Now the Provincial knows, the whole parish will know. They're finding me a locum priest to take the services here.'

'I hope he's good.'

'Good enough not to drive people away. But not so good that they don't want me back,' he said, still peering at his typewriter.

Agnes smiled at him. 'Anyway,' she said, 'I'll be there, at your bedside.'

He looked at her then. He seemed to be about to speak, then went back to his typewriter and took the piece of paper out of it. He stood up. 'I assume you're joining us for mass.' He crossed the room to the huge church cupboard that lined one wall. He opened the cupboard, then turned back to her. 'I see you've been with Athena again.'

'How can you tell?' Agnes tucked her feet under her.

'It's that shopping bag that you're trying to hide under your chair.'

'I didn't pay for it,' she said.

'Stealing, eh?'

She laughed. 'No. Although we did consider it.'

'You mean, Athena paid.'

'She's about to go to Barcelona,' Agnes said, as if in explanation.

Julius took two new candles from the cupboard. 'I hope she's not intending to stay there,' he said.

'I hope so too,' Agnes said.

He glanced across at her, suddenly serious.

'Don't say it,' Agnes said.

'I wasn't going to. Come on, I should get ready for mass.'

They went through, into the darkened church. Julius flicked the heavy light switches for the Lady Chapel. Agnes sat in a pew and watched him potter by the altar, arranging the cloth, the candles, lighting incense.

But he was, she thought. He was about to say, you can't afford to lose both of your two best friends.

The incense smoke rose softly in the columns of light. Julius moved behind the altar, preparing to repeat once more, as he had done for years, the timeless sacramental rites of their shared faith.

Behind her, the church door creaked as the first few parishioners arrived for mass.

Agnes blinked back tears, watching Julius. Without him, she thought, what would I be?

After mass, she walked back towards her flat. In her mind she saw the curls of incense smoke, the soft candlelight. She heard the words of the mass, that by Jesus's death our death is destroyed; that in rising from the dead he restores our life: the promise of eternal life in the eucharistic chalice.

For a moment, her mind held the possibility of life without Julius, life without Athena; and it was as if a door slammed shut, as if a convent cell had walled her in.

Life is nothing without love, she thought.

She reached the river. She sat on the embankment wall, under a street light. There was a mild fresh breeze, promising spring. A young couple ambled past, entwined.

I am nothing without love, she thought.

She thought about what Alasdair had said, that the poet can pass through the circles of Hell because he is saved by love. She wondered what Alasdair really thought about Laura in Paris.

She remembered she'd told him she was going to visit

Sean and Janet. She got down from the wall and left the river behind her, passing the hostel, crossing the road to Janet's flat. She could see the tattered brown curtains in the first floor window, a light on behind them.

She rang the bell marked Flat Two. She waited. A dog barked. She rang the bell again. She heard a door open, footsteps, then a rough-looking man of about forty answered the door.

'I weren't expecting no one,' he said. A cigarette stub stuck out of the corner of his mouth.

Agnes tried to speak, failed, tried again. 'Janet?' she said. 'I was looking for Janet. And Sean...'

'Gone,' he said. 'I moved in yesterday, didn't I.'

He began to shut the door.

'You don't know where they went, do you?'

He shrugged. 'Don't make it my business to know too much,' he said.

'Where did you find out about the flat?'

He took the cigarette out of his mouth and pointed it at her. 'Listen, flower, I ain't asking you no questions. You don't ask me none? OK?'

Agnes looked at him. She nodded. 'Thank you for your help,' she said, turning away. She heard the door slam behind her. She walked past the hostel, wondering whether Jeanie had been in touch, knowing that if she had, someone would have told her.

Chapter Sixteen

'They've gone,' Agnes said, into her phone. She sat on her bed, looking out of the window into the London night, hearing Alasdair's surprise.

'Who?'

'Janet. And Sean,' she said.

'Where have they gone?' Alasdair sounded annoyed.

'They've vanished. I went to the flat. There's a new tenant, since yesterday. He wasn't very forthcoming. The upshot is, there's no sign of Janet and Sean, and I've no idea where they are.'

Alasdair was silent against the background traffic rumble. 'Oh,' he said. 'Now what?'

'I don't know.' After a moment, Agnes said, 'Did you mean it when you asked me to pray for you?'

'Did you pray for me?'

'Sort of,' she said.

'I expect better than that,' he said.

'If you must know, I thought about life and loss and death, and the path we take to redemption. And I concluded that without love, it means nothing.' She watched a police van screech and flash around the corner. 'Are you still there?'

'Yes,' he said. 'I'm still here.' Another pause. 'Your priest,' he said. 'Julius, isn't it. How is he?'

'Not well. He's going into hospital next week.'

'I should have asked before. I'm sorry, I've been preoccupied.'

'That's OK,' Agnes said. 'You've got a lot on your mind.'

'Not as much as you, I imagine. If someone you care about is facing...'

'Death?'

'The possibility of death,' he said.

'Yes,' she agreed, feeling tears in the back of her throat, 'it's very hard.'

'Do you think people join religious orders so that they don't have to lose the people they love?'

'Well, if that's the plan, it doesn't work.'

'No,' Alasdair said. 'I can see that.'

'And even out in the world...' she began.

'The fact is,' he said, 'just to love is to know loss. Dante in real life loved Beatrice for years, but she married someone else and died young.'

'And you?' Agnes said.

There was a silence. 'Me?' he said. 'I'm the one who should join a religious order, I think.'

'It's not an escape,' Agnes said.

'Then there's no hope for me,' he said. When he next spoke, his voice was abrupt. 'I'll see you tomorrow,' he said. 'At Braybrook's club.'

'Yes, of course. What time?'

'10:30, he said, he's going back to the country after that.'

'I thought he lived at his club.'

'So did I, but it seems he has a wife somewhere. Suffolk, I think he said.'

They rang off, and she switched off her phone. She went to her kitchen and poured a large whisky and twisted ice into it. She sat in the the chair by the window, twirling her glass, watching the golden flecks of light across her desk.

She thought about how Alasdair didn't drink. She thought about what he'd just said, that if you avoid love then you escape the possibility of loss. She remembered what he'd said before, about drinking too much; about loving life too much.

She sipped her drink and thought about the hostel residents, and wondered when a glass of whisky ceased to be a pleasure, ceased to be the waters of life, and became instead the entrance gate to the road to Hell.

She drained her glass and went to bed.

Shafts of sunlight spilled through the revolving door of the club, as Major Braybrook greeted them in the grand hallway. He held a cigar between two fingers. 'Yes, yes,' he said. 'Been thinking, you know. Had a bit of a drink last night, with this fellow from the barracks twenty years ago. He reminded me of a few goings on there, thought you ought to know, may shed some light on all this business, yes, yes...' He led them into the lounge, which was almost deserted. An elderly gentleman sat in the far corner, struggling with a large and chaotic heap of newspaper. There was a sofa and some armchairs by the bay window, and the Major settled them all there.

'Thing is,' he went on, 'bullying in the barracks.' He lowered himself into an armchair with a heavy sigh. 'Wouldn't have thought of it myself, get used to this kind of thing, young men left to themselves, you know how it is.' He paused to relight his cigar. 'But the Colonel reminded me, at the time those boys started their training, bit of nastiness at the barracks. Someone found dead with gunshot wounds, only a young lad. Suicide, they said, and I'm sure they were right, but as old Jackson said to me last night, you have to ask yourself, what leads a kid like that to do it? And then I fell to thinking, about the way it was in those barracks, and the things that McFadden wrote in his diary that you showed me.' He blinked at them. 'We in the forces, we have a responsibility to our young men. And sometimes, I feel that we let them down. Too often, we let them down.'

Outside, St James' Park was green and sunny. Women walked with pushchairs, fathers laughed.

'Was Andy involved with bullying, do you think?' Alasdair leaned an elbow on the arm of his chair.

'Was it connected with someone called Billy Lee?' Agnes added.

Major Braybrook drew heavily on his cigar, breathed out.

'I don't know the chap's name. But, Jackson led me to believe that it was about a relationship. This chap Lucky, in the jottings you showed me... Jackson seemed to think he was, involved, shall we say, with another lad. Yes,' he added. 'Billy. Rings a bell, must say.' He puffed on his cigar. 'It's what they call a culture, isn't it, a culture of bullying. And I imagine, from what I know of chaps in the barracks, that two of them being closer than what one might call natural...' He paused, glanced at Alasdair, then went on, 'it might cause trouble. From the sound of it, one of them was driven to suicide. And it was a Scottish regiment, sometimes these divisions get rather tribal...' He sighed, breathing out blue smoke. 'That's really all I can tell you. May not be any help at all. It's all so long ago, you see. I just thought it was worth mentioning, that's all.' He brought out a pocket watch on a chain and peered at it, then put it away. 'Promised the wife I'd catch the 11:40, I'd better step on it.'

In the hallway of the club they shook his hand. The mahogany banisters shone with polish with the morning light.

'I'm afraid I've been no help at all,' the Major said. 'Too long ago. And rather shrouded in secrecy these things, at the best of times.'

'It was nice of you to spare the time,' Alasdair said.

'And anyway...' The Major led them towards the doors. 'What good does it do to pursue these things? Some of the bravest men I've ever met have died when it wasn't their turn to die. At the time, one wants to shake one's fist at the heavens, demand that whoever it is up there takes a bit more care in how he organises things down here. And then you think, how else could it be? We seem to be destined to get it wrong, time after time. Each war ends with the promise of peace. And each war leaves scars which makes peace impossible. A world without wars is a world without mankind.' He gazed out beyond them into the park. 'Do let me know how you get on.' He shook their hands, and turned back across the marble floor. The revolving door flashed brass and sunlight, and then they were outside, descending the stone steps, crossing the green lawns of the park. Alasdair lit a cigarette.

They walked in silence. Agnes watched a group of children throwing a stick for their cocker spaniel. The stick was retrieved, and thrown again. No one seemed to tire of it.

'But would someone come back, all those years later?' she said.

'Sorry?' Alasdair turned away from watching the dog and the stick and the children.

'Whatever happened at the barracks when they were new recruits, would it affect them now? Even if Lucky was part of it, even if Andy felt strongly about it, which he did, you can tell from the writings, would someone have sought him out now, after so many years?'

Alasdair's gaze had returned to the dog. 'I doubt it,' he said.

'If only we could ask Sean. He was there, wasn't he?'

'Yes.'

'They must still be in London.'

Alasdair breathed in his cigarette. 'They might have gone back to Scotland.' He began to walk again.

Agnes fell into step beside him. 'If you were Janet, would you just run away? Surely she wants to know the truth about Gordon's death?'

Alasdair shrugged. 'Perhaps she'll get in touch with you.'

'When you heard about Andy's death, you needed to know, didn't you?'

He took a long drag on his cigarette. 'I did, yes.'

She glanced at him. 'You mean, you're not so sure now?'

He paused, mid-step. 'All I mean is, it won't bring him back.' He turned off the path, towards the main road, and Agnes followed him.

'You heard what Braybrook said, about the futility of searching the past,' Alasdair said. He turned to face her. 'He's right. He has the wisdom of someone who knows that if you search the past for reasons for war, you just find more war. It's the history of humankind.'

'Mankind,' Agnes said, tight-lipped.

'Oh, you think so?' Alasdair stood in the sunlight, his cigarette making curls of smoke across his face. 'You think if it was up to women there would be no wars?' He began to walk again. 'Women don't need to wage war. They don't need to avenge their dead sons, because they have men to do it for them.'

They walked on in silence, until they reached the Mall. He stopped, as if making a decision. 'I've reached the limits of what I can do,' he said.

'What do you mean?' Agnes stared up at him.

'Braybrook has clarified something I've been thinking for some time. What truth am I searching for? Even if I find out about Andy's death, it won't bring him back.'

'But – ' Agnes reached her fingers towards his sleeve, then withdrew them. 'I can't do this without you,' she said.

He looked down at her. He smiled a brief smile. 'You don't have to. You can just go back to your ordinary life, your work at the hostel.'

'But Andy was in our care – '

'That doesn't make you responsible.' They crossed the Mall, into Carlton House Terrace. He set off up the steps towards Charing Cross. They came out on to Pall Mall, into the sunlight and the Sunday traffic.

He stood before her. The wind ruffled his hair. He shrugged. 'Bye, then.' He seemed to be about to go, then faced her again. 'You should just sign that letter. The one from the order, about your house. It will be a resolution.' He squeezed her arm. 'I'll be in touch.'

'It's that woman, isn't it?' Agnes was aware that her voice was loud; people turned to stare.

He turned back to her. 'Which woman?'

'The Italian. The one who lives in France.'

'What about her?' he said.

'Something has made you change your mind. About all this.'

'It's got nothing to do with her,' he said.

'What's happened?'

He sighed. 'She wrote to me. From Paris.'

'And?'

'I'm afraid I really don't want to talk about it.'

Agnes looked at him. Again, the shutters, the veiled detachment. 'You're right,' she said. 'It's none of my business.' She turned away from him, just as he said, 'She's very unhappy.'

Agnes faced him, in the jostling crowd.

'She's been unhappy for years,' Alasdair went on. 'She thought of writing to me before, but she was frightened to disturb things, as she put it. And now she says she's more frightened that things might stay the same, so she's prepared to take the risk.'

'What are you going to do?'

He looked away from her, back towards the park, the distant treetops. 'I don't know,' he said. He watched the branches sway. 'Years ago, it was my greatest hope, that she would want me after all.' He turned back to Agnes. 'But now...'

'You'll go and see her.' It was a statement of fact.

He looked at her. 'Yes. I will.'

'And I will sign my house over to the order.'

He almost smiled. 'Will you?'

'What else can I do?'

'What else can either of us do?' He bent and briefly kissed her cheek. 'I'll phone you,' he said. Then he'd gone, merging with the crowd, disappearing towards Haymarket.

She went straight to the hostel. There was no news of Jeanie. She picked up the phone and dialled Sheila's number.

'I wish I could say we've made some progress,' Sheila said.

'No sightings of her?'

'Nothing.'

'Did you have a contact number for Janet, Gordon's wife?' Agnes asked.

'It'll be in the file – shall I get back to you?'

'She's vanished from the flat they were staying in. They've all gone.'

'I'll phone you back.'

She sat, holding the phone, and then dialled Haz's mobile number. It rang and rang, and then she heard his voice.

'It's Sister Agnes,' she said.

'Oh. Hi. How's things?'

'OK. I wanted to ask you about when you were recruits in the army.'

'Sure. Long time ago, though.'

'Alasdair and I met Major Braybrook. He was from your regiment. He said, in the barracks where you trained, there was a bullying problem. Someone died. Lucky was very upset.'

'Yeah. I remember. Trouble, man.'

'There was someone called Billy Lee. He was involved with Lucky.'

There was a silence on the end of the phone. Then Haz said, 'I remember. Billy Lee was the guy who killed himself. And then Lucky left after that. Bloody hell, I had no idea.' She heard him breathing. 'It kind of explains things,' he said. 'Lucky was in a hell of a state when he left, you know. And when he had the accident, some of us wondered about it. We thought maybe he'd been drinking or something. Still,' he said, 'it can't be connected, can it? I mean, what happened to Andy, all these years later, it's not going to be about something that happened when we were all kids.'

'Who else was in the barracks then?'

Haz was quiet, thinking.

'It was a Scottish regiment.'

'Yeah, there was us lot, but there were the lads that Andy knew from before.'

'Iain,' Agnes said. 'And Sean – '

'Sean. He was great, he was. He rescued me once, we were on an exercise, crossing a river, water up to our waists, we'd been marching since the day before. And I'd had it. It happened to people, you'd kind of seize up. You'd start crying and that. And Sean had crossed the river, and he looked back and saw me, standing there, frozen, crying. And he waded all the way back out again, and talked me through it. One step at a time. It felt like days. I never forgot that, you know.'

He was silent at the other end of the phone.

'If when Billy died,' Agnes began. 'And Lucky left after that...

would Andy have held a grudge of some kind? Or would someone have had a grudge against him? There's a lot in the writings about revenge.'

'Revenge? Andy was always going on about revenge. Blokes who'd picked a fight with him, blokes who'd looked at him the wrong way, blokes who'd driven too close when he was on his bike. He hated authority, don't know how he lasted in the army. But you see, his dad died when he was a kid, and he idolised him, it's like no one else could ever measure up. His stepdad worst of all, he talked about him like he was the very devil. He fell out of a window, his stepdad, wouldn't be surprised if Andy had pushed him himself. But one of the lads said that to him one day and he really went into one, one of his rages. So we didn't mention it after that.' Agnes could hear voices in the background. 'Yeah, yeah, OK, I'll be right there. Got to go,' he said.

'Who do you think killed Andy?' Agnes said.

'Maybe it was Mitch. Maybe it wasn't. Scott reckons it wasn't, he said he's talked to a copper about the way Andy died, and he said you couldn't get that sort of injury with a broken bottle.'

'Why does Scott need to know?'

'He needs to know everything. It'll be about money, he'll think there's some connection between Andy and Trina which will benefit him. He wouldn't be bothering otherwise. I'm sorry, I've got to go into a meeting. Later, OK? Nice to talk to you.'

He rang off. Almost at once her phone rang. It was Sheila.

'I only have the address you've tried. And a mobile number, but it seems to be Gordon's. It was stolen in the attack. The number's void, we've tried it. Sorry.'

'Why would Janet have vanished after such a tragedy?'

'It seems odd,' Sheila said. 'It's much more normal to hang about obsessively. She's bound to contact us soon, I'd say.'

'Yes. I suppose so.'

'Keep in touch.' Sheila rang off.

Dan came into the office clutching a large mug of coffee, and collapsed into a chair. 'It would be nice sometimes just to lock the door,' he said. 'We could just sit in here, drinking coffee, reading the papers.'

Agnes smiled at him.

'You might as well go,' he said. 'Petra and I are both on tonight.'

'I'm just worried that if I go – '

'You might miss something exciting?'

She laughed. 'Not exactly.'

'I know what you mean,' he said, serious again. 'But you might as well get some rest.'

'I won't be around much in the next few days,' she said. 'Father Julius is going into hospital – '

'Julius? Is he OK?'

'Yes. I expect so.' She tried to keep her voice light. 'I just won't be so available for a while.'

'Sure. That's fine.'

She got up, and picked up her coat. 'Phone me if there's any news from Sheila.'

She walked back to her flat. The afternoon had clouded over. She thought about going to mass, then realised it wouldn't be Julius. She wondered what sort of replacement they'd found for him, and how long Julius would be off work.

She let herself into her flat, switched on lights and heating, turned on the oven, opened her freezer, took out a pizza. She went to her fridge and found a bottle of white wine still half full. She poured herself a glass and went into her living room and flung herself into the armchair. She reached for the phone and dialled Julius's number.

'Hello,' he said.

'It's Agnes.'

'How lovely,' he said. 'I feared you were a tetchy parishioner.'

'I could be tetchy if you like.'

'I know.'

She smiled into the phone. 'Julius, I've been thinking. It's Sunday now, you're going in on Tuesday, we've got lots to do.'

'We have?'

'You know what hospitals are like these days. I've cleared my work schedule so that I can bring you food – '

'Agnes – '

'And these days the wards are so short-staffed you need an advocate just to get basic care –

'But Agnes – '

'So I thought I'd base myself there, catch up on some reading – '

'But I don't want you to.'

She looked at her phone, then put it back to her ear. 'What do you mean?' she said.

'I don't want anyone there,' he said.

They were both silent for a moment.

'I'm sorry,' he said.

'But surely you need – '

'No. I've never had a general anaesthetic in my life. I'm absolutely terrified. And when I come round it's even worse, so they say. Pain from the wound, and my guts won't be working, days on a drip... I'm going into the dark spaces of Hell, and I hope to come out again, but it's something I have to do alone.'

'But on Tuesday I can bring your things in for you – '

'No. It's very sweet of you, but no. By the end of the week I might be off the drip, you can come and see me then.'

'But Julius...' Agnes felt the tears coming.

'I appreciate it, of course – '

'I need to be there.' The words seemed to burst from her.

'And I need to be alone.' She could hear his quiet determination. There was another silence, then he said,

'Every night these last few days, I've woken up at five past three. I don't know why. I go from deep sleep to wide awake, and I look at my clock, and it says, 3:05. And it's as if he's there, the Grim Reaper, sitting on the end of my bed. Waiting.' She heard him breathe, then he spoke again. 'And all I can think is that they're going to put me under, and send me into some hazy underworld where I'm going to meet him face to face. You see, I'm scared. Terrified. And the worst thing is, that at three in the morning Our Lord is powerless in the face of my terror.'

After a moment, she said, 'But isn't that exactly why you need a friend?'

'You don't understand. For fifty odd years, I've talked about the Christian message of eternal life. I've used the phrase as if I knew what it meant. I thought I did know. I believed that beyond this earthly life, beyond the simple truth that we will, of course, all die, there is still some kind of light, or love, that lasts, that endures into infinity. And at three in the morning, I am defeated by the knowledge that all this will come to an end. That the self that I am, that has had such a wonderful bloody time living this life, will come to a full stop. And I think about our Lord, who seems very far away just now; and I look at the hooded figure sitting at the end of my bed. And the hooded figure sits there patiently. And he looks back at me. And he just shrugs.' His voice at the other end of the phone sounded very far away. 'I'm on my own with this,' he said.

Agnes blinked back tears.

'You could come and see me tomorrow,' he said. 'I'll be in the office, clearing my desk.'

'Do you want me to?'

'Yes,' he said. 'Yes. I'd like that.'

She hung up. She buried her face in her hands and let the tears come.

O Lord, she began, but there were no words. Instead, an image, of Mary the Mother of God, at the foot of the cross.

Is that how we all die? she thought. On our own, at a distance from those that love us, with no one there to see us out of this life and into the next?

She lifted her head and dried her face. She drained her glass of wine and went into the kitchen. She saw the pizza sitting on the shelf. She picked it up, put it down again. She refilled her glass.

Another image, this time of a dark-haired woman singing a lullaby, the paving stones around her wet with blood.

We don't always die alone, she thought.

And anyway, she thought, standing in the bright light of her kitchen, he's not going to die. Silly old Julius. He's going to be OK. In a month I'll go to see him in his office and he'll be bashing away at that stupid typewriter as if nothing has happened.

She unwrapped the pizza and put it in the oven.

Chapter Seventeen

'There are people you hate. Certain NCOs in my battalion I could mention, you hate them and they hate you. Even in war. The rules don't change. I remember one night, all we heard was a plane, low overhead, and there was this sergeant who'd always had it in for me, and he hits the mud, throws himself on the ground, shaking. And I laughed. Even though I was shaking just as much as he was...

'I still shake even now. Fireworks. Cars back-firing. You're on a knife edge, you can be set off by someone jostling you in the street, nothing at all. It doesn't go away, see? I've met the old boys from the second world war, and they're still living with it. But, what I think is, life has to go on. I owe it to the blokes that died there, and to the others, those Argie boys...

'Sometimes when a plane goes overhead and I find myself shaking and I think about that sergeant who hated me and I think, wherever he is, I bet he's shaking too.'

Agnes turned a page. The name Lucky caught her eye.

'...They say that three's an unlucky number, but me and Lucky and Billy Lee, we were all right. Until Billy Lee died, and Lucky left the barracks. Then it was just me. Three was lucky for me. Two would have been lucky, if I'd married the only girl I loved. My unlucky number turned out to be the number one.'

Agnes turned the page. The other side was blank. She noticed a pencil mark across the writings. Someone had tried to cross out the words 'the only girl I loved.' She wondered if it was Janet.It was Monday morning. Outside the streets were steely with rain. She went into the kitchen to make some coffee. She stood by her sink, listening to the rain against the window, the kettle's stirring.

Perhaps Alasdair's right, she thought. Perhaps we've come to the end.

It's a pretty silly end, she thought. Dante's quest ends with the Truth, with Enlightenment, even with the hope of union with God himself. How strange that Alasdair should settle for so much less.

We're always drawn to the thing we can't do, he'd said, the gap we must cross.

She thought about the sheets of paper she'd just put down on her desk, Andy's writings. For all these weeks she'd been studying them in the belief that they would shed some kind of light on Andy's death, that under their chaotic scribble she would find order and reason; and explanation.

She spooned coffee into the cafetiere. She thought about Julius, with the grim reaper sitting waiting on the end of his bed.

People die, she thought. Quite randomly. Random collections of cells, randomly growing. Random accidents. Random acts of violence.

I thought that in Andy's notes I would find the truth, if only I knew how to look for it. And now it turns out that his writings might be, after all, just the angry, sorrowful ramblings of a terribly damaged man.

The kettle boiled and she poured water into the cafetiere.

Tomorrow Julius goes into hospital, she thought. She glanced up at the window. Skeletal black branches threw raindrops at the glass.

She went back to her desk with a mug of coffee, just as the phone rang.

'Hi, it's Dan. We've got a friend of yours here. Trina. She's in a bad way, she's asking for you – '

'When you say bad way?'

'She won't explain. But, you know – '

'Black eyes? Torn hair?'

'Exactly.'

'I'll be right there.'

Trina was hunched in the office armchair, a mug of coffee clutched between her fingers. She looked up as Agnes came into the room. Agnes took in the wrecked hair and swollen face, the tears that welled as she saw herself through Agnes's eyes.

'Bloody hell, Trina.' Agnes went to her, crouched down by the chair and took her hands.

Trina shook her head. She muttered something about Scott.

'What did you say?' Agnes leaned towards her.

It was barely audible, but Trina seemed to be saying, 'He didn't mean it.'

'He didn't mean it?' Agnes echoed. Trina nodded. Agnes stood up and found one of the office chairs and brought it close. 'You mean, usually when he hits you, it's in places which no one will see?'

Trina appeared not to hear. 'He was cross about Eileen's will,' Trina said, not lifting her head.

Agnes frowned at her. 'What do you mean?' she said.

'He said I wasn't helping, he knows that now Andy has gone there's money owing to me...' She winced, and put one hand up to the side of her face.

'You ought to see a doctor,' Agnes said. Trina flashed Agnes a look. 'No,' she said.

Agnes went to the sink in the corner of the room, found a clean tea-towel, soaked it under the cold tap and squeezed it out. She brought it to Trina, who held it against her face.

'Is that better?' Agnes murmured, and Trina nodded.

'I shouldn't have come here,' Trina said. 'He'll be livid if he thinks I've told you.'

'You can't go back there,' Agnes said.

'What else can I do?'

'Does he know you're here?'

Trina shook her head. 'Afterwards...' she winced. 'After the row, I mean – he went out. He thinks I'm still there, probably.'

'Then you can stay here, can't you.' Agnes did a quick calculation about bedspaces.

'He's right, really,' Trina said. 'He's only thinking of me. Like he says, it'd be stupid if there's money sitting there with them lawyers and I didn't claim what was mine.'

She spoke in a blank, empty tone, and Agnes glanced across at her.

'So he's only thinking of you when he gives you a black eye, then?' Agnes said.

'It's not like him,' Trina said. 'He was upset. It'll be different when I get home. He'll pour me a gin, that's his way of saying sorry, and he'll ask me what I want for tea, and he'll phone the pizza place and order my favourite, that one with the anchovies.'

'You can't go back.' Agnes tried to keep her voice steady, but in her mind she was twenty again and married to Hugo. She saw the kitchen floor of the house in France, the old stone floor, so cool against her cheek – lying there with her eyes closed, trying to keep still, thinking that perhaps if Hugo thought she was dead he wouldn't hit her any more; thinking that it was all her fault.

'It's not your fault,' Agnes said. She felt the tears come.

'But I shouldn't have kept it from him – ' Trina said.

'It's not your fault.' Agnes almost shouted, and Trina looked up at her, startled to see that Agnes was crying.

Agnes found a handkerchief, dabbed her eyes. 'I always blamed myself,' Agnes said. 'You do, don't you, if it goes on long enough? Over the months, the years, you start to believe it must be your fault, because that's what he's telling you. My ex-husband always chose a moment when I'd burnt the steak or broken a plate...' She dried her eyes, feeling the images fade, wondering once again at the power those memories possessed to catch her off-balance even after all these years.

'Your ex-husband...?'

'He never got caught out like Scott. I never once appeared in public looking like a battered wife. Long sleeves, of course, high necks, otherwise the marks would have shown.'

Trina pulled at her black polo-neck jumper. 'I'm not a battered wife,' she said.

'No,' Agnes agreed. 'Of course you're not. None of us are. There's always a reason. If we hadn't broke that plate... or if we'd told him what he wanted to know...' Agnes stopped. Something about this story, about the will...

'He's only thinking of me,' Trina said, but her voice carried less conviction now.

'Yes. My husband cared about me, too. He cared so much he almost killed me.'

Trina opened her mouth, closed it again. She stared at Agnes for a moment. 'But I don't want to be a nun,' she said, suddenly plaintive.

Agnes leaned across and took her hand. 'You don't have to be. It's not a path I'd recommend, to go from violent husband to convent cell.' She thought of the acceptance form she'd filled in for the order, lying on her desk, ready to be posted. 'All you have to do,' she went on, 'is stay here for a day or two. And have a think. And then if it turns out that Scott really is the man for you, you can go back to him, can't you. And no harm will be done.'

Trina's eyes widened in panic. 'But he won't know where I am, he'll kill me—'

Agnes looked at her. Trina lowered her gaze, stared at her lap.

They were sitting like that, Agnes with her hand on Trina's, when Dan put his head round the door.

Agnes looked up at him. 'Dan, is Aberdeen Bob's room still free?'

Dan looked at Trina, then back at Agnes. 'But—' he began.

'Just for a night,' Agnes said. 'Trina needs to stay here, don't you,' she said.

Trina nodded, hunched in the chair.

'I'll ask Mary to make up the bed,' Dan said.

Agnes left Trina with Mary, then went back to the office. She put in a call to Sheila, who was off duty, and left her a message to say she'd phoned.

She left the hostel and went home, buying a sandwich on the way.

She settled at her desk at home, and took out Andy's writings again. She stared at them for a while, thinking about Trina. This story about the will, she thought. None of it made sense. Scott could easily find out about the will without Trina's help. Why would Scott dish out that sort of violence, for something so minor?

She picked the tomatoes out of her sandwich and put them carefully on the side of the plate, then unfolded a page of the writings.

'Yesterday my counsellor asked me, what do I want? I said, what do you mean, mate? I want not to feel like this any more. I want no more fucking nightmares. He said, for your future. What do you want? I said, I want to go back. I want to go back to war. Then he said, why do you think you feel that way? And I said, because I didn't die. I waited for him to go on about survivor's guilt, like the bloke they sent me to before, but he didn't. He just sat there. After a while we both just looked out of the window and thought about the dead, and what it's like to stumble out of a dark and shuddering field seeing only blood, hearing only screams...'

Agnes thought about what Alasdair had said, about the wrathful in Dante's Hell, submerged in mud, rejecting pity, refusing to accept their guilt.

Guilt, Agnes thought. Andy McFadden lived with guilt.

That's what was wrong with Trina earlier. For Trina to get a beating like that, it must have been something more, something much more important, something that Trina was very reluctant to tell him. She put down the writings. She remembered Trina mentioning Jim's accident. She remembered Alasdair's reluctance to talk about his father's death.

She got up, pulled on her coat and went out. It had come on to rain. She walked fast, arriving at the hostel damp and out of breath. She went into the office, and found Mary sitting at the desk.

'How's Trina?' she asked her.

Mary looked up. 'As well as you'd expect,' she said. 'She's in the kitchen with Archie.'

Agnes hung up her coat and went out to the kitchen.

'... And then there was the Derby, in '82, I got the first three winners on the Tote,' she could hear Trina saying. Agnes appeared in the doorway.

'... and everyone said it was fluke, but it wasn't, because the next National, I got the winner, only it was each-way and I'd only put a fiver on him – hello,' Trina said, looking up at Agnes. She was sitting with her feet up on one of the chairs, and Archie was sitting opposite her. He had taken off his glasses and was polishing them on his sleeve.

'Tea, anyone?' Agnes went to put on the kettle.

'I'm tea-d out, me,' Trina said. 'It's all anyone does here, isn't it, drink tea? I suppose if you're all off the sauce, what else is there?'

'Smoking,' Archie said, putting his glasses back on and standing up. He bent and shook Trina's hand. 'It was a pleasure talking to you,' he said. 'I've got a meeting to go to.' He nodded at Agnes, then left the room.

Agnes sat down with her mug of tea.

Trina looked at her. 'It's nice here,' she said. 'Shame I can't stay.'

'You can stay as long as you need to,' Agnes said.

Trina shook her head. 'You know that isn't true,' she said. 'I've got to go back to him. I always talk of leaving, I was telling Mary about it, she's nice, isn't she, she told me about her chap who died, very sad isn't it... but how can I leave Scott?'

'Very easily, I would have thought.'

Trina met her gaze. 'You never left, did you? From what you were saying, you didn't leave until you was nearly dead and they had to carry you out.'

Agnes stared at her mug. 'Trina,' she said, after a moment, 'if you go back, he'll hit you again. Unless you tell him what he needs to know.'

Trina drew a circle on the table with her fingertip.

'And,' Agnes went on, 'it seems to me you don't want him to know about how Jim Brogan died.'

Trina's finger continued to follow its path.

'Is it money?' Agnes said. 'Does he think that knowing about Jim's so-called accident will benefit him in some way?'

Trina bit her lip, still tracing circles.

'Was it Andy who told you?' Agnes tried.

Trina's finger came to a halt. At last she spoke. 'Walker told me, yes. Once, when we was together, when we were... lovers, you know... I was asking him about Alasdair, because there was always trouble there, they were kind of close, like brothers, but edgy with each other too. And he said that Jim Brogan was murdered, and it was Alasdair who did it. And that's all I know, and I'm not having Scott getting the money off Alasdair that way, it would be blackmail, wouldn't it? And anyway, I didn't know no more than that, and he can hit me all he likes but I can't tell him more than I know, can I?'

'Jim fell out of a sixth floor window.'

'Seventh,' Trina said.

'Did Alasdair push him?'

'I don't know. Andy said there was a fight of some kind in the flat on that estate in Scotland, both the boys were there and Jim was drunk, and then he fell out of the window.'

'And he died of his injuries,' Agnes said.

'He lingered, he did. But he never spoke again. And then he died. That's what Eileen told me anyway.'

'Did she suspect anything about his death, do you think?'

Trina looked up at her, then looked away. 'Once she said something about having to get out of there, get away from the estate, because of the whispering, she said.' She shrugged. 'You can know something and not know it at the same time, can't you.'

'Yes, I suppose you can.' Agnes sipped her tea.

'Mary was telling me about the girl who's gone missing.'

'Was she?'

'Yeah. About some bloke she's frightened of, and that's why she's run away. She really cares, doesn't she, Mary?'

Agnes turned her mug around in her hands. 'Yes,' she said. 'They all do, the people who work here.'

'My Scott could do with coming here. That would make him think about his drinking, wouldn't it?' She laughed.

'And then you could go home and stay there in peace.'

'I'd love that, I would,' Trina said, but then her smile died. 'It'll never happen, though. He'd never let that happen. Do you know,

Mary said a strange thing. She said, if a man hits you, it's only because he knows he can. She said some women will go through life and no man will ever lay a finger on them. And then she said I had to change my destiny.'

Agnes looked at her. 'How odd.'

'What makes me laugh, though, is that she said you were someone who a bloke would never hit.'

'Me?'

'Yeah. She said "like Agnes".'

Agnes smiled. 'Perhaps I changed my destiny,' she said.

Walking back to her flat, she thought about Alasdair.

It would explain why he'd always been so wary of Trina, she thought. It would explain his sudden veiling of himself, his ability to hide.

And yet... in what sense could it possibly be the case that he killed his own father, however awful Jim was?

And if it were true, how much was Andy involved? Did he help Alasdair to cover it up? Is that why they were so complicit as teenagers, when they hardly knew each other?

And how much did she trust Trina's account of anything, she wondered, taking out her keys as she reached her block of flats.

She wondered whether she should phone Alasdair; wondering what she'd say if she did. The answering machine was flashing, and she pressed Play.

'It's, um, Julius. About four o'clock. I'm kind of – sitting here. Wondering if you're going to come over, because I've finished. Everything. Perhaps you could, um, phone me?'

She dialled his number.

'I thought perhaps I'd offended you,' he said.

'No,' she said. 'We're beyond that, aren't we?'

'I hope so.' There was a pause. 'Do you want to, um, have a cup of tea, maybe? Here?' he said.

'Now?'

'Only if you're not busy.'

'No,' she said, 'I'm not busy.'

On the way she stopped at the new patisserie in Borough Market and bought two slices of chocolate mousse cake. She arrived, breathless and windswept, opening the door of Julius's office, seeing him sitting at his desk as if nothing was wrong.

'I wasn't sure you could eat these,' she said, unwrapping the exquisite white box with the lemon yellow ribbon.

'Isn't that the funniest thing?' Julius said. 'Since my diagnosis, I seem to be able to eat whatever I like. I've just developed lots of new symptoms instead. None of it makes sense,' he said. 'I've always looked for meanings, for some kind of structure in this life called Father Julius. And it turns out there is none. I've made the tea,' he added.

Agnes poured two mugs of tea and put the cake on a plate each, with a fork.

They sat in silence, eating cake. 'I didn't know I had forks,' Julius said, after a while.

'You need a fork with a soft cake like this,' Agnes said, as her eyes filled with tears.

'I'll be all right,' he said.

'Of course you will,' she said, but the tears still fell.

'It's a gamble,' he said. 'It always has been. In the old days, when I thought I'd live for ever, it was a different kind of risk. Fox-hunting in Ireland, flinging yourself at fences without a thought in your head that anything might go wrong. Now it's just me and the Grim Reaper, playing dice in the small hours. But he's very polite, he is. A gracious winner, you might say.'

'He might turn out to be a good loser,' Agnes said, dabbing at her eyes with a handkerchief.

Julius shook his head. 'He's always going to win in the end, isn't he? I suppose that's why he can afford to be so polite now.'

She glanced up at him. I can't bear it, she wanted to say. She noticed a smear of chocolate just under his bottom lip. She leaned over and dabbed at it with her finger. He caught hold of her hand and held it against his cheek.

They sat there like that, as the daylight in the little leaded window above them faded and thickened with the dusk.

He released her hand and picked up a piece of paper. He wrote down a name and a phone number. 'That's the ward in the hospital. It's named after some famous Englishwoman I've never heard of.'

Agnes read it. 'No,' she said. 'Me too. But then, you're Irish and I'm French, it's not surprising. Foreigners both of us. And Athena too.'

'And yet Londoners through and through. All three of us.'

Agnes smiled at him, resisting the urge to ruffle his soft white hair.

'I go in in the morning,' he said. 'I'm nil by mouth all day. It'll be early Wednesday morning that they...' His voice tailed off.

It will be all right, she wanted to say. Julius, it will be all right.

He leaned across and kissed her cheek. 'It'll be all right,' he said. 'Come on, I'll walk you home.'

He'd said goodbye at the gateway to her block.

'Thursday, or so,' he'd said. 'You can phone to find out how I am. If you're at all interested.'

'I'll pray for you,' she said. 'Unless you don't...'

He'd smiled. 'I need all the help I can get,' he'd said.

He'd held her then, and she'd clung to him, and then he'd gone, walking away from her back to the main road, his footsteps fading into the traffic's roar.

Now she stumbled into her flat, in the dark. She paced the tiny space, muttering, crying, in her mind a woman's voice, singing a baby to sleep; singing a grown man out of this world and into the next.

She stopped still in the middle of the room.

Singing a baby to sleep.

She went to her desk, switched on the lamp, flung herself into the chair, leafed through the biro scrawl and the shabby scraps of paper.

'...the only girl I loved,' she read, through the pencil scratchings that had tried to cross it out.

She opened the copy of the *Purgatorio* that Alasdair had given her.

'...I had come so far within the ancient wood that I could no longer see the place where I had entered. There appeared to me a lady, all on her own, singing and picking flowers...'

A lady, all alone, singing.

Agnes thought about Julius, on the brink of his own descent into Hell. She thought about Andy, emerging from the blood-soaked fields of war, but in his mind still living in the inferno.

The churches of the city were chiming six o'clock. Agnes lit a candle and turned the pages of her prayer book.

'Lord let me know my end, and the number of my days;

So that I may know how short my life is.

We walk about like a shadow, and in vain we are in turmoil; we heap up riches and cannot tell who will gather them.

And now, what is my hope?

O Lord, my hope is in you.'

Agnes thought about Julius playing cards with death. She imagined the hooded figure, flitting through the dark London streets where Andy had met his death, lurking by the window at Jim's drunken fall, standing by the tree as Jeanie's boyfriend hurled his car into it.

And when it comes to it, we will all pick up our cards and play. Even those, like Chris, who play to lose.

Agnes stood up and put out the candle.

'...The storm will quieten with the daybreak,

The waves' roar will be a whisper when you awake...'

O Lord, my hope is in you, she thought.

The thinnest, most fragile hope, she thought. But hope all the same.

Chapter Eighteen

'I'd like to book a sleeper train to Glasgow, tonight, please.' Agnes tucked the phone under her chin. 'Sorry? No, of course I don't want to share a cabin... How much? That's fine. Yes... OK. 11:45. Euston. OK– An hour before? OK. Thanks. Goodbye.'

She rang off. She wrote "11.45 pm" on a scrap of paper. She took a large swig of coffee, then picked up the phone again. She was half-way through dialling Alasdair's number when she stopped. She put the phone down.

She went into the kitchen, which was bright with morning sunlight. She buttered a piece of toast and brought it back to her desk. She drew out her carefully written letter addressed to her French lawyers that she'd printed off on the computer at the hostel. "Messieurs", it said: "With regard to the property I own in Provence..." It went on to say that in a few weeks she would be taking final vows, and that she wished the property to be given to the order. She was enclosing the appropriate forms, duly filled in, and awaited their response... Yours, etc.

A description of the house was enclosed. Six bedrooms, acres of grounds including orchard; stable block and paddock.

It's not as if I was ever happy there, she thought. A solitary only child of eccentric and ill-matched parents, whose marriage drifted from disappointment to bitterness to eventual separation.

The smell of lavender across the valley; the heat rising from the red tiled roof; burying her face in her pony's neck.

It's past, she thought. It was over long ago; years ago.

She signed the forms and the letter and folded it all into a large envelope, which she addressed to her lawyer in Paris.

She picked up the phone and dialled Alasdair.

'It's Agnes,' she said.

'Hello,' he said.

There was a pause, before she said, 'I've been talking to Trina.'

'Poor old you.'

'She told me about your father. About how he died.'

The line crackled in the silence. 'She has all sorts of interesting theories about that,' Alasdair said at last. 'I hope you found them amusing.'

'I wouldn't say amusing – '

'Shakespearean, even. The patricide of Hamlet, the dysfunctional siblings of King Lear...'

'Are you going to tell me what happened, Alasdair?'

'Would you believe me if I did?'

She was silent.

Alasdair went on, 'Trina was in love with Andy. He never loved her. He always loved Gemma. Trina's always blamed me for that, for some reason, but he was a man who knew his own mind. Until it got screwed up by going into battle.'

'I'm going to Scotland,' Agnes said. 'Tonight.'

'Whatever for?'

'I'm not sure,' she said.

'Isn't your friend Julius in hospital?'

Agnes tried to keep her voice steady. 'He doesn't want me there.'

'Just him and God, eh?'

'I think it may be just him on his own.'

'Dark night of the soul and all that.'

'Please don't laugh about it,' she said, hearing her voice tremble.

'I wasn't laughing.'

The conversation seemed to have come to an end. After a moment, he said 'Agnes?'

'Yes?'

'I'm very grateful to you,' he said. 'I'm grateful for the way you believed, the way you became my guide through it all.'

'But – '

'Not just Andy.' She heard him breathing. 'I'm – I'm going to Paris,' he said. 'I'm going to see Laura.'

'When?'

'This afternoon.'

'Oh.' Agnes couldn't think of anything to say.

'Do you remember what you said about loving the rose. Taking the risk to love something for what it is, even though it won't last?'

'Yes.' Agnes could barely speak.

'Your words must have worked within my soul,' he said.

'Julius's words,' she said.

'But expressed by you. Without you, I don't think I'd have dared,' he went on. 'You've always said you believe in love, and risk, and taking a chance. I'm grateful for that.' He paused, breathing. 'Are you still there?'

'The thing is,' she began. 'It's not over. Unless you really have decided to believe that Andy was killed by Mitch in a drunken brawl.'

'I think it's just that I'm moving on.'

'Moving on?' She was trying not to shout. 'Regardless of the truth about Andy's death? I'm beginning to see all this more clearly. I'm beginning to realise that your loyalty to Andy was nothing to do with brotherhood and everything to do with you. You being stuck. And now, because some woman's written to you from Paris, you've decided you're "moving on", just because it suits you.'

'You're being unreasonable – ' he began.

'I don't know why I bothered,' she said. 'I don't know why I believed you at all. You won't even tell me the truth about your father – '

'My father was a drunk. He fell out of a window. You can think what you like – '

They were both shouting now. 'I will think what I like,' Agnes said. 'I'm still here, still caring about Andy and Mitch and Sean and Janet and Gordon – '

'I cared.' His voice was loud. 'I cared about Andy, more than you'll ever know. But in the end, I have to rescue myself. I've been burdened by it for so long, weighed down by it, my mad mother and my hopeless father, and Andy being so damaged by the war... And now Laura is giving me a chance. It's as if for all these years the past has gripped me in its tentacles, and now I can free myself at last.'

'But Mitch is going to be found guilty for something he hasn't done. And Janet has been widowed, and we don't know why – '

'Look, Agnes – ' his voice was harsh. 'Just because you're about to shut yourself away from life, that doesn't mean I have to.'

Agnes looked at the envelope on her desk, at the creamy weave of its texture in the sunlight. She thought about the form inside, signing her house away.

'I think we're both freeing ourselves from the past,' she said. 'But I'm running towards my future; and you're still running away.' She put the phone down.

She sat by the phone and put her head in her hands. She felt like crying, but no tears came. The phone rang, and she jumped. She picked it up.

'Sweetie, it's me.'

'Oh.'

'Are you all right?'

'No. I've just put the phone down on Alasdair.'

'How awful. And I'm just sitting here with several suitcases and a whole heap of clothes, wondering what one wears to start a new life. Do you think lime green is a good colour for Barcelona? And Nic said it was raining there when I spoke to him last night, I almost cancelled my ticket.'

'Just because of a bit of rain?'

'No.' There was a pause. 'Not because of the rain.' She sighed. 'I almost cancelled my ticket because he was being such an idiot on the phone.'

'Do you want a coffee?'

'What a brilliant idea.'

'Let's go to that one with the terrace, the one tucked away in that side street; we can sit in the sun and feel smug that we live in London instead of Barcelona.'

'Half an hour? I'll be there.'

Athena was wearing her lilac cashmere sweater and linen trousers. Agnes was wearing her camel cashmere sweater and jeans. For some reason they found this funny, pointing at each other and laughing.

They settled outside on the terrace with large white cups of coffee. Across the road, the lady from the florist's was outside watering her window boxes of daffodils.

'Men, eh?' Athena said.

'Men,' Agnes agreed.

They sipped their coffee. 'So,' Athena said, 'you're off on the train tonight?'

'Mmm.'

'Why didn't you fly?'

Agnes frowned. 'I did think of it, but... I like trains,' she said. 'When I was a child we went everywhere by train, Switzerland, Italy...' She felt tears well in her eyes.

'What is it?' Athena's hand touched hers.

'When I was a child,' Agnes repeated. 'There is no one alive who can tell me how it was. There is only that house that stands as testimony to my past... And now...'

'And now you're getting rid of it,' Athena finished for her.

Agnes nodded, dabbing at her eyes. 'I'm right, though,' she said, after a moment. 'Today Alasdair said the past was like tentacles wrapped around him – '

'Bloody poets,' Athena said.

'And I think maybe there does come a time when you have to free yourself.'

'And is that why he's running away?'

Agnes swirled a spoon around in her coffee. 'It's this woman from his past.'

'They're always the worst,' Athena said. 'He'll learn the hard way that octopuses are easier than women when it comes to escaping.'

Agnes laughed. 'He said tentacles, not octopuses.'

'Is it octopuses? Maybe it's octopii?'

'You sound like Julius,' Agnes said.

'What I don't understand,' Athena said, 'is why does Alasdair need to run away from you?'

'Oh, that,' Agnes said. 'It's because I found out from Trina that he killed his father.'

'Good heavens,' Athena said. 'I thought this was Dante's Divine Comedy and now it's become Oedipus or the Return of the Jedi or something.'

'It can't be Oedipus, no one's yet accused him of marrying his mother.'

'It might explain – '

'Don't even go there, Athena.'

They both started to giggle, as the waitress refilled their cups.

'I'll miss you,' Agnes said.

'It's only a few days. And if Nic carries on the way he was on the phone I'll be on the first flight home, I can tell you. It's a very dodgy time to travel, you know, there's a lunar eclipse tomorrow night. It makes the moon turn blood red. Oh, dear, when's Julius's operation?'

'Tomorrow. He's there now, he's being monitored or poisoned or whatever they do first.'

'Oh dear. Sweetie, I really think you should have a word with the surgeons, get them to put it off a day or two. People shouldn't have surgery when there's an eclipse. And as for me, I don't know what I'm thinking of, starting a new life at a lunar eclipse and wearing a lime-green suit. The omens are not great.'

'It'll be good with a tan,' Agnes said, 'the lime-green.'

Athena frowned. 'Do you think so? Perhaps it's worth the risk. Maybe with sugar-pink lipstick and matching pink bag?'

'And shoes,' Agnes said.

'Yes. The right shoes are very important. Actually, I hear Barcelona's quite good for shoes.'

Out in the street they hugged each other.

'Let me know how it all goes,' Agnes said.

'Do be careful up North, won't you,' Athena said.

'Say hello to Nic.'

'Look after Julius.'

'When he lets me,' Agnes said.

'He'll realise he needs you.'

Agnes shook her head. 'He's a stubborn old man, he really is.'

'That must be why you're friends.' Athena kissed her on both cheeks. 'I'll phone you.' She set off down the street, then turned to wave, her black patent leather bag swinging from her shoulder.

'I thought you were away.' Petra looked up from a mountain of paperwork as Agnes walked into the hostel office.

'Just sorting out a few things. How is everyone?'

'Bernie's been putting his old photographs into an album. It's taken him all day. Archie's at another meeting. It's either AA or Gamblers Anonymous, or maybe it's his group therapy, no that was this morning, oh, I don't know, I lose track. Trina and Mary have gone for a walk. Trina's horrible boyfriend has been phoning her mobile all day, and Mary suggested they throw it in the canal, they may have gone to do that. Jayce is in his room listening to music.'

'But –'

'Headphones,' Petra said.

'Obvious, really.' Agnes sat at the other desk.

'And this is for you.' Petra pulled a scrap of paper out of the heap. 'Sheila Kelly phoned about Jeanie. Do we want to register her as a Missing Person, it means there can be publicity –'

'I would have thought it would make Jeanie run even further away.'

'That's what I said, but I thought I'd check with you. Trina said in her view Jeanie won't have gone far, what with her being pregnant and being terrified of Ash and everything.'

'How does she know?'

'Oh.' Petra shuffled some papers in front of her. 'I thought you'd told her.'

'No. Only the basics.'

'Mary?' Petra glanced at Agnes.

'Mary's been the model of discretion.'

'Until now.' Petra smiled. 'I can see your friend Trina's going to be like bloody Mary Poppins. How long is she staying?'

'At least till I'm back.'

'It's just – with the paperwork – it's all a bit unorthodox.'

'The order will pay.' Agnes put her feet up on the desk.

'But – ' Petra began.

'If I'm going to sign my life away to them, it's the least they can do in return.'

Petra laughed.

'Don't let Trina go back home,' Agnes said.

'She's showing no signs of wanting to. She went shopping earlier, she appeared with masses of stuff for her room. Lampshades, cushions. And who do you think bought Jayce the headphones? See what I mean about Mary bloody Poppins.'

The sun was throwing deepening pink shadows when Agnes left the hostel. She'd had a quick word with Trina to say she'd see her at the end of the week.

'Did you talk to Alasdair?' Trina had said.

Agnes had hesitated. 'He didn't want to talk about his father,' she'd said.

'Yeah, well, I'm not surprised.'

'He's going to France to visit some woman.'

Trina scowled. 'He was always like that. You never knew where you were with him.' She'd patted Agnes's arm. 'Have fun in Scotland, won't you. And don't you worry about me, I'll be fine.'

'Did you get rid of your phone?'

Trina had laughed, producing the phone from her pocket. 'Mary wanted me to throw it in the river, but I've switched it off, that's all. He can stew, he can.'

Back at her flat she packed some basic clothes into a small case, smiling at the thought of Athena and her many suitcases. Jeans. Gloves. A thick cableknit sweater. An A-Z of Glasgow she'd bought at London Bridge station that morning.

She heated a carton of organic carrot soup and sat at her desk. She got out the phone number that Julius had given her and dialled it. The ward sister answered.

'Is it possible to speak to Father Julius?'

'Who?' The voice was abrupt.

'Father Julius.'

'I can't hear you. Is he a patient? It's their supper time,' said the harsh voice.'

'But – '

'Oh. Did you say Father Julius?' the voice said, suddenly softening. 'I'll just get him.'

There was background shuffling and then Julius came on the line. 'It had to be you,' he said. 'You're the only person I know tough enough to get through.'

'Are they looking after you?'

'Yes. They are. It's fine.'

Agnes watched the steam rise from her bowl of soup. 'Good,' she said, after a while. He seemed to be somewhere very far away.

'Athena said it's a lunar eclipse tomorrow,' she said, for something to say.

'Is that a good thing?'

'Yes,' Agnes lied.

'I bet she said it was a terrible bad thing.'

'Julius – '

'I'll ask my hooded friend tonight about lunar eclipses and their bearing on survival, I'm sure he'll agree that the difference in terms of risk is marginal.'

'Are you really all right?'

'I'm bloody starving. And I'm terrified. But in fact, when I think about it, I'm no more terrified than I've been these last few weeks.'

'I'm going to Scotland. Tonight. On the train.'

'Oh.' He breathed.

'You've got my mobile number, haven't you?'

'Yes,' he said. 'When will you be back?'

'In a couple of days. But I'll phone the ward tomorrow.'

'You'll be back by Thursday?'

For the first time in their conversation, she smiled. 'By Thursday,' she promised.

When it was dark, she went out. She walked through the fresh night air to the post box, and posted the letter to the French lawyers. There was one thing left to do, and that was to phone Connor. Tonight, she thought, I'll be on the train. She walked back to her flat through the city streets, and wondered whether this sensation of freedom was to do with the train, or the letter, or both.

Much later, she sat in the train's bar, sipping whisky, watching the northern suburbs of London slip past in the night. She had the address that Connor had given her over the phone, and that was all. She hoped it was enough.

Her words came back to her in the rhythm of the train, the words she'd said to Alasdair about running away from his future. She looked out at the smears of light in the darkness, and felt suddenly weighed down by doubt, by the thought that it was she who was running away, not Alasdair at all.

Chapter Nineteen

'Well, pet, you'd better come in.'

The old woman stood at the door, the smoke from her cigarette curling upwards. She had bright blue eyes, a lined, amiable face, hands that were twisted with age.

She showed Agnes into her hallway.

'You go and sit in the lounge, I'll put the kettle on,' she said, ushering Agnes into a boxy room of clashing floral patterns.

Agnes felt suddenly tired. She put down her bag, took off her coat, and curled into a chintz armchair. She felt dizzy from the train, although it seemed a week ago, a lifetime ago, that she'd boarded the train at Euston in the middle of the night and woken up in Scotland. She'd wandered out of the station at seven that morning, wondering where she'd stay that night, wondering whether to reserve a room, wondering what on earth she was doing here. She'd gone to a large hotel near the station and ordered bacon, eggs, coffee. Then she'd found a taxi and asked to be taken to Castlemilk. She'd given the address that Connor had given her.

The taxi had driven for miles, until at last she stood in the grey, windswept street. Pale houses curved away from her down the hill; beyond them, the greying walls of the flats, the remnants of the high-rise dream, fifty years on.

And now, here she sat, in Kathleen's front room. A vase of dried flowers sat in the unused fireplace. Above the mantelpiece there hung a wooden crucifix, dark and shiny with age. On the mantelpiece there were photographs: monochrome children in long shorts and stubbly hand-knitted pullovers; two smiling gap-toothed auburn-haired girls; a faded woman with elegant hair, in a full skirt and tight-waisted jacket, laughing at a spaniel puppy.

Agnes stared at the faces of these other people with their private, hidden stories. London seemed to be very far away, and here she was, among strangers, searching for truths that were not hers to find.

'Tea or coffee?' Kathleen called from the kitchen, and Agnes called back coffee and then regretted it but felt it would be rude to change her mind. She noticed another photograph, placed on the television in a smart wooden frame: a young man in army uniform. She wondered if it was Lucky; if it was the photo that Betty wouldn't show because it wasn't true.

Agnes looked at the open, confident face, and for a moment the past floated, whispering, in the bright room. The rattle of Kathleen's tea tray dispersed it.

'You did say coffee, didn't you pet?'

Agnes took the cup and saucer she was handed, and Kathleen sat down in one of the armchairs and sighed with the effort. 'So,' she said, 'A nun are you?' She cast a glance over Agnes, the baggy sweater and jeans, the soft leather boots.

'Yes,' Agnes said, and for some reason glanced at the cross on the wall.

Kathleen's question passed unasked. Instead, she noticed Agnes's gaze on the crucifix. 'Family heirloom,' she said, nodding towards it. 'Came from Ireland, from my mother's family, no one knows how old it is. Rosewood. Supposed to be hewn from a holy tree, our mam said.' She glanced up at it, and then back to Agnes. 'Betty said to expect you,' she said. 'She phoned last night. What can I do for you?'

'You'll know,' Agnes began, 'about Eileen McFadden's boy Andy?'

Kathleen nodded. 'Our Betty told me. A wicked world. And that nice boy that Betty knows, Connor, it was his brother, they say.' Her bright eyes seemed to cloud at the world's wickedness.

'You see,' Agnes said, 'Andy's brother believes there's more to it, and he thinks it might be to do with something else in Andy's past, when he was in the army with Lucky.'

Kathleen shot a glance towards the photograph on the television. She took a sip from her cup and sighed again. 'We never thought it could be so bad,' she said. 'Betty and me, we lived through a war, with our dad away fighting, and thank God he came back to us. If you'd told me that all them years later our Betty's lad would be killed not even fighting for his country, I'd have wondered then and there what it were all for.' She sipped her coffee. 'Andy's brother, you say? You'll be meaning Jim Brogan's boy?'

Agnes nodded.

'Not his brother at all, then?'

'No,' Agnes agreed. 'But there's no one left,' she added, as if in explanation.

'Aye,' Kathleen said, and then was quiet.

'Do you see much of Betty?' Agnes asked, for something to say.

Kathleen stared into her lap, and her eyes moistened. 'All those miles,' she said, almost to herself. 'London. It's so much further than you think.' She raised her eyes to Agnes. 'We were so close as children.' She blinked back tears. 'I see her boy, Doug, he's on the rigs. He pops in when he's passing. Nice boy, he is. He was born within a month of my Stevie, he's done well for himself too, our Stevie, lives in London with his lassie and their kids.' She picked up her tea cup and stared at it. 'They don't marry, do they, the young? We've had to get used to it. Cannae imagine what you people make of it.' She looked at her cup in surprise and put it down again.

'So,' Agnes said, 'how did you meet Eileen?'

'In Govan,' Kathleen said. 'Her Robbie, her first husband, he was a Govan boy, he'd got work in the docks in London, that's how they met, but after they married they moved back to Govan. She had her boy by then, her Andy, and I had our Janice. We'd meet doing our laundry. And then they were clearing Govan and we took a three-apartment up the road there, and Eileen and Robbie got on the list, and after a while they got a four-apartment over by Glenacre. Ooh, you cannae know how it was. The day of the flit, my mam came to see, she got the bus from Govan, and she thought it was the other end of the world. We had a budgie, Joey, and he caught a chill and died, and I'm sure our mam thought the same thing would happen to me.' She laughed. 'It didn't work for everyone, there were some as went straight back home after a week. But I liked it, the fresh air, and you had a front and a back door for the first time in your life. I liked it.'

'And then Eileen's husband died?'

'Dear oh dear, Robbie McFadden. He was in the yard, the shipyard, you know. Great lumps of iron swinging above you there were. And one broke loose...' She smoothed her skirt across her knees. 'She got some money, the unions were stronger in those days than they are now. But not much money,' she added, 'Not much for someone left with a wee lad to bring up on their own.'

'How did she meet Jim?' Agnes asked.

Eileen pursed her lips. 'There was a pub, corner of Dougrie Road. She took to going in there. Near the bowling green, where the old witch used to live,' she added, then laughed. 'When we first came here, there was nothing there, you cannae imagine. Mud,' she said. 'And down there, where the bowling green is now, there was an old cottage. It had been there for years. For centuries, maybe. And an old woman lived in it, she had snowdrops and kept hens. You wouldn't believe it now. The weens always had it she was a witch, she'd chase them with her broom. She wouldn't let them knock it down, her pile of stones.'

'What happened to her?'

'She must have died, in the end. One minute it was there, next it had all gone. Snowdrops and all. And they built the bowling green.' Her gaze settled on the wall behind Agnes, her eyes distant, seeing some other scene, some other time.

'Did you know Jim Brogan?' Agnes asked.

'Not to speak to, no. People said he'd married an Italian girl from the Gorbals, one of those ice-cream families. But no one saw her. Eileen said that she was crazy, he'd had to lock her up. It would be enough to drive anyone mad, if you ask me, being married to him. But he had a way about him, from what they say, he charmed Eileen right enough. They took up together. People talked, of course. He had that boy you mentioned, a bit older than Andy, wasn't he?'

'Alasdair.'

'Aye, Alasdair. No one saw him either, he was away at school. Clever lad, they say.'

Agnes smiled. 'Yes,' she said. 'Clever lad.'

'And then some time after that he was widowed, and so they got married, and they moved into his flat, it was one of the high flats in Dougrie Place. Eileen never liked it, she said you couldn't hear the television when the wind was high.' She leaned forward to put her coffee down, her fingers rattling the cup in the saucer. 'And then,' she said, settling back into her chair, 'And then...' She shook her head. 'After Jim's fall, Eileen couldn't settle. She'd been the butt of gossip for long enough, and now widowed twice, it was more than she could bear. And there was nothing to keep her here, sitting on her own up there in those flats. She started to go on about going home. "I want to go home, Kathleen," she used to say to me. Not that she'd got anyone left there, her mum dead, her bits of family scattered. So I said, if you're going back there, our Betty will look after you. She'd settled there with her Alf by then. And so I lost a friend, and Betty gained one.' She laughed. 'I remember the day she went, she got into a taxi with all that she could carry, never a backward glance.' She picked up some imaginary dust from the table with a shaky finger. 'Not the same for her lad, though. I've never seen anyone more loath to leave Castlemilk.'

'Andy?'

'Aye. He'd become one of us. He'd have been going on sixteen by then, this was all he'd known. And they were good kids round here in those days, not like now. People said he was sweet on Beattie Mitchelson's lass, Gemma. Lovely girl, she was. She married one of the Moir boys in the end, moved out to Clarkston. I think one of her brothers signed up to the army too, but he came back alive.'

'Do you mean Sean?' Agnes asked.

'Aye, that'll be the one. Lovely boy. Two or three brothers, she had, I seem to remember, but they lived over the other side. They'd go to the East Parish church, and we were St Margaret Mary's.'

'You wouldn't have an address for her, would you?' Agnes asked.

Kathleen shook her head.

'Or for any of the Moir family? I'm trying to find Janet Moir too, she was living in London but she may have come back here?'

'I wouldn't know, pet. To be honest, we didn't have much to do with that family. The Moir lads, and the McLeod boys, and some of the others. I mean, it wasn't as bad as they say, with the gangs and that, folk said it was worse in Easterhouse, but we had our share of it. Some of the families they moved in here, they were troublemakers, you see, didn't know how to behave.' She tutted, then went on, 'Mind you, it's worse now, with the drugs everywhere, some of these kids don't know right from wrong. Sometimes I wonder, what's to become of them? I see how some of them go on, downright wicked some of them, and then I think about our Betty's boy signing up and never coming back, and I wonder at the justice of it all.' She glanced up at Agnes. 'In your line of work, you must wonder too.'

Agnes smiled. 'I do,' she said.

Kathleen stood up. She began to load things on to the tea tray. 'Aye, wondering is all there is left.' She looked up at the crucifix on the wall. 'That there cross saved my life,' she said. 'My mam told me, when she was giving birth to me, I was laying all wrong in the womb, she said, and all the women gathered, they thought she'd die. And she held that cross so tight against her hand it drew blood. And then suddenly, I came out, happy as you like, and the women said it was a miracle.' She laughed. She finished loading the tea tray, and Agnes carried it out into the kitchen for her.

Kathleen stood in her kitchen, rubbing her back. 'You cannae know what it was like, when we first came here, to have a kitchen like this,' she said. Out in the street, the wind played with the litter. 'The folk who come here now, they take it all for granted.'

At the door Kathleen took Agnes's hand in her gnarled fingers. 'I hope you find what you're looking for, for Eileen's lad,' she said.

'Thank you,' Agnes said.

'You could ask at the church about the Moirs, if you wanted. It's a bit of a walk, right down the bottom of Ardencraig. Mr Reid was their minister, I don't know who's there now. Mind you, you'll be lucky to find anyone there, all the churches are locked and barred these days.' She looked up at the grey sky. 'I thought it would rain but it hasn't,' she said. She turned and went into her house.

When Agnes looked back from the street, she was still there, standing at her window, her hand raised in a brief wave.

She followed Kathleen's directions and came out on to the main road by the bowling green and the shops. She thought about the old woman with the hens and the broom. She wondered how deep you'd have to dig to find bits of the old stone cottage underneath the supermarket car park.

The church was bolted up. The street was deserted. Agnes checked her watch and realised it was lunchtime. She watched a group of kids who had gathered on a scrubby patch of grass and wondered whether to ask them where she might find the minister.

On the peeling church door was a notice with an address. A few moments later Agnes was knocking at the door of a house a bit further down the hill.

'Can I help you?' The door was opened by a young man with unruly blond hair and black polo-neck jumper.

'I'm looking for the minister,' Agnes said.

'That's me. Mark Kimber. What can I do for you?'

She refused his offer of tea, but explained what she was looking for. 'The Moirs have all gone,' he said. 'I did know them, I knew old Mr Moir before he passed away. The Mitchelsons? Old Mrs Mitchelson is still alive, I can take you over there if you want.'

'Kathleen said you might know her,' Agnes said. 'Kathleen Dougal.'

'Ah.' Mark Kimber nodded. 'Not one of ours, of course.'

'Sorry?'

'Catholics, they are. They're St Margaret Mary's. We're the Protestant church.' He stood up. 'Come on, let's go and see if Mrs Mitchelson is at home.'

They stood by a terrace of faded, two storey homes, knocking at a door. The door was opened, eventually, by a fragile elderly lady in black who greeted the minister, then peered up at Agnes through delicate spectacle frames. At Mark's urging, she agreed to give Agnes Gemma's address. 'Though, you're not to bring her any more trouble. She's had trouble enough, our lassie.'

A thin afternoon sun was breaking through the clouds. The taxi dropped her off on the Greenwood Road. She walked up a tidy, tree-lined street until she reached the number that Mrs Mitchelson had written down for her. She glanced up at the house, with its air of neglect, its dark green painted windows and stubby roses in its small front garden.

Agnes sat on the front wall. She tried to remember what had brought her this far. London was so very far away. She felt weary, and faint with hunger.

Somewhere, Athena is on a plane, Julius is in an operating theatre and here I am sitting on the front wall of an anonymous little house on the outskirts of Glasgow in the hope of finding some kind of answer, when I don't even know the question.

She checked the house number, and rang the bell. The door was answered by a woman with short grey hair and big brown eyes. She was dressed in black trousers, a black jumper, and an amethyst hung on a silver chain at her neck.

'Yes?'

Agnes found her voice. 'Are you Gemma?' she said. The words sounded rough, uncouth.

'Who are you?' the woman asked.

'I'm Sister Agnes. I know Janet,' she added, 'and I knew Gordon, and I met Sean your brother, with Alasdair Brogan...'

The dark eyes were frowning at her. 'Alasdair? When? When did all this happen?'

'I work at the hostel where Andy was staying. Andy McFadden – '

'You're a nun?' The brown eyes widened. 'Andy?' she repeated. She put out a hand and drew Agnes into the house. Agnes followed her down a musty hallway into a sitting room at the back of the house. It had a worn, red, patterned carpet, and it overlooked a narrow, overgrown garden; beyond that loomed a distant row of poplar trees.

Agnes sat down on the sofa. She thought she could hear the sound of a baby crying. Gemma checked her watch. 'I only just put him down,' she said. 'He's been restless all day.' She sat down. 'I'll see if he settles again.' She glanced at Agnes, then laughed, nervously. 'Oh, no, he's not mine, I'm past all that now, my two are in their teens now, well the younger one is twelve. No, this is my neighbour's wee lad, I'm doing a bit of childminding for her.' She tilted her head, listening. 'He's gone off now, I thought he might.'

She sat down on a chair opposite Agnes, straight-backed, her knees tight together, waiting.

'I was hoping,' Agnes began, 'that you might know where Janet is.'

'How did you know I was here?' Gemma's gaze was piercing.

'I saw Kathleen, on the estate. Eileen's old friend. And then I met the minister of your church. And he took me to see your mother. And she told me.'

Gemma continued to eye her. 'You must have an honest face, for my mother to tell you where I am. And, in answer to your question, I don't know where Janet is,' she said. 'I heard about Gordon, our Sean told me. He said it was some thieving drug dealer. They should never have gone to London.'

Agnes watched Gemma fidget her fingers on her knees. 'I just thought it was odd that Janet and Sean left the flat when the police are still trying to find out what happened, when Gordon's not yet buried...'

Gemma shrugged. 'Perhaps they found somewhere better, our Sean said it was a dump.' Her hand went to her mouth; she began to bite one of her nails. 'I'd offer you something to eat, but I've not got much in,' she said.

'You haven't been here long, have you?'

Gemma looked at her, her finger poised in her mouth. She looked away again. 'No,' she said. 'I left my husband last week. I'm renting this.'

'Where did you live before last week?'

'Not far, just off Eaglesham Road. A few streets away.'

'Is Iain still there?'

'He can rot there as far as I'm concerned,' Gemma said. 'He won't give me anything towards our keep, that's why my friend is helping me out, paying me to have her wee boy.'

'Would Iain know where Janet is?' Agnes watched Gemma shift on the edge of her chair.

'I've no idea.' She fiddled with the worn weave of the armchair, as if trying to make up her mind. 'I've got a mobile number for her,' she said. 'I'll write it out for you.'

The sun went in. The room seemed to shrink. Agnes breathed a deep breath. 'Alasdair told me you loved Andy,' she said.

'It was a long time ago.' Gemma was cast in shadow.

'There's a man called Mitch O'Grady who is about to plead guilty to having killed him. I'm here because I want to prevent an injustice.'

'Was this Alasdair's idea?' Gemma's voice was harsh.

Agnes was silent.

'He never had his feet on the ground, that boy,' Gemma said. 'He's obviously not changed.'

'Andy knew secrets, from the barracks,' Agnes said. 'We've spoken to his commanding officer, Alasdair and me.'

Gemma sighed. 'Andy was a loyal friend,' she said. 'If it's Lucky you're talking about.'

'It is.'

Gemma met Agnes's gaze. 'Andy knew about Billy Lee who died. He knew about the bullying. He'd tell me about it. He knew about the relationship between Lucky and Billy. He told me not to tell anyone else. But that was years and years ago.' She began to bite her nail again. 'I can't see what that's got to do with him dying now.'

The thin sound of the baby crying filtered into the room.

'Gordon wanted to tell us something, before he died – ' Agnes raised her voice above the child's audible distress.

'I'm sorry – ' Gemma stood up, dabbing at her eyes. 'He's not going to settle...'

'Gemma, Mitch has this memory of the night that Andy died – '

'I wish I could help. Really I do,' Gemma said, heading for the door as the crying became a loud wail. Agnes heard her go upstairs.

Agnes got up from the sofa. She stretched her legs, standing in the gloom of the room. A bookcase stood in one corner, its shelves almost bare. A dusty glass vase, an empty photo frame, a couple of paperback novels. A pack of photos lay next to the frame and Agnes picked it up. As she did so, some of the prints fell out. She began to put them back into the folder, then stopped. In her hand she was holding an image of three people standing in a sun-lit garden; a laughing boy in his mid-teens, a girl a bit younger, and in between them, an arm round each, a woman in her forties, wearing a striped sun-dress, with long dark hair.

Last week, Agnes thought, Gemma left her husband. Last week, or perhaps the week before, Gemma cut off her long, dyed hair.

Agnes could hear Gemma moving around upstairs.

The woman who sang the lullaby, holding Andy, drenched with his blood.

Hush, my baby, hush, my pretty one,

Soon it will be dawn...

The staircase creaked.

Agnes looked up as Gemma came back into the room, holding a tearful, blinking baby boy. She was singing to him.

'... The waves' roar will be a whisper when you awake,
The ships will come back safely in the morn...'

Gemma met Agnes's eyes. Her expression seemed to empty. She stood in the room, looking at Agnes, seeing recognition in her face.

She sat heavily into her chair. The baby began to play with the necklace.

The stillness hung heavy in the room.

'It was you,' Agnes said at last. 'It was you who held Andy in your arms, when he was bleeding to death. It was you who sang him that song.'

Gemma's face was white. She began to cry, in wrenching, gulping sobs. The baby turned to Agnes and smiled at her, then went back to the necklace. Gemma disentangled him and sat him down on the floor, where he began to pat the rug with both hands.

'Who killed him?' Agnes said.

Gemma bent her head towards her knees, her hands clutching her hair, still weeping. 'I see it all the time,' she said, her voice muffled with tears. 'I can't sleep for seeing him, for seeing the life drain out of him.'

'Who was it?' Agnes insisted.

Gemma shook her head.

'Is that why you left Iain?' Agnes said, aware of a shrill trilling noise, realising it was her phone.

She snatched it from her bag and pressed the button.

'Sister Agnes? I'm Margaret Lacey, ward sister. We have your name as a contact number. It's about Father Julius -' 'What?'

'There's been a problem – '

'What problem?' Agnes heard the nurse's voice, so faint, so far away. 'What problem?' she shouted.

'Can you get down here?'

'I'm in Scotland,' Agnes said, and the words sounded so strange she wanted to laugh.

'How soon can you get a flight?'

'What's happened?'

'He's had a bad reaction to the anaesthetic.'

'How bad?' She seemed to be shouting into a fog.

'It is quite serious, Sister. He's in the ICU. We only have your name, yours and – '

'I'll be there.' She rang off. Gemma had raised her head from her knees and was staring into space, her face drained, chalk-white. The baby had crawled over to the french windows and was watching a fly, which buzzed loudly in the corner of the peeling ornate frame.

Chapter Twenty

The green trace of Julius's monitor kept up its steady rhythm. Agnes found herself staring at it for minutes a time, soothed, hypnotised. Then she'd blink, and her gaze would travel back to the figure lying on the bed.

She looked at Julius now. His skin was yellow and waxy, his eyes tight shut. Wires and drips surrounded him. He didn't move, and she wondered whether, in the absence of the comforting beep from the machine, she'd think he was dead.

The nurse sitting at the end of the bed glanced across and smiled at her, and Agnes felt tears well in her eyes.

'What time is it?' she asked the nurse, whose badge declared her as Teresa.

'Nearly ten o'clock.'

Agnes glanced up at the windows, the night sky black against the bright fluorescence of the ward.

She'd left Gemma's house in a taxi, had gone straight to the airport, straight to departures, straight on to the next plane back to London.

Then it was Stansted, more queueing, another taxi, and at last the hospital, as the dusk gathered over the river and the crowds inched their way homewards.

Staring unseeing at the trace of Julius's monitor, she recalled her words to Gemma, as she'd stood in her hallway and asked her, again, 'Who killed him, Gemma? Who killed Andy?'

And Gemma had stared at the crimson sworls of rented carpet. 'You were there,' Agnes had insisted. 'You must know.'

Gemma had lifted her pale, tear-stained face to Agnes and had taken both her hands. 'Please don't ask me,' she'd said, 'please don't make me say it.' Her voice was barely a whisper, drowned out by other sounds, the baby beginning to cry again, Agnes's taxi drawing up in the street outside.

An uneven blip in the beeping on the screen brought Agnes sharply back to the present. Nurse Teresa was on her feet, and took hold of Julius's hand. He didn't stir, but the monitor settled back to a steady rhythm.

The nurse smiled at Agnes and went back to her place. Agnes stared at Julius's lifeless face and wondered where he was. 'In the midst of life we are in death.' The words came to her, and she imagined him floating, somewhere, between this world and the next, and then imagined him telling her off for being fanciful, and then smiled as she thought that of all people, she and Julius had earned the right to believe in whatever fanciful notions of the afterlife they chose. She thought of him, surrounded by cherubim and seraphim playing harps on fluffy clouds, and wanted to laugh out loud, but found that her eyes had filled with tears instead. Because, of course, she thought, staring at his peaceful, empty face, you and I, Julius, given the choice between life and death – angels or no we will choose life.

'You can have a break if you want.' Teresa spoke softly. 'Go for a walk, or have a coffee or something.'

Agnes dabbed the tears from her eyes. 'Thank you. I will.'

Her feet took her out of Intensive Care, down the corridor to the main staircase, and then to reception. She found herself outside the hospital, in the chilly night. On the wide pavement that skirted the embankment, she was aware of gathered crowds, all staring at the sky. She followed their gaze, and wondered at first what she was seeing; a blood-red shadowed circle in the sky.

The eclipse of the moon.

She thought of Julius, wired to a membrane between life and death. She looked up at the darkened moon, remembering the terrible warning, was it from Revelation, about the sun being turned into darkness and the moon into blood.

She began to walk along the embankment, dodging the sky-gazing crowds. She glanced up at the moon again. The words came to her: 'The sun shall be turned into darkness and the moon into blood, before the great and terrible day of the Lord comes.'

She thought of Andy, wading through the mud and blood of war, pulling his friends' bodies from the wreckage.

She thought of Gemma, the woman of Mitch's memories, singing, blood-soaked, to the man she loved as the life ebbed from him.

Agnes looked at the milling, murmuring people. No one seemed that bothered about great and terrible days, she thought. Everyone seemed to be rather enjoying the spectacle. Perhaps none of these people were burdened by thoughts of loss, and grief, and war, and murder.

Perhaps none of these people had left the person they loved most in the whole world in intensive care.

She turned back towards the hospital. A tiny crescent of white was appearing at one edge of the moon.

She headed along the hospital corridor, passing a sign marked 'Chapel'. She turned back and went in.

It was a low-ceilinged room, softly lit, with square purple seating. A lighting arrangement in one corner looked a bit like a crucifix, in a modern, secular sort of way. In front of it was a rack of small candles. Agnes thought about the universal nature of candle-lighting: a cry from the heart, regardless of faith; a prayer in the darkness.

As she struck the match and watched the flame gutter into life, she remembered doing the same in the church in the village in Provence. She remembered the cool stone shadows of the church, the paintings on the wall, the sufferings of Our Lord in ghoulish reds and flesh pinks, the thorns and the nails and the bleeding heart of Our Lady. She remembered praying for her pony when he was ill, she must have been about seven at the time, and her pony Caspar was lying in the field, not eating, not getting up to greet her, praying to Our Lady because she would know, she would understand, that without Caspar there would be no one left in the world who loved her, who truly loved her, who would let her nuzzle his soft neck and whinny in reply, and that if her Son could rise again from the dead it wasn't much to ask that a pony with colic might get better again, too, was it?

Agnes sat on the purple cushions. She wondered how her seven-year-old self had perceived, so clearly, that Caspar's love was true, unlike the distant, unreliable attentions of her parents. She realised that her seven-year-old self had fully expected her prayers to be answered, because God, too, was love, and if you were good, He would answer your prayers.

If you were good. Already, that worry, even at seven. Already that creeping sense of the tightrope to be walked between doubt and faith.But Caspar had survived, and faith had triumphed, this time, at least.

Agnes looked around her at her muted surroundings. For a moment, she yearned to have that faith again, to fling herself upon the garish sufferings of our Lord and ask that in the battle with Death, Julius might triumph too. She found herself wondering whether, if she prayed in that church, her church at home, with the faith of a child, her prayers might be answered.

I can't sell that house, she thought. My freedom is not in cutting myself off from my past, in severing myself from my stories; my freedom is in their continuance, their validation, like the crucifix above Kathleen's fireplace that had saved her life; like the photographs on her mantelpiece.

As she walked back along the corridor towards the ICU, she had a sense of someone at her side. She turned her head, but saw only the edge of a white coat, hanging inside the open door of someone's office.

When she got back to his bedside, Julius hadn't stirred.

She felt a gentle touch on her arm.

'You fell asleep,' Teresa was saying. 'I'll get you a cup of tea, the trolley's just outside.'

She left the room. The sky outside was softened with a grey dawn. Agnes blinked, straightened herself in the chair, tried to ignore a general ache that seemed to have taken hold of all of her. She had the impression she'd been dreaming of her mother. The first light of the day brushed Julius's face, and Agnes thought she saw his lips move.

He opened his eyes, and his hand moved weakly towards her. She took hold of it. He tried to speak, failed, almost smiled, then closed his eyes again. The monitor settled back to a sleeping rhythm.

'He woke up.' Agnes almost shouted at Teresa as she came back into the room. 'He opened his eyes.'

Teresa handed her a cup. 'Good,' she said. 'I thought he might.'

The hospital was stirring, waking, strip-lights flickering into life, bustle and trolleys and the smell of toast. Agnes walked the corridor from time to time, always returning to Julius's side after a few minutes. Later in the morning, he opened his eyes again. He took hold of her hand, and said, 'Don't give them your house.' Then he went back to sleep.

Teresa looked at her.

'It's a long story,' Agnes said.

Later in the day, Agnes looked up to see Athena appear in the doorway of the room.

'What – ?' Agnes wondered if she'd fallen asleep, if this was another hospital dream. 'What are you doing here?'

Athena shook her head. She looked very tired. 'I spoke to the hostel,' Athena said. 'That nice young man. He told me everything.' Her glance went to the sleeping Julius. 'Is he – will he be – ?'

Agnes couldn't think of anything to say.

Athena sat down next to her and took her hand. After a while, Agnes said, 'What happened, then?'

Athena sighed. 'It was as bad as I thought. Worse. Nic's business partner seems to think you can run a therapy centre from an old stable block on the edge of a deserted village, with a couple of hippy-chicks and some scented oils. I pointed out to Nic that it wasn't going to work, he got cross with me, really cross, I haven't seen him like that, not ever, I said I wasn't going to be spoken to like that, he didn't apologise, I booked myself into a hotel in the town, it's nice, Barcelona, bit edgy but fun, had a couple of phone calls with him which didn't solve anything, got the first flight back. How was Scotland?'

'I met Gemma. She was in love with Andy, she was there when he died.'

'So – ' Athena's eyes were wide. 'So, she'll know – '

'She wouldn't tell me.'

'Wouldn't tell you?'

Agnes shook her head. 'It was all in the middle of a phone call from here, telling me about Julius, I was trying to get a cab, it was madness. She's left her husband, she's living in a rented house with her children.'

'What happens next?'

'I just want to stay here,' Agnes said. 'One of the doctors here, she came to talk to me earlier. She said they just have to see how he is when he comes round.'

'And the cancer?'

Agnes glanced at Julius. 'They're doing tests on the bit they removed. They're looking for clear margins, whatever that means.'

'Will you go back to work?'

'Tomorrow,' Agnes said. 'I'm supposed to be there tomorrow.'

'Hadn't you better get some sleep at home?'

'I just don't feel I can leave him. Nice shoes, by the way.'

Athena considered her feet, which were tucked into a pair of kitten-heeled pink round-toed shoes. 'Thank you,' she said.

At nine the next morning, Agnes walked into the kitchen at St Christopher's.

'There you are.' Trina looked up from a cup of coffee. She was sitting in the sunny kitchen, her feet up on the table, wearing an extravagant black sweater with silvery sequins sewn on to it. 'Did you have a nice time?'

Agnes smiled at her. 'Yes. Sort of.'

'You look very tired.'

'I've been sitting by a friend's bedside. I didn't get to bed till about four.'

'We found Jeanie,' Trina said.

Agnes blinked at her. 'You found Jeanie? Where is she?'

'Oh, she's not here, she wouldn't come back with us. Poor kid, she's that scared she is. Mary tried to talk to her, but it was no good. What I thought we could do is, go back with you, later on today, if you want.'

'Where is she?'

'There's a bit of wasteland, at the back of the railway, not far, Mary thought of it. It used to be allotments, she said, there are sheds and that. It's no place for a kid. She might listen to you, if you come and get her back.'

'OK,' Agnes said.

'Do you want a coffee?' Trina went over to the kettle.

Agnes settled at the table. 'Have you heard from Scott?'

'Have I heard from him?' Trina rattled coffee mugs. 'He's been phoning everyone I know, making a right bleedin' nuisance of himself.'

'What will you do?'

Trina shrugged. 'I don't know. Have you spoken to Alasdair?'

'He's in Paris.'

'Good luck to him.'

Trina stirred the mug of instant coffee, then handed it to Agnes.

'Trina – '

'What?' Trina sat down again.

'It was Scott, wasn't it, who broke in here two weeks ago.'

Trina stared into her mug.

'He thought Andy's writings would reveal something about Eileen's money.'

'He's a bleedin' idiot.'

'He didn't find anything.'

'Nah.' Trina looked up. 'Scott's all mouth, he is. He's lucky he weren't done for it, he cut himself smashing the window, and then he goes and nicks the bleedin' printer, tries to sell it down the pub, he does, no one'll touch it. You can have it back if you want, it's sitting in our front room.'

Dan put his head round the door. 'The hospital's just rung,' he said. 'Julius is out of intensive care – here's the ward number.' He handed her a piece of paper.

Trina stood up. 'Come, let's go and find Jeanie. Then you can visit your mate.'

They crossed the main road, and made their way under the railway arches towards the river. Trina was carrying a large plastic zip-up bag. They turned off along an overgrown pathway, skirted a fence, and reached a broken gate.

'It's this way,' she said.

They walked along a muddy path. Sunlight flickered through branches above them, trains rumbled past in the distance.

'How did Mary know about this?'

Trina shrugged. 'From talking to the residents, I think.'

'She doesn't talk to me,' Agnes said.

'No.' Trina stepped over some brambles. 'I've told her, she's got to stop living in the past. She's got to get over it. I've told her, there's worse things than losing your man. She should try living with mine, I said.'

'What did she say?'

Trina edged past a clump of nettles. 'She thinks it's her fault, that's the problem. I've tried to tell her, if she'd promised to stay with him, he'd have died anyway. But she thinks she killed him by staying with the nuns. It's guilt, you see. Us Catholics, it never goes away. You must be the same,' she said, standing aside to let Agnes catch up. 'Here we are.'

They'd reached a patch of overgrown grass, a couple of tumbledown sheds.

Trina stopped. 'Jeanie?' she called.

A door wobbled open, and a pale face emerged.

'I've brought Sister Agnes,' Trina said.

'I can see that.' The figure that stepped towards them was bony, lank-haired, her face shadowed with hunger or dirt or both.

'I've also brought this.' Trina opened the bag and produced a rug, a thermos and some food. She spread out the rug, and poured tea for Jeanie. Jeanie sat cross-legged and drank, thirstily.

'Want a crisp? They're salt and vinegar.' Trina opened a packet and handed them round. Jeanie ate a large handful of them.

'You've got to come back with us, you know,' Trina said.

Jeanie shook her head. 'He'll come after me.'

'He can fuck off,' Trina said. 'You've got to think of your baby.' She reached over and patted Jeanie's stomach, which had a noticeable curve in her skeletal frame. 'It's Chris's baby,' Trina went on. 'You can't let Ash ruin this too.'

'How can you know that?' Jeanie's eyes were huge as she looked across at Trina.

'I just do. And anyway, there's that copper, she'll stand guard at the hostel, won't she, Agnes?'

Agnes nodded, wondering whether Sheila would agree to be Jeanie's personal bodyguard.

Jeanie picked bits of fluff from the rug. 'I don't know what to do,' she said.

'There's no argument,' Trina said. 'You're coming with us.'

They made their way back along the path, back to the road, under the railway arches. Trina took Jeanie's arm and she leaned on her.

At the hostel Trina ran Jeanie a hot bath, while Agnes went to the office and phoned Sheila Kelly.

'Jeanie's here,' she said.

'Great,' Sheila said.

'We need security,' Agnes said.

'I can see you might.'

'It's a matter of time before Ash shows up,' Agnes said. 'I reckon hours rather than days.'

'I'll see what I can do. I'll ring you back.'

'I'll be on my mobile.'

The hostel was fragrant with lavender bubble-bath.

'Don't leave her side,' Agnes said to Trina.

'Where are you going?' Trina was whispering, outside Jeanie's room, where Jeanie had been tucked into a clean bed and was already fast asleep.

'To see Julius.'

'Don't be long, I'm anticipating trouble.'

'I've told Sheila that Jeanie's here,' Agnes said. 'And Dan's down in the office. And Mary's due in later on.'

'That Ash is bad,' Trina said. 'We'll need more than a young thin bloke, a couple of middle-aged women and a nun to fight him off.'

'You'd be surprised,' Agnes said. 'I'll be back.'

She walked along the embankment towards the hospital. She paused by the river wall, watching the Thames, the silvery water ruffled by the wind. She took out her phone and dialled Alasdair's number, but there was no answer and she didn't leave a message.

She walked through the wide hospital doors, up flights of stairs, following endless signs to the ward that Dan had written down for her. Once more she felt the hospital enclose her, and it was as if she'd never left after the vigil in Intensive Care, as if she'd been pacing these corridors ever since.

He was lying in bed, his eyes closed.

'Julius?'

His eyes opened, and he smiled. 'There you are, then,' he said.

She sat down by the bed and took his hand. She sighed, smiled, shook her head at him.

'I'll try not to do it again,' he said.

'What, nearly die?'

'But I can't promise,' he added.

'It must have been a very tense game,' Agnes said.

He frowned at her, then remembered. 'Oh, the card game. My

hooded friend.' He raised himself slightly on his pillows, causing the festoon of drips to sway. 'Actually, when it came to it, he was nowhere to be seen. Perhaps Death is a coward too.'

'Did you really nearly die?'

'So they tell me. These anaesthetics are perfectly safe in most cases I'm told. I think it must be my fault for being so old.'

'And – and the other thing?'

'The cancer? They have to check the lymph nodes and things. I'll know soon. The liver looked clear, they told me. I think they're so glad they didn't bump me off, they've forgotten I might still be terminally ill – ' he winced as Agnes started to laugh. 'It's not funny,' he said, laughing too.

'So, any sightings?' Agnes said.

'Of what?'

'Oh, you know, heaven. Angels. That sort of thing.'

'I don't think I got near enough.' He shook his head. 'No,' he said. 'No such luck.'

'Perhaps if one's faith was stronger...'

Julius laughed again, winced again.

'Do you remember telling me not to give away my house?'

He frowned. 'Yes,' he said. 'When was that?'

'Some time during that night. You woke up, told me not to sell my house, went back to sleep.'

'It feels like weeks ago. You haven't given it away, have you?'

She stared at the white blanket on his bed.

'Oh well,' he said. 'Never mind. It's only a house.'

'It's my past. It's part of my story, my history.'

'Ah yes,' he said. 'Our beginnings, middles and ends.'

'Only not yet,' she said. 'No ending yet for you.'

'No,' he agreed. 'Not just yet.'

He took her hand again.

'I was aware of you,' he said, after a while. 'I knew you were here. I seemed to be able to see you, walking along the corridors.'

'No wonder you didn't have a vision of heaven,' Agnes said. 'You were stuck here with me.'

'Ah well,' he said. 'I can think of worse places to be.'

It was getting dark when she left, and the wind had chilled the air. Again she skirted the river towards London Bridge. She wanted to dance, to jump up on the embankment walls, to tap-dance along them. She laughed at the thought. She laughed to think that Julius was still here. She thought about her fears, that Julius would die in months or years, and smiled to think that here he was, back from the dead; that just to have him back with her, just for now, for one more day, was enough to make her want to salsa down the street.

How the Gods must laugh, she thought. We can be grateful to be granted another day, and yet ungrateful for a whole lifetime. She thought about Andy, staggering away from the fields of war, a survivor, only to have the life drained out of him on a London street, twenty years on. She thought about the meaning of his life, held in a web of threads, the threads of the people who'd reared him, the women who'd loved him, the soldiers who'd been his loyal friends; the friends who'd faded away as the trauma of war destroyed him over the years.

It's guilt, Trina had said. Catholic guilt. It never leaves us.

The meaning was there. It was there in the shadow of his writings, it was there in what was unsaid about Lucky's death, it was there in Betty's memories and Kathleen's photographs, and in Gemma's song.

She has to tell me, Agnes thought, turning the corner of the street towards the hostel. Gemma has to tell me.

Chapter Twenty-One

The hostel was quiet. In the kitchen, there was the sound of supper being washed up. Agnes went straight to the office and dialled Gemma's number, which, to her surprise, was answered.

'I can't talk to you,' Gemma said.

'You don't have to,' Agnes said. 'All you have to do,' Agnes said, willing her to stay on the line, 'is tell him the truth.'

'Tell who?'

'You know who. Tell him that a man is about to be given a life sentence because of what he did. You know he's a decent man. You can't protect him for ever. And anyway, he needs help. He's not a bad man, is he, not deep down. A man like that, whatever you think of him, he can't walk around for the rest of his life knowing that he killed a man and that another man got put away for it.'

'Agnes, I've tried. I've tried to talk to him. Why do you think I've ended up living here – ' she stopped herself.

'Try again,' Agnes said.

There was a silence. Then Gemma said, 'Pray for me.' She rang off.

Agnes sat in the quiet of the office. She thought about what Alasdair had said about the meaning of Beatrice in Dante. That through loving Beatrice, the poet finds redemption.

Is it that simple, she wondered, resting her head on one arm, listening to the rhythms of the house around her.

A smash of glass.

A male voice, shouting, abusively.

Another smash of glass.

A woman's voice, screaming.

Agnes flung open the office door. There was another crash, more glass. 'What the hell's going on?' she yelled.

She could hear shouting, Dan's voice from the kitchen, Mary's too. More screaming. Jeanie, she thought. At the sound of more glass breaking, another window, another tirade of abuse, Agnes raced back to her desk and dialled Sheila's number.

'Quick,' she gasped. 'The hostel. Ash, smashing windows, Jeanie's terrified –'

'We'll be right there.' Sheila rang off.

Ash's voice was outside. 'Where are you? Bitch. You told them. Bitch. You told them I knifed him –'

Agnes went into the hall, which was showered with glass. 'I've phoned the police,' she shouted.

'What the fuck are we going to do?' Dan was yelling, as a missile bounced off the front door.

'Oh my God.' Trina appeared from the kitchen. Her hands went to her face. 'Oh my God. Where's Jeanie?'

'In her room, I hope.'

Agnes and Trina ran up the stairs. 'It's us, love,' Trina shouted.

'I told you.' Jeanie was crying on the other side of the door. 'I told you it was no good.'

'Let us in, there's a good girl.' Trina tried the door handle, which eventually opened.

'Where is he?' Jeanie was shivering with fear. She went and sat on her bed.

'He's out the front of the house.'

Another smash of glass.

'We've called the police,' Agnes said.

'He won't stop. Not now. He never gives up. I know him.'

Then there were police sirens, blue lights flashing in the gathering darkness. Cars pulled up outside, a male voice shouted. A single gunshot. Silence.

'Oh no.' Jeanie buried her head in her hands.

Trina ran across the landing to the front of the house, opened one of the bedrooms and peered out of the window. There was another gunshot, and she ran back.

'Bloody hell,' she said. 'He's got a gun. He's firing into the air if anyone goes near him. The police are sitting in their car. Radioing for help, I hope.' There was more shouting in the street, a hammering on the front door. Trina ran to look.

'He's asking for you,' she said to Jeanie, coming back. 'He's threatening all sorts unless you go out.'

Jeanie stood up, her arms limp at her sides.

'Where do you think you're going?' Agnes grabbed her hand.

'Out there.'

'Why?'

'Because it's no good me staying here. He'll start shooting at the house in a minute.'

'You're not going nowhere, missy,' Trina said, reaching for her, but she ran past them both and dashed to the front window.

Agnes and Trina ran after her. There was a shout from the street, another shot, an explosive crack, as the window shattered from a hole at its centre and a bullet smashed into the wall behind Jeanie.

In the cotton wool silence that followed, the three women stared at the deep dent in the wall. Then, bit by bit, the glass from the window began to fall onto the floor, leaving gaping, jagged air.

Out in the street, a shriek of brakes and sirens. A megaphone, a police voice calling to everyone to keep away from the windows. Then, oddly, the sound of someone singing.

'That's him singing. He's laughing at them,' Jeanie said. 'He's got a gun. He's off his bloody face. What can they do?'

Trina and Agnes led Jeanie back to her room. They all sat on the bed. Jeanie held out her hands in front of her, watching their shaking.

The voice from the megaphone seemed to be addressing Ash, suggesting he put his gun down. In answer there was more laughter, another shot. Agnes crept back to the broken window. Ash was swaggering to and fro outside the house, waving his gun.

He had shorn blonde hair, narrow eyes. The street was deserted. Up and down the road, nervous faces peeped through upstairs windows.

The megaphone once again began to negotiate. Ash lost his air of cheerfulness, switching to sudden threat. He began to shout at the police van, then ran up the steps and held his gun to the lock of the front door. He began to yell abuse at the house, demanding to be let in, demanding that the bitch come out.

In her bedroom, Jeanie began to cry.

Agnes heard the front door open, then shut again.

'Someone's let him in,' she said, her voice weak with shock. 'Why should anyone – ' She looked down, and saw that Mary had come out of the house and was now standing on the front steps, facing Ash, who had stepped back in surprise.

She held out her hand. 'Give me the gun,' she said.

The street seemed frozen in silence.

'Give it to me,' she said.

Ash took a step back from her. He levelled the gun and pointed it at her. 'Send the bitch out to me,' he said.

'She's not a bitch,' Mary said.

'You going to get hurt, you are,' Ash said. He steadied his aim of his gun.

'It's over, Ash,' Mary said. 'Jeanie's finished with you. You might as well accept it.'

Jeanie and Trina had crept out of Jeanie's room, and were now standing at a distance from the broken window, watching the scene in the street.

'You can fuck off,' Ash was saying. 'I don't have to take nothing from you meddling fucking cow.'

There was movement from the police van.

'I hope they're radioing for some guns,' Trina said.

'Send her out,' Ash was saying to Mary. 'I can kill you too, I don't care.'

'I'll do no such thing.'

'She ain't nothing to you anyway, she's a junkie whore and she's carrying my baby.'

'Don't be ridiculous.' Mary's voice was so firm, so calm, that Trina started to giggle. 'It's not your baby,' Mary said. 'You know that very well.'

Jeanie's gaze was fixed on Mary.

'It's the end, Simon Ashleigh,' Mary said. 'You might as well give up now.'

'I ain't giving up nothing, man – ' Ash flicked his head, aware of movement behind him. One of the policemen had crept out of the van and was sheltering behind it. Ash whirled on Mary. 'You think you're so fucking clever – ' He lurched forward and grabbed Mary and held the gun to her head. She looked suddenly very small, held in his huge grip at the foot of the steps.

The megaphone now spoke. 'Put the gun down,' it said. 'Put the gun down. Release the lady.'

Ash laughed. 'She's dead,' he said.

Agnes saw his finger twitch on the trigger. In a flash, Mary reached up and grabbed the barrel of the pistol. Trina screamed, her hands in front of her mouth. The gun fired once, a loud crack, the bullet buried in the wall behind Mary. Ash tried again, and there was a click. Then nothing.

Ash yelled a stream of abuse, standing, rigid, trying to fire his gun. 'What you fucking done – '

He took the gun away from her head and held it in front of him, racking it with both hands. More loud clicks followed. Mary was frozen, standing absolutely still.

And then, from nowhere, a policeman flew at Ash and tackled him to the ground, and then there were others piling out of the cars, and in a hail of shouts and abuse, Ash was disarmed and handcuffed. He was bundled into the van, blinking, muttering threats. The van sped away, siren blaring.

Agnes, Trina and Jeanie raced down the stairs.

Mary was standing in the street, motionless. Jeanie flew into her arms and held her, and Mary seemed to collapse in slow motion, swaying forward until Jeanie was taking her entire weight. Trina ran to help, and they laid her out on the ground, and Dan came out with blankets and covered her up.

Sheila Kelly stood with the policeman who'd tackled Ash. She began to radio for an ambulance. 'Is she hurt?' she called.

'Don't think so,' Trina said. 'Just fainted. I'm not bloody surprised.'

'What happened?' Dan said.

The policeman standing next to Sheila sat down on the wall. 'Feel a bit shaky now,' he said.

'What did you do?'

'It weren't me,' the policeman said. 'This lady here – ' he indicated Mary who was still unconscious. 'She must have released the magazine, when she reached up to the barrel. It fired once and missed her, but it couldn't fire again. When he was racking the gun, that's when I realised he had a problem. Seized the moment, I suppose.'

Sheila patted his shoulder. 'Brave man, our Pete,' she said.

Mary stirred and murmured and then sat up. 'Am I dead?' she said, provoking a wave of laughter. Jeanie laughed most of all, crouching down next to her on the pavement, holding her hand.

They trooped into the house. Kettles were boiled, tea was made, glaziers were phoned, statements were taken. Petra appeared and began to make toast for everyone. Dan wandered around the kitchen, writing lists of damage.

'There are two bullets in the walls, one in the top front bedroom, the other outside by the front door.' He scribbled a note on his list.

'We should keep them there as souvenirs,' Petra said.

'I'm not sure I want to remember,' Mary said, sitting at the kitchen table.

'What were you thinking of?' Sheila turned to her.

Mary stared at the table, tracing circles with her finger. 'I can't imagine,' she said. 'I just wanted to put a stop to him.'

'You were very brave,' Sheila said.

Mary shook her head. 'It wasn't being brave,' she said. 'It was not caring whether I lived or died.'

'But you do now.' Jeanie was sitting next to her at the table.

'You do want to live, now, don't you?'

Mary turned to her and smiled.

Agnes's phone shrilled, and she went into the hall to answer it.

'It's Haz.'

'Oh. Hi.'

'Listen, I've just come from the Rising Sun. Your mate is in there, the Scottish one, Andy's sort-of brother.'

'Alasdair?'

'Yes. He's drinking like the world's about to end. We tried to get him to leave, but he got angry. They'll be closing soon—'

'Thanks for telling me.' Agnes rang off.

She walked through the dark streets, pushed open the bright doors of the pub. She scanned the faces until she saw him, hunched over a glass of spirits, a cigarette in his other hand.'

'Alasdair?' She approached his table.

He looked up. He was unkempt, hair awry, shirt oddly buttoned. 'Oh.' He screwed up his eyes as he stared at her. 'It's you. Have a drink.' He began to stumble to his feet. She pushed him back down in his seat. 'I'll get them,' she said.

At the bar she gestured towards him. 'How long's he been here?'

The barman shrugged. 'Couple of hours, I guess.'

'You should go home,' she said, returning to Alasdair's table.

'Home?' He gazed at her.

'What happened?'

'What happened when?' He drained his glass.

'In France.'

He slammed his glass down on the table. 'Nothing. Nothing happened in France.' He laughed. 'Do you want a drink?'

'You're not having any more,' Agnes said. 'We're going.'

'Oh,' he said. 'We're going, are we?'

'Come on,' she said. She helped him to his feet, and he stumbled out of the pub, raising his hand here and there in a farewell wave.

'It's bloody freezing,' Alasdair said. 'Where are we going?'

'We're walking,' Agnes said. She set off in a determined manner, and he followed.

'Well,' she said, as they came out of Abbey Street on to Jamaica Road, 'I don't know what happened in Paris, but you've missed a lot here.'

'You're walking too fast,' he mumbled.

'Ash came to the hostel for Jeanie and missed shooting Mary by about half a millimetre. Mary was extremely brave and extremely stupid but survived. Ash seems to have admitted, in the middle of all the shouting, that he killed Gordon.'

'He killed Gordon?' Alasdair stopped still, swaying slightly.

'We'll see,' Agnes said. 'He's been arrested now. And Julius nearly died. And I went to Scotland, to Castlemilk, and I met Kathleen Dougal, Betty's sister. And then I met Gemma.'

'Gemma?'

'Yes.' Agnes kept walking, past Bermondsey tube, then north towards the embankment. Alasdair stumbled after her.

'Why did you meet Gemma?'

'Because it was her, of course. She was the lady who sang to Andy in his dying moments.'

'But – but they'd have said. Janet would have said.'

'They've all been trying to protect someone. Gemma most of all. But of course, they can't hide away for ever. Gemma's split up with Iain,' she added.

'Good.' Alasdair's pace was becoming steadier in the cold air. 'She should never have married him in the first place.'

'And Laura?' Now it was Agnes's turn to stop, as they reached the river, which flowed black and slow in the darkness.

Alasdair was silent, his gaze fixed on the lights across the river. 'I believed in the rose,' he said, after a while. 'After everything you said, I thought, yes, it's all about loving the transient rose. I went to see her, and on the train over there I imagined myself throwing myself on her mercy, and saying, this is what I am. It's not much, but it's yours.'

'And?'

They took a few steps towards the water, and sat on a low wall.

'She's lovely,' Alasdair said. Beneath them, the waves lapped quietly. 'She's forty-two, she works in the University, in the Italian department. She has a teenage daughter, with the husband from whom she's just separated.'

'And did you offer her your love?'

Alasdair managed a smile. 'It's a threadbare thing,' he said.

'So, she didn't accept it?'

'It's not that. She told me, that all her life she's dreamed of me. All her life, I was a possible future. A different future from the one she was living. Her husband is a difficult man, he's a lawyer, quite eminent. She's always held me in her thoughts, she said.'

'How poetic.'

'Oh, in Italian, very poetic. I've known her since Oxford, she did part of her Masters degree there. We talked for days,' Alasdair said. 'I only got back this morning. My God – ' he turned suddenly and grabbed her hands. 'Did you say Julius nearly died?'

Agnes smiled at him. 'Yes. He's OK. He had a bad reaction to the anaesthetic.'

'And the cancer?'

Agnes shrugged. 'They removed it. They have to see whether it's spread.'

A distant barge sounded its horn, a melancholy note in the damp air.

'Her husband is the man she loves,' Alasdair said. 'She'll get back together with him. She needed me to be there in order to find that out. She's lived with all these possible worlds, and she's found out that in the end you have to choose just one.'

'I've given away my house,' Agnes said, after a moment.

Alasdair nodded. 'There you are, you see.'

'And you?' Agnes glanced at him.

He sighed, crossed and uncrossed his legs on the wall. 'I am destined to follow Dante, who is driven by love and faith and hope, while having none of that myself. If you look at Dante's poem, you can see, very faintly, following in the footsteps of the poet, a shadow of a man. That's me. A threadbare shadow of a man.' He laughed, briefly. 'I seem to have sobered up. Shall we go?'

They stood up, shaking the chill from their legs.

'You won't start drinking again, will you?' Agnes looked up at him, as they began to walk along the embankment.

He stopped, and stared out towards the river. Then he turned back towards her. 'I used to drink because I loved life. I used to drink in celebration – in thanksgiving, you might say. "To life," I'd say, as I raised my glass. And then it turned out, I loved life too much. This morning, I got off the train at Waterloo, and had to face another London day. And another after that. And all I could think was that I'd left my best self behind, the self that Laura loved; the self that she still might believe in, if only I was worthy of it. And there I was, in Waterloo station, this other self; my true self. A lesser man, who, in the end, was too scared to take the risk; too scared to love. Someone who has gazed upon the rose, and seen only decay.' He looked at her. 'And so next thing I knew, I'd found a pub right by the station, and I'd ordered my first drink of the day. If you hadn't found me...'

'It's not up to me. It's up to you,' Agnes said.

'Yes,' he said, as they began to follow the river again. 'It's up to me.'

They walked in silence for a while. From time to time they could hear bells chime the small hours of the night. They passed Tower Bridge. The heights of the City glittered across the river. Alasdair paused.

'You were right,' he said. 'Of course.'

'About what?'

'About my father.'

'It wasn't an accident?' Agnes glanced up at him. His face was pinched and thin in the street light. He took out his cigarettes and lit one.

'Andy and I were in the flat that night.' His voice was a monotone. 'I was eighteen, I was just finishing my exams. Andy was fifteen. My father came stumbling home as usual, I don't know where Eileen was, probably taking refuge in the pub. It was a Saturday night. He was drunk, of course.' Alasdair took her hand and started walking again. 'You have to understand,' he said, 'it grinds you down. The violence against Eileen, the threats of violence against us boys, the constant background fear, it makes you ill. It drove my mother mad...' He stopped, drew his hand across his face. 'That night, he started on us. Again. His favourite theme was how I was jumped up and poncy like my mother. She'd only been dead less than a year, she'd been in a mental hospital for some time before that...' His voice trembled. 'I'd got my place at Oxford, and he couldn't bear it. He hated me. He hated me more than he hated my mother, I think. Or perhaps it was because I was so like my mother. I was due to study Classics and Italian, he hated that too... And anyway, after quite a lot of this, I hit him. I'd never fought back in my life, even earlier that year when he was beating Eileen, Andy and I stood by, helpless. We were so scared of him. You can't know, that fear. It paralyses you, it convinces you that the abuser is so much bigger and stronger than you are – '

'I do know,' Agnes said, quietly.

He looked down at her. 'I forgot.'

'So, you hit him.'

They walked a little way until they found a bench. 'Yes.' Alasdair sat down. He took a long drag of his cigarette. 'It was like unleashing a monster. I thought I'd be killed. Until Andy intervened. Andy was standing by the window, they were big plate glass windows, we were seven floors up. And Andy just started shouting abuse at him, calling him all the names you could think of. And he left off me, this big, lumbering, raging, drunken man, and he just sort of charged. At Andy. By the window. Seven floors up. And Andy stepped aside, and he went right through.' He ran a hand through his hair. 'There was a tiny balcony, bits of railings, but he was going so fast, he went over them all. It was the noise, the sound of him landing. I can still hear it. A sort of crumpling, cracking noise... terribly loud. It's in my nightmares.' He shook his head.

'What did you do?'

'Andy and I looked at each other. And we didn't say anything, we just tidied up the room and left. We crept down the back stairs, out towards the garages. No one saw us. We walked to the edge of the estate and got a bus to Glasgow. We joined the Saturday night crowds, and came back in the small hours. And they told us my dad was in hospital, and we feigned surprise, and then some days later he died. Andy and I, we didn't look at each other for all those days, not once. We didn't dare. And not at the funeral, either.' He stamped out his cigarette.

'Did you ever talk to each other about it?'

'No. Never. I think we wanted to believe our new version, the version we pretended.'

'But Andy told Trina. Trina knew you were both in the flat when Jim died.'

Alasdair nodded. 'Andy was close to Trina. And there came a time when he had so many ghosts, I suppose he felt he should lay some of them to rest. I think that's why he told her.' He sighed. 'Poor Andy.'

'So why are you so cross with her?'

He looked at her. 'No,' he said. 'I'm not cross with her. But I know Scott. He'll use anything for his own gain. If he got a whisper of the truth...'

'Scott doesn't know. That's why Trina was in such a bad state when she turned up at the hostel.'

'It would be nice to think she won't go back,' Alasdair said. 'But she will. We all seek redemption, and then when we catch a glimpse of it, we run away.'

'Except Dante.'

'He has Virgil to keep him there. And then Beatrice.'

They sat and listened to the river's gentle tide, the sleeping city.

'Scott thinks there's money,' Agnes said.

'I know.' Alasdair smoothed his coat over his knees. 'My mother had money. Her father's family came from Italy in the twenties, they set up in Glasgow selling ice-cream. They did very well. It became a huge family catering business. And my grandfather believed in education. My mother was a cultured and quite wealthy woman.'

'How did she meet Jim?'

'Those Catholic circles were small. My father was a charming

Irishman.' He shrugged. 'At least to start with. When it all went wrong, it went very wrong. My mother would speak to me in Italian, and my father hated it. When I was little, I associated hearing Italian with a kind of deep, trembling fear.'

'What made you study it, then?'

'I didn't want him to have won. He drove her mad, you see. She was an open, emotional, passionate woman. When her dreams all died, one by one, she retreated into a private space. By the end, she was unreachable.'

'When your father died – '

'She was dead by then. She'd died alone. One brief phone-call from the mental hospital, that's how we found out. And then it turned out that when she was first admitted to the hospital, she'd settled all her money on me. She got one of her uncles to tie it all up in a trust. No one ever believed it, perhaps because she seemed so fragile. But even when she seemed crazy, there was a kind of steely resolve about her too. So everyone thought my father got money, then everyone thought Eileen got his money, and because Eileen was so kind to Trina, I suppose Scott thinks, in his stupid, grasping way, that there's a fortune of Scots-Italian ice-cream money still swishing around East London.'

A distant police siren broke the silence, echoing away into the night.

'I never forgave my father.' Alasdair's hands were clasped tight together on his lap. 'That night he fell through the window... it was in slow-motion, he seemed to rise up against the glass and then somehow float through it, so slowly I knew I had time to prevent it. And I chose not to.'

'But that's not true. It would have taken barely a second.'

'But that's how it felt.' Alasdair turned to her. 'It felt like a choice, to let him die. And Andy was there, and he saw it. He kept my secrets...' His voice cracked. 'That's why I owed him, that's why I came to you after he died. He was the sole witness to my crime, my sin, if you like...' He put his hand to his face, and Agnes saw there were tears in his eyes.

'Not sin.' Agnes spoke quietly.

'If not sin, what?'

'In Dante's *Inferno*, the sinners are entrapped by their sin.'

He looked away, across the river. 'You mean I have hope?'

'Didn't we agree we were happier with Purgatory?'

He smiled. 'Yes,' he said. 'We did.'

'Come on.' They stood up, and he took her hand, and they continued their walk, and the dome of St Paul's glowed against the indigo sky.

Chapter Twenty-Two

The phone shrilled through the late morning birdsong. Agnes reached out and answered it.

'Mmm?'

'Sweetie, is that you?'

'I've just woken up.'

'Wonderful news. Loads to tell you. I'm on my way round with croissants and champagne – '

'But – '

'Of course you're allowed champagne, sweetie, it's Saturday.'

'But – '

'No arguing, I simply have to see you.'

'But – Alasdair's here.'

'Oh. WHAT?'

Agnes looked at her floor. Alasdair's tousled hair was just visible under her spare duvet.

'Oh, sweetie, good heavens, and you supposed to be taking final vows – '

'He's sleeping on the floor.'

'Which floor?'

'I only have the one.'

'Oh. Yes. Of course.'

Agnes started to laugh. 'You can't really have thought...'

'I don't see why not. With you anything's possible. I'll get an extra croissant and I'll see you in half an hour.'

Agnes hung up. She sat up in bed, looked at the still-sleeping Alasdair and smiled. Then she tiptoed to the bathroom to get showered and dressed.

She was making a large pot of coffee when she heard him stir. He was sitting on the floor, the duvet wrapped around him up to his neck.

'God,' he said. 'Hangovers. I'd forgotten this.'

'Well,' she said. 'You'll have to hang on to your resolve. Athena's on her way round with champagne.'

'Oh no.' He rubbed his head. 'Whatever for?'

'Something to celebrate, apparently.'

'I'm glad someone has.' He pulled the covers around him. 'What are we going to do?'

'About what?'

'Everything. Gemma, mostly.'

'I'm giving her time.'

'Do you really know what she's going to do?'

'I don't know anything.' Agnes went into the kitchen and came out with two mugs of coffee. 'If I knew anything for certain, I'd have gone to the police myself.' She put his mug down on the table. 'Now be a good boy and get showered and dressed before Athena comes, I don't want her teasing me about having men in my room.'

When Athena arrived, Alasdair was sitting by the window, with another mug of black coffee. Athena was wearing a black polo neck jumper and black jeans and pink sparkly vintage earrings.

'Croissants,' she said, handing Agnes a large paper bag and kissing her on both cheeks.

'Athena, this is Alasdair. Alasdair, Athena.'

'I've heard – ' Athena began.

' – a lot about you,' Alasdair finished, in unison.

'Champagne.' Athena produced a chilled bottle from her bag. She looked at them both. 'What? What's the matter?'

'I think you're on your own with the champagne,' Alasdair said.

'Well, that's very boring of you both.'

'Coffee, I think,' Agnes said.

'This better go in the fridge, then.' Athena handed her the bottle. 'For when we all feel like celebrating, and not just me.'

'So,' Agnes called from the kitchen, as Athena settled down in an armchair, 'what are you celebrating?'

'It's all off. The Barcelona plan. Nic's coming back to London.'

'How wonderful,' Agnes said. 'What witchcraft brought that about, then?'

'Oh, just one of my usual everyday spells. Looking gorgeous and being right, it's quite an easy one if you know how to do it.'

'It's all right,' Agnes said to Alasdair as she reappeared with a pot of coffee, 'she's always like this.'

Alasdair smiled, accepted the mug of coffee she poured, refused a croissant. He took out his packet of cigarettes and tapped them on the desk.

'Nic's terribly depressed, of course.' She crossed her legs. 'As I thought, the whole plan was completely potty. Those hippies he'd teamed up with had no business plan at all, they thought that just because the two of them and a couple of their dippy friends were interested in drumming and massage therapy, the whole of Spain would flock to their door. Then, yesterday, the farmer up the road switched off the water supply to the barn they were hoping to use. And they got a letter from the authorities saying the building was unsafe. I think it's all fishy, Nic said that the farmer's donkey was back in the barn within hours of them giving notice.'

'Perhaps the donkey's interested in drumming and massage therapy,' Alasdair said. He opened the packet of cigarettes, closed it again.

Athena laughed. 'At least someone is.'

'And what happened to the blonde Swedish masseuse,' Agnes said, 'the one with interesting theories about internalising family dysfunction into physical symptoms?'

'Ah, well,' Athena said. 'Even better. She met some swarthy spaniard in a bar who claimed to be a bull-fighter, and so now she's gone off with him to the South in search of the real Spain. Nic said she had a theory about how bull-fighting represents the search for the true male self, the mythic hero, I think he said, but I was only half-listening, of course.'

Alasdair looked from one to the other. 'Are you two making this up?'

Athena sighed. 'If only, darling. How often I wish I could be ordinary.'

'No you don't,' Agnes said.

'Of course, the problem now is what to do with Nic, who's going to be hanging about in London being morose, and there's a very real danger it will all start to be my fault, because I'm the one who was right – what are you doing?'

Agnes had crossed to the desk, picked up the phone and was dialling a number.

'I know what she's doing,' Alasdair said.

'Hello – is Sister Christiane there? Yes, thank you, I'll hold.'

Alasdair leaned across to Athena. 'She's giving you – '

'Ah, good morning, Sister. Yes, it's Agnes here. I'm sure you're aware that I've given permission to my French lawyers to hand over to the order my property in France. And I just wanted to let you know that that's no longer the case... Yes, I will be taking my vows, it's just that my property in France is going to be donated to a very deserving cause – yes, a charity, Sister, that's right... Yes, I thought so too. Thank you so much. Goodbye.'

'She's giving you her house,' Alasdair finished.

'What, for Nic?' Athena was wide-eyed.

'It's much nearer than Spain,' Agnes said.

'And you can invite the donkey and the bull-fighter,' Alasdair said. 'And people can pay a fortune to re-enact stories from Greek mythology, like Theseus and the Minotaur, and discover their inner hero.'

Athena looked across at Alasdair. 'I do believe he's getting the hang of this,' she said. 'Would you like to go into business with Nic? He needs someone sensible. Doesn't he?' she called to Agnes, who had gone into the kitchen.

'I'm not sensible,' Alasdair said.

'But you're a Capricorn or something.'

'No, I'm not.'

'What are you, then?'

Alasdair stood up, went over to Athena and whispered in her ear.

'Oh,' Athena said. 'Of course. Of course you are. It all makes sense now.' She looked at him. 'So, the woman in Paris, you still feel a kind of connection with her, but you know in your heart that as a real relationship it would never have worked.' Alasdair stared at her. She nodded at him, and went on, 'Yes. That's typical of your sign, it explains everything.'

Alastair sat down again, still staring at Athena.

'Right.' Agnes emerged from her kitchen and went over to her desk. 'I've got to phone the French lawyers to cancel the previous instructions.' She turned to Athena. 'And you'll have to sign something to take possession of the house.'

'But I thought it was for Nic – '

'Do you think I'd trust him with my house? No, he can be your tenant.'

'How exciting,' Athena said. 'I've never had a tenant before. Although, isn't it rather ageing to be a landlady?'

'And the good thing about this plan,' Alasdair said, picking up his packet of cigarettes, 'is that you can give back the house when Agnes changes her mind.'

Athena looked at him. 'How well you know her – '

'Oh,' he said, 'it's typical of her sign.'

The phone rang, loudly, and Agnes picked it up.

'Hello? Sheila, hi. Yes. Yes, I have got a number for her. Hang on.' Agnes opened a notebook, and read out a number. 'It's a mobile,' she added. 'Yes. Oh, right. OK, thanks. Bye.' She looked at Alasdair. 'That was Sheila Kelly. Ash is denying having anything to do with killing Gordon, she wants to talk to Janet.'

'Will Janet know any more than we do?'

'No, I don't suppose so. But Gemma gave me her mobile number, Sheila might as well have it.'

'Surely there'll be a DNA connection?' Alasdair fiddled with his packet of cigarettes.

'She said they were following that up, and she'd keep me posted. Oh, for God's sake have a fag,' Agnes said.

Later, Athena went off to find Nic and tell him the good news. Alasdair said he ought to go home and find some clean clothes and remember what he was supposed to be working on. Agnes was left alone in her flat.

She cleared up the bedclothes, washed up the coffee things. Waiting, she realised. Waiting for a word, a phone call, a message.

What if I'm wrong, she thought.

She sat at her desk and pulled out some pages of Andy's writings.

'... because I know this like I know the back of my own hand. I know it like the blood in my own veins, that evil begets evil. What I've thought, in my life, and what I've said, and what I've done, is written in my destiny. And what he's said and what he's done, is written in his destiny. And you can't rub it out, can you? I know that on my dying day I will see his face. But him, on his deathbed, what will he see?'

Agnes folded the pages away, picked up her coat, and went out.

Julius was sitting up in bed with a newspaper, doing the crossword.

'You're doing what?' Agnes came up to him, clutching a bunch of flowers.

He looked up and smiled. 'I know. I've never done one of these in my life. I think I must have been given someone else's brain during surgery, by mistake.'

'Why, have you become brilliant at crosswords?'

He shook his head. 'No. Absolutely hopeless. As ever.'

'Same brain, then. You're just bored. That's my diagnosis.'

'Thank you, Doctor.' He laughed, winced.

'Does it still hurt?' Agnes pulled up a chair by the bed.

'I think if you take out several inches of someone's gut, it might hurt for quite a while, don't you?'

Agnes shuddered. 'And does the crossword take your mind off it?'

'Not really, no.'

'Are the test results back?'

He shook his head. 'Tomorrow, maybe. Tomorrow I'll find out if I'm dying. Which, of course, I am. It's just a question of how fast.' He shifted, slowly, in his bed. 'Have you seen the chapel here?'

'Yes,' she said.

'One does yearn for something more Catholic,' he said.

She smiled at him. 'Perhaps we're out of touch,' she said. 'Perhaps nice purple seating is more appropriate to our times than bloodthirsty depictions of the sufferings of God.'

'More appropriate to a hospital, perhaps,' Julius said. 'We have enough blood and suffering on the wards. Aren't you going to put those in water?' He pointed at the daffodils she'd brought.

'I'll go and find a vase,' Agnes said.

She came back a few minutes later with a vase full of water, and began to unwrap the flowers.

'It's not the crossword,' Julius said.

'What do you mean?' She glanced at him. He looked suddenly pale and tired.

'It's not doing the crossword that makes me think I'm different.' He lay back on his pillows. 'It's that I have a terrible need for certainty. Whenever a doctor comes past, I have an overwhelming impulse to grab them by the sleeve and insist on the Answer. "Tell me, doctor, am I dying? And when? When will it be? I don't want ifs and buts about lymph nodes and margins. I want to know." In fact, what I really want someone to tell me, is that I have years left to me – decades, even. When I was first diagnosed, death cast its shadow over me. And now I want time off. Time out of the shadow, back in the light. I want it guaranteed. I've never needed guarantees before. "My heart is sore pained within me; and the terrors of death are fallen upon me..."' He stopped, breathless with effort.

She watched him for a moment. 'Oh, Julius,' she murmured.

'I know,' he agreed. 'There are no certainties. In the midst of life we are in death. I used to know all that. "Darkness and Light to You are both the same..." It just doesn't feel quite like that at the moment.'

They sat in silence. After a while Agnes finished arranging the flowers and placed the vase on his bedside locker.

He gazed at them for a while as the colour returned to his face. He looked across at Agnes. 'Mind you,' he said. 'There are times when one can discern a pattern in the meaninglessness. Look.' He pulled out the crossword puzzle, pointing. 'Isn't the answer to that clue "hermeneutic"? It must be, I can't see what else will fit.'

She began to laugh, and he tried not to laugh, but did anyway, wincing.

It was sunset when she emerged from the hospital and switched on her phone. She'd left him still struggling with the crossword, promising that she'd visit tomorrow. The wind had got up, rippling the Thames into foamy waves.

Her phone trilled, breaking the silence. She pulled it out of her bag. 'Hello? Ah,' she said. 'Where are you? Good... Yes, of course. Can you get to the hostel? It's across the road from where the others were staying. Good. I'll be there. And, thanks.' She rang off.

The Answer, she thought. The end of uncertainty. The beginning of meaning. I must tell Julius.

Ten minutes later, Agnes was pacing the office at the hostel. She could hear loud, tuneless voices from the kitchen as Trina and Jeanie prepared supper together, singing along to the radio.

Dan put his head round the door. 'Can I come in? I'm due to have a session with Archie.'

'Dan – ' Agnes looked at him. 'Is the lounge free? I kind of, um, need this room.'

He glanced at her, then nodded. 'Sure.'

Agnes went out to the front steps to wait. The street lamps were coming on, faint points of pink in the gathering rainclouds. Gusts of wind threw litter into playful circles.

There they were, turning the corner into the street. Three

figures, small at first, approaching. Gemma, flanked by two men. Sean, on one side of her. On the other, a thin, red-haired man, his hands in his pockets. Then they'd arrived, Sean pointing at the house, hesitating when he saw Agnes; Gemma smiling, coming up the steps to shake her hand. 'I've brought them,' she said. 'Sean and Iain.'

Agnes held open the front door for them, then led them silently into the office. 'Can I get you anything?' she said, but they all shook their heads. Gemma sat down, and the men too. Iain stared at the floor, Sean perched stiffly on the edge of his seat.

Agnes drew up a chair. For a moment there was silence in the room, the noises of the house muffled behind the closed door.

'Have you talked to the police?' Gemma's fingers were clasped tightly in her lap.

'No,' Agnes said. 'Not yet.'

'Oh.' Gemma glanced at Sean, at Iain. Iain didn't look up.

Agnes took a deep breath. 'Do you want to talk about Lucky?' She addressed the top of Iain's bent head. There was no answer.

'If you don't tell her, I will,' Gemma said.

Iain's head flicked up. 'If it weren't for you, I wouldn't be here.'

'She came to see me,' Gemma's eyes flashed anger. 'I didn't ask her to.'

Sean held up a hand. 'We've had all this. We've reached a decision. Iain?'

Iain's gaze came to rest on Agnes. His eyes were a dull, empty blue. 'They all joined up, see. Andy and the rest, the London laddies. Andy said Scots Guards to the wee chappie in the recruitment office, so we all ended up training together. Andy could hack it, but them other lads, och, they just couldna take it. Lucky was one of them. A bare few weeks he lasted, and he was off.'

Iain seemed to have run out of words. He fell silent again.

'He was bullied very badly.' Gemma's words hung in the still air.

Iain shook his head.

'They were both bullied, weren't they?' Gemma's voice was steady. 'Lucky and Billy Lee. They really cared about each other. And they both ended up dead.'

Iain blinked at her.

'I've kept your secrets long enough, Iain Moir.' She faced him, her lips tight.

Iain opened his mouth to speak, then shook his head. 'It wasn't me,' he said.

'Billy was found dead,' Agnes said. 'By the perimeter fence of the barracks. Shot.'

Gemma was staring at Iain, but Iain said nothing.

'And then,' Agnes went on, 'Lucky left. And some months later smashed up his bike.'

'It was an accident,' Iain said.

'No one knows that,' Gemma said.

'Andy knew.' It was Sean who spoke. 'Andy knew the truth about Lucky's death.'

'And it died with him, you mean?' Iain seemed to be smiling at Sean. 'No one smashes themself into a tree on purpose. Like I said, it was an accident.'

Agnes thought of Jeanie's Chris.

'An accident?' Sean was staring at Iain. 'Like an SA80 just happens to go off and leave a man dead?'

'Billy killed himself,' Iain said.

'And why did he kill himself?' Sean's fists were clenched.

'You always were a bully, Iain.' Gemma said.

Iain jumped to his feet. 'You said, if I agreed to come here with you, you'd give it a rest. You made a deal with me.' He stood, breathless, leaning heavily on the back of his chair.

It was Agnes who broke the silence. 'So,' she said. 'You all had an unhappy training. Andy, and Sean and Iain, and Lucky and Michael and Haz. And Billy. And the bullying got out of hand, and Billy was found dead. And Lucky left, and later died. And Iain, you did your tour of Belfast and left.' Iain sat down again.

'It's you, in Andy's writings, isn't it? When he swears revenge on someone, it's you.' Iain's hands were clenched together in his lap. Agnes went on, ' As Major Braybrook says, there was a culture of bullying. And you were at the heart of it. And Billy Lee was your first victim – '

'It wasn't just me.' Iain didn't look up. 'It was all the lads. Billy Lee and Lucky, we didn't want that in our company. It wasn't just me,' he echoed, staring at the floor.

Agnes glanced at the window, black with the night. 'Andy was very close to Lucky. When Lucky had that accident, Andy changed. Everyone says so.' She looked at Iain, who continued to stare at his knees. 'And then your platoon went their separate ways. Some left. Some went to Belfast. Sean went to Bosnia. And Andy served in the Falklands. And you, Iain, you married the woman he'd always loved.'

Iain shifted in his chair.

'And Andy, already damaged by war, sought revenge.'

'It was his fault.' Iain raised his head. 'That fight-'

Agnes held up her hand. She continued, 'We're talking about now. It was now, now that he'd finally begun to get his life together again, that was when he made contact with you, Gemma, didn't he? And you, Gemma, you came to London to meet him, because he promised you he'd stopped the drinking and he'd stopped the rages. And because you still loved him.'

Gemma looked up at Agnes. She blinked away tears. 'Go on,' she said, her voice quiet in the hush of the room.

'It was a tragedy, Andy's death.' Agnes met Gemma's gaze. 'You'd arranged to meet in a particular pub, in the West End. He got into a muddle, he got the wrong pub. He thought you'd stood him up, he started to drink. You were the only thing he was still living for, and you'd gone.'

'I hadn't gone, I was pacing the bloody streets looking for him – ' Gemma burst out. Sean put his hand on her arm.

'He drank all night,' Agnes said, 'came back to the hostel, drank some more, rowed with us all, gave me his writings and went out again that next night. He never came back.'

'I was searching for him,' Gemma said. 'I was asking for him in the streets, I never gave up...'

'Janet came to warn him,' Agnes said.

Gemma opened her mouth, the question unasked on her lips. She turned to Iain. Iain shrugged. 'Janet's a true friend,' Gemma said, then turned away from Iain. 'It's just a shame she was too late.'

Agnes faced Sean. 'You were all in the house across the way there, weren't you.'

'Iain had followed me from Scotland,' Gemma said. 'He knew what I was planning. I had no idea he knew. And then Janet came too because she was anxious about – '

'About what might happen? And it turned out she was right to be anxious.' Agnes looked at Gemma.

Gemma stared at her hands. 'I found him, that night. He was on the streets, drinking, with a friend.'

'Mitch,' Agnes said.

'Yes,' Gemma said. 'And some others. I saw how drunk he was. It broke my heart. I'd given him so many chances. I'd run out of chances to give him. So I ran. I was crying, and I ran. And he ran after me. And then Iain and Sean were there, because they'd followed me, and we all ended up under the railway there, and there was a big fight...'

Gemma looked down, tears welling in her eyes. Iain flashed a glance at Sean. The room was quiet. Then Iain said, 'I married her. She's my wife.'

'You'd already come to blows, hadn't you,' Agnes said. 'Some years before. Andy did time inside for fighting you.'

Iain nodded.

Sean spoke. 'We wanted to look after her. She's my sister, for Christ's sake. And he was never – '

'One of us?' Agnes turned to him. 'He was Catholic, you mean. And you were all Protestant.' She turned to Gemma. 'Poor old Eileen didn't understand, did she. She sent him to your school, because it was nearby – when all the Catholic kids used to take the bus to the other school. He was never "one of you".'

'I loved him.' Gemma was staring at her lap, her voice barely a whisper. 'I didn't care.'

Agnes waited a moment. 'So, this fight,' she said. 'It was chaos. Andy drunk. Mitch drunk. No one knowing what they're doing. Shouts and rage and bloodshed.' She glanced at Iain, then went on. 'And you, Iain, were shouting at Andy, and he was shouting back, and Gemma was screaming to you both to stop it, and then there was the knife and the blood, and Mitch standing there with a broken bottle...' Agnes looked at Sean. He was staring straight ahead of him, his knuckles white at his sides. She spoke again. 'Just the noise of people screaming, and fighting, and someone getting killed – '

'No.' Sean put his hands to his ears.

'Sean – ' Gemma put her hand on his arm, but he shook her off.

'No.' Sean's voice was loud, hoarse, echoing in the quiet of the room. After a moment, he spoke. 'I didn't mean to kill him,' Sean said. His eyes were unseeing, his hands clenching the side of his face. 'I didn't know what I was doing...' He sat there, motionless. 'I didn't know.' He began to cry, dry-eyed, sobbing with pain.

Gemma put her arms around him and burst into tears.

It was Iain who spoke. 'I was going to say it was me. I love her, you see. I thought, if I said it was me...' His voice tailed away.

'I know,' Agnes said.

'I got them all away from there.' Iain's voice was a monotone. 'I was the only one thinking straight. Gemma was holding Andy, trying to keep him alive, Sean was standing there with the knife, my knife, I was such a fuckin' idiot for bringing it. In all the fighting and the shouting he'd got it off me. I heard the sirens and we legged it, and there's me dragging them all away, and that poor wee man with the broken bottle standing there. If the coppers had done a test on the blood they'd have found it was mine, on that glass, that laddie took me on in the brawl, scratched my arm. But what did the police care, what was Andy to them, eh? Just another drunken ex-squaddie washed up in a fight. They didn'a care.' He glanced across at Gemma, at Sean, who was hunched in his chair, his hands across his face. 'She was never mine,' Iain said. 'It made me angry at times. Very angry. But when I saw him there, dying – you can tell when a man's dying... all the anger went. Emptying out of me. And I looked at Sean, at Andy, at Gemma, and I thought, who's the fucking victim here? Them two laddies, Sean and Andy, chewed up by the fuckin' army and spat out again. Sean here, he's seen things that would drive the strongest man crazy. Peacekeeping, they call it. At least the word war has a dignity. Sean's had to stand by with his mates and see the worst that man can do to man, and they're under orders to do nothing.'

'He was twelve,' Sean said. His voice seemed to come from somewhere far away. 'The kid they killed. I was about as near to him as here to there – ' he gestured to the limits of the room. 'And I ran forward, I had my rifle, I was going to kill the guy who was doing it. And the sergeant shouted, and I obeyed orders. Orders – ' the last word was a sob. 'The guy, he was a Serb, he laughed at me, and pulled a knife, and the kid was slaughtered like an animal...' He began to cry, his eyes wet with tears. 'I used to tell myself a different version, that I bayoneted the man and saved the boy. Plunging the knife in. It was so real, my version, that I could feel how it was... The blade going through the flesh. And then, that night with Andy, I could hear the screaming and the noise, and it was real. It was more real than anything around me. Bayoneting the man. The knife in the flesh. Saving the boy. Only there was no boy. No one to save...' He covered his face with his hands and cried. Gemma tried to comfort him, but it was as if he didn't notice her. He sat stiffly, unseeing, in the room, the only sound his muffled sobs. Outside the night was dark and wet, flinging rain against the windows.

Chapter Twenty-Three

'Will you hand him over?' It was Gemma who broke the silence, much later that night. Agnes had made them coffee, venturing out into the kitchen. The house was very quiet. Dan had gone to bed. She feared that Trina and Jeanie had gone out celebrating.

She came back into the office. Gemma, Sean and Iain were sitting in the gloom, the solitary desk lamp casting long shadows. Agnes handed out the mugs.

Gemma sipped her coffee, as they all waited for Agnes's answer.

Agnes looked at Sean. 'You could escape,' she said.

He turned to her, his eyes dulled with weariness. 'Could I?'

'You'd be a free man,' Iain said.

'I haven't been free for years.' Sean stared into his mug.

'If you go to prison, your life will be over,' Iain said.

'My life is over. My life ended when that lad's life ended.'

Gemma dashed tears from her eyes.

'If I run away,' Sean said, 'then that other bloke gets done for murder, doesn't he. It seems to me there's only one path open to me.'

Gemma put her hand on Sean's arm.

'What will our Janet say?' Iain looked at Sean. 'After all she went through, covering up for you. And her Gordon too.'

'Gordon didn't cover up for him,' Gemma said. 'That's why he's dead too. That's what comes of trying to lie, that's what Janet said at the time, and she was right. We should have listened to them two, so we should.'

'When Gordon was on his way here, that evening...' Agnes began. She looked at Gemma, at Sean. 'What was he going to tell us?'

Gemma stared at the floor. 'He didn't like what had happened. He guessed you knew more than you were letting on, you and Alasdair. We argued with him, didn't we. Sean here nearly came to blows with him. We made him promise not to see you, and then I suppose he decided to after all.'

Iain shifted on his chair. 'He shouldn't have died.'

'The police are going to charge someone with his murder.' Agnes was aware of their sharp attention.

'Aye, that's what Janet said.' Gemma nodded at Agnes. 'They think it was a robbery gone wrong.'

Agnes saw Sean glance at Iain.

'And is that what you think?' she asked.

Gemma looked at the men, then at Agnes. 'If you mean, do I think anyone in this room is capable of killing one of their best friends...' Her voice faded away.

Iain broke the silence. 'No one here killed Gordon. If it's Andy's death we're talking about, what is there to say?'

Sean sighed, a deep heavy sigh. 'No,' he said. 'There's nothing more to say.'

'I don't believe you.' Alasdair's voice on the phone was loud with shock. 'Sean?'

Agnes looked out of her window. The morning sun danced on the towerblocks, sparkled on the glimpse of the river.

'Gemma brought him to see me, him and Iain. We sat up most of last night.'

'Where are they now?'

'In the hostel.'

'He might run away.'

'We discussed it.' Agnes yawned. 'He might. But it's unlikely.'

'Have you told the police?'

'I'm just about to.' Agnes hesitated. 'Though, I don't really want to.'

'But Mitch – '

'I know.'

There was a silence between them. 'Are you still sober?' Agnes asked.

'Miraculously, yes.' Another pause. 'What shall we do now?'

'Can you – are you – ' she began. 'What I mean to say is, I – I need you. Now. For this bit.'

She heard him breathing. 'I'll be at the hostel in half an hour,' he said.

The hostel was lively with Sunday breakfast. When Agnes came into the kitchen, Jeanie jumped up and gave her a hug. Trina was sitting at the table, mug of coffee in one hand, cigarette in the other, tapping her feet on the floor in their diamante high-heeled sandals.

'No, you're wrong,' Archie was insisting to her. 'Say you've got money on five horses, and they all come in, first, second, third, fourth, fifth – '

'But that isn't going to happen, is it? Trina said. 'You're better off buying a lottery ticket.'

Archie shook his head. 'The odds on the lottery are terrible. Absolutely bloody terrible...' He took a large bite of toast.

Jeanie was whispering something to Agnes.

'Sorry?' Agnes turned to her.

'Ash, right.' Jeanie dragged Agnes over to the window. 'They can get his DNA, can't they. Now he's inside.'

'Yes, I suppose so.'

'So,' Jeanie went on, still whispering, 'if they checked the baby too, they'd know. Who the father is.'

Agnes stared at her. 'I'm not sure that legally they can just-'

'Legally?' Jeanie's voice was suddenly loud. 'The bastard raped me. I don't care about what's legal.'

Agnes looked at her. 'No,' she said. 'I don't suppose you do.'

'You will ask that copper, won't you?'

'Yes,' Agnes said, hearing a knock at the door. 'I will.'

Dan met her in the hallway.

'It'll be Alasdair,' Agnes said. 'Are the new residents still upstairs?'

'As far as I know,' Dan said, opening the door.

'Morning,' Alasdair said.

'I'll tell them you're here,' Dan said.

Agnes and Alasdair stood in the sunlit hallway, waiting. 'You look much better,' she said to him. He was newly-shaven, wearing a fresh linen shirt. He was about to reply, but then his attention was caught by something beyond her. Agnes looked up, to see Gemma descending the stairs, her eyes fixed on Alasdair. She was dressed all in black; slim black jumper, black skirt. Wordlessly, she walked towards him, took his hands, and gazed up into his face. The noise in the house seemed to fade to silence. Then she said, 'My brother.'

Alasdair stroked her hair. 'I know,' he said.

Her eyes searched his. 'I loved only him, only Andy.'

'You loved the man he was,' Alasdair said. 'Before the war – '

'No,' she interrupted him. 'I loved him to the end. Always. For ever.' She pulled at her jumper. 'See? A widow.' Her eyes filled with tears and she turned away from him.

'Does Sean want to see me?'

She shook her head. 'He wants the police to come,' she said, addressing Agnes. 'He wants to get it over with. He can't face seeing you,' she said to Alasdair. 'I asked him. Iain's up there with him.'

'If it helps,' Alasdair began. 'If it's any consolation, when my father – when my father died...' He took a deep breath. 'It is like climbing a mountain, forgiveness. Forgiving other people, is one thing. Forgiving oneself... a lifetime. A long, slow, painful climb.' He shook his head. 'I'm sorry, I'm not making much sense.' He took hold of Gemma's hand again. 'Your brother may think he's trapped by what he's done, but tell him, from me, there's hope. Really, there's hope...' Alasdair's voice shook.

Gemma looked up at him. 'Thank you,' she said. 'I'll tell him.' She kissed him on the cheek.

Alasdair blinked away his tears. 'I'll be in the office,' he said to Agnes.

She heard the office door shut behind him.

Gemma turned and fled up the stairs.

When Sheila Kelly arrived, it was Agnes who greeted her, Agnes who went upstairs and found Gemma and the others, Agnes who wished them goodbye from the steps of the house as Sean was led away to the waiting police car, Gemma and Iain following.

When they'd gone she went into the office. Alasdair was sitting at the desk, staring into space.

'I wonder,' he said, not looking up.

'What?' She sat down next to him.

'Purgatory,' he said. 'I might be wrong about it.'

'Why?'

He rubbed his face, then looked at her. 'Circles of Hell. When I think of my mother's life, all her hope, her life, fading away in a lunatic asylum. And then, my father, Jim Brogan, his madness passed itself on, didn't it. Until Andy and I did what we did, and he died. It's in human nature to be sinful, it seems to me. We can't escape. And then Andy thought it would be a good idea to be a soldier, like Sean, like Iain. And look at how their Hell played itself out... Do you think Sean will get life?'

'I think not, if he gets a good enough lawyer, and if the court accepts Post Traumatic Stress Disorder.'

'Circles of Hell, you see. We are all trapped by our sinful natures.'

'But Dante's right,' Agnes said. 'It's what you said, weeks ago. That we're living Hell, and Purgatory, and Paradise, all the time. Now, continuously. There is always hope of redemption.'

'Did I say that?' He smiled.

From the kitchen, Trina's voice rose up loud and out of tune as she did the washing up.

'What's she singing?' Alasdair said.

'Something about love being for ever, I think.'

Alasdair laughed. 'Perhaps Trina was Beatrice all along,' he said.

'I don't know,' Agnes said. 'I can't see her getting very far up a mountain in those shoes.'

'Alasdair's worried about circles of Hell,' Agnes said to Julius that afternoon.

'Is he?' Julius smiled up at her.

'What on earth is all this?' Agnes gestured to his bedside table, the tray across his bed, all covered with vases of flowers, festooned with cards. She picked up one of the cards.

'Word got out,' Julius said. 'I tried to keep it quiet in the parish, but the visiting has started. I'm exhausted. Every well-meaning person from the congregation has been since yesterday.'

Agnes inspected the displays. 'Why has Mrs Featherstone sent you thistles?'

'They're not thistles, apparently. She took great pains to explain. It's all the rage in flower arrangement these days to have things that are sparse and spiky like that. It's very Japanese, she said, very fashionable.' He laughed.

'You look much better.'

'Test results,' he said.

Agnes sat down heavily. 'And?' She felt the colour drain from her face.

'It's really not bad. The resection margins were all clear. Apparently it's very good news. And there were no lymph nodes involved. I've been very lucky, it turns out. Now it's just a matter of whether the joining up bit has worked. They keep trying to get me to drink tea to get me off all these drips.'

Agnes tried to speak, stopped, felt her eyes fill with tears. He reached across the bed and took her hand. After a while, he began to murmur.

'What did you say?' Agnes leaned towards him.

'"Thou has turned for me my mourning into dancing; thou hast put off my sackcloth and girded me with gladness."' Julius met her eyes, then looked away again, still grasping her hand.

They were sitting like that when they became aware of

someone approaching the bed. Agnes saw the swing of a black coat from the corner of her eye.

'Alasdair.' She turned to greet him. He was carrying a brown paper carrier bag.

'Hello.' He rested his hand briefly on Agnes's shoulder, then reached across to shake Julius's hand. 'I'm Alasdair Brogan.'

'I've heard a lot – ' Julius began.

' – about you,' Alasdair joined in. He pulled up a chair.

'How did you know to find us here?' Agnes smiled at him.

'I asked. It's easy. Everyone seems to have heard of you,' he said to Julius.

'Oh, nonsense.' Julius smiled at him.

'Julius has had his test results back. It's very good news.'

'It's not cancer?' Alasdair was wide-eyed.

Agnes laughed. 'Of course it's cancer. It's just the spread of it all was about as minimal as it could be.'

'It means I might still be here next year,' Julius said. 'Even the year after. God knows it makes my heart dance just to think it.'

'I was right,' Agnes said. 'Dante was right.'

'Really?' Alasdair laughed. 'You and Dante both, then?'

'Hell, Purgatory, Paradise. life and death, darkness and light. It's a continuum.' She looked at Julius. 'Alasdair's been worrying that we get trapped in the circles of Hell, by our own sinful nature.'

'But we can choose,' Julius said. 'Sin is dying to life. "When the wicked man turneth away from his wickedness that he hath committed, and doeth that which is lawful and right, he shall save his soul alive."'

'It's an empty promise,' Alasdair said. 'Why should we believe in eternal life?'

Julius met his eyes. 'Before I got ill, I would have argued with you. But it's true, these last few weeks I've stared into a black pit of emptiness. Death, pure and simple. Ending.' He gazed at Mrs Featherstone's thistles. 'But you see,' he went on, 'That's why Dante is right. Surely the whole *Divine Comedy* is about Love? Somewhere in the *Purgatorio*, doesn't Virgil explain to the poet all about Love? And, you see, the nature of sin, as described in Purgatory, isn't it all about love, in fact? Love that's out of balance – excessive love, or love for the wrong things? Sure, we are sinful human beings. But we can also love. That's our salvation, even if it's only here, only in this earthly life.'

Alasdair thought for a moment. 'But people do terrible things,' he said.

'Terrible things happen,' Julius agreed. 'And people are moved to compassion. In the face of suffering, people's souls stir towards the good. Why, even here – ' he gestured to the armfuls of flowers in front of him. 'Just because I might have died, all the worthy women of my parish have brought all these.'

'So I see.' Alasdair eyed the flowers. 'It makes my contribution seem rather paltry.' He opened the carrier bag and produced a narrow glass vase in which there stood one rose stem; a full, heavy-petalled white rose.

Agnes and Julius stared at it. Agnes stood up and cleared a space amongst the other vases, and Alasdair placed it on the tray in front of Julius.

'It's – ' Julius tried to speak. 'It's very kind of you.' He blinked, his eyes moist. 'You can't know how beautiful that seems to me...' He stared at the rose, swallowing tears.

A single petal fell from the rose and rested there in front of him. For a long time, no one spoke.

'Oh sweetie, I'm so glad.' Athena gave Agnes a big hug. 'You see, God needs Julius here with us mere mortals. At least for a bit longer.' She flung herself into one of Agnes's armchairs. 'I've brought cake for tea, it was to celebrate the house and Nic and everything being lovely again, but of course, Julius coming back to life is much more important.'

Agnes took the cake and went into her kitchen. 'I've spoken to the lawyers, you'll get various forms to sign,' she said, putting on the kettle.

'And you can trust me, honestly sweetie, any time you want to leave those horrible nuns you can have the house back, I'll write an agenda on the form.'

'Addendum,' Agnes said.

'Sorry?'

'Technical term,' Agnes said, coming back into the room with two plates and handing her one. 'Like hermeneutic.'

'Sometimes I haven't a clue what you're talking about.' Athena picked up a forkful of chocolate mousse. 'Are you really going to take final vows?'

'In two weeks,' Agnes said. 'It's all set up.'

'Is it like a wedding?' Athena said. 'Will there be a party? What shall I wear?'

Agnes laughed. 'It is like a wedding, in that I'll be making promises that are very difficult to keep. But no, not really a party. Just close friends.'

'When is it?'

'Saturday week. At the convent house, in Hackney.'

Athena picked up another forkful of cake and frowned at it.

'Will you be there?' Agnes said.

'Oh yes. Absolutely. I'll be there.'

At eight the next morning, Agnes appeared at the hostel for work. The house seemed subdued. Jayce sat at the kitchen table eating cereal, his head bobbing to the beat in his headphones. He nodded at Agnes, raised a hand, carried on eating.

There was no one in the office. Agnes sat at the desk and looked at the weekly schedule. Mary was supposed to be on with her this morning, Petra this afternoon.

She heard singing on the stairs, as Trina emerged from her room.

The phone rang.

'Good Heavens,' said a voice, as Agnes answered, 'you start work early.'

'Morning Sheila.'

'Just thought I'd keep you up to date. We're going to charge Ashleigh with the murder of Mr Tait. It has all the hallmarks. Baseball bat. Typical bloody crackhead. We're hoping for a DNA match when the labs send their results back. And it looks like Mr O'Grady is going to be released without charge later on today.'

'Mitch?'

'Yes. Mr Mitchelson's pleading guilty to manslaughter, diminished responsibility.'

'Oh.' Agnes watched the sunlight flicker on the window. 'When Gordon died – it really was Ash, then?'

'It really was Ash. Sometimes bad stuff happens for no reason at all,' Sheila said. 'Must go, I'll speak to you soon.'

Agnes put down the receiver. The sun went in again, and the room was cast in shadow. She put on her desklamp.

The office door opened and Mary came in. She smiled at Agnes and sat down at the other desk.

'First day back,' she said. 'They insisted I rest over the weekend.'

'I'm not surprised.' Agnes picked up a pen from her desk, turning it over in her fingers. 'You were very brave,' she said.

'No,' Mary said. 'Foolish. Not brave.'

'Without you – '

'Without me the police could have moved in as they wanted to. As it was, I nearly died. It was sheer luck that last bullet went into the wall.'

'Did you know how to stop him firing?'

She smiled, shook her head. 'Did I heck. I just wanted it to stop, but apparently I released the magazine, they told me, when I grabbed the gun.'

'It was still very brave.'

Mary shook her head. 'It was a death-wish. I've been re-living it, when I close my eyes at night. The sound of that gun firing so close...' She shivered. 'There was a kind of ping when it hit the wall. I think I thought I'd been shot. And the funny thing is, it was then that I came to my senses, but it was too late then, I was standing there with that horrible young man. And that's when I thought, I don't want to die.'

'Jeanie's a new person,' Agnes said. 'Singing, dancing.'

'I hope they lock him up and throw away the key. I'll go and get some tea, do you want some?'

Mary went out of the room. Agnes sifted through the papers on her desk. She found the referrals list and went through it. Trina's room was available, in theory. And Jeanie shouldn't be here when the baby comes, she thought. She needs a proper mother and baby unit. Except, they're always full.

Mary came back in and put a mug of tea down next to Agnes. She sat down and watched her for a while. 'I'm sorry,' she said at last.

'You don't have to apologise,' Agnes said.

'I wanted to blame someone. I wanted it to be someone's fault. I wanted to blame anyone other than myself.'

'It was no one's fault.'

'That's what she said,' Mary said. 'That Trina.' She gestured with her head towards the door. 'She said, there was no point being stuck in the past, that I would never have known how it was going to turn out, even if I had married him. She said, he'd probably end up a right old misery like all men do.' She managed a smile. 'I think she's wrong about that bit, but I could see what she meant. Mind you, she's a fine one to talk. That Scott's been whispering sweet nothings on her phone, and she's talking of going back to him.'

'Is she?'

Mary shrugged. 'She claims he loves her really. I've told her what I think, but I'm not sure she'll listen.'

Agnes sipped her tea. 'Mary – I'm taking final vows in a couple of weeks. I'll understand if you don't want to be there, but I'd be very pleased, I'd very much like it – if you could be there.'

Mary smiled at her. 'I'd be glad to. Don't expect me to believe in your God too, but it's high time I went to a party.'

Chapter Twenty-Four

Agnes walked down the aisle of the convent chapel. It was the 21st of March. Bright spring sunlight spilled through the high windows. The organist was playing a Bach prelude. The hush of the chapel began to be fractured with noise, people getting up out of their chairs, some of the sisters coming to greet Agnes with a kiss or a hug. She saw Father Julius, sitting near the back; Nic, who waved. There was Athena, but she seemed to be leaving.

Sister Christiane came over and kissed her on both cheeks and then went to talk to the bishop. Sister Madeleine took both her hands. 'See?' she said. 'It's easy.'

Agnes went to find Julius, who was still in his pew. He looked well, pink-cheeked but thinner.

'Well, I thought that went very well,' he said. 'You managed to say all the words without a fluff.'

'I'd been practising all night. Are you all right?' she asked.

'I'm fine. And you,' he said. 'Do you feel different?'

She shook her head. 'Should I?'

'No,' he said. 'Not at all.'

Alasdair appeared. 'Athena wants you outside,' he said.

'But – I have to sign the book,' Agnes said.

'Well, after that. We're going on.' He smiled at Julius.

Agnes looked at him blankly. 'Going on?'

'Athena's booked some restaurant in Shoreditch. Taxis waiting and everything. I've had to ask everyone who knows you, I've been on the phone for a fortnight.'

Julius started to laugh. 'I might have known,' he said. 'Final vows, followed by a champagne reception. Only Agnes could do it...' He laughed some more.

'Don't blame me,' Agnes said. 'Blame my friends.'

'Come on.' Alasdair offered Julius his arm.

'Oh, not me, I couldn't possibly... ' Julius got to his feet. 'I'm doing the evening eucharist in my own church this evening.'

'Julius, if you don't go, then I won't.' Agnes glanced up at Alasdair, who took Julius's arm.

'I mean, it's not as if it's a wedding...' Julius grumbled, as Alasdair led him away towards the waiting cars.

Agnes's car was the last to arrive. She walked through the doors of the restaurant to be greeted by glasses of champagne, sunlit white tableclothes, trays of canapes. And there was Athena, in her lime-green suit and pink shoes, with Nic at her side.

Agnes went straight to her and hugged her. 'Julius is appalled,' she said.

'Oh nonsense, sweetie, of course he isn't. He's having a lovely time. Look.'

Julius was holding a glass of champagne, sitting at a table, deep in conversation with Trina. Behind her Scott hovered, clutching a glass of beer.

Nic took Agnes's hand. 'Thanks for everything,' he said.

'It's the least I can do,' she said. 'You look well,' she added, taking in his well-cut suit in navy linen, his hair streaked blonde by the sun.

'It's love,' Athena said, and kissed his cheek. 'I must just check what's happened to the crab filo pastries, I ordered them to go with the champagne. Later on there's goat's cheese and saffron roulade. Nic, go and talk to one of those women over there, they're looking lost.'

'It's Sister Madeleine,' Agnes said. 'And Petra. I wouldn't describe either of them as lost. Ever.'

The door flashed with sunlight, and Jeanie appeared, with

Mary. They blinked at the waiters, took a glass each of champagne, sought out Agnes.

'I shouldn't really,' Jeanie said, giggling as she took a large swig from her glass.

'We're celebrating,' Mary said to Agnes.

'What are you celebrating?'

'Jeanie's going to come and live with me. Her and the baby. I've been rattling around in a huge old house on my own for too long.'

'She's going to be its nana,' Jeanie said.

Mary was wearing her hair loose. It framed her face in soft curls. 'Do you know, I can't remember when I last drank champagne,' she said.

Jeanie took Agnes by the arm. 'I'm celebrating something else,' she said. 'It's Chris's baby. I found out yesterday. Mary took me to the clinic, we got the results, we spoke to Sheila like you said. And he'll be a summer baby.'

'He?'

She laughed. 'They said did I want to know that too, as I was there, and I said, I want to know everything. Everything you can tell me. And so then I got in touch with Chris's mum in Essex, and I told her everything. And she's going to be his other nana. Ooh, look, there's Trina, we want her to be godmother, come on.'

Mary and Jeanie moved off to speak to Trina.

Athena appeared at Agnes's side. 'Are you having a lovely time?'

'Yes,' Agnes said. 'I am. Who's that talking to Alasdair?'

Athena followed Agnes's gaze. Alasdair was holding a glass of orange juice, standing with a young woman with long blonde hair. She was wearing a strappy floral dress which revealed tanned legs, and high-heeled shoes.

'Oh, that,' Athena said. 'That's Kirsten. She's Simon's new assistant at the gallery, she's been such a sweetheart helping me organise this, it was only kind to invite her. She's got a PhD in Art History, something about abstract art in New York in the 1960s, but she's an absolute love. How funny that Alasdair should be talking to her.' Athena raised an eyebrow.

They laughed so loudly that Alasdair glanced across at them.

Later, Agnes found Julius. He raised his glass. 'I've had a wonderful time. All final vows should feature a party organised by Athena, they should make it part of the deal. I met a charming woman from the East End, and her husband, common law husband, she insisted on telling me, but I reassured her that in the eyes of God it's the same thing. She said her mother was a Catholic, and she feels a deep yearning to return to the faith, so we had a bit of a chat about that. Charming woman.'

'Did you talk to Scott?'

'Her chap? Yes. He was very sympathetic when I told him what I earned. Offered all sorts of career advice if ever I chose to leave the cloth.' He looked at his watch. 'I really ought to leave if I'm going to celebrate the eucharist this evening.'

'I'll come with you,' Agnes said.

'Really, it's your party, you don't have to – '

'I want to.'

They left towards the end of afternoon, the wide windows ablaze with the setting sun. There was music, and Agnes saw Trina dancing with Scott, Athena dancing with Nic, Jeanie giggling with Petra, Mary talking to Sister Madeleine, Alasdair dancing with Kirsten. As she stood in the doorway with Julius, Alasdair crossed the room to find her.

'You're not going?' He put his hands on her shoulders.

'I am.' She smiled up at him.

'But – '

'But what?'

'There's so much still to say.' He gazed down at her.

'And there'll be time in which to say it.'

'I'll phone you,' Alasdair said.

'I hope so.'

At the door she turned. He was still there, a glass of orange juice raised in his hand. 'I'd avoid Athena,' Agnes called to him. 'She'll try to tell you Kirsten's star sign. It might be bad news.'

She knelt by the altar rail of Julius's church. The stained glass window was black against the twilight sky. The incense curled softly through the points of candle flame.

For the second time that day, she awaited the eucharist, the communion; for the second time as a full member of a religious order.

"'...all things come of thee. And of thine own do we give thee...'"

Julius moved across the altar, preparing the wafers and the wine. Agnes saw the white cloth, the crystal jug of water, the chalice. She heard the words of the service; the murmured responses of the congregation.

The body and the blood. The God who dies so that we might live. The memorial of a terrible death; the promise of new life in the breaking of the bread.

We are still here, she thought.

After the service she sat and waited for him, as he blew out candles and turned out lights, and the church was gradually enfolded in darkness.

They walked down the main aisle, arm in arm, and came out into the night, the promise of spring in the freshening air. They looked up towards the sky, towards the stars.

Julius locked the church, and they made their way down the gravel path, through the gate, out into the London night.

THE END